WHAT WE LEFT BEHIND

LUISA A. JONES

*To Nic
With much love from
Luisa
x*

Storm
PUBLISHING

This is a work of fiction. Names, characters, businesses, places, events and incidents are either the products of the author's imagination or used in a fictitious manner. Any resemblance to actual persons, living or dead, or actual events is purely coincidental.

Copyright © Luisa A. Jones, 2025

The moral right of the author has been asserted.

All rights reserved. No part of this book may be reproduced or used in any manner without the prior written permission of the copyright owner. This prohibition includes, but is not limited to, any reproduction or use for the purpose of training artificial intelligence technologies or systems.

To request permissions, contact the publisher at rights@stormpublishing.co

Ebook ISBN: 978-1-80508-704-5
Paperback ISBN: 978-1-80508-706-9

Cover design by: Sarah Whittaker
Cover images by: Arcangel, Shutterstock

Published by Storm Publishing.
For further information, visit:
www.stormpublishing.co

ALSO BY LUISA A. JONES

The Gilded Cage
The Broken Vow

Goes Without Saying
Making the Best of It

"A single act of kindness throws out roots in all directions, and the roots spring up and make new trees."

AMELIA EARHART

For my parents, with love.

ONE

LONDON, FRIDAY 1ST SEPTEMBER 1939

Olive

It was strange to be packing when no one knew where they were going.

Eight-year-old Olive swallowed the last mouthful of her bread and margarine, then licked every trace of crumbs and grease off her fingers. She watched her mother shake out two pillowcases. One of Mum's eyelids was swollen and red this morning. With her eyebrow puffed out and misshapen, her face looked like a half-deflated balloon. She'd have a real shiner in a day or two. Still, she was on her feet. Olive had seen her look worse.

"You'll have to carry your stuff in these pillowcases. I'll tie 'em up with string before you go. Don't know where they think we'd get two suitcases from. Bleeding ridiculous, it is. And expecting us to pack spares of everything! I suppose the powers that be imagine the servants will put your spare shoes in your cases along with your diamonds and pearls, Ol."

Despite her obvious agitation, Mum kept her voice low to avoid disturbing Dad, whose snores reverberated from the bedroom. It was never a good idea to wake him. He'd come in late from the pub last night, and as usual Olive had cowered under the bedclothes, pressing her good ear against the pillow to muffle the sound of blows and her mother's cries from the tiny kitchen in their flat.

The paralysing, helpless terror Olive felt whenever Dad was violent was sickeningly like the way she'd felt on the day her younger sister Irene died, four years earlier. Perhaps it was the way his voice went in an instant from a low growl to a roar. It was like the whoosh of the flames that had scorched Olive's face when Irene's toes caught in her hand-me-down nightdress, pitching her little body from the hearthrug into the fire.

That terrible day had taught Olive how easily catastrophe could strike. Now, it could soon be falling from the skies. The government said children's best chance of safety from firebombs and poison gas was to leave London. But Mum wouldn't be coming with them, and no one had told them where they'd be going, or how long they'd be away. All kinds of dreadful possibilities had raised themselves in Olive's mind. Today she'd find out if her fears were justified.

"You'll have to share the soap and the toothpaste," Mum went on. "I'll put those in *your* pillowcase, Olive, so mind you look after them. Don't let the teachers split you up, or Peter won't have none. And don't let any bugger pinch your comb, neither."

Olive nodded as her mother tucked the small pink tin into her pillowcase. They usually made do with a bit of salt to clean their teeth – if they bothered at all. The tin was joined by a toothbrush, a flannel cut down from an old towel, and a new bar of pungent yellow soap. In went the comb, then Mum slipped a handkerchief, a clean vest and knickers, a pair of socks and a pullover into each pillowcase.

Seven-year-old Peter craned to peer into his pillowcase. "You'd better not have forgotten I'm taking Ted," he said, a scowl on his freckled face that made him look disturbingly like their father.

"Course I ain't forgotten. He's already in."

Gracie was still on Olive's pillow, grubby pink cotton limbs spreadeagled. Olive thought of fetching her, but the fist-sized dent in the door of their flat's only bedroom made her pause. She bit her lip, reluctant to risk disturbing Dad's sleep. Trying to ignore the jitters in her stomach, she reasoned that they couldn't be going wherever they were being sent off to for more than a night or two. Hopefully she could manage without her rag doll for that long.

"Lord! It's half six already. You'd better get your coats and plimsolls on, kids. And don't forget your gas masks."

Gas masks – another thing to remember. They'd been practising memorising their home address all week. Olive slung the string carrying her gas mask box over her shoulder. With one final check, Mum made sure they had their identification cards: blue for Peter, biscuit-coloured for Olive. She thrust their bulging pillowcase bundles towards them.

"Now, it'll be like I told you. You'll line up in the school yard with the other kids, like you been practising, then you'll all walk to the station to catch a train for a little holiday out in the countryside where it's nice and safe. Some of your teachers will go with you. Make sure you behave for them and don't go giving them none of your cheek, Peter. Do as you're told in your new place, and I'll see you soon," Mum said.

She seized them each by a shoulder and squeezed hard. "Whatever you do, do *not* let them split you up," she said, as if it was very important. "D'you hear me? Stay together and don't let no one tell you different. Keep hold of Olive's hand, Peter. Give him a clip across the ear if he doesn't do as he's told, Ol. Make sure you look after him."

Mum's eyes seemed to bore into Olive, as if she was deciding whether she could be trusted with such an important task. More than anything, Olive knew she mustn't fail. She'd been careless with Irene, too busy with her own game to pay attention to her little sister. But she wouldn't be careless with Peter. It was down to her to keep him safe.

"I will," she whispered, holding back the tears that threatened in her throat.

Mum nodded and looked away. When she spoke, her voice sounded thick and strange. "Best you get going. Be careful on them stairs – and go straight to school. No dawdling on the way. You don't want to be late and miss the train."

Olive opened her mouth to say goodbye, but the front door was already closing, shutting them out on the landing. Through the frosted glass pane she saw the strange sight of their mother's silhouette sinking downwards as she slid down the wall to sit on the floor.

When would she see her again?

TWO

Olive

Olive had never seen so many people in one place. The mothers who'd walked along with the seemingly endless line of schoolchildren and their teachers weren't allowed to follow into the depths of the Tube station. A few wept, and Olive looked away after reading the lips of one woman who cried: "Oh, I can't bear it." The pain in her expression confused Olive. Why was the woman so upset if the children were only going away for a few days to stay with nice, kind people in the country?

While the children swarmed over the platform to await the train, ladies wearing smart green hats handed out little packets of cream crackers. It couldn't be more different from the usual morning routine, when they'd troop silently into the school's assembly hall to say prayers and sing hymns.

A ripple of excitement greeted the steam train as it groaned and hissed to a halt beside the sooty platform. Any prospect of remaining in their assigned groups had gone. It was impossible to keep hold of Peter's hand in the jostling as the massed children climbed into their carriages, and Olive's pulse ramped up at the thought that he might get lost in the crowd. Lunging for the string on his gas mask box, Olive towed him until she found enough space in a compartment further along the carriage for them to sit together. She dropped their packed pillowcases onto two seats to claim them before tugging his arms out of his coat sleeves and ordering him to sit.

Crowing with delight at the prospect of their first ride on a train, Peter climbed up to stand on the seat, ignoring her pleas to get down. The biggest boys had already bagged the seats nearest the windows; a lanky boy carrying a bucket and spade lunged past and clambered to claim a position in the luggage net above their heads.

"Watch out, you clumsy twerp!"

Olive flinched away too late to dodge his feet as they sprawled into her face. Pain seared as one boot made contact. She covered her mouth with her hand, plopping onto her seat as her knees gave way. Her lip throbbed, already beginning to swell.

Peter tried to wrestle her hand away, eager to see the damage. "Gi's a look, Ol. Cor – you're bleeding like a stuck pig. I thought he might have knocked your teeth out."

He sounded almost disappointed. Olive had learned long ago that it was pointless to expect sympathy from her younger brother. Their dad had brought him up to have no patience with weakness or feminine tears.

"I'm alright," she mumbled, even though she felt far from it. "Sit down and eat your crackers."

Her head swirled at the pain and the sight of blood on her fingers. She fumbled up her sleeve for her handkerchief and dabbed at her mouth, sending fierce glares upwards towards the boy in the luggage rack. He hadn't even noticed what he'd done, was too busy pulling faces and boasting that he was the only kid who'd thought to bring a bucket and spade to play with when they reached the seaside.

As the guard blew his whistle and the train lurched into motion, the other children sent up a cheer. Olive didn't join in. Her teeth felt numb; over and over, she ran her tongue around her puffy mouth, across the gap at the front where a couple of adult teeth had only recently emerged, hardly daring to believe they hadn't been loosened by the blow a few moments earlier.

"I'm thirsty," Peter grumbled beside her. He had already finished scoffing his crackers. A green column of snot hung from each nostril, and before she could remind him to use his handkerchief, he swept his tongue across his top lip to clear it. They hadn't been offered anything to drink as the lady giving out crackers had said they wouldn't all have time to go to the toilet before the train had to depart.

"I expect they'll give us a drink soon." Olive said, hoping this would be enough to head off one of his tantrums. It would also be welcome to wash the taste of blood from her mouth. She'd been looking forward to her crackers, but her lip was too sore to think of eating now.

She brightened a little as she spotted Miss Summerill approaching. Dumpy and grey-haired, the teacher swayed with the movement of the train and gripped the backs of the aisle seats as she moved along the carriage. Olive had liked being in her class when she was small. Perhaps she would be able to do something about the boy in the luggage rack.

The teacher's hands fluttered as she spotted him.

"What are you doing up there, Sidney? Please get down this instant. Oh my, whatever has happened to you, Olive?" Her eyes had widened at the sight of the blood on Olive's handkerchief.

"I walked into a door, miss," Olive mumbled, dipping her chin towards her chest. Mum always gave the same excuse when anyone remarked on her cuts and bruises, and with Sidney still waving his feet around she didn't dare invite any further injuries by telling tales.

Miss Summerill frowned. "Really? Sidney, you should get down, dear..." She wrung her hands, but to no avail.

Sidney merely laughed but stopped abruptly when all the children in the compartment fell silent in the same instant.

Olive's breath caught in her throat at the sight of the stern face looming above them. Mr Winter had a way of looking at a child as if he knew every misdeed or bad thought that had ever crossed their mind. His faintly menacing presence was heightened by his distinctive way of speaking, like a character in a New York gangster movie. She'd never heard him shout; he was one of those teachers whose manner was so forbidding, he didn't need to. Every pupil dreaded the prospect of being sent to him for a misdemeanour, far more than they feared being sent to Miss Maybank, the school's headmistress.

"You, boy. Down. Now." Although Mr Winter had not raised his voice, the colour drained from Sidney's cheeks and he swung down from the rack with a sullen expression. "Find a seat someplace else," Mr Winter said, the dangerous gleam in his eyes making the boy slink off along the carriage with all his former bluster gone.

Olive let out her breath in a rush, then held it again as Mr Winter's cool gaze turned upon her.

"What do we have here?" he asked.

"She says she walked into a door." Miss Summerill sounded doubtful. She staggered as the train jerked.

One of Mr Winter's thick brown eyebrows arched slightly, and he stooped to examine Olive's swollen lip.

She stiffened, pinned by his gaze, pressing the back of her head against the high back of the seat.

He hitched his trouser legs and dropped to crouch before her, then reached out a hand to cup her chin. Instinctively, she flinched, ready to cower. It took a couple of heartbeats before she registered that his fingers were gentle. His gaze held hers as he tilted her chin, the expression in his silvery grey eyes softening. Something flickered in them, and she had a feeling he knew why she'd been afraid to say what really happened. She watched him closely until his hand dropped, the muscles in her jaw and shoulders only relaxing when he let go and stroked his lip thoughtfully.

"It doesn't need stitches. It'll be sore for a few days though, I shouldn't wonder." Straightening, he glanced around the compartment. All the children sat still, hands folded in their laps like angels. "Best behaviour now," he said. "I don't want to have to speak to any one of you. And we want everyone in one piece when we get to Wales."

The children exchanged eager glances.

"Wales, sir?" one of them risked asking. "Is that where we're going, then?"

Mr Winter nodded, but there was no time to find out more as the sound of shrieking laughter further down the carriage drew him away with Miss Summerill close on his heels.

"Wales! That's where we're off to, Ol. Is it far away?" Peter bounced in his seat.

"Not *very* far," she murmured, not wanting to admit that she wasn't sure where Wales was, or how long it might take to get there.

Three children had claimed the seats opposite, the eldest of them a boy with scabby knees bulging from skinny legs like knots in a length of twine. He and the girls alongside him all had skin the bronze colour of an old penny, and they looked so alike that Olive guessed they must be siblings.

"They wear big black hats in Wales, like witches," one of the girls said, the rich brown of her freckled cheeks turning faintly rosy at the attention this earned her. "It's true, ain't it Michael?"

The boy Michael nodded solemnly. "Tall black hats, and shawls," he said. "And they don't speak English."

"How the hell will we know what they're saying to us, then?" Peter asked, frowning.

Michael's large, expressive eyes were almost as black as his tightly curled hair. "I dunno," he said, spreading his hands. "But I suppose if that's where they're taking us, we'll soon find out. At least we'll be safe in Wales. German planes can't fly that far west."

Olive swallowed hard and gazed at her hands where they twisted in her lap. About a week ago she'd heard her parents arguing about them being evacuated. Dad had been against the idea, saying if they were going to be blown to bits or gassed by the Germans it would be better for them all to go together. But Mum had insisted she and Peter would be safer in the countryside. She'd already lost one child, she said. She didn't plan to let the others get killed if there was a chance to save them.

The idea of their dad being bombed left Olive unmoved. She'd once seen Mum telling Auntie Winnie that he was a nasty bastard. At least if he got blown to pieces or buried under rubble, she wouldn't feel the sting of his belt lashing the back of her thighs again. It was his fault she couldn't hear properly: her right ear had stopped working after he slammed her head into a wall for accidentally dropping a plate when she was six.

Mum, though, was a different matter. The lump rising in Olive's throat threatened to choke her at the thought that they'd left her in danger. With her wheezy chest, Mum wouldn't be able to run quickly down the three flights of steps from their flat to the new shelter that had been dug under the grass outside their block. The thought of her being far away, and maybe even killed, brought the familiar sick feeling back to Olive's stomach. She swallowed hard, wiping her palms on her dress.

Any day now, the war might start. Who knew how long they'd have to stay away, or what might happen while they were gone? Hitler might invade, as everyone said he'd done to Czechoslovakia, and if that happened even Wales wouldn't be safe. Again, the question arose in her mind: would she and Peter ever see their mother again?

Olive kept quiet, her thoughts churning and her senses alert as she watched the other children in her carriage. The elder of the two girls opposite was fussing with the younger one's frizzy pigtails, retying the pretty yellow ribbons and maintaining a cheerful chatter as if to keep up her spirits. In spite of the general hubbub of chatter, which made it even harder to pick out individual conversations, the lipreading skills Olive had had to develop after her ear was hurt revealed that the older girl, who looked about her own age, was called Barbara. The younger, whose cheeky, gap-toothed smile flashed often, was Shirley.

They changed trains at Paddington Station, where tables of refreshments were served by more ladies in green hats. Peter wolfed down orange squash and jam sandwiches, but Olive only nibbled at hers, wincing at the pain in her lip. Her stomach clenched in increasing trepidation at the prospect of going to a place where they wouldn't understand anyone.

Before boarding their next train, one of the ladies gave each child a heavy paper bag with instructions to hand it over to their host family on arrival at their destination. Olive had to help Peter with his, as well as managing her own. She felt weighed down with too much to carry, and too much to wear, and on top of all that too much to worry about, not least trying to keep an eye on Peter, who could no more stand obediently in line than he could pat his head and rub his tummy at the same time.

Soon they were seated on the westbound train and the tall, sooty chimneys of the city started giving way to open spaces and patches of greenery. Curiosity got the better of them, and the children couldn't resist peeking into the paper packages they'd been given. There wasn't much of interest, only corned beef, a tin of condensed milk, a packet of Marie biscuits and a package of tea. Olive was packing hers back up when Michael gave a shout and pointed towards the window.

"Look – cows! And see how big the fields are."

Everyone crowded to peer out of the smut-stained pane.

"Cor! It's true what the teacher said – they really do eat grass. How funny!" Barbara said. She and Olive giggled together with little Shirley, whose long-lashed brown eyes were round with surprise at the unfamiliar sights from the window.

"Are they really cows, Mikey? Are you sure those ain't pigs?" Shirley asked.

"Definitely cows, Shirl. Pigs are pink, with curly tails. I been reading about them this week. Cows have got four stomachs, you know."

"Four! They must have to eat all day."

"I suppose so. And they make milk. The farmer has to squeeze it out of them."

Olive was awed by Michael's knowledge as much as his confidence. It must be a remarkable feeling, to be able to have all eyes on you without cringing. She rarely spoke up to offer an opinion or to show off a snippet of knowledge, knowing it to be a sure-fire way to earn criticism or enmity. Still, there was a part of her that wished Michael knew she, too, enjoyed reading books and learning about things. Part of her longed for him to look up and see her, to nod in her direction and give her one of the earnest smiles he readily gave to his sisters.

For a brief, luxurious moment she forgot how sore her mouth was: it felt full of words she might share. Bold, clever words gleaned from books of stories and true facts; ones Michael would probably appreciate if he heard them. They fizzed temptingly on her tongue until, as always, she swallowed them down. The feeling would go if she focused on something else. It always did. Better to go unnoticed. Life was safer that way, both at home and at school.

After a while several of the children had fallen asleep,

including Peter, whose head lolled heavily against Olive's arm. Her own eyelids drooped as the carriage became stuffy and warm from the sun glaring through the large windows. The rhythm of the train had become soothing as the line of carriages creaked and groaned along, accompanied by a constant hiss of steam. The sight of telegraph cables rising and falling between their tall poles alongside the track was almost hypnotic. Olive had never seen so many trees or so much grass before. Nor had she ever seen such an expanse of uninterrupted sky. It was disconcerting, like finding herself in a film. She half expected to glimpse magical creatures, or a tornado, or a battle between cowboys and Indians.

Looking round, Olive noticed that Shirley had folded her arms over her belly. Her face had gained a strange, waxy sheen.

"Is she alright?" Olive asked.

Barbara glanced up, following Olive's concerned gaze just as Shirley's stomach contents erupted from her mouth. A stinking mess of undigested jam sandwich and cream crackers splashed into her lap, drenching the paper bag of food for her hosts. It might have been funny if it hadn't smelled so awful, and if Shirley hadn't then bawled so loudly, waking Peter who now complained that he, too, felt sick. While Miss Summerill was fetched to help clean Shirley up as best she could, Olive could do little but advise Peter to breathe through his mouth and try not to think about it.

Unlike the first train, this one had no compartments or corridor.

"Oi! Miss! I need to pee and there's no carsey on this train," a boy shouted.

Miss Summerill, crimson-cheeked, snapped at him uncharacteristically. "You'll have to wait until the next station," she huffed, and headed back to her own seat.

After a pause, the boy swaggered over to the open window and Olive averted her gaze while he relieved himself through the gap. Within moments there was a queue of boys jostling and jeering to follow his lead, and she had little choice but to let Peter join them when he claimed to be bursting to go.

"It's alright for you," she muttered when he sat back down, clearly delighted with himself. "What about me?"

"Just pull your knickers down and stick your arse out," he said, laughing when she rolled her eyes.

More time passed, and Shirley started jiggling in her seat. Her legs were crossed, and she clutched herself with one hand, grimacing. It wasn't hard to guess the reason for her distress, but they could hardly tell her to pee out of the window as the boys had done.

"You'll have to hold on," Barbara muttered to her.

Olive sent a sympathetic glance her way. She was uncomfortable herself. How long would it be before they reached their destination? It felt as if they'd been travelling all day. At last, Shirley's little face crumpled, and tears flooded her cheeks. Olive's nostrils twitched as the stink of vomit was supplemented with a new smell of urine.

Michael looked away, gazing out of the window with his mouth set in a line, while Barbara passed her sister a handkerchief and shifted to the farthest edge of the seat away from her.

At intervals, the train stopped and groups of children were called to disembark. Each time, Olive tensed, wondering if it would be her turn, and if she and Peter would be called at the same time, or if they'd be separated as their mum had feared. It was teatime when their turn finally came.

More matrons in green hats waited on the platform, and as the dishevelled children tumbled from the train they were directed to line up before being marched two-abreast up a hill. Several were hollow-eyed and stinking, and Shirley was not the only child to have disgraced themselves in the absence of a toilet.

Olive dragged Peter along. She didn't know whether to be

relieved or disappointed that they were still together. Peter was a snotty, smelly, grubby little tyke, and his whinging grated on her nerves, but at least she would be able to do as Mum had asked and look after him.

"I'm too tired to walk up here. I've had enough of being evacuated now. I want to go back home," he whined.

The cobbled road uphill was steeper than any she'd seen in London, and there was no way of telling how far they'd have to walk, or where they'd end up. This town seemed to be as grey and dirty as their part of London had been, but without the comfort of any buildings she recognised. The shops they passed were unfamiliar, with a few people staring from windows and doorways as if they'd never seen children before. Not a familiar face anywhere, except those in the line of kids, who'd soon disperse goodness knows where. Trudging along, puffing as they wound their way uphill, Olive could spare little energy to take in their surroundings.

Half-dazed, they crossed sharply sloping side streets of low terraced houses, slate-roofed and with front doors right on the pavement. No blocks of flats like the one she and Peter lived in. Would there be anything nice to do in this bleak place? Were there any cinemas or places to play?

At the head of the line of children, a foot taller than Miss Summerill, marched Mr Winter in his navy-blue suit and brown fedora hat, his coat draped over his arm. Olive fixed her gaze on him. All they could do was follow and hope everything would work out for the best.

THREE

Dodie

Dodie's heart sank as she approached the white-haired man in the reading room. His head had been resting on the table without moving for at least an hour. It wasn't unusual for library patrons to fall asleep over the newspapers, but she felt a moment of trepidation every time she had to touch one of them on the shoulder. It was the fault of Mr Gibson, the librarian, for suggesting she wake them up a good while before closing time in case they were actually dead.

It wasn't only the thought of finding a corpse that bothered her, but the prospect of Mr Gibson's wrath at the bureaucracy and late finish that would ensue. The library was due to close in less than half an hour, and immediately after locking up she needed to fulfil the mission delegated to her by her sister, so this chap had better not have expired over today's *Western Mail*.

The tapping of her heels on the parquet flooring failed to wake the man before she reached his side, so she stooped to take a closer look. His hollow cheek was rough with white stubble, and thinning hair had been combed across his pate. A grubby woollen cap lay on the polished oak table beside him. His gnarled hand with black-edged nails, swollen knuckles and scars suggested a life of toil. Probably a former miner or factory worker, like so many of the patrons of the library in Pontybrenin. They came in for many reasons: some to improve their education by reading, hoping thereby to improve their lot in life; many, she suspected, simply to pass the time in a warm, peaceful environment which must feel like paradise compared with their years in a colliery or factory.

To her relief, a discreet cough stirred the man into wakefulness. Dodie smiled.

"I'm sorry to disturb you, sir, but we'll be closing soon. If you'd like to borrow anything, you'll need to bring it to the desk in the next few minutes."

Blinking, he nodded and sat up. "That's alright, flower. I'll have another look tomorrow. Might try the *Express*, see if that one's any better for keeping me awake." With a wink, he picked up his cap, stuffed it onto his head and shuffled towards the main doors.

Dodie gathered up the newspapers and abandoned books to return them to their shelves. The reading room had a smell of its own: musty wool, stale sweat and tobacco. It clung to patrons' clothes and mixed with the smoke of the coal fire in the corner and the distinctive dry smell of books. It was a calming smell, one she had come to associate with routine and quietness. She slotted a book neatly between its companion volumes, then paused, realising someone else had come in.

The newcomer's voice was familiar and unmistakable. Strident, and very English, unlike most of their patrons whose more melodic Welsh voices were reverentially hushed in the pillared surroundings of the library.

"Good evening, my good fellow. I'm looking for Miss Fitznorton." Venetia's patrician voice carried clearly across the reading room from the reception desk. Dodie could imagine Mr

Gibson's annoyance at the disturbance, but he wouldn't dare express it to such a prominent figure – a former mayor no less, and still a town councillor and magistrate.

Venetia was unusually tall for a woman, but it wasn't only her height, her confident voice and the metal brace on her leg that made her stand out. She exuded a restless and dynamic energy that drew the eye and made people notice her. Her clothes were plain, but well-cut and of a quality that few in Pontybrenin could afford; her fair hair was always immaculately set and her homely face, bare of make-up, was remarkably unlined for a woman of fifty-one. Dodie was fonder of her than of almost anyone. Of all the adults who had featured in her childhood, Venetia had been the one on whom she could most reliably depend.

Mr Gibson, stiff in his old-fashioned starched collar and bow tie, looked pointedly at his fob watch, replacing it in his waistcoat pocket before replying. "Miss Fitznorton's shift doesn't end until half past five, Miss Vaughan-Lloyd. But you're welcome to wait until then."

"Ordinarily I would, of course. However, today is no ordinary day. Miss Fitznorton's sister, Mrs Charlotte Havard, has requested that she collect two of the poor children who have arrived in town this afternoon. The little mites have left their homes to travel nearly two hundred miles into the unknown and are waiting at the church hall as we speak. I wouldn't ask you for my own sake, or for Miss Fitznorton's, but it would be an act of Christian charity on your part to allow her to go a little earlier than usual. For the children's sake."

Mr Gibson's hawk-like eyes had spotted Dodie hovering beside one of the tall oak bookcases. It was clear from his expression that he dearly wanted to keep her there until half past five on the dot, but to deny Venetia something she wanted was not easy. "Very well. You may go now, Miss Fitznorton," he said through lips tight with disapproval, as if he could hardly bear to say the words.

Dodie thanked him, knowing he would more than likely ask her to make the quarter hour up on another occasion, and hurried to collect her bag, coat and hat.

Venetia frowned as the door closed behind them. "That man is deliberately obstructive, simply for the enjoyment of exercising a little power."

"Oh, he is. But my previous boss was worse, so I can't complain." Dodie spared her the details of her previous supervisor's wandering hands and suggestive remarks. As much as she was wary of Mr Gibson's sharp temper and strict ways, she felt safer working at the library than she had in her former post as a junior clerk in the London office of a commercial firm. At least here she didn't have to be constantly on her guard, wary of turning her back in case her bottom was groped, and ridiculed if she raised an objection to such demeaning treatment.

"So, how are you settling into the job? I imagine Pontybrenin seems dull to you after the excitement of London. You were always a bookish child, but does it suit your temperament to work in the library?"

"I'm fine. Honestly. I enjoy helping people find books they'll enjoy. Many of them seem so lonely, and the library is a place where they can have a little conversation."

"Loneliness is a curse. And, in my experience, a broken heart can be equally painful, and may take a long time to mend."

Dodie remained silent, unwilling to reward Venetia's attempt at fishing. Her heart was mending, but still fragile. Raking over the coals of her recent humiliation could only cause pain. Having decided when she returned to Pontybrenin to put thoughts of romantic attachments aside, she was ploughing her energies into forging her own way in the world and finding satisfaction in doing so. She'd had to learn at a young age how to rely on herself. She told herself now that she didn't need a man in her life, or indeed anyone else who might let her down or reject her.

And ironically, her work here made her less lonely than she'd been for most of her life. It connected her with people. With patrons asking her about books, there were always new topics to find out about and puzzles to solve, whether it was someone offering only the vaguest description of a book – "it was red, with gold embossing on the cover" – or a request for volumes on diverse topics, from ancient Welsh folk tales to Keynesian economics. Queries took her out of herself, and away from the sort of thoughts that had led her to flee London.

With hard work and dedication she might one day work her way up. While her options might be limited by her sex, she had achieved good marks at school and then at secretarial college, so perhaps in the future she might even take over Mr Gibson's post or join the civil service or local council. But for now, being a library assistant in Pontybrenin would have to be enough.

"You seem lost in your thoughts, my dear. A penny for them."

"I was just thinking it was brave of you, convincing Mr Gibson to bend the rules like that," she hedged, slowing her steps to match the other woman's limping gait as they made their way along the uneven flagstone pavement towards the church hall.

Venetia raised an eyebrow. "We'll all need to muster a little courage in the coming days and months, I daresay. Have you heard the news on the wireless today?"

"No. We've been busy. I know about the evacuation, of course."

"Hitler has sent his troops into Poland, blast him. Parliament meets at six this evening, but we all know what the inevitable consequence will be. He's hardly likely to turn his armies around and claim it was all an unfortunate misunderstanding."

This was it, then. They were on the brink of war, as so many people had predicted. It was less than a year since the prime minister had promised the nation a long-lasting peace.

Venetia's expression spoke volumes of what another European war would mean. Dodie was too young to remember much about the Great War, but she'd heard stories aplenty.

Dodie reached out to squeeze her arm.

Venetia sighed. "Thank goodness the government is thinking of the children, finding them homes outside of London for their safety. I gather Charlotte has volunteered to take two children?"

"She has, but she couldn't collect them herself. Something about her committee work. The Women's Institute this time, I think? You know Charlotte – always occupied with something or other, but not necessarily the most important things." Dodie rolled her eyes.

"Now, Dodie. The WI will play an important role in keeping us fed if the Germans blockade our ports and sink our shipping, as they did in the last show. You should be proud that she's doing her bit."

"It won't be Charlotte who bears the brunt of the hard work of looking after the children, though, will it?"

"I think sometimes, having been away from home for much of your life, you forget quite how much she's achieved. When I first knew her, she was a silly young girl who'd been brought up to believe marriage should be the pinnacle of her ambition, and yet look at her now: heading up countless committees and keeping that frightful old house going. She even brought up three children despite being so tragically widowed. Not many people could do it."

"The way I remember it, she rarely did much of the nursing and child-rearing herself." Dodie muttered the words under her breath, reluctant to quarrel with Venetia, whose loyalty to Charlotte ran deep. She knew it pained her to hear such old resentments, but it was impossible not to see a bitter irony in Charlotte offering to care for strangers' children when she'd failed her own infant half-sister.

It wasn't that Charlotte had ever been cruel to Dodie. As she'd often been reminded, Charlotte had taken her in when she was only a few days old. The death of their father, Sir Lucien Fitznorton, followed by Dodie's mother only days after Dodie's birth, had left her an orphan. Naturally Dodie was grateful to the older half-sister who'd been the closest thing to a parent she'd ever known. But the wrench when Charlotte sent her away to school only a few years later had cast a shadow over not only their relationship but Dodie's whole view of the world.

It was all too easy for Dodie to imagine how the children gathering in the church hall might be feeling. Lost, bewildered, hoping against hope that the strangers charged with their care might show them kindness. They'd be dreading what lay ahead for them, and what might befall those they'd left behind. They faced a future over which they had no say and no control. It made her mouth dry to think about it, bringing back unwelcome memories of that awful day, aged four, when her own world fell apart. Charlotte might do her duty and provide materially for their new evacuees, but Dodie feared she wouldn't give them what they needed most.

Whatever happened, Dodie would make sure the children billeted in their home were well cared for. However long they ended up staying, she'd do her level best to help them feel safe and secure, and never to make them feel that they weren't wanted or welcome. As she pushed open the door to the church hall, she made this her promise to herself.

FOUR

Dodie

The church hall smelled of disinfectant and floor polish, and something much less pleasant that made Dodie wrinkle her nose. A motley bunch of children were lined up as if they were on display. There were fewer than she'd expected: presumably most had already dispersed to their new homes, or else the predicted number of evacuees had been exaggerated. All those remaining looked grubby, their faces and hands covered in grimy streaks from their long train journey. The smallest wore a coat bearing dubious stains down the front, as if she'd been sick or spilled something that had left a nasty mark when it dried.

A man hailed Venetia, and Dodie recognised him as one of the local police constables.

"Ah, Miss Vaughan-Lloyd. What do you think of all this, eh? I must say, I have grave reservations about the number of strangers coming into our town. This lot today, and more due tomorrow. It strikes me that this evacuation programme could enable all sorts of undesirables to move around the country, and no one would think to question it. Is there anyone checking that these people are who they say they are? Are there any guarantees that we won't end up having to house criminals and degenerates?"

Venetia stared at him and raised an eyebrow. "Good evening, Constable Todd. I appreciate your concern. However, isn't it rather unlikely that any undesirables would wish to come to such a dull little town as Pontybrenin?"

This answer didn't seem to mollify him. "Who knows what goes on in the minds of these people, miss? The kinds of people who want to spread dissent or radical views would be only too happy to have the chance to take them all over the country. You only have to look at what's been happening in Coventry and Liverpool this past week, with the IRA bombing and murdering innocent people. Our mine and factories could be a target for Fenians, or Nazi sympathisers, or Communists."

"I have every confidence that your vigilance will keep us safe, Constable. And to judge by the evacuees here this evening, I think we have little to fear from such young children, or from their teachers." Venetia's firm tone brooked no argument, and he nodded and finally allowed them to pass.

It seemed that while they'd been waylaid, several more children had been claimed by local hosts. A woman Dodie recognised as a library patron and an avid reader of gruesome murder mysteries rushed past, leading a pale, frightened little girl by the hand.

"You might regret leaving it until now, Miss Fitznorton," the woman said in her lilting Welsh accent as she left. "All the best ones have already been taken."

The best ones? These were children, not goods for sale.

A smartly dressed woman pointed a gloved hand towards a scrawny girl of about six or seven, whose eyes seemed too big for her thin brown face.

"I'll take that one. She seems to be the cleanest out of a sorry bunch," she declared, her decision apparently made, then turned towards a table where two adults sat with pens and paper.

A tumult of emotions crossed the girl's face.

The woman was occupied in giving her details to the man at the desk and didn't notice the child's reluctance at first. "Look sharp, now," she said, glancing back to see the girl still standing in line. "I haven't got all day."

The girl took a faltering step towards her, but a younger child, a scruffy little girl with tightly curled black hair in pigtails tied with yellow ribbons lunged forward to tug at her hand.

"You know what Mum said," the younger one insisted, then turned to the lady who had claimed her sister. "We all have to stay together. Please, missus. Mikey, tell her," she added, turning to the taller boy beside her.

He put a protective arm around her shoulders. "Our mum and dad said all three of us must stay together. You can't take her without us," he said, with a quiet determination that brought a lump to Dodie's throat.

The chosen girl glanced from her two siblings to the woman, as if torn between family loyalty and obedience. Picking up a battered canvas bag, she murmured something to the younger girl, whose shoulders slumped in response. The younger one's face screwed up as she clung to the boy, and Dodie guessed she was trying not to cry as their sister left them behind. Dodie's heart thumped wildly as her own memories of abandonment flooded back. Surely the girl wouldn't be forced to go without her siblings?

Realising she was blocking the way, Dodie stepped aside for the woman to pass. A waft of expensive perfume surrounded her, and her nose was stuck up in the air as she went by. The beady glass eyes of the fox-fur stole around her neck seemed to glare even more fiercely than the woman herself. She didn't show any sign of sympathy for the girl, who let out a sob and faltered, reaching for her siblings' hands as if she couldn't bear to let go.

The boy fumbled in his pocket, then the three children huddled together, whispering.

The woman paused, annoyed at being delayed. "Come along, now," she snapped.

All three children shook their heads.

The boy spoke up, his chin tilted upwards and his nostrils flaring in defiance even though his eyes were wide with fear. "Only if you take us all," he said.

"Don't be impudent. I never heard of anything so silly."

It didn't strike Dodie as silly at all. Of course they didn't want to be severed from the people they loved. They'd already been forced to leave their parents and homes. What was silly about them clinging to each other?

"I've told you I can only take one. Do as you're told and be grateful to be offered a billet. There are many who wouldn't be so generous." The woman grabbed the little girl's forearm, only to exclaim impatiently and call out to the teacher. "Look here. He's tied them together!"

Dodie saw that the boy had indeed tied his wrists together with those of his sisters. It would be easy enough for an adult to cut the string, but her heart went out to them at the thought of how desperate they must be even to think of trying such a thing. She knew all too well how frightening and lonely it was to arrive in unfamiliar surroundings far from home and face unsympathetic adults.

Charlotte had specified that Dodie should accept two children, but one more wouldn't make much difference. It would be worth a little extra temporary inconvenience to spare siblings the anguish of separation.

"I could take all three," she blurted out, before she had any more time to think about it. She kept her gaze on the teacher and the impatient woman, in case her offer was turned down.

She didn't want to see the children's faces if their hopes of staying together were dashed. Experience had taught her how little say children usually had in what befell them. Adults controlled everything.

The woman huffed impatiently, but she allowed herself to be persuaded so quickly that it seemed she was more relieved than disappointed. "Be my guest. I wouldn't want to take on such a cry-baby, in any case. I wish you luck with this bunch. You'll have your hands full with them." Marching back to the man at the desk, she announced the changes to the arrangements. "I can only take one, and I should be grateful if you could make it a decent one," she announced, and was quickly allocated a more biddable child. She stalked out with the chosen boy dragging his heels behind her.

A middle-aged woman and a sour-faced farmer were making their selection, choosing the two tallest boys in the rapidly dwindling line. Dodie hoped they wouldn't be expected to serve as unpaid labourers on the farm but had a suspicion their introduction to country life would be a harsh one.

"Well done, Dodie," Venetia murmured. "My, isn't this ghastly? It's like a slave market in here, with traders examining the goods. I hate the idea of having to choose one in front of the others."

"It looks as if your choice will be limited," Dodie replied grimly. "There are only two left." Her heart sank as she realised the last remaining boy was clinging to the girl beside him, who must be his sister. She was a little taller but equally skinny and dressed in ill-fitting clothes which looked as if they'd been repeatedly darned and patched. The buttons on the boy's jacket were mismatched, and his sister's shabby overcoat appeared to be several sizes too small.

Venetia only had one spare bed in the house she shared with her lodger Maggie, Dodie's former nanny. She wouldn't be able to take both.

"I don't see any other hosts coming forward," Venetia said, looking back towards the open doorway.

A young woman wearing a green hat denoting her role with the Women's Voluntary Services called them to the table. "You'll need to register your details before you take the children home," she said. "We'll note it on a postcard for each child, so that they can let their parents know their addresses, and the billeting officer will update our records. Will you take these last two, Miss Vaughan-Lloyd?"

Venetia grimaced. "I'm awfully sorry, but I only have room for one, and after seeing the other child so upset at the prospect of separation from her siblings, I should hate to be the cause of any further distress."

"You could take one of the teachers?" the volunteer suggested. "There are two, Miss Summerill and Mr Winter. Reverend Appleton has said he'll take Mr Winter; as a bachelor it wouldn't be proper for him to have a single woman living at the vicarage. No one has offered to host Miss Summerill yet."

Venetia nodded. "An ideal solution. I'd be pleased to offer her a room." As they followed the volunteer towards the table, Venetia whispered into Dodie's ear. "Do you think me awful for being relieved? I can't say I relished the prospect of dealing with a child. At least I'll be able to make conversation with a teacher. We might even enjoy each other's company, if three women in one household doesn't prove too much of a crowd."

Miss Summerill shook Venetia by the hand and thanked her, then took Dodie's details for the three children waiting in a huddle near the doorway. The teacher looked wan with fatigue, and thin strands of greying mousy hair escaped what looked as if it might have been a neat hairstyle that morning.

"It's so kind of you to take the three, Miss Fitznorton. An odd address – *Plas Norton*. But – isn't Plas a German word? Doesn't it mean town square, or something? Are you... are you *German?*" Her eyes widened and her cheeks turned pink.

Dodie shook her head hastily. "No, I'm not German, and it's *Plas*, not Platz. *Plas* is a Welsh word. It means…" She hesitated, struggling to come up with a definition that didn't sound boastful. "It means… mansion."

"Well, that's good. You won't have any difficulty in accommodating three, in that case."

The billeting officer's ears had pricked up. He thumbed through his sheaves of papers. "Ah yes, Plas Norton. When I visited, I discussed the possible number of billets with… let me see, now. A Mrs Havard, according to my records."

"My sister," Dodie said. "She offered to take two children, but to avoid separating siblings I've agreed to take three."

It wouldn't do to sound as if they didn't want to do their bit. When she'd discussed it with Charlotte, they'd both agreed that this was important war service. They'd have been willing even if it wasn't compulsory. It was one of the few things they did agree upon.

The man sent her a stern look over his reading glasses. "The capacity of the house suggested to me that there was sufficient room for several more. I understand the house was run as a hospital in the last war, accommodating a dozen or so convalescent officers. Even with four adults in the family, and two members of household staff living in, there are still several bedrooms standing empty."

There was an awkward silence in which Miss Summerill and the WVS volunteer exchanged a speculative look.

Dodie swallowed. "I've already taken one more than my sister agreed to…"

"But given that you're the last host to come forward, and you do have plenty of space… Even if you could take them just for tonight, it would be a great help. And then if you find you don't have room, we could make enquiries tomorrow to find alternative accommodation. A hostel, perhaps." The volunteer's smile seemed artificially bright.

The billeting officer didn't smile. "The hall closes at six. If no one else comes forward, we'll have to march those last two around the streets and knock doors until we find a household willing to take them in. It seems a shame to put them through that when you can see they're already exhausted and hungry. Especially as you are fortunate enough to have the capacity in your... mansion."

Dodie's stomach plummeted. So far, the fellow had refrained from pointing out that accommodating a child was compulsory if there was sufficient capacity in the billet. For all she knew, he might have the right to impose a fine if she refused. There didn't seem to be a way to avoid taking all five children.

"Look at the poor little things," the WVS volunteer added. "Think of the day they've had."

The vicar had come in, jangling a large bunch of keys in his hand as if he was impatient to lock up. "It's five to six. Are we all done?" he asked.

"I think we are, Reverend. Are we?" The billeting officer addressed Dodie with a persistence she had to grudgingly admire. He held his pen poised over his papers.

"I suppose we are." She sighed. "For tonight, at least."

She'd have until they got home to work out how to explain this to Charlotte.

FIVE

Olive

Olive had never been in a car before. Nor had she ever seen one like this in real life. Peter's eyes and mouth were as round as the wheels when it drew up beside them, its sleek lines so graceful it looked ready to take off and fly. Its long, shiny blue nose was flanked by sweeping running boards which dipped below the doors and came to rest at the equally elegant rear wheel arches. Large chrome headlights were mounted either side of the tall front grille with its Riley badge, all polished to a dazzling mirror-brightness. The five children gawped, speechless.

It came as a surprise when an ordinary-looking man climbed out of the driving seat. Olive had expected a vehicle so beautiful to be driven by a movie star like Cary Grant or Ronald Colman, but this fellow wore a scruffy tweed jacket with corduroy patches at the elbows, and a flat cap such as Dad wore to the pub. He removed it, revealing thin, sandy-coloured hair that was white above his ears, and turned it over in his hands before speaking to the posh young woman who had collected them from the church hall.

"Am I seeing double? Must be time I got my eyes tested. Only, I could have sworn Dolly said you'd be getting two, and... well, blow me down if that doesn't look suspiciously like five," he said with one bushy eyebrow raised, pointing along the row of children as if he was counting them. His voice sounded almost musical, like the billeting officer's, but deeper.

"The original intention was to take two, Ivor," the woman replied a little sharply. "However, we now have Michael, who's ten, and his sisters Barbara and Shirley, who are seven and..." She paused, and all three Clarke children helpfully chimed in with the answer "six."

"And these two are Olive, who is eight, and her brother Peter, who is seven, like Barbara." Her smile looked tight. "This is Mr Griffiths, children. He and his wife work for us, so you'll see a lot of them during your stay."

Mr Griffiths opened the luggage compartment, stowing each child's bag or pillowcase bundle inside. Then he turned the shiny silver handle to open the car's back door, revealing a leather seat like a sofa.

"You'd better pile in then, kids," he said.

Peter and Shirley rushed to clamber in.

"Feet off the seat!" he boomed in a voice that made even Peter obey.

After some squirming, the five children rearranged themselves so that Peter sat on Olive's lap and Shirley sat on Barbara's. The other girls' skinny legs were almost the same shade of tan as the leather seat, unlike Olive and Peter's pasty, bowed limbs. Olive breathed through her mouth to avoid the sharp odours clinging to Shirley's clothes.

They all stank after having their hair combed with methylated spirits in the church hall, to combat lice. It had been a humiliating experience after the strain of the journey, later crowned by having to wait in line to be chosen by strangers. As other children were chosen first, each new pair of eyes skating past Olive as if she was invisible or worse, repulsive, Olive had felt something inside her shrink smaller and smaller until she'd wondered if she might actually disappear unnoticed by anyone in the world, no more important or substantial than a puff of smoke or a breath of wind.

The adults wound the front windows down, making a fierce breeze ruffle Olive's hair as they drove along. Presumably they, too, weren't immune to the pungent smell emanating from the children. Olive appraised the young woman in the passenger seat. She'd introduced herself as Miss Fitznorton and explained that they were welcome to stay with her and her sister Mrs Havard for as long as they needed.

Miss Fitznorton was pretty, or at least she would be if she'd stop frowning and biting at her lower lip every time she looked over her shoulder at the children in the back. She wore a blue jacket over a dress sprigged with flowers, and a dainty hat with a bow which Olive noticed picked out the exact shade of dusky pink on her dress. Her chestnut-brown hair fell in soft waves to just below her shoulders, pinned back in rolls at the front to frame her face. To Olive she looked so perfectly put together she might have been a mannequin from a shop window come to life, right down to the gloves and smart little bag. She'd never seen anyone look so fresh and lovely before. The women in Olive's block of flats rarely wore anything more sophisticated on their heads than a hairnet or headscarf, and their clothes didn't fit so beautifully or have that perfect finish and sheen. Usually they covered themselves with a wraparound apron, except when they went to Mass on Sundays. None of them had such straight white teeth or smooth, rosy cheeks. Miss Fitznorton was a vision of a different world. A different life. What must she think of these five rag-tag kids she'd been so obviously reluctant to take home in her glamorous car?

Olive picked at her fingernails as the car purred along through the town, past the terraced rows of almost uniform slate-roofed cottages, past bigger, semi-detached houses with mock-Tudor gables and long front gardens, out into country lanes with high hedges and only a few other vehicles. It wasn't only the increase in speed that made her nervous. She recalled observing Miss Fitznorton's arrival at the church hall, alongside an even taller woman who'd had a leg in a brace and a walking stick. The tall woman had leaned towards her and said something about a slave market. Although she didn't manage to lipread the whole sentence, those two words had made Olive's blood chill. Where were they being taken to? Would they be slaves? Would Mum ever know where they were?

Hills rose all around them, forbiddingly dark against the orange-streaked evening sky. They sped past fields, some grazed by sheep, and then crossed a river over a stone bridge. For a while the charcoal-grey waters flowed slowly alongside the road, banked by trees with leaves in myriad shades of green. A few showed signs of turning brown, but only here and there, as if they still clung to summer. When they slowed to pass a clutch of houses and shops, Miss Fitznorton inclined her head.

"This is Bryncarreg," she said. "There's a post office where you'll be able to send letters to your parents, a grocer's and sweet shop, and the school you'll all attend while you're staying at Plas Norton. Although the village is a couple of miles from the house, there's a shortcut across the fields past Home Farm. I'll show you the way, either tomorrow or on Sunday. I hope you've brought some sturdy shoes."

Olive and Peter exchanged a look. They didn't possess any other shoes but the canvas plimsolls they both wore every day. A glance at the other children revealed that they were wearing boots, but Michael's had a hole in the toe and Barbara and Shirley's were little better.

Beside her, Shirley belched ominously. "I feel sick again," she said with a whimper.

Both adults' heads whipped round, and the car juddered to a halt, but too late to prevent the inevitable.

"Bloody hell, Shirley, you stupid idiot!" Peter swore, flicking lumps of half-digested cracker off his shorts.

Olive nudged him for being so rude and was rewarded with a kick on the shin that made her suck in her breath.

"Out! Out!" Mr Griffiths urged, leaping from the car to wrench the back door open.

The children bundled out and stood helplessly beside the car, Barbara sniffling miserably and dabbing her handkerchief down their soiled dresses while Shirley wailed.

"You can explain this to Mrs H," Mr Griffiths grumbled, fetching a cloth from the front of the car and wiping the seats and carpet down. "As if I won't have enough to do setting up three extra beds, now I'll have to clean the ruddy car as well."

Miss Fitznorton grimaced, then reached out to pat Shirley on the shoulder. "There there, now. You couldn't help it," she said, before turning back to Mr Griffiths. "You know I'll help you with the beds. And yes, I'll take responsibility. But there's no need for Charlotte to even know... Dolly will know a way to get rid of the smell. We'll keep the windows open and drive a bit slower. If we sit this one near the window for the rest of the journey, we should have time to stop and let her out if she feels sick again." She turned back to Shirley and dropped to a crouch in front of her, dabbing at the little girl's tear-filled eyes with a lacy handkerchief. "You will tell us if you feel poorly again, won't you?"

Reluctantly, everyone clambered back into the car, this time with the back windows open as well as those at the front. Shirley buried her face against Michael's shoulder, sniffing. Mr Griffiths drove cautiously, and in the mirror which sat above the dials on the polished wooden dashboard Olive saw him cast frequent, worried glances back towards the children.

It must have been only a few minutes later, although it seemed longer, when Mr Griffiths swung the wheel around to turn into a narrower lane. This road was bumpier, and he drove much more slowly. To one side was woodland with tall trees and dense undergrowth of tangled brambles. On the other, between the road and the glowering hills, lay a low, grassy valley sprinkled with white clover. It seemed a vast expanse, almost like a prairie in a cowboy movie. It couldn't have felt more alien to any child who'd only known the city.

In the distance, Olive noticed a group of brown animals she'd never seen before. She pointed towards them.

"What's those brown things over there?" she asked.

"They're deer, they are," Mr Griffiths said.

Olive frowned. Did he mean they were expensive? Why would anyone want to buy them?

"Fallow deer. We get venison from them," Miss Fitznorton added.

Olive had never heard of venison. Perhaps it was some kind of milk, although they looked nothing like the cows she'd seen from the window of the train.

On they went, until they rounded a bend and saw a building in the distance. Built of stone, with four towers and tall chimneys, it looked like a castle from a storybook. Staring, Olive forgot about the long train journey and the fear she'd felt in the church hall. She forgot to worry about her shoes or what venison might be, or Mum, or how her legs were getting pins and needles from Peter sitting on her lap for so long. As they drew closer, passing through metal gates onto a wide sweep of gravel in front of an arched porch of pale stone, her jaw hung slack. She half expected to see the King and Queen appear on the roof of the porch, like the newsreels she'd seen of them waving from Buckingham Palace with the princesses in their pretty frocks. Beside her, Barbara gasped, while Peter started bouncing, his feet kicking against her shins. Even Shirley stirred and looked up, rubbing puffy brown eyes with her fists.

"Here we are," Miss Fitznorton said. "Welcome to Plas Norton, children."

SIX

Olive

Mr Griffiths left Miss Fitznorton at the porch before driving around the corner of the house to a flat cobbled yard edged by buildings in need of a fresh coat of whitewash. The lower edges of their wooden doors were ragged, as if they'd been gnawed away, and the paint was flaking off in patches. Weeds sprouted between the cobbles and from the guttering edging the slate roofs. He stopped the car outside what looked like a workshop with a tool bench, then hopped out and opened the back door.

"Out you get, now, you 'orrible lot. You'll be wanting your tea, I reckon, and then a bath and bed. My Dolly will soon have you whipped into shape."

Olive slipped warily down from the car. Although Mr Griffiths had called them horrible, the gleam in his eye and the hint of a smile on his cheeks suggested he was teasing.

"Fall in, troops. Quick, march!"

Peter grinned and immediately fell into step behind Mr Griffiths, swinging his arms and stamping his feet like a soldier. With the circulation flooding back into her calves in a rush of pins and needles, Olive trailed after the others round a corner and into the big house.

Her eyes widened. There wasn't much time to take in the details of her surroundings beyond scrubbed grey flagstones and blue-painted walls in a long, high-ceilinged corridor. It led past a series of rooms to the biggest kitchen she'd ever seen. Warm rays of evening sunshine slanted through a row of tall windows set high up on the walls and bounced off the gleaming white tiles which stood shoulder-height to Mr Griffiths. In the centre of the room was a pine table, its scrubbed surface bigger than Mum's entire kitchen at home. Dozens of copper saucepans and jelly moulds sat on thick wooden shelves above cupboards around the edges of the room. An enormous black range dominated one wall, with a smaller electric cooker beside it.

A dark-haired woman wearing a white apron turned from her task of stirring the contents of a huge saucepan as the children lined up beside the table, eyes darting everywhere to take in their new surroundings.

The woman held up two fingers to Mr Griffiths, who stood with his hands in his pockets and eyed her with his twinkling half-smile.

"How many fingers am I holding up?" the woman demanded.

"Two," he answered.

"That's right. This is what two looks like. And that"– she pointed towards the children – "that is *not* what two looks like. Arithmetic was never my strong point, but even I can see that that looks like considerably more."

"Well, Doll, it's like when Mrs H goes on one of her shopping trips, see. She goes out intending to get two dresses and comes back with five. In the full range of colours." He gave a wheezy cough into his handkerchief, then wiped his mouth, his eyes gleaming as if he had been stifling a chuckle.

"Very funny, I'm sure. But where does she think we're going to put them? I've only aired two beds."

"I'll sort it."

"Five! I ask you. It's alright for her. She isn't the one who'll be doing the cooking and the washing. What does she think they're going to eat tonight? One loaf I've got, that's all. It would have been enough if there'd only been two. If I'd known…" She threw up her hands, then wiped one across her forehead.

"We'll talk about it later."

A lump of despair rose in Olive's throat. It was obvious they weren't wanted here. Their unexpected arrival was inconveniencing everybody. Mr Griffiths seemed to find it amusing, but his wife clearly didn't, and all the way here Miss Fitznorton had looked as if she was recovering from a shock.

Olive had never wanted her mum so badly. Her chin started to wobble, but she swallowed her tears down. She had to be brave, for Peter and for Shirley, who looked as if she might start bawling again.

"Soda bread," Mrs Griffiths announced, as if she'd suddenly found the answer to all their problems. "I can have it done in under an hour."

Mr Griffiths nodded, then winked at the children and gestured for them to sit. "I'll get them all a glass of milk and rustle up some biscuits to keep them going while you get on. They've had a rough day, by the looks of them."

"And then you'll have to find some more mattresses from the attic. There won't be time to air them properly, and the bed frames will have to wait until tomorrow. But look at the state of them: practically poleaxed, by the look of that little one. What's all that down your front? And what on earth happened to your face, flower?" She spoke rapidly, firing questions while weighing out flour in a set of brass scales.

"She walked into a door," Peter said.

"Did she, indeed? You're a bold little lad, aren't you? Now, drink your milk, but don't go thinking you'll eat a single crumb at my table with hands like that. You can give them a good wash first. The scullery's through there..." She pointed with her chin, her hands busily working dough in the biggest mixing bowl Olive had ever seen.

Having poured glasses of milk from a large jug, Mr Griffiths vanished somewhere beyond the kitchen doorway. Michael and his sisters slurped their milk down eagerly while Olive sipped hers. She wasn't keen on the milk they were given at school, which was warmed by keeping the bottles on top of a radiator before they were given out by monitors. This, though, was cool. It tasted much nicer. She wiped her top lip and motioned to Peter to drink up.

"I'm not drinking that," he said. "It's disgusting."

All the other children stared at him. Olive's cheeks grew hot. Mrs Griffiths had clearly heard him, as she sent a glare over her shoulder before slamming the oven door and wiping her hands on her apron.

"Time to wash," she said sharply.

The scullery was bigger than Olive and Peter's kitchen at home, yet it seemed to be only for washing up. Huge racks stood to one side, with plates of all sizes. Three deep metal sinks were set in a long wooden counter. Mrs Griffiths pulled a stool up to the first sink and started filling it with hot water from the shiny brass taps. Lathering up a small brush using a block of soap, she passed it to Peter and then picked him up by his armpits to plonk him down on the stool.

"Get scrubbing those hands, little *mochyn*. You won't be touching anything else in this house until they're clean. Make sure you give those filthy nails a good going over. Ivor could grow spuds under those, boyo... Are you his sister?" she asked, turning to Olive, as Peter started feebly stroking his fingernails with the brush.

Olive nodded.

"You help him then, while I help the little one. And while you're washing, you can all tell me your names and how old you are. I'm Mrs Griffiths, but you can call me Auntie Dolly. Uncle Ivor is my husband."

"Is this your house, Auntie Dolly?" Shirley asked, as she was lifted onto another stool in front of the next sink.

"Goodness me, no. I only work here. I started when I was thirteen. There were a few of us to share the work then – not as many as there'd been in old Sir Lucien's time, of course. It used to be a grand old place, but now it's just me and Ivor to do pretty much everything – so don't you lot go making a mess, or you'll have me to answer to. The house belongs to Mrs Havard and Miss Fitznorton. They're sisters, although you wouldn't think it to look at them."

"We met Miss Fitznorton," said Barbara. "She was the lady who brought us here."

"Course you did. She's got a soft heart, that one. I expect that's how she ended up with all of you, instead of just two." She tutted and shook her head, but Olive noted that she didn't seem cross, and she was being quite gentle with Shirley's hands.

"What's this stuff in your hair?" Auntie Dolly asked, lifting a lank strand of Olive's mousy locks.

Olive gazed at her fingers in the soapy water, remembering the rough ministrations of the nurse when they arrived in the church hall.

"They said we had lice," Barbara whispered.

Auntie Dolly took a step back. Olive cast an uncertain glance over her shoulder and watched a series of expressions cross her homely face.

At last, Auntie Dolly sniffed and pursed her lips. "I think perhaps we'll bring bath time forward," she said.

SEVEN

Dodie

Dodie squared her shoulders, preparing to confront her sister. She had only just hung up her coat and hat when Charlotte emerged from the drawing room, elegant as always in a jewel-bright silk blouse with a long string of pearls. Her make-up was as immaculate as her permed blonde hair, making Dodie feel shabby by comparison; but then, Charlotte hadn't been out at work all day.

"Ah, there you are, Dodie. I thought I'd heard the car. I've just poured tea. Come and tell me all about our new acquisitions. I take it you've sent them to the kitchen with Ivor?"

Typically, Charlotte didn't pause to give Dodie an opportunity to answer, but disappeared back into the drawing room, leaving a cloud of floral scent in her wake. Dodie followed, her feet moving reluctantly over the worn patches of carpet. She sat down in the somewhat saggy armchair opposite her sister and accepted a cup and saucer.

"Tell me all about them. Do you think they'll settle in

quickly? I hope they aren't too frightfully dirty. One hears such stories. Did you manage to get a boy and a girl?"

"I need to discuss that with you—" Dodie said.

Charlotte sat back, her forehead creasing in a frown. "That sounds ominous. You didn't get two boys, did you? I specifically asked you not to."

There was no point putting it off any longer. "As a matter of fact, two of them *are* boys, yes. But the other three are girls." She lowered her gaze and sipped her tea to avoid seeing Charlotte's expression.

"I'm sorry. I've surely misheard or misunderstood you. Two boys and three girls would make *five*."

"That's right." Dodie leaned forward to put her cup and saucer down on the low table between them. Shifting in her seat, she crossed her legs and folded her arms across her lap.

"Dodie! Whatever possessed you?"

"I wasn't given a choice. The billeting officer said we had more than sufficient space, and I didn't care to push him on it in case he decided to allocate even more to us, or worse. We could be fined fifty pounds for refusing, remember? Or even sent to prison for three months."

"Don't be ridiculous. No magistrate in the district would dare."

"Whether or not that's true, I could hardly deny that we have enough rooms. Everyone in town knows you accommodated an awful lot more than five patients in the last war."

"Those were officers, Dodie – not slum dwellers! Convalescent officers who understood how to behave in a house such as this."

Charlotte jerked to her feet, then crossed to the window as if she couldn't endure the sight of her younger sister for a moment longer.

Irritation flared in Dodie's chest. Someone needed to help

these poor, skinny little children, and if Charlotte wouldn't help, then she'd manage without her.

"As I understand it, Charlotte, you provided those officers with shelter here as your way of serving your country. Now, we have the opportunity to shelter the needy for the war effort again. Or are they too *low class* to deserve such a thing?"

"Stop trying to make it sound simple. It isn't only their class, but their age. It's alright for you, you'll be out at work all day—"

"When they'll be at school."

Charlotte tutted impatiently. "The point remains that you won't be the one most affected by this. What about Dolly? Think of the extra burden you're placing on her shoulders."

That touched a nerve: Dodie was keenly aware that the children's arrival would add considerably to their housekeeper's workload. She picked at a rough bit of skin on her finger, where a paper cut had dried and healed over.

"How old are they? I trust they're of an age to be helpful, if Dolly is to be saddled with all this extra work?"

"Well... they're not quite the age we anticipated."

"What does that mean?"

"The youngest is six. She's called Shirley."

"Six! But I thought—"

"And the eldest is Shirley's brother Michael. He's ten."

"We were led to believe they'd be eleven or twelve, at least. It sounds as if they're barely out of infancy."

Dodie refrained from pointing out that she had been even younger when Charlotte sent her away to school. It was pointless to get embroiled in that old argument just now.

"There's something else I should probably tell you, although you'll see it for yourself soon enough. Three of them are coloured."

"Good grief! They'll stick out like Mae West in a nunnery. It would be difficult for any city child to settle in the country, without people staring at them wherever they go. Whatever were their parents thinking, sending them somewhere like this?"

"Presumably they were thinking that it's better to be stared at than to be bombed or gassed? Just as the white children's parents must have done."

"Dodie, you can't possibly imagine that we can keep them all. I know you like to be helpful, and of course we must do our bit, but honestly – there are limits."

Frustrated, Dodie cast about for a convincing response, one which Charlotte couldn't refute. Her eyes flickered towards a framed sepia photograph on the mantelpiece of Charlotte's late husband Kit Havard, whose image was displayed in almost every room of the house. It showed him as handsome but serious, with wire-rimmed spectacles above finely chiselled cheeks. The portrait seemed far removed from the smiling, kindly man Dodie recalled in snatches of memory from her early childhood. She had no doubt he would have been on her side about this. In the industrial Welsh valleys community where he had worked, Kit had been a champion of the poor. If he'd lived, he might even have gone into politics to further their cause. But he'd died of Spanish flu only three months after marrying Charlotte. In a grim example of Fitznorton family history repeating itself, Charlotte's twins had been born after their father died, just as Dodie had been. But at least they still had their mother.

"What would Kit say about this, do you think?" Dodie asked.

Charlotte flinched, following her gaze.

Already regretting the question, Dodie watched her sister walk over to the photograph and touch it with her fingertips.

Charlotte's elegant face had set hard. "We'll never know the answer to that, will we? It's one of many things we'll never get to know about him."

"I think he'd have been proud of us. He'd have said taking the children in was the right thing to do. If I hadn't taken them, they'd have been separated from their siblings, and I couldn't allow that. Goodness knows they'd already been through enough. You may not agree with me, Charlotte, but I honestly think if you'd been there... if you'd seen them... you'd have done the same. Ask Venetia if you don't believe me."

Charlotte gazed silently at the image of her husband, forever frozen in time.

Dodie snatched up her handbag and headed to her room, hoping that time to reflect would bring Charlotte round to her point of view. But after freshening up and changing into a house dress, she was startled to hear shrieks and cries from one of the bathrooms further along the corridor. Following the sounds, she put her ear to the door.

"I'm not going in there! You ain't gonna make me. Olive, don't let her drown me!"

"I'm not trying to drown you, you silly boy! Anyone would think you'd never seen a bath before." Dolly's exasperated voice cut across the hysterical fury of a child's cries.

Without knocking, Dodie opened the door and was confronted by the sight of two of the arrivals, Olive and Peter, dressed only in grubby knickers. Both were pitifully skinny and bow-legged, with straggly hair and patches of raw skin on their elbows and knees.

Steam rose from the bathtub, and a crimson-faced Dolly was attempting to wrestle Peter into the water.

"Get into the bath, you little devil!" Dolly exclaimed, then yelped as Peter lashed out and caught her a blow on the side of the head.

"Peter! You must do as Mrs Griffiths asks," Dodie said, taken aback.

"She's trying to bloody drown me, she is. I know her game."

"Of course she isn't. Why should anyone want to drown you? Olive, is he always like this at bath time?"

His sister hugged herself. "At home we just wash with a flannel at the kitchen sink," she whispered.

Dolly gave up her struggle. As soon as she dropped her hold on Peter he bolted for the door, trying to shove Dodie aside with his wiry little arms.

She dropped to her knees and caught his fists as gently as she could. For a small child he was surprisingly strong.

"Peter, dear, there's no need to be frightened. No one wants to hurt you. The warm water will feel lovely, I promise. When I was a child, I had a little wooden boat, and I loved to sail it in my bathwater. You're a brave lad, I know you are. If you'll be brave now and let Auntie Dolly bathe you like a good boy, I'll give you my boat for the next time."

He paused, freckled forehead puckered in a ferocious scowl. Dodie had a feeling he was calculating his options. "Why can't I have it now?" he demanded, as if he'd decided it could be worth bargaining with her.

"I'm not sure where it is right now..."

His scowl deepened and he started pushing her again.

She rushed on: "I'll look for it in my old things, and if I can't find it, I'll buy you a new one. I don't mind giving it to you as a present, as long as you do as Auntie Dolly asks. Olive can go in the bath with you, so you won't be in the water by yourself. You'll be perfectly safe in the tub if you sit nicely."

"Will you stay with us?"

Dolly sent her an emphatic nod behind his back.

"If you'd like me to."

It still took a while to convince both children to climb into the bathtub, and then only after they'd swished the water about with their hands and splashed each other a bit. Olive was the first to climb in, clinging to Dodie's hand and sucking in her breath as she sank into the warm water. Once she was in, and almost smiling in spite of her swollen lip, Dodie started to relax. Now it would surely be easier to persuade her brother.

"It's not scary, silly," Olive said, then squealed as Peter threw caution to the wind and leaped into the tub with a snarl, causing a wave of water to slosh over the side and into Dolly's lap.

"I'm not scared! I'm not a bloody chicken!" he shouted, seizing Olive's head in the crook of his arm and trying to force it under the water.

It took both Dodie and Dolly to prise his arm from around her neck and make him sit down at the other end of the tub. By the time he had acquiesced, glowering, poor Olive was trembling and Dodie felt almost as badly shaken herself. Fetching towels, she handed one to Dolly, whose curls now straggled limp and wet down her face.

Worse was to come after the next challenge of shampooing the children's hair was done.

Rubbing water from his eyes, Peter scowled up at Dodie. "Right," he said. "You got what you wanted, you bitch. Now piss off and fetch me that bloody boat."

EIGHT

Patrick

Patrick winced and swore as his borrowed bicycle bounced along the lane. Every bump and pothole jarred his weary muscles and threatened to leave bruises. He wasn't entirely sure he was on the right road but had to rely on his memory of the vague, hand-drawn map Reverend Appleton had provided along with the bicycle when it was still daylight.

He'd been stopped as he cycled through Bryncarreg village by an overly officious policeman: a gut-twisting moment considering his history, but somehow he'd resisted the urge to pedal as fast as he could and hightail it out of there when the man held up his arm and ordered him to stop.

"I recognise that bicycle," the policeman said, eyeing him suspiciously from the pavement. "What are you doing with it? I don't know you, do I?"

Patrick reminded himself to breathe. He'd done nothing wrong this time and should have nothing to fear.

"Good evening officer," he responded, as if dealing with a cop didn't make his heart skitter and thump. "I arrived in town with the evacuees today, and this bike belongs to my host, the Reverend Appleton. I'm borrowing it to check on the welfare of my pupils billeted around the village."

Predictably, his unusual accent had caused the man's eyes to narrow. "You don't sound like a Londoner to me. What's your name, son, and where are you from?" He took his notebook out of his breast pocket.

"My name is Patrick Winter. I've lived in London for the past thirteen years, but I spent most of my childhood in New York. I'm an elementary school teacher in Stepney, and I volunteered to come here along with a colleague who's also been billeted in Pontybrenin."

The man's only response was to look him up and down and take down some notes.

"Do you mind if I continue, officer?" Patrick prompted him, after half a minute or so. "I'm sure the Reverend will be happy to verify my story. It's been a long day, and if you don't mind, I'd like to carry on visiting as many of the children as I can before it gets too late this evening."

"That depends if everything is in order. If you're an American, I trust you have your alien registration card about your person?"

"I do." After only the briefest hesitation he reached into his jacket and pulled out his wallet with his registration card, then waited, on edge, while the other man made a meal of taking out his spectacles and checking the card on both sides.

"Hmm. It all seems to be in order," he said at last.

Patrick nodded and plucked the card back from the policeman's grasp, then tucked it into his wallet and swung his leg back over the bike.

Unfortunately, the policeman hadn't quite finished with him. "I'd advise you to attend the police station tomorrow morning to confirm your new address, Mr Winter. I'm sure you're aware that a failure to notify the authorities of a change of address will result in a caution."

Patrick had the sense he was enjoying this opportunity to exercise a little power. "I'll be sure to come along tomorrow, officer." He'd have agreed to anything to get the guy off his back.

"Ask for Constable Todd. And I suggest you bring the Reverend with you, to corroborate your story. I'll keep a look out for you!" the policeman called after him, sending a shiver down Patrick's collar as he rode away.

He hoped Miss Summerill's evening had been less strenuous and stressful than his. It had fallen to Patrick to check on the children billeted in the village of Bryncarreg, while she visited those near her billet in the larger town of Pontybrenin. He could hardly expect her to cycle around unfamiliar country lanes in the twilight, calling on strangers in their cottages and farmhouses.

Now his calves were burning after cycling up and down these Welsh hills, and the billets he'd visited so far had been almost primitive. The last one especially so, where he'd found the eleven-year-old evacuee was expected to sleep on a mildewed mattress in the cellar. He'd been reluctant to leave the lad behind, knowing he wouldn't rest easy until he could go back and check if the grim-faced farmer's wife had kept her grudging promise to let him sleep upstairs.

Come hell or high water, he'd make sure the kids under his care were well-treated. Leaving their families hundreds of miles away to face the possibility of Nazi bombs would inflict enough suffering, without them having to endure a frigid welcome from strangers who were, after all, being paid to keep them.

Without warning, Patrick's tyre struck a stone and catapulted him off the saddle, launching his outstretched arm into a hedge full of brambles and nettles. Clambering back to his feet, he tucked his injured hand under his armpit, sucking his breath between his teeth at the stings and cuts.

He picked up the bicycle with his good hand and peered at the wheels, hoping against hope that they might have escaped damage. It wasn't to be: the remaining light was just enough to reveal a puncture. *Dammit.* He'd only had use of the bike for a couple of hours, and now it was banjaxed, with his hand not much better. Flexing his sore fingers, he had little choice but to start walking, gripping the handlebar as he pushed the wobbly bike along.

He hadn't gone more than ten yards when he noticed that he'd lost his hat. *What an eejit.* Gritting his teeth, he retraced his steps, peering through the dim light into the hedgerow and the ruts on the road until he spotted it amongst some leaves. Scooping it up, he realised too late that they, too, were nettles. Within seconds his hand felt as if it were on fire: he blew on it, but there was nothing to be done. Ramming his hat down onto his head, he resumed his plodding march along the uneven lane.

One by one, stars began pricking holes in the darkness. He never got to see them in London, any more than he had in New York. His steps slowed as he marvelled at the vast expanse of sky above him, interrupted by not a single building, only the somewhat sinister shapes of tall trees to his left and hills in the distance to his right. Silhouetted against the petrol-blue vastness, bats fluttered overhead, darting out from the trees at a remarkable speed as they whizzed in seemingly random and tangential directions. A city dweller all his life, his heart swelled as if nature was putting on a grand performance especially for him. Yet he felt, at the same time, that he'd never been further from any semblance of home in all his twenty-six years.

What was he even doing here? He'd let himself be persuaded to accompany the children, most of whom weren't even in his class. And look where that had got him.

How many miles had he travelled today? On foot, by train and by bicycle – he'd been on the move for hours. His body had started rebelling, his blistered feet smarting with every step in his cheap shoes. His shoulders had stiffened, as if his muscles resented what he was putting them through. The scratches and hives covering his right hand burned where he held on to the wobbling bike, the cool evening air doing little to soothe the damaged skin.

Then, rounding a bend, he glimpsed the cosy glow of lights: several of them, over two floors.

Patrick's pace picked up. This must be the big house he'd been aiming for, where five of the school's young pupils had been taken. His attention had been diverted when they were allocated their billet, and from what the billeting officer said when Reverend Appleton locked up the church hall, their host had been reluctant to take them on.

He set his jaw. Would these children be better housed than the lad at the farm? They'd better be – he was in no mood to stand for any nonsense after the day he'd had.

As he drew closer to the building, its grand size became even more obvious. There were more rooms, and more floors, than the lights had initially suggested, and even tall turrets at the corners, shadowy against the sky. He shivered at the eerie sound of an owl's *hoohoo*, then shook himself. Just because this place looked like a haunted house or vampire's castle from a movie, complete with bats, it didn't mean there was any danger.

His feet crunched over deep gravel that dragged at the tyres on the bicycle, then finally he arrived beneath the shelter of an arched stone porch. He propped the bike against one of its pillars, lifted his hat briefly to smooth his dishevelled hair with his good hand, straightened his tie and adjusted his cuffs. After ringing the doorbell he stepped back, hoping this visit wouldn't take long. He was already dreading the long walk back to the vicarage.

A scraping sound, followed by a thud, suggested a bolt being drawn back before the door opened. Framed in the warm yellow light of the open doorway stood a woman, as far from the conventional view of a vampire or ghoul as he could imagine. She was elegantly dressed, a single strand of pearls the only adornment over a sapphire blue blouse that had the delicate sheen of silk. Her blonde hair was set in soft waves that framed an attractive face. Long lashes fluttered as she looked him up and down. A corner of her red-painted mouth lifted.

"Good evening," she said.

Patrick lifted his hat in greeting, his gaze flickering to her left hand where it toyed with her necklace. He was pretty sure he hadn't misinterpreted a flirtatious interest in her smile, despite the gold band she wore on her wedding ring finger.

"Good evening, ma'am. My name is Patrick Winter. As one of the teachers who accompanied the schoolchildren evacuated today, I'm here to check on their welfare."

She arched one delicately plucked eyebrow. "Are you really? I hadn't imagined that anyone would visit so soon."

With that plummy voice, and those expensive clothes, he could only assume she was the mistress of the house.

Stepping aside, she gestured for him to enter the impressive hallway. "Do come in, Mr Winter. I'm Mrs Havard. Welcome to Plas Norton." She extended her right hand and he shook it without thinking, the pressure on his bruised and grazed fingers making him wince.

"Are you alright, Mr Winter? My goodness, look at that poor hand. Have you had some sort of mishap on your way?"

She looked him up and down, and he realised his trousers were muddy at the knee where he'd landed on the ground.

He swallowed his pride. "Reverend Appleton lent me his bicycle, but I'm out of practice, and especially on bumpy country lanes," he said. Tucking his injured hand against his side, he gazed about, trying not to look awed by the faded grandeur of his surroundings.

Ahead of him stood a large, polished table with a tall porcelain vase generously filled with flowers. Portraits lined the walls to the side and above the wide, carpeted staircase. An elaborately carved newel post drew his eye towards an ornate balustrade leading upwards.

"You may leave your hat and coat here if you wish. The children are already in bed, I believe. As you might expect, at this hour."

"Thank you." Glancing down at his fedora in his left hand, he tried to push a dent out before hanging it along with his coat on the hall stand. He'd wiped his feet on the coir mat near the door, but checked the soles of his shoes again, just in case.

Looking up, he noticed another woman on the staircase with slender legs and a pretty flower-sprigged dress with a skirt that swished around her knees as she descended lightly in her low-heeled green shoes.

"Ah, there you are, Dodie – this is Mr Winter, the children's teacher. Mr Winter, this is my sister, Josephine Fitznorton."

Patrick bid the newcomer a good evening. She looked younger than the blonde, not merely due to the fresh peachiness of her complexion and longer hair, but also the comparative lack of sophistication in her clothes and her slight air of awkwardness. Where her sister had sized him up with a self-assured smile, this one hesitated.

"Mr Winter would like to reassure himself that we haven't chained the little darlings up in the attics or made them sleep in the stables." Mrs Havard spoke playfully, but there was an edge that made him suspect she found his unexpected arrival something of an imposition.

"But they're asleep. They're exhausted after their long day," the younger one said, glancing at her wristwatch.

He drew a finger along one eyebrow, irritated. "I'm sure they are, but if you don't mind, I'll look in on them anyway. After the trouble I've gone to to get here, I'd hate it to be a wasted effort." Exhaustion made his voice came out sharper than he'd intended. He'd like nothing more than to be tucked up in a warm and comfortable bed, preferably with a belly full of food, but he doubted he'd have any prospect of either for hours yet, given that he had no idea how long it might take him to trudge back to the vicarage in the dark, unfamiliar lanes.

Mrs Havard sighed. "While my sister takes you to inspect the standard of our accommodation, I'll fetch some antiseptic for that hand of yours, Mr Winter. We wouldn't want it to give you any bother – not after all the trouble you've gone to to get here," she said, with an arch expression.

"I don't want to inconvenience you," he mumbled, his foot already on the bottom stair.

"Not at all," she replied, sweeping gracefully towards a door at the end of the hallway. "By the way," she added, making him turn halfway up the stairs. "Have you eaten since you arrived in Pontybrenin? You look a trifle pale."

"Well, no, but—"

She cut him off. "We were about to eat when you arrived. I'm sure our cook can make it stretch to an extra portion."

He was on the point of refusing, but she'd already disappeared through a doorway, presumably to find the cook, and Miss Fitznorton was frowning down from the top of the stairs. Was she merely reluctant to delay her meal, or could there be a more worrying reason for her apparent reluctance to show him up to the children's rooms? Remembering the mildewed mattress at the farm, he quickened his pace up the staircase.

She paused with her hand on a brass doorknob some distance along the landing, dark-lashed hazel eyes large and troubled, as if she were about to protest again. Presumably she read the resolve in his face, for she twisted the doorknob without a word and pushed the door open for him to enter.

Treading softly to avoid waking the children who lay tucked under brightly coloured quilts on two metal bedsteads, he noted these were the boys, Michael and Peter. The room was carpeted, with a couple of chests of drawers and a solid wooden armoire. It looked comfortable. In fact, he had to admit it was rather better than comfortable. With its delicately patterned wallpaper and long curtains, it looked luxurious.

Despite his care, a floorboard creaked under his foot, and young Peter sat bolt upright, rubbing his eyes.

"Who's that?" he squeaked.

Patrick supposed it was natural for the boy to be nervous at finding someone unexpectedly entering his room at night, especially after such a tumultuous alteration in his circumstances.

"It's Mr Winter. I've come to check you're okay."

Michael sat up too, squinting at the sight of his teacher.

"We're alright, sir. Thank you."

Patrick nodded, noting the courtesy. "How are you settling in, boys?"

"I don't like *her*," Peter said, pointing at the young woman silhouetted against the light from the doorway.

Patrick noticed she put a hand to her throat, as if this pronouncement had shocked her.

"Why not?" he asked.

"She promised to give me a toy boat. I had to take all my clothes off, in front of her and the other woman, but she still never gave me the boat."

Ignoring the gasp from behind him, he kept his gaze on the boy. "Go on," he said.

"And then you should've seen the food they tried to make us eat. It looked like the stuff Shirley puked up."

Patrick's own stomach lurched at the thought of them not being fed well. Being made to strip off like that had set off alarm bells, too.

The light from the doorway brightened and he realised the woman had gone. A guilty conscience, perhaps, now that Peter had blabbed?

Michael cleared his throat. "We all had a bath and our hair washed," he said. "Peter didn't want to, so they let him go in with his sister, but he still didn't like it. And then they gave us stew with carrots and spuds and bread and butter. I thought it was nice, but Peter didn't want any." The boy's wry expression and Peter's answering scowl told Patrick what he needed to know.

"Well, now. Those beds look pretty comfortable. I guess you two had better get some sleep after your busy day. I'll look in on the girls and then get going. Behave yourself, young Peter, or else, make no mistake, I'll get to hear about it."

The boys lay down and he returned to the landing, pulling the door closed behind him.

Miss Fitznorton's face was ashen. She pushed the next door open, saying nothing.

This room was equally large and well decorated, but this time there were no bedsteads. The three girls lay on mattresses on the floor, tucked under blankets, their heads on plump pillows. All were asleep, so he tiptoed back out again and faced the young woman.

"We hadn't expected more than two, so we only had two beds set up. We'll have the other bedsteads in place by tomorrow evening. I wouldn't want you to think—" She paused, her hands twisting.

Patrick waited. Over the years he'd found silence to be an effective way of making people talk themselves into a corner when they had something to hide. She'd obviously been embarrassed by Peter's less than enthusiastic testimony, but then Michael had put a different spin on the tale. He was prepared to give her the benefit of the doubt.

"What Peter said. It wasn't the way he made it sound. His sister – Olive – she's a dear little thing. She said they don't have a bath at home. He was rather reluctant to get into the water, so I promised him a toy boat for next time if he'd behave himself. Unfortunately he was rather rude, and we had great difficulty managing him. I assure you our only concern was for the children's health and hygiene. After the journey, and having their hair deloused, they were all—" She had been speaking softly, but lowered her voice still further, pink patches appearing high on her cheekbones. "Well, to be blunt, they were all rather dirty and smelly. We couldn't let them go to bed without first having a bath."

Patrick rubbed his chin, but quickly dropped his hand, conscious of the rasp of stubble after his long day. He'd never taught Peter Hicks, but the boy had a reputation for being difficult. His colleagues had often complained despairingly in the school's staffroom about the lad's behaviour and his use of foul language.

He nodded. "Shall we go back downstairs? I'm satisfied that the children's accommodation is of a suitable standard."

He hadn't, perhaps, been as friendly as he might have been. Certainly Miss Fitznorton's rigid posture and the way she led the way down the wide staircase and along the corridor without uttering another word suggested he hadn't won her over.

The dining room was outrageously large. A pristine white cloth covered a table surely long enough to seat at least eight or ten diners. Three places had been laid with silver cutlery and sparkling crystal glassware. Patrick stood awkwardly behind the chair Miss Fitznorton indicated.

"It's very good of you to offer me a meal, but I really think I should go," he said. "Reverend Appleton will be wondering where I've got to."

"I've telephoned the reverend to explain," Mrs Havard said from behind him. "And our cook will be most put out if you don't eat the dinner she's about to serve. I'm sure it will be a comfort to poor Dolly if we adults show a little more appreciation for her culinary skills than some of the children did this evening."

Mrs Havard had covered her silk blouse with a snowy white apron. She pulled out the chair beside his and laid a folded towel on the tabletop, along with a white enamel bowl. Steam rose from it, smelling strongly of Dettol. As she slipped into the seat beside him, she pulled a pair of tweezers, a wad of cotton wool and a bandage from her apron pocket.

"This isn't necessary," he began, but she cut him off with a stern glare.

"Nonsense. Now, hold out your hand please, Mr Winter. While I'm checking for thorns and cleaning up those scratches, you can entertain us by explaining why an American is accompanying children from the most deprived parts of London to this part of Wales."

NINE

Patrick

The way Mrs Havard ignored Patrick's protests that a bandage was unnecessary for a few minor scratches and grazes made him suspect she'd deliberately prolonged the contact. *God preserve him from lonely forty-something women.*

A couple of years ago he wouldn't have been averse to taking such an attractive woman up on the kind of unspoken offer he'd read in her eyes. These days, though, he preferred to avoid such entanglements. He'd allowed himself to be toyed with before, and hadn't enjoyed the difficulties of extricating himself, contending with not only shrill hysterics but also threats to reveal aspects of his past he should never have disclosed in pillow talk. He wasn't about to tread that path again.

Inwardly Patrick chided himself for bolting the tender lumps of beef, vegetables and potato so quickly. He shouldn't let old habits overcome his manners. The heavy silver fork felt awkward in his bandaged right hand, but it would take more than that to stop him polishing off every morsel of such hearty fare.

"This stew is delicious," he said, only just remembering not to speak with his mouth full.

"Dolly must take the credit," Mrs Havard replied, from her place at the head of the table. "Neither of us has much experience in the kitchen."

"I cooked my own meals when I lived in London," Miss Fitznorton piped up. There was a defensive air about her, much like that which he'd seen upstairs when Peter made his accusation against her. Interesting that she felt a need to prove herself to her sister, who merely knocked back a mouthful of red wine and continued as if she hadn't spoken.

"It's a pity your pupils didn't find the food equally delicious, Mr Winter. What can you tell us about them?"

She was watching him eat, one eyebrow slightly raised as if in disapproval. Belatedly he realised these two would expect him to eat slowly, as if he'd never been hungry in his life, with the knife and fork held in both hands throughout the meal. Doubtless she thought him an uncultured Yank for using only his fork, but she was polite enough to rearrange her expression when she caught him looking.

"None of your evacuees were in my previous class," he said. "But Michael Clarke would have been one of mine from the beginning of this term if things had gone the usual way. I teach the ten- and eleven-year-olds. From what I've been told, he's a good kid. Polite, eager to learn, and quick to catch on. Good at math, and a capable reader. I doubt he'll give you any trouble, although..." He frowned as the image of Michael at the church hall entered his mind. Tying himself to his sisters had been a neat trick, but hardly compliant. Ah, well. Patrick shrugged. "He seems close to his sisters, and I haven't heard a word against either of them either. The other girl, the one with the bruise on her mouth—"

"Olive," Miss Fitznorton interjected.

"That's right. Olive Hicks. She may be a cause for some concern. I suspect all is not rosy at home."

"Her brother Peter swore like a sailor on the way here, and even more so at bath-time. He completely refused to eat his stew. I shouldn't be surprised if he's the one to give us the most trouble," she continued, her smooth forehead furrowed. "But then, sent away to an unfamiliar place, without their loved ones, not knowing what they would find... They're bound to find it distressing." She spoke with a fervency that surprised him, then set down her cutlery with her meal unfinished, her mouth twisting as if she couldn't stomach any more.

Mrs Havard toyed with her wine glass; after gulping back the contents, she set it down and immediately reached for the bottle to top it up.

"Children are resilient, fortunately," she said.

"Or is that merely what adults like to believe when they send them away?" her sister said softly.

"It's better for a child to go somewhere safe than to stay, if home is a place of turmoil and upset."

Unexpectedly, the atmosphere between the two women held a charge that made Patrick itch to push back his chair and make his excuses. He considered leaving, but he was still hungry, and the stew was good, and he didn't know when he'd next get a meal this tasty. The vicar was a skinny fellow, as if a strong gust of wind would topple him. Either he was a man of frugal appetites or his cook was awful. Suppressing a sigh, Patrick dug in with his fork and chewed a little faster. Whatever was going on between these two had nothing to do with him.

"I still find it intriguing that a New Yorker should be here during these troubled times. Haven't Americans been advised to leave Britain, given the danger of war with Germany?"

"They have, but I've lived in London longer than I lived in New York. I figure my life is in this country now."

"And yet you said your mother is Irish, not English?"

"That's right." He took a sip of wine to buy himself a few moments. Given that he'd never managed to rid himself of his accent, it was inevitable that he was asked questions about his origins from time to time, but he always kept his answer brief and changed the subject as quickly as possible.

Mrs Havard was more persistent than most, though, and he owed her after she'd pulled a couple of thorny splinters out of his palm, patched him up and fed him. He doubted her younger sister would have done the same, given the defensive glances she kept sending his way along the table.

"My mother's family moved from Kilkenny to London to find work. She met my father there, and they emigrated to New York with dreams of a better life. We came back after my grandmother fell ill." It wasn't a lie, even if it was far from the full truth, and if he'd implied that his father had returned with them... well, it was easier than explaining what had actually happened.

"I always wanted to visit New York, but after the Crash... Unfortunately, it wasn't to be." Mrs Havard sounded wistful.

Patrick had had enough of discussing his birthplace. "You said it had been a while since you'd ministered first aid, but you applied this bandage like an expert. Were you ever a nurse?"

"Not a nurse, exactly. But this house was a convalescent home for officers during the Great War. I learned first aid at that time."

The mention of war made all three pause.

"I don't suppose you'll have to fight, Mr Winter? Being a teacher. And an American."

He thought he detected a note of disapproval in Miss Fitznorton's tone, whether of his job, his nationality, or his ability to escape the violence he couldn't tell.

"That's right, at least for now. I guess we're all still hoping no one else will have to fight, either."

"We're praying that my nephew Christopher will be spared military service, given that he's studying medicine."

"He'll be far more useful to his country if he's allowed to finish his medical training," Mrs Havard said, her voice clipped. Patrick guessed Christopher must be her son. Although she looked more glamorous than motherly, he supposed she could be old enough to have an adult child.

There was nothing maternal in the way she was watching him again, though. He held her gaze thoughtfully for a moment, then dropped it to his plate, reluctant to engage in that kind of intensity.

Reaching for the wine bottle, Mrs Havard left her seat to pour more into his glass with a hand that was noticeably less steady than it had been when she bathed his palm.

"No more for me, thanks," he murmured, gesturing for her to stop. "I'll have to go soon, and I wouldn't want to arrive back at the vicarage intoxicated on my first night."

"Oh, you shouldn't worry about Reverend Appleton. He isn't as stuffy as he looks. We've known him leave here positively mellow after a few sherries. And you won't have to find your way back in the dark: Ivor will drive you and repair the bicycle for you to collect it another day. It will give you an excuse to visit us again. To satisfy yourself… as to the children's welfare, I mean."

He kept his expression blank, as if he hadn't understood the flirtation, and left the wine glass untouched.

She leaned her hip against the table, twirling her string of pearls, until her sister spoke up.

Miss Fitznorton's tone seemed calculated to chill any possibility of ardour. "Christopher is following in his father's footsteps, becoming a doctor."

As Mrs Havard straightened and returned to her seat, Patrick pictured an older, retired gentleman and wondered if he'd get to meet the doctor this evening.

"My husband sadly passed away." Mrs Havard waved away Patrick's murmured condolences. "He left me a very young widow. A few months later I found myself with three small children to support: newborn twins Christopher and Louise, as well as Dodie here, my half-sister."

Miss Fitznorton's lips tightened and Patrick saw a flush creeping up her neck. His fleeting amusement was swept away and drowned in the undercurrents between the two women. Hurriedly, he steered the conversation into what he hoped would be safer waters.

"You said your son is studying to be a doctor. What about your daughter?"

"Louise is more interested in languages than medicine. She's due to travel home from a trip to Switzerland any day now," Mrs Havard replied.

"It was Loulou who first called me Dodie, do you remember Charlotte?" Miss Fitznorton almost managed a smile then, but it faded as soon as she turned her attention back to Patrick. "My given name is Josephine, but Loulou found it too hard to pronounce when she was small. It probably didn't help that I was away a lot of the time when we were young."

"They were difficult times for all of us, as you might imagine, Mr Winter." Mrs Havard left a frosty pause. "My sister is a librarian."

"A library assistant, actually."

Mrs Havard continued as if her sister hadn't interrupted. "Until a few months ago she was a junior clerk in London, but now she's returned to dreary old Plas Norton and one can hardly blame her if it's a disappointment after all the excitement of the capital. I say, I wonder if you two lived in the same parts of the city? You might even have passed one another on the street without realising it."

"I doubt it," Patrick said. He couldn't imagine a young woman as refined as Josephine Fitznorton living or working in

Stepney or Whitechapel, with their poverty and densely packed, overcrowded tenements.

A knock at the dining room door heralded the arrival of Ivor Griffiths, a sandy-haired Welshman who appeared resigned to driving their unexpected guest back to town through the now pitch-dark lanes.

Patrick laid down his napkin and jumped to his feet. He'd satisfied himself that the children were being suitably housed, and was grateful for the meal, but fatigue and the simmering tension between the two sisters made him glad of the chance to depart. As he bid them farewell and retrieved his belongings from the hall, he couldn't help hoping that he'd be able to avoid seeing them again when he called at Plas Norton to collect the bike from Ivor.

TEN

Olive

Olive had found it strange having a whole mattress to herself. Despite being worn out, falling asleep had been hard, especially without her doll. She hadn't missed Peter's wriggling or his tendency to spread himself out and hog the bed, but she'd longed to hold Gracie to her nose and breathe in the scent of home. Hearing Barbara sniffling in the night, she'd asked her what was wrong, and the other girl had sobbed that she missed her dog, Rusty. Olive had always found dogs frightening with their big teeth and the way they'd bark suddenly when she walked past, but she thought it must be hard to be parted with one that was a family pet.

When she woke and felt her pyjamas cold and wet, she'd thought she might die of shame. Shivering, she'd wriggled out of her sodden pyjamas under the sheets, then dragged the bedding into a ball and tucked it into a corner before hastening to put on the clean clothes which had been laid out by Auntie Dolly the night before. They dragged on her sticky, smelly skin, but she couldn't bear the thought of anyone seeing her naked on the way to the bathroom. Hopefully the mattress, quilt and sheets would dry out by bedtime, and then no one need ever know what she'd done.

She'd been the first of the children to arrive in the kitchen for breakfast, where she found Auntie Dolly busily preparing food. Eyeing the plates and dishes in the middle of the table, she knew she'd never get used to the sight of so much grub – and all for just one meal. Peter claimed four of the freshly baked bread rolls in their cloth-lined basket by licking his finger and jabbing it into them as soon as he joined her in the kitchen, only stopping when Auntie Dolly spotted him and swatted his hand away. As soon as her back was turned, he stuffed two into his pockets, and Olive wondered if she should do the same. At home, there was no guarantee of a decent meal in the evening. But perhaps here, with this feast spread out before them, they wouldn't need to keep anything hidden for later?

There were two pots of jam – raspberry and damson – and marmalade, too. A golden block of butter sat in its own rectangular container, with its own special horn-handled knife. Beside it stood a blue and white striped jug containing fresh milk, covered with a little net edged with brightly coloured beads. By the time Miss Fitznorton and the Clarkes came to take their seats Auntie Dolly had lined up several slices of perfectly browned toast in a metal rack, and now scooped brown things out of a saucepan, deftly dropping them into little cups and setting one on each child's plate.

"Salt's in the middle of the table," she said, turning back to the stove to fill the teapot with freshly boiled water.

The children eyed each other, and Michael shrugged. Picking the rounded brown object up, he quickly swapped it to his other hand and held it with only his fingertips, as if it was hot. With his face puckered, he bravely took a bite.

"Whatever are you doing, Michael?" Miss Fitznorton

exclaimed, as he grimaced and spat the mouthful of food back into his hand.

Olive froze, afraid to reach for any more food in case she might do something wrong, too.

"Sorry, miss. I didn't mind trying it, but it's horrible."

"Have you never eaten a boiled egg before? You don't eat the shell – no wonder it didn't taste very nice. Here, I'll show you."

Olive watched as Miss Fitznorton neatly sawed the top off one of the brown eggs, revealing a golden core nestled within a white ring.

"You can dip fingers of bread into the yolk before scooping out the white. Go on, try one," she urged with a smile.

Barbara and Shirley reached for their knives. Copying the young woman's movements quickly became a game, and Olive joined in when she realised Miss Fitznorton was playing along, making them giggle by pretending to miss her mouth with her spoon. Olive's swollen lip hurt but smiling still felt good. Her shoulders loosened a little.

She'd never eaten so much for breakfast, and soon her stomach was so full of eggs and toast that it bulged against the thin fabric of her dress. She copied the way Miss Fitznorton dabbed at her mouth with a napkin and set down her cutlery, sitting up straighter in her chair as if she were the young woman's reflection in a mirror. She looked so pretty in her fresh, summery dress and with her shiny brown curls swept up at the sides with tortoiseshell combs. While Olive aped her by sipping daintily at a cup of tea, setting it carefully on its saucer between mouthfuls, Peter carried on stuffing toast and jam into his face with no care for manners at all.

Michael and Barbara exchanged glances across the table.

"Miss Fitznorton... will we be able to send our postcards today, please? We need to let our parents know our address. They'll be wondering."

"Of course you may, Michael. I should have thought of it myself. As soon as you've all helped Auntie Dolly clear the table and wash up, fetch your postcards and your outdoor shoes. I'll bring pencils and once you've written your messages, I'll show you the way to the village. Although you won't have to go to school next week, after that you'll be attending the local elementary school, so you'll need to know how to get there. What do you say to visiting the sweet shop as well as the post office, to make an adventure of it? They'll both be open until lunchtime."

Olive joined in the excited squeals at the prospect of sweets, but her full tummy clenched at the thought of starting at a new school. Barbara and Shirley chattered while helping to clear the table, but Olive remained silent. Peter's initial refusal to help to do "women's work" was met with a stern word from Uncle Ivor, who had come in for a cup of tea, so he had to join in, however sulkily. By the time they'd finished putting all the dishes away, five pencils had been placed on the table along with a metal pencil sharpener, and the children ran to their rooms to fetch their postcards.

"How many kisses will you be putting on your postcard?" Shirley asked, as she fished her postcard from her bag and tried to smooth out the creases.

"I don't know," Olive replied, puzzled.

"She doesn't know about the code, silly," Barbara said.

"What code?"

Barbara tugged her into a huddle.

"Mum said if we don't like it here, she'll come straight away and bring us home. But she said the people we're staying with will more than likely read what we write on our cards, so we'd better not say straight out if we ain't happy. We've worked out a code to use instead."

Olive hadn't thought of the possibility of her messages to her mum being read. But then, her mum hadn't said she'd come to fetch her and Peter if they were unhappy. "What's your code, then?" she asked.

Shirley started whispering it into her deaf ear. She had to turn her head and ask her to repeat it.

"If we like it, we'll put two kisses. But if we don't, we'll put one."

"If we really hate it, we won't put any at all, and then Mum will get on the next train," Barbara added.

Olive nodded. "So, how many kisses will you put?"

Barbara bit her lip.

Shirley stifled a giggle. "I really love it here so far. I've never eaten so much, and this room is lovely."

"I thought we'd arrived at Buckingham Palace when we got here," Barbara agreed. "And that car! We'd never get a ride like that back home."

"And Miss Fitznorton's lovely, isn't she? I think I might put *three* kisses on mine."

Barbara frowned. "I'm not sure you should. Mum might be upset if she thinks we like it *too* much."

Shirley's smile drooped, and Olive could understand why.

How many kisses would I put? she wondered. Miss Fitznorton was nice, that was true, but the house was a bit scary, with its long, silent corridors and all those faces glaring down from the paintings on the stairs. It was nice knowing Dad couldn't hit her or shout at her, but she was still stuck with Peter, and when she thought about her mum and Gracie it was as if something pulled at her insides, making her feel horribly far away.

In the end, after copying their new address in her neatest handwriting and writing *The house is very cumfy and the food is nice*, she put two kisses at the bottom. She didn't want her mum worrying. It gave her a warm feeling to picture her reading the postcard in a day or two. Would it make her smile? Would Dad be interested in what they'd written, or would he just shout at Mum to get on with his tea?

A few minutes later, Miss Fitznorton reappeared, wearing a striped cotton blouse and wide-legged navy-blue slacks with a sturdy pair of shoes. The addition of a scarlet beret together with her red lipstick gave her a glamorous look. Olive felt a glow of excitement at the idea of an adventure with her, although she wasn't sure how she felt about visiting a sweet shop without any money in her pocket.

"Make sure you're all carrying your gas masks... Oh, my – don't you have any proper outdoor shoes?" Miss Fitznorton asked, as Auntie Dolly shooed them out of the kitchen towards the door that they'd used to enter the house the day before.

Olive looked down at her canvas plimsolls, then at Barbara and Shirley's boots.

"Never mind. We'll have to get you some new shoes in Pontybrenin next week. I'll speak to my sister about it later." Miss Fitznorton marched out into the cobbled courtyard, setting a brisk pace as they passed the run-down outbuildings. "Watch where you step: we don't want you getting muddy," she added.

Uncle Ivor grinned from the doorway of one of the buildings, a tool bag in his hands. "Dolly'll flay you alive if you traipse muck through the house."

Olive wasn't sure what flay meant, but the meaning was clear. She trod carefully.

Soon they left the cobbled surface behind and were walking across grass, lush and springy like the carpets in the house. Now and then Miss Fitznorton pointed out something of interest: "The lake is over there. Don't go that way by yourself, or near the river, in case you fall in" and "the rhododendrons are quite spectacular in the spring, but hopefully Mr Hitler will see sense and you'll all be back at home with your families by then."

The air was extraordinary, as green as the vast expanse of lush grass extending across the deer park and over the hills. It even tasted different to London, as if they'd landed on another planet. It was so much fresher and brighter than what they were used to.

After a few minutes they reached a gate, and Miss Fitznorton told them firmly not to leave open any gates they found closed, or to close any open ones.

"Why?" asked Shirley, her shorter legs pumping faster than anyone else's to keep up.

"Because there might be animals who could escape. You wouldn't want them to get out and be run over, would you?"

Shirley's eyes widened as she scanned the fields. "But there aren't any roads."

"Oh, there are, even if you can't see them just here," Miss Fitznorton said, laughing lightly. "Cows and sheep can run quite fast, you know, much quicker than the farmer. So if something frightens them and the gate is open, they'll be gone before he can do anything to stop them getting to the road."

"My dad would like it here," Barbara said. "He always says the blues where he's from are bluer, and the greens are greener than anything he's ever seen in London. So I suppose Barbados must be like this."

Miss Fitznorton's cheeks, rosy from the walking, dimpled prettily. "Goodness. I should think Barbados must be much nicer. It might look lovely here today, but it can be bleak when it rains, and in the winter these hills will often be covered in snow for weeks."

Olive couldn't imagine so much green turned white.

"Are we near the seaside?" Shirley asked, only to be met with another soft laugh.

"Not really, sweetheart. I'm afraid the sea is twenty or thirty miles away, at least."

The boy from school with the bucket and spade would be disappointed, then. Olive had no sympathy; it served him right for kicking her in the face.

Soon they reached a low stone wall surrounding a knot of buildings with small windows and lichen-spotted roofs. The largest was a house, its white walls stained with green, as if the country air had somehow coated it the way soot had blackened its two squat chimneys. A scruffy black and white dog lolled on the doorstep, but at their approach its ears pricked up and it lifted its nose to bark a warning. Hens squawked, flapping their wings in a dash across the yard.

"What are those?" Olive asked, pointing.

"I think they're chickens," Michael said.

Miss Fitznorton confirmed it.

"I always thought they'd have four legs, not two," Peter exclaimed. "They look funny."

Before they'd crossed the farmyard, a boy of about eleven or twelve appeared from inside the house, wearing stout clogs. On spying them, he called back through the doorway, and another four children and a solidly built dark-haired woman all came out to stare.

Peter scowled back. "Ain't you never seen other kids before?" he shouted, once they'd been left a safe distance behind.

"Not brown ones!" the farm boy yelled back.

"Up yours!" Peter retorted, sticking two fingers up and waggling them provocatively in the direction of the farm until Miss Fitznorton seized him by the shoulders and hustled him along ahead of her. Her already fresh complexion had flushed scarlet right up to her hair.

Michael said nothing, but Olive noticed he had put his arms out to shepherd his sisters closer. She frowned, puzzling over what the boy had said. In her street there were lots of brown kids, and everyone played together without thinking there was anything strange about it. But now she came to think about it, she hadn't seen any other people with dark skin since they'd arrived on the train.

They all picked up their pace, left uncomfortable by the inquisitive stares of the family at the farm, and no one spoke until they reached a stile. Miss Fitznorton showed them all how to climb over it.

"Don't step in the cow pats," she warned them, pointing to a greenish-black splat of dirt on the grass. It didn't look very nice, covered in flies, and Olive screwed up her nose at the smell. There were lots of them, dotted about all over the field. Some were dark, whilst others had obviously dried in the sun, as they looked faded and stiff.

"What's a cow pat?" Shirley asked, peering at it.

Again, Miss Fitznorton's cheeks turned pink. "It's dung," she said, then rolled her eyes a little at their blank faces. "Cow poo. You might think it's funny now, but you won't be laughing like that if you step in it. So watch where you're walking, please."

For the rest of their walk the children debated animals and their poo, or "droppings" as Miss Fitznorton seemed to prefer to call it. They didn't see any rabbits, but there were little black pellets aplenty.

Sheep, they discovered in the next field, were bigger than Olive had expected, and they had funny eyes as well as surprisingly loud, harsh voices when they bleated.

On the outskirts of the village, rows of squat, slate-roofed houses lined the road. After a hundred yards or so they reached a crossroads with a cluster of shops. Olive didn't recognise any of the names above the doors, but the window displays showed the nearest was a baker, and there was also a greengrocer, grocer, butcher, and a post office with a red pillar box outside the door. That, at least, looked the same as the ones back home. One by one, the children slipped their postcards into the slot, and Olive's eyes pricked as she heard hers land like a whisper on the pile of mail within. Strange to think that it would soon be held in Mum's hands, with them so far away. Her chin drooped, but soon lifted again when Miss Fitznorton pointed out the sweet shop on the other side of the road.

They were able to cross straight away – no waiting for traffic to pass, with the roads so much quieter than those at home – and as Miss Fitznorton pushed the shop door open a bell jangled to announce their arrival.

"Good morning, Miss Fitznorton. This is a lovely surprise. I see you've—" The large woman behind the wooden counter stopped speaking abruptly, her mouth hanging slack like a pair of knickers with the elastic worn out as the children squeezed into the tiny shop. "Well I never," she murmured, raking them all with a glance.

"We've come to buy a half-pound box of Black Magic chocolates for Mrs Griffiths, and some sweets for our guests, please, Mrs Lee. Now, children: you may each spend thruppence. Choose whichever sweets you like, but remember you'll need to make them last until next weekend."

Thruppence! Olive caught hold of Peter's arm. Her eyes must surely be shining as brightly as his. She joined in the chorus of thanks as all the children craned to examine the large glass jars on shelves behind Mrs Lee, who stood on a wooden step stool to reach for the Black Magic chocolates on the highest shelf.

Peter pressed his nose against the glass counter to view the rows of chocolate bars displayed like ingots of treasure. "I want a Kit Kat!" he shouted, only adding "please" after Olive nudged him with her elbow.

"Where have you three come from, then?" Mrs Lee asked, her attention glued to Michael and his sisters.

"They're all from London," Miss Fitznorton said.

"But where are they from originally? Where – are – you – *really* – from?" She strung out the words, speaking louder and more slowly than before, as if all three were stupid or deaf.

"We're from London, like she said," Michael replied.

"Really, though?"

"We're from Stepney. Same as Olive and Peter."

"I assure you they're telling the truth, Mrs Lee. All five of our new guests are as British as afternoon tea."

Mrs Lee pursed her lips in the face of Miss Fitznorton's insistence.

"Well, I never saw the like. Not since that Paul Robeson fellow sang in Mountain Ash..." She shook her head, as if perplexed, but as it wasn't clear what had confused her, Olive focused on choosing from the array of confectionery on the shelves.

Shirley pointed at a large glass jar of Brazil nut toffees on the counter.

"Don't touch that!" Mrs Lee snapped. Her lips pursed up as if she'd smelled something nasty.

Shirley's hand jerked back to her side, and she edged closer to Barbara. Olive saw them look at each other, something flashing between them.

Mrs Lee picked up the jar and wiped it with her handkerchief. It seemed strange to Olive, who reasoned that a snotty hanky would surely be dirtier than Shirley's finger.

Miss Fitznorton frowned.

Michael cleared his throat before asking for Liquorice Allsorts, waiting stiffly while they were weighed out. Mrs Lee tossed the paper bag onto the counter as if she didn't care to hand it to him.

Barbara and Shirley both chose fruit drops, their voices more subdued than before.

Unlike Peter, the Clarkes had each chosen a bag of sweets which could be eked out over the course of a week, and Olive decided to do the same.

Mrs Lee's hard face softened a little when Olive asked for Jelly Babies. Watching her sweets tumble from the jar onto the scales and then into their paper bag, Olive marvelled at the array of colours. She'd never had so many all to herself before.

"They used to be called Victory Babies," Mrs Lee said. "We'll be needing to pray for victory again soon enough, I don't doubt."

Miss Fitznorton took out a small cloth purse she'd been carrying in her trouser pocket. "Let's hope it won't come to that," she murmured, laying several coins on the counter before picking up the paper package containing the box of chocolates. She thanked Mrs Lee, but Olive noticed her tone was cooler than it had been when they arrived, and guessed she was disappointed by the unfriendly way the shopkeeper had spoken to Shirley.

The bell on the door tinkled as Michael opened it and stood aside to let his sisters pass. His face was troubled and downcast. Olive saw that Miss Fitznorton had noticed it too, and that it made her pause.

"Would you mind waiting outside for a moment, children? I just need a quick word with Mrs Lee," Miss Fitznorton said, folding her hands and waiting until the door had closed behind them before turning to speak to the shopkeeper.

Olive watched her through the glass panel in the shop door. She couldn't see Miss Fitznorton's face, but Mrs Lee's expression was a picture, wide-eyed and then crimson.

Moments later, Miss Fitznorton emerged. "If you have any more trouble with Mrs Lee let me know, won't you Michael?" she murmured. "There's another sweet shop in Pontybrenin."

Michael and Barbara exchanged a look.

"Why did you buy Black Magic for Auntie Dolly?" Shirley asked Miss Fitznorton as they continued their walk. "Is it her birthday?"

"No, it's just to show appreciation for all her hard work, with all the extra cooking, cleaning and laundry she'll have to do while you're staying with us. I thought you children could give it to her this evening before you get ready for bed. She'll like that, I'm sure."

It sounded a nice idea, giving someone chocolates just to say thank you. Her dad had never given her mum chocolates. But then, he'd never given her anything much, apart from bruises.

Miss Fitznorton pointed towards a grey stone building with tall, narrow windows and a row of four gables along its roof. It was surrounded by a concrete yard, edged with a low wall topped with metal railings.

"That will be your school while you're staying with us," she said.

"It's not very big." Peter's lip curled. "Our school in London is much bigger."

As he spoke, a tall man wearing a dark blue suit and a brown fedora hat rounded the corner and paused.

"Mr Winter!" Shirley dashed across the road and flung her arms about his legs.

Miss Fitznorton's smile vanished. She directed the rest of the children across the street and crouched beside Shirley, who had fortunately let go of Mr Winter's leg by now and was holding out her bag of sweets to invite him to take one.

"Shirley! You must never run across the road like that without looking."

"But there aren't any cars." Shirley looked from one adult to the other, her chin wobbling.

"That's immaterial. There might have been. I'm sorry, Mr Winter. I don't know what she was thinking, running into the road and grabbing you like that."

"No harm done. But Miss Fitznorton's right, Shirley," Mr Winter said, tugging a neatly folded handkerchief from his pocket and using it to dab her eyes. "Don't cry now. No one's cross. Just remember, your parents have sent you here to keep you out of danger. It wouldn't do to get yourself hurt on your very first day now, would it?"

His face softened, not quite into a smile, but Olive was reminded of his gentleness when he examined her swollen lip on the train. He hadn't seemed quite so scary since then.

"How is your lip today, Olive?" he asked, as if he had read her thoughts.

"Bit better, thank you," she murmured, grateful that he'd remembered.

Miss Fitznorton raised an eyebrow. "Your hand is better, I see. You've dispensed with the bandage." Her voice sounded more clipped than usual.

"Ah, yes. It was kind of your sister, but..."

His voice trailed off as if they were talking about something awkward, and Miss Fitznorton nodded, her mouth tight, like the way she looked when Peter was rude and made everyone uncomfortable. She didn't seem inclined to stay and talk to Mr Winter but mumbled something about having to get back to Plas Norton for lunch. It was disappointing, as Olive would have liked to hear more about his mysterious bandage. As Mr Winter tipped his hat and Miss Fitznorton set off in the opposite direction with the children following, Olive was left wondering why they both suddenly seemed so shy.

ELEVEN

Dodie

On Sunday morning, the adults gathered around the wireless in the drawing room. Ivor had heard there would be an important announcement at ten o'clock, but it was delayed until eleven. Dodie wished she hadn't had breakfast: her stomach churned with unease.

Charlotte was pacing the length of the room, to and from the window, her arms folded as if she was hugging herself. She'd be frightened for Chris and Loulou, of course. Now and then Dodie noticed her sister casting yearning glances towards the cabinet where the sherry was kept, but it was too early to start drinking alcohol, even for Charlotte. Even on such a nerve-racking and potentially momentous occasion.

Dolly had removed her apron and tidied her hair to listen to the Prime Minister. She stood beside Ivor, fiddling with her wedding ring and occasionally scowling. Dodie wasn't sure if it was the prospect of war that made her look so angry, or the radio programme about using tinned foods in recipes.

Ivor's usually cheerful face was grim and pale. Having been

lucky to survive being gassed at Ypres, he, better than any of them, knew what war could mean. The thought of gas being used again, not only against soldiers but also against civilians, made Dodie's blood run cold, and she rubbed her arms to warm them. After Guernica, everyone knew how dreadful the destruction unleashed by fascist armies might be. Even little Shirley and Peter must be aware of the risks to their parents if bombs fell on London. She'd overheard them whispering about Hitler and invasions, and the air raid shelter that had been built outside Olive and Peter's block of flats.

At last the cookery programme ended, and an authoritative voice addressed them. "This is London. You will now hear a statement by the Prime Minister."

Now they would know, once and for all, what was to come. Dodie's mouth was dry while she listened to Mr Chamberlain's message. He sounded weary and bitter as he announced that Britain was now at war with Germany; that Hitler would not see reason and had lied about his wicked intentions towards Poland.

They all listened in silence until the end, then Charlotte sank into the nearest chair and covered her mouth with a hand that trembled noticeably.

"That's that, then. It's really happening," Dolly said, her voice hoarse with repressed emotion.

Dodie swallowed hard to suppress the pent-up feelings threatening to burst out in a flood: weeping wouldn't help anyone, as much as she wanted to let the tears out.

"Got to be done," Ivor said. "It's time for old Adolf to get a good licking. He's bitten off more'n he can chew now, with Britain and France against him." He sniffed and patted his jacket pocket to find his pipe. "I'm going out for a smoke while I still can. I expect baccy'll be rationed soon enough. Once I've done that, I'll go up to the attics and fetch the bedsteads down. Looks as if those five kiddies will be staying with us for a while."

"If I could get my hands on Hitler, I'd kill him myself," Dolly growled, before stomping off to start cooking dinner.

"We'll have to put up the blackout material and tape up the window frames this afternoon, I suppose." Charlotte's voice sounded thin, lacking her usual confidence. She gnawed at her thumbnail.

"I'm sure the children will help with that," Dodie said.

"Would you mind asking them? I'm going to lie down for a little while. I've been fighting a headache all morning."

Dodie arched an eyebrow as her sister slipped out of the room with a hand to her brow. How typical of Charlotte to retreat to her room to avoid dealing with the children. She'd managed to avoid having much to do with them so far, apart from breezing into the kitchen now and then to dazzle them all with a smile and a quick hello, like a visiting princess. It seemed it would be left to Dodie to explain the news and tend to their needs. She swallowed the sharp retort hovering on the end of her tongue. Now wasn't the time for bickering. Not with the world plunging into a war that promised innumerable hardships and griefs. Alone in the drawing room, she permitted herself a few moments of weakness to bury her face in her hands, releasing a sob into her handkerchief.

Please, God – keep Christopher safe. Keep us all safe from invasion.

The idea of Nazi tanks and soldiers on the streets of Pontybrenin or Bryncarreg was too terrifying to contemplate. It wouldn't do to give in to dire imaginings. Somehow, Britain, her Empire and allies would pull together to see off the threat. She had to hold on to that. Blubbing wouldn't help anyone. After mopping her eyes, she sucked in some deep breaths and straightened her back before venturing outside to find the children.

They were on the wooden jetty near the boathouse, throwing morsels of stale bread into the lake and laughing as the ducks honked, wings flapping as they raced to scoop up the crumbs from the surface of the water.

Dodie couldn't help but smile. "The ducks must be delighted to have you staying with us. Be careful near the water, though. It's deep in some places."

"What did the news say?" Michael asked. He sent a worried glance towards his sisters as Dodie's smile faded.

"I'm so sorry. I'm afraid it wasn't the news we've all been hoping for," Dodie said with a sigh. She'd have given anything not to have to say the dreaded words aloud. "As we feared, Britain has declared war on Germany."

The sight of Olive's stricken face made Dodie reach out to squeeze her hand.

Barbara pulled Shirley close and hugged her, dark eyes wide and brimming with tears.

"It will be alright though, won't it?" she asked, her voice catching on the words.

Dodie gazed into each child's face before answering, infusing her voice with a confidence she wasn't sure she felt but which she sensed they needed to hear. "I'm sure it will be. Hitler will realise he can't possibly defeat us. It's disappointing that this has had to happen, but we've been preparing for this day for some time, haven't we? London will be well defended, and you must remember we have the best armed forces in the world, and right on our side."

Michael nodded.

She squinted against the bright sunlight reflecting off the lake and tried to inject some lightness into her voice. "Right, well we need to start putting blackout coverings on the windows, and Ivor will be busy this afternoon setting up bedsteads. I wondered if you might help."

"I'm not helping you with nothing. You still haven't given me that boat," Peter replied with a mutinous glare.

Dodie blinked. "I'll go up to the attics with Uncle Ivor later and look for it. But only if you promise to be good."

"Believe it when I see it," he muttered.

"There's no need to be rude," she said, exasperated, but he was already stomping off the jetty towards the house.

"We'll help, won't we Mikey?"

"Thank you, Barbara."

Not for the first time since their arrival, Dodie felt a rush of warmth towards Barbara for her irrepressible positivity. She and Shirley must be feeling as worried as their solemn-faced brother, but they were still determined to be cheerful. Olive, by contrast, stood silently gazing after her brother with those great, sad green eyes that Dodie had hardly seen smiling yet.

Dodie's concerns about Olive and Peter had kept her awake for ages the previous night after Dolly had discovered a bundle of wet bedding hidden beside Olive's mattress, and Peter's behaviour had been rude and uncooperative. She so wanted them to be happy, but with her lack of experience with young children, she had no idea how to help them. It was obvious that Olive was deeply troubled, and Peter's rudeness surely stemmed from anger. It wasn't hard to imagine that being sent so far from their parents and their home could have had such an effect. But what could she do about it?

TWELVE

Dodie

As soon as she could, Dodie took refuge in action and climbed the stairs to the attics, where Ivor was working up a sweat tugging metal bedsteads out from storage.

Wheezing from the effort and the dust, he mopped his forehead. "I'll sort these, miss. No need to trouble yourself with it."

"I'll willingly help you carry them down, Ivor. But I've actually come up to find something else. Do you know where my old toys might be?"

He pointed out some trunks and packing cases in a corner, and reluctantly accepted her help to carry the bedsteads down to the girls' bedroom. Within half an hour, he was assembling the bed frames while Dodie tackled the boxes in the attic alone.

The first was a dusty wooden trunk. Dodie heaved open the lid. Inside, nestling amongst layers of tissue paper, were her mother's things. The sight of them made her heart skip. She stroked a neatly folded piece of brightly coloured, exotic silk. It must be a garment of some sort. Lifting it out, she gasped as the gorgeous fabric swirled and flowed to the floor. As she held it up, she realised it was a kimono woven with chrysanthemums and cherry blossom. She gazed wistfully at the beautiful design, wishing she could picture her mother wearing it. But it was impossible: she had so few photographs of Rosamund and all of them were stiff and formal, with no colour images to help her visualise the living, breathing woman. Burying her nose in the fabric, Dodie released a disappointed sigh. It smelled only of mothballs. What else had she expected? Some lingering fragrance that might remind her of the mother she'd only known for a matter of days? Reverently, she folded it back up and set it aside before delving into the trunk again.

A packet of letters was tied with a ribbon. She opened a few. The handwriting was familiar, and sure enough a glance at the signature confirmed that the correspondence was from her godfather, Ewart Rutledge. She had never met him, but he sent her brief letters each year on her birthday and at Christmas, sometimes enclosing a pressed flower from his home Ambleworth Hall, where her mother had spent a happy childhood. The tone of these letters seemed friendly, even affectionate, which was hardly surprising given that Rosamund had asked for him to be one of her daughter's godparents; but there was no time for reading them now. With a sigh, Dodie laid them back in the trunk along with a gauzy shawl and the few books which had been packed along with them: a Bible with an embroidered cover, a couple of volumes of obscure medieval tales, and a motoring handbook for ladies which would be too dated now to be useful.

It was frustrating to have so little to connect her to the woman who gave her life. Hardly anyone among Dodie's acquaintances had known Lady Rosamund Fitznorton, apart from Charlotte, who had always been guarded when questioned about her stepmother. Venetia had met Rosamund once or twice when visiting Plas Norton as a girl, but she hadn't known her well.

She found her old toys in a box half-hidden behind a perambulator, which she presumed must have belonged to her or the twins. Lifting out a doll with a china face which had been her treasured possession as a little girl, she smiled and hugged it. The doll's soft hair and cold cheek against hers transported her back in time. *Juliet*. She had no idea what had inspired the name.

She thought of the evacuees: Barbara and Shirley each had a doll, and Peter had a threadbare teddy bear with only one ear and a nose that was half worn away, but Olive and Michael hadn't brought any such comforts with them. Michael, perhaps, was too old to take a toy to bed, but Olive... Olive was clearly troubled. She rarely spoke, flinched at loud noises, and the dark shadows under her eyes had grown worse with two nights away from home. She'd wet the bed on both nights and tried to hide the evidence, cringing away when Dolly questioned her about it. If ever a child needed the comfort of a doll to hold at night, it was scrawny, sad little Olive.

There were several other toys in the box. Dodie supposed she'd been spoiled, compared with the evacuees from Stepney, who had so little. Most of the items were made from painted wood, relics of the carpentry workshop in the stables which provided therapy for the shell-shocked officers who had recuperated at Plas Norton during the last war. There was an ark, with a set of little animals in pairs and Noah and his wife. There was also a box of dominoes; a draughts board with its black and white pieces; a snakes and ladders game; and a wooden horse on wheels. At last she found the boat, its paint flaking off a little when she brushed it with her hand. She could only hope that Peter would value it and stop using such horrid, insulting language.

Beside the boat was a car her mother's chauffeur had made for her, shiny dark blue with a red coachline. The windows had been painted to show a lady wearing a hat, and a driver with a chauffeur's cap. It had wire axles and wooden wheels which still turned. The weight of it in her hand, the smoothness of its paint, and the colours, all brought memories flooding back. The Fitznorton family's motor car had looked just like this when she was small. A stab of pain knifed through her as she remembered her most significant journey in it, on the day she was sent to school.

The twins had been small babies, only a couple of weeks old, and four-year-old Dodie had barely seen them or her sister since their birth. Maggie had been busier than usual, doubtless struggling with the leap from one to three children in her charge. She'd said nothing as she packed a trunk with Dodie's clothes and led her by the hand to say goodbye to the servants. She wasn't taken to bid farewell to Charlotte, but Dodie only thought of that later, after the excitement of a long journey in the rear compartment of the car with Venetia.

Venetia and Cadwalader, the chauffeur, had made a fuss of her; stopping for a picnic on the way was fun. On arriving at the imposing red-brick building which she was told was to be her school, she'd tried to run back to the car. Cadwalader had kissed her tear-streaked cheeks and turned away; it was left to Venetia to lead her inside and abandon her to her fate.

Dodie shoved the car back into the depths of the trunk, unable to look at it. Sitting back on her heels, she rubbed her breastbone, then doubled over at the waist, her body folding in on itself to ease the bitter grief that memories of that day still evoked. Surely the memories shouldn't still have the power to cause her such pain twenty years on? She'd been a happy child until that day. Despite the lack of a mother or father, and despite the loss of Charlotte's husband Kit, she'd felt secure. She'd believed herself to be loved by Charlotte and Venetia, and by Maggie and the other household staff. She'd been petted; cared for; indulged, even. And then, abruptly, she'd been wrenched away from everything she knew, and told to be brave and that it was for the best. *Best for whom?* Dodie was sure it hadn't been best for her. Even now the thought of that cataclysmic day made her want to howl.

Like Alice falling down the rabbit hole into Wonderland, she'd tumbled headlong into a different world, one in which she felt uncomfortably out of place. One in which there was little kindness, and absolutely no love. No physical affection. No more climbing onto Maggie's lap or being hoisted into Cadwalader's arms. A world in which she couldn't remember ever wanting to smile. She'd wondered for years what she had done to deserve the punishment of being sent away. If she had, perhaps, unknowingly caused Kit's death. After all, she'd caused her mother's by being born.

In the long years at school she'd been criticised for being tall, skinny and shy, and bullied for being able to play the piano better than other girls in her year, until she'd felt she must hide any talents away. She made herself invisible by being unexceptional.

When she returned to Plas Norton in the school holidays, the twins were so perfectly at home there that they provided a poignant reminder of everything of which she'd been deprived. They weren't unfriendly, but they were strangers to her. They had their own bond. She'd had no one. She'd sought comfort in books, losing herself in stories. When she was old enough to leave school and had completed her training at secretarial college, she'd been eager to get away from the house and estate that reminded her so painfully of the life she should have had. She'd found a job in London and felt proud of herself for striking out on her own and proving that she didn't need Charlotte or anyone.

If only she hadn't been so pathetically vulnerable to male attention. She'd made the dangerous mistake of falling in love with Lionel, the handsome under-manager, who'd turned her head by showing her kindness when their boss upset her with his disparaging remarks and his wandering hands. How thrilled she'd been when, after several months of stepping out with her, Lionel proposed marriage. She'd believed she'd found someone to be her best friend and confidant, her rock in times of trouble. Believed she'd never feel lonely again. That she was loved, and she'd make her own family. They'd have children and a home of their own, and she'd hardly ever need to go back to Plas Norton, except to show them all what she'd managed to achieve without them. She'd pictured herself returning with Lionel at her side, showing off a beautiful diamond ring. But he'd sworn her to secrecy, telling her it wasn't the right time to announce an engagement just yet. Soon he'd be promoted to manager, and then would be the moment to share their good news with the world. It had been disappointing, but for a few happy weeks she'd accepted it.

Emboldened by their secret understanding, Lionel hadn't wanted to wait until they were married to proceed to a more physical relationship. He'd said if she loved him, she would allow that intimacy now that he'd proved his love by asking her to marry him. She'd come shamefully close to giving in to the wanton urges that had made her melt when he kissed her.

But when she'd baulked at giving Lionel everything he wanted, he'd decided she wasn't right for him after all. *A tease*, he'd called her, leading him on only to frustrate him. She'd choked him like a clinging vine, he said, with her desperate need for affection. He'd berated her for her many failings. Too keen to throw herself into arrangements for their wedding and talk of their planned future together. Too boring, with her nose forever stuck between the pages of a book. Sluttish, the way she'd responded with such enthusiasm to his caresses. Stupid, too... He'd been right about that, if nothing else. She'd been so foolish to have allowed herself to be taken in.

When he told his friends in the office that she'd visited a hotel room with him, they'd drawn their own conclusions. In the face of their open contempt and after a humiliating dressing-down by the senior manager, she had little choice but to leave the whole experience behind: her engagement, her job, her lodgings in London, her hopes of a family, and the few friends she had made there before Lionel made her focus her every spare moment on him. Memories of everything he had cost her made her pound her fists on her thighs.

Back at Plas Norton, no one knew her secret shame, even if Charlotte and Venetia had their suspicions. She'd been building a life again, settling into her quiet routine and working hard to gain the respect of Mr Gibson and her patrons at the library whilst grieving the loss of an imagined future that had glimmered so brightly on her horizon. Now, there was a war on. Who knew what fresh terrors the future might hold?

All she could do was try to be a light in the darkness for the five evacuees in her care.

She packed the animals into the ark: Shirley would enjoy playing with it, she was sure. Peter would have the boat, of course, and Olive could have Juliet. Michael could have the dominoes, and Barbara the snakes and ladders. And at the library on Monday, she'd see if there were any books that they might enjoy reading. She knew from bitter experience just how much a child sent away from home could benefit from losing themselves in a story.

THIRTEEN

Olive

The other children seemed to find it fun walking to school across the fields. Barbara and Shirley held hands, Barbara laughing often at her little sister's exuberant chatter. Over the past week, Olive had noticed they hugged each other a lot. It must be nice having someone to hug. An actual person who wanted to hug you back, not just a doll with a cold, hard face and limbs that wouldn't bend. Peter was more likely to give her a shove than a hug.

It was strange to walk along footpaths, tracks and lanes to school, instead of along streets busy with women scrubbing their front doorsteps and traders calling out from market stalls. In the golden light of early morning, the fields were alive with flies and grasshoppers which leapt away as the children skirted the edges, careful not to touch the barbed wire fence strewn with sparkling cobwebs and clumps of wool. Olive's canvas plimsolls were soon soaked with dew right through to her socks.

Peter found a stick, amusing them all at first by using it as a staff, pretending to be an old man. Olive stopped finding it funny when he poked her in the ribs with it.

"I'm a shepherd," he jeered. "Go on, sheep, get a move on."

"Don't," she complained, but the more she batted it away and scowled, the more he seemed to enjoy prodding her back and bottom, then swiping it across her bare calves. Her eyes burned from holding back tears. Trying to angle her body so that he wouldn't be able to get to her so easily didn't work, and she finally made a dash past Michael to put herself out of reach.

Michael's brown eyes met hers as if he'd noticed what was happening for the first time. "That's enough now, nipper," he said to Peter, like a grown-up taking charge.

Peter's grin vanished. "You can't tell me what to do," he said.

Olive's shoulders tensed.

"No, but I can race you to the farm. Bet you I'll get there first."

Michael took off and with a frustrated howl, Peter dropped his stick and took to his heels, chasing after him. The cardboard gas mask boxes strung over their shoulders bumped wildly as they ran, hooting with glee. Peter's shorter legs pumped just as quickly as Michael's but, caught off guard like that, he had no hope of catching up.

Olive let out her breath. At least the stick now seemed to have been forgotten.

"Your Peter's a right little rascal, ain't he?" Barbara said. "If you ever need help to sort him out, you just ask Mikey. He's good like that. Hates bullies, he does."

They continued in silence until they reached the edge of the farmyard, where both boys were waiting, panting.

"You won't beat me next time," Peter declared, holding his stomach.

"Bet I will!"

Their laughter faded as the farm boy appeared in the

doorway and called out to them, using a nasty word that made Shirley cling closer to Barbara's side and Michael pick up his pace. The five children walked quickly, the girls casting glances behind.

"He's coming!" Shirley exclaimed.

Rapid footsteps crunched along the lane behind them, too many to be one person. Sure enough, the boy from the farm had been joined by three others, all of them shorter by varying degrees. His brothers, Olive guessed. They followed, heckling. Small stones pinged off the ground and off Michael's back, making Olive flinch. Michael, though, kept his head held high and didn't respond except to herd the younger children ahead of him.

By the time they reached the end of the lane and emerged at the village, Olive's heart was hammering. To her horror, the farm lads followed them right into the school yard, then trotted up to a group of loitering boys they didn't recognise. All of them stared.

The five evacuees stood together. Even Peter licked his lips nervously.

More children trickled into the walled school yard, most of them unfamiliar, until to their relief they recognised a few others from London and quickly beckoned them over. After eight days and nine nights in their billet at Plas Norton, Olive and her fellow evacuees had had plenty of time to explore the house and its grounds, but apart from their single encounter with Mr Winter on their outing to the sweet shop and postbox, they'd had no opportunity to see anyone they knew from back home. In this bigger group of familiar faces, Olive felt somehow less vulnerable, the prickling between her shoulder blades lessening now, her chest lighter. Eagerly, they exchanged snippets of information about their various billets, and it became clear to Olive that she, Peter and the Clarkes were the luckiest by far.

"There's no tap water in the house I'm staying in," Jimmy

told them with a groan. "And to go to the jakes you have to go to a hut at the end of the garden. It's full of spiders! And it doesn't flush. You have to chuck a scoop of earth on top after you've been."

Olive shuddered.

"I have to go out right after breakfast, and I'm not allowed back in until teatime," Audrey said, her voice little more than a whisper. "Then I have to go straight to bed. I've tried to write and tell me mum, but the old bag read my letter and ripped it up." Her chin wobbled as if she was trying to hold back tears.

"That sounds horrible," they all agreed.

"Our billet is like a castle!" Peter boasted, earning himself a nudge from Michael that made him fold his arms and glower, scuffing his toes in the gravel on the yard. "What do you do all day, Audrey?" Barbara asked.

"I just wander about," Audrey said. "Sometimes I sit by the river. When it rained the other day, the old cow still wouldn't let me in, so I went to the church and sat under a big tree. It was dry under there. Not much fun, though. I get awful bored."

The other girls all murmured sympathetically. Barbara reached out and patted Audrey's shoulder.

Audrey listened, agog, as Michael told her about their own adventures. "You should come over our way. We've found a little wooden place on a hill, like a posh shed – or used to be. It's a bit rotten now. Auntie Dolly, what cooks our dinners, says it's an old summerhouse, and her feller Uncle Ivor ain't got the time to fix it, so we can play in it all we want. It's our den now, and our hideout in case the Germans invade. We'll see them coming a mile off from up there."

Before they could say any more, they were interrupted by the clanging of the school's bell being rung by a thin, stern-looking woman with scraped-back, greying hair tied in a bun. With her black skirt almost down to her shoes, and a severe, dark-grey jacket, she looked like a ghost from a bygone age. A second woman came out to stand beside her, half a pace behind. This one looked down her nose at the gathered children through thick, tortoiseshell-framed spectacles. Both women raked the yard with fierce glares like gorgons from the story book Miss Fitznorton had read aloud the evening before.

The Bryncarreg pupils chorused out: "Good morning, Miss Honeycutt. Good morning, Miss Bright." They then formed two lines, one of boys and the other girls. Olive realised there were hardly more than twenty children in each line, the whole school totalling about the number that might be in one class back in London. The dozen or so evacuees moved to join them but were immediately ordered to line up separately.

It was a relief to see Miss Summerill and Mr Winter emerge from the building. Miss Summerill smiled somewhat nervously. Mr Winter gave them an approving nod, then lifted his chin. It was as if he was a ringmaster whose silent command reminded them how to perform at their best: instead of huddling anxiously, each evacuee stood straighter and taller. Olive sensed that the others felt as she did: that he'd reminded them they didn't need to be ashamed of being who they were. Yes, they were different. They were out of place, unwelcome even. But that simple gesture from Mr Winter was a reminder that not only could they hold their heads high, they absolutely should.

Bryncarreg school was tiny compared with the one they'd been used to in Stepney. It had only two classrooms, separated by a wooden partition through which the other teacher could easily be heard. One classroom had rows of sloping desks with inkwells for the junior children, aged seven to eleven, while the other had low wooden tables and chairs for the infants to sit in pairs. Dark wooden panelling lined the walls up to the height of the windowsills, with a few printed maps, some pictures of Biblical scenes, and an alphabet pinned above, barely covering patches where the gloomy green paint had flaked away to reveal bare plaster. The windows were criss-crossed with tape in case of air raids, as they now were at Plas Norton and all the houses and shops they'd passed in the village. Beside the door, Olive noticed buckets of sand, a couple of pails of water, and a stirrup pump. This stark reminder that bombs could start fires made her stomach lurch. Instinctively, she hugged her arms about herself. She mustn't think about what had happened to Irene now. She and Peter weren't going to burn. She wouldn't let him.

After traipsing inside for a short assembly, the dull hymn and even duller prayers were soon followed by an unenthusiastic speech of welcome by Miss Honeycutt, the headteacher. She explained that a lack of space and chairs meant the visiting children would spend the morning outdoors with their own teachers while the Bryncarreg pupils worked indoors at their desks.

First, they had a gas mask drill, practising putting their horrid-smelling masks on as quickly as possible at Miss Honeycutt's signal, receiving a scolding for being too slow.

"It's imperative that you learn to put on your gas mask at a moment's notice," she said. "We shall practise every week, and I expect you to practise at home... or at your billet, of course... to ensure that you can do it quickly. Hitler will not wait for you to be ready."

While the local children sat at their usual desks, Olive and the other evacuees filed through the main door to sit cross-legged on the concrete in their two groups for their first lesson. It was strange to have no exercise book, no pencil, not even a desk to sit at. There was no blackboard or chalk, and whenever Olive glanced over at the infants' group to see how Shirley was faring, she looked bored.

There was no time for the older children to get bored with Mr Winter in charge. He soon organised them into teams and had them racing to complete mental arithmetic problems.

"This afternoon, we'll go for a walk," he told them. "I'll set you a challenge to collect a leaf from as many different trees as you can. Then, we'll see how many we can identify using the books in the reading corner. Tomorrow, if the weather is fine, I'd like you each to bring a wax crayon to school, and we'll head out to the woods with some paper to make some bark rubbings from the trees you can name."

After a stodgy school lunch which was barely edible compared with Auntie Dolly's tasty cooking, the evacuees clustered together in the yard. With the obvious exception of the Clarkes, Olive noted that they all looked pasty compared with the local children, whose ruddy, freckled cheeks and wiry, golden-brown legs made them look as if they must spend every day out of doors.

"What you looking at, then?" one of the sturdier local girls called out, seeing Olive's furtive glances. A shiver sliced down Olive's spine as the girl marched over to her, together with several of her friends. They were immediately followed by a group of boys who nudged each other and grinned, as if they planned to enjoy some fun at the evacuees' expense. Within moments the evacuees had been surrounded by jostling locals.

"You lot stink," the girl said, her lip curling with distaste as she looked Olive up and down. "Pooh!" She pinched her nose between her thumb and forefinger, and the others immediately joined in.

"We do not!" Peter snarled back, his fingers curling into fists.

Olive lunged for his arm. He'd only cause more trouble by lashing out.

"I bet they're all crawling with nits, too. And fleas. That's what my mam said," another girl chimed in, causing much hilarity. "You are, aren't you?"

"My dad said you was from London, but you three look like you're from the jungle," a boy said, pointing at the Clarkes.

His friend started scratching his armpits and making monkey noises.

Olive felt sick. She moved closer to Barbara and Shirley, wanting to show loyalty but scared to speak out for fear of attracting equally cruel taunts.

The boy opened his mouth to say more, but snapped it shut with one glance towards the school door, where Mr Winter had appeared and was watching them with narrowed eyes. As if by magic, the circle of jeering children fell silent and drifted away to play at the other side of the yard.

"Are you alright, Barbara?" Olive murmured.

Barbara only turned away.

FOURTEEN

Olive

Nearly two weeks had passed since their arrival at Plas Norton, and there had been no letter from home. The Clarkes had had three letters already, and now a fourth was causing excitement at the breakfast table, with Michael taking responsibility for ripping it open and reading it out to his sisters. It was a wonder Mrs Clarke could afford the stamps to write twice weekly. Olive couldn't understand why there had still been no word from her parents when letters were obviously getting through without any difficulty.

Barbara's excitement as Michael read the letter didn't last long. Tears rolled over her chin and into her bowl of cornflakes at the words he read aloud.

You'll be pleased to hear that your brother Francis is settling into his new job in the factory and the foreman is pleased with him. Kathleen is talking much more now, and she has learned to count to ten. I show her your photo every day. But I'm sorry to tell you Rusty has had to be put to sleep.

Michael's voice snagged on the words.

We've heard that Hitler is planning to send rabies into Britain, and I didn't want him to catch it. And if we end up with food being rationed like it was in the last war, there might not be enough to feed him. People have to be fed first. I know how upset you'll be but try not to be sad. He didn't suffer.

"Poor Rusty!" Shirley wailed, as her brother's voice faltered.

Barbara put her arms around her and sniffed, wiping her nose on her sleeve. Olive saw that Auntie Dolly had noticed, her mouth opening as if she was on the point of telling her to use a handkerchief; but she turned away and said nothing, just filled the kettle with water and set it on the hotplate.

Olive bowed her head. She'd never had a pet, but she could see from the way Michael's jaw trembled as he folded up the letter that he was as sad as his sisters. Maybe even sadder than she was about not receiving any word from Mum yet.

Was Mum alright? According to the news, there'd been no bombings or gas attacks yet in London, and Hitler hadn't invaded. She should be safe. She would have received their postcards ages ago. So why hadn't she written back to say she knew they were being billeted together, and to send news from home?

It didn't upset Olive not to have heard from their dad. She still hadn't quite got used to not having to listen out for his heavy tread. Uncle Ivor teased her for flinching at every loud noise, like when he dropped a tray with a clatter onto the flagstone floor of the kitchen and she'd covered her head so quickly with her arms that she'd almost overbalanced off her chair. She'd been nervous around Uncle Ivor at first, but he seemed easy-going. Now and then he'd raise his voice at Peter and threaten to give him a clip across the ear, but that was to be expected considering Peter was so often naughty. He was always getting told off for being rough or rude. He'd shoved Olive and pulled one of her pigtails yesterday and it had been all Miss Fitznorton could do to stop Auntie Dolly putting him over her knee and spanking him.

Miss Fitznorton had knelt in front of him and grasped his arms. "Why do you do it?" she'd asked, a pained look on her face as if he'd caused her almost as much as pain as he'd done to Olive. "It's wrong to be so mean. We aren't here to hurt each other, but to look after one another."

Miss Fitznorton had a soft heart, that much was clear. Not that Olive was complaining; so far Miss Fitznorton hadn't told her off for the wet sheets Olive had woken up on every morning. She'd just quietly asked her to take them down to the laundry room and put them to soak, instead of leaving them in a bundle next to the bed, then went out and bought a rubber sheet to cover the mattress. And Olive had thought her heart would burst when she was given the most beautiful doll that she'd ever seen to take care of. Juliet had wide blue eyes, blonde ringlets and a lace bonnet that tied under her chin. She wore a frilly dress over her lacy petticoat and brown leather shoes. Her head was made of porcelain, so when they weren't playing, Olive kept her safely tucked away in a shoebox Uncle Ivor had given her, with a soft yellow duster under her head to protect it.

She couldn't remember anyone ever being quite so kind before. To Olive, Miss Fitznorton seemed like an angel, with her lovely, smooth, clear skin and her warm smile, her rich brown curls and her gentle voice. With her, Olive felt safe. She'd like nothing more than to spend all day with Miss Fitznorton, soaking up her presence.

After they'd helped clearing up the breakfast things, the children lined up to collect zinc buckets from Uncle Ivor, who was going to lead their planned expedition to collect blackberries. Earlier in the week they'd helped to collect apples from the Plas Norton orchard. It had seemed strange, seeing apples growing on actual trees and not simply piled on a greengrocer's barrow.

"Are you sure they're really apples?" Shirley had asked, pressing a doubtful finger to her lower lip. "They're not poisonous, or anything?"

"They won't hurt you, but the wasps might. Watch out when you're picking them up, in case you get stung," Uncle Ivor warned them. He puffed as he dragged a heavy wooden ladder out and leaned it against one of the trees, nudging it with his boot before starting to climb with a bucket over his arm.

As the eldest two children, he put Michael and Olive in charge of picking the fruit from the lowest branches. "It has to be done carefully, mind. No dropping them into the bucket. Put them in gently, as if they were made of glass. If they get bruised, they won't keep."

Barbara, Shirley and Peter were tasked with collecting what Uncle Ivor called windfalls. "You'll still need to be careful with them, but it doesn't matter quite so much if they get bruised, because they're going to be taken to the village hall to be dried or made into blackberry and apple jam by the Witches' Institute."

The three girls gaped at him.

"The Witches' Institute?" Barbara repeated.

Goosepimples rose on Olive's arms. She didn't like the idea of witches in the village hall one bit. Yet Uncle Ivor was laughing.

"Don't go telling Mrs H I called them that," he said. "She'd have my guts for garters. Off you go now, see who can be the first to fill their bucket."

He couldn't have said anything better to make Peter join in. He'd folded his arms and jutted his lower lip out at the idea of being asked to help with anything, but the chance to compete in a race was a different matter. He dashed around seizing apples and hurling them into his bucket, even the wormy ones and the ones with squishy bits. He was soon ahead of his rivals, who preferred to work steadily rather than throwing themselves into the task; but by the time his bucket was half full, he was already starting to lose interest in their new game.

"This is boring!" he said, putting his hands on his hips and squinting at Michael, who was twisting apples on their stalks to detach them from the tree and then laying them carefully in his bucket.

"You can't stop now, the girls will beat you," Uncle Ivor called from his vantage point up the ladder.

Olive kept quiet. She knew there was no point trying to convince Peter to help with a job if he didn't want to, and if she said anything to make him look small, he'd punish her for it later.

Peter picked up a stick and started swiping at the apples still hanging on the lowest branches, trying to knock them down. One or two bounced onto the ground.

"*Diawl bach!* Stop that, you little bugger," Uncle Ivor growled.

"You're helping Hitler, you know, by spoiling those apples," Barbara said, shaking her head. "He wants to starve us into submission, our mum says."

Although she was unsure what submission was, Olive was pretty sure Peter had grasped the message, just as she had.

Poking his tongue out, Peter held his thumb to his nose and waggled his fingers at Barbara before blowing a defiant raspberry and stalking away beyond the trees.

Wary of what he might get up to unsupervised, Olive kept half an eye on him but continued plucking apples from the boughs she was able to reach. Their smell was sweet and ripe in the warm morning air, luring wasps, and she made sure not to grasp the fruit carelessly, but to mind where she put her fingers. Soon her bucket was too heavy to hold, and she had to put it down on the ground. Reaching up to pick the fruit, each shiny apple looked deliciously tempting, but she resisted, pride filling her chest at the knowledge that she was doing a good job. Uncle Ivor would be pleased with her.

She almost dropped an apple when a piercing yell carried across the orchard from Peter's direction. Something terrible must have happened. Why, oh why hadn't she paid more attention to what her brother was doing? The palms of her hands turned suddenly clammy. She wanted to run to Peter, but her legs refused to move.

"Argh! Help me! It's a bloody snake!" Rapid footsteps pounded their way and Peter swerved around a tree, his face ashen and eyes wide. "It's bit me!"

Uncle Ivor's ladder wobbled precariously, and Olive's breath caught in her throat, only releasing it when she saw that he'd managed to steady himself by grabbing onto the tree.

"*Duw!* What's all this fuss?" He climbed down the ladder remarkably quickly; but the children's eyes were no longer on him. All their horrified attention was focused on Peter and the sinuous, sludgy-green creature writhing from his outstretched hand.

"I tried to pick it up behind its head, but it twisted round. It won't let go! Am I going to die? Is it poisonous?"

The colour had returned to Uncle Ivor's cheeks. He climbed down the ladder, put his hands on his knees and peered at the snake.

Olive hugged herself, fighting the urge to be sick as her head throbbed with fright. She'd thought the wasps would be the worst danger they'd face today, but it seemed the countryside was full of hidden perils. The sight of the snake clinging to the skin between her brother's thumb and index finger made her whimper. It was horribly long – a yard or more – and it thrashed in mid-air, resisting all Peter's wild attempts to shake it off.

"Well, I'll be blowed," Uncle Ivor said. "I've never seen a grass snake bite anyone before. You're alright, lad, it's perfectly harmless. If it'd been an adder, it might've been a different story, mind. Let this be a lesson to you, not to go messing with snakes. Or any other wild animal, for that matter."

Olive dared to breathe again. But still the snake dangled, its jaws clamped firmly onto Peter's hand.

"I won't touch any ever again, I promise – just get it off me!" Peter wailed.

Uncle Ivor straightened, then took off his cap and scratched his head. "I'm not sure I want to touch it if it's in a biting mood, to be honest."

"Does it hurt, Peter?" Michael asked, curious now that it seemed there was no immediate danger.

"Not really. But I don't like it. Bastard thing, you've got to help me get it off."

"Well now – if you're going to use language like that, it can stay there."

To Olive's surprise, Peter apologised. He must be really scared. Barbara and Shirley had linked arms with her, one on either side, and she squeezed her elbows in, comforted by the contact.

"Perhaps if you run it under the tap, it'll let go to breathe?" Michael suggested, putting his hands on his hips in an unconscious mirroring of Uncle Ivor's posture.

"Hmm. That's not a bad idea, boyo. Or we could just chuck young Peter here into the lake, and see if it has the same effect?" Uncle Ivor had already started chuckling, but now wheezed with laughter and coughed all the more as Peter's face contorted into a furious scowl at this suggestion. "Come on, now. Off to the tap with you. Let's see if we can get it off without hurting it."

The girls followed close behind. Barbara and Shirley's eyes shone with excitement now that they knew Peter wasn't about to drop dead from a venomous bite, and they chattered eagerly either side of Olive about his latest scrape. But Olive couldn't say a thing. Her legs moved stiffly, her knees wanting to lock. Sweat cooled on the back of her neck, making her hair stick to her skin. She wanted to hide away, to curl up under her pretty pink eiderdown with Juliet and pretend that none of this had happened. With a gulp, she swallowed a rush of bile and prayed her parents would never know how badly she'd let them down. There might be no lasting harm done this time, unlike the time she hadn't been quick enough to stop Irene stumbling into the fire, but once again, she'd failed to prevent one of her siblings falling into danger. Somehow, she would have to do better.

FIFTEEN

Olive

Ever since the incident with the snake, Olive had suffered nightmares, sometimes more than one in a single night. If she wasn't being chased by an unseen monster, or wandering lost and alone in a dark forest, or trying to find Peter in a milling crowd of faceless strangers, she was awake and imagining real dangers: bombs falling on her flat in London, or hordes of Nazis charging across the fields towards Plas Norton. Although Peter hadn't come to any lasting harm this time, she had to do more to protect him. It was what their mum would want.

There was a red notice outside the post office in Bryncarreg saying *Freedom is in peril – Defend it with all your might,* and she'd noticed several people talking about the invasion, and what they'd do in the event of it.

Once, after Uncle Ivor had mentioned that he'd stocked up on shotgun cartridges, Auntie Dolly had sniffled into her handkerchief and left the room for a good few minutes. Mrs Havard had made a list of all the provisions in the cellar, "just in case". Uncle Ivor was turning over the flowerbed for growing more vegetables, which had made Miss Fitznorton look sad. But if Hitler arrived on their doorstep, the number of pots of chutney in the cellar and the loss of a few roses would be the least of their worries. Even snakes wouldn't seem all that scary then.

"We need more defences in case the invasion comes," she said, looking over Michael's shoulder at the illustrated library book he was reading about castles. "Like a moat, maybe."

"Plas Norton isn't old enough for a moat, but it has the ha-ha," he pointed out.

"But that's just to stop sheep or deer getting into the gardens and eating the veggies. It wouldn't stop a person. It won't stop the invasion."

He spread his hands and carried on reading.

"We could build some hidden traps," Olive said, thinking aloud. "With five of us to do the work, it shouldn't be that hard. We could put them around the house and disguise them so the Nazis won't see them until it's too late." She thought of scenes she'd watched in films, with people's feet caught in ropes that pulled them up into the trees, trapping them in a big net. But that might be a bit tricky to set up. Even if they could find a big enough net, there weren't any tall trees near the house.

With Michael finally curious enough to put his book down, they went to find the others. After swearing them to secrecy, they shared their plan. No one must know about the traps, otherwise they might not work. Then, energised by their secret mission, they asked Uncle Ivor to let them do some digging, and he seemed more than pleased to let them borrow spades, forks and trowels from one of his sheds. He even pointed out which flowerbeds needed digging over.

"But won't the Nazis use the paths?" Shirley said, looking doubtful, when they headed out to the gardens and looked for somewhere to dig.

"Not if they're storming the house," Peter replied scornfully. "They ain't going to be holding the gate open for each other and saying, 'After you, Fritz'. They'll be rampaging across with their tanks, and they won't care about our spuds and carrots when they attack. Besides, if we mess with the paths, they'll spot the traps a mile off."

The others agreed. They decided to dig shallow trenches and then to disguise them.

"Like they do in the films," Michael suggested, sending Barbara and Shirley to gather sticks and leaves from the edge of the woods nearby.

Digging was surprisingly hard work, even with three of them to share the task. The earth was heavy and littered with stones, and the sides of the trench kept falling in. With the autumn sun on their backs, Olive and the boys were soon hot and fed up.

"This is hopeless," Peter said, wiping his arm across his forehead and leaving a muddy smear. "We'll never manage to make a trench all the way round the house. We could dig till Doomsday and still not finish the job." Olive guessed he was already on the point of giving up, bored now that he'd realised the task was harder than he'd expected.

Michael leaned on his spade the way they'd seen Uncle Ivor do. "What if we just make pits? Even if we dig them a few yards apart, we'll still catch some of the enemy. It will be enough to slow down their advance while Uncle Ivor reloads his shotgun."

"It's not a bad idea," Olive agreed. It certainly seemed more manageable than their original plan, which had rapidly started to feel like an impossible task. They might be able to build more defences over time, but at least this was a start.

When the younger ones returned, arms laden and pockets full, the girls knelt and carefully laid a lattice of sticks across the shallow pit that had been dug so far. It was about a foot deep, and a yard or more long, with the boys making progress on another a couple of yards away. Soon both pits were covered over with sticks and leaves. A light scattering of loose earth on top made them look less out of place with the rest of the soil in the flower bed.

Michael nodded approvingly, then put his hands on his lower back and stretched. "Phew! Time for a drink, I reckon. Good work, everyone."

Olive couldn't suppress a giggle. "You sound like Uncle Ivor," she pointed out.

"He does! Next thing you know, he'll be cussing in Welsh. It'll be all *Duw Duw* and *Bobol bach* before you know it." Peter sniggered and Michael nudged him good-naturedly with his elbow, laughing it off.

The children trooped indoors, leaving their tools where they were and kicking off their muddy footwear in the boot room. After washing their hands and faces in the scullery, they sat around the kitchen table pouring beakers of cold orange squash from a jug. Olive kept quiet while the others chatted, content to know she'd done something that would help to defend not only Peter but the freedom that the poster said was in peril.

"You lot finished already?" Uncle Ivor stumped through the kitchen. "Hope you've cleaned my tools and put them back?"

The children exchanged glances.

"Whoops. Sorry. We were just having a drink, but we'll do it once we've—"

Muttering darkly, Uncle Ivor disappeared.

Olive drained her beaker. "Perhaps we'd better go and tidy up," she said, her stomach knotting at the thought that they might have got into trouble with Uncle Ivor. He'd never hit any of them like Dad would, but still she hated the idea that he might think she'd been naughty.

Huffing, the others pushed back their chairs and followed her outdoors after retrieving their boots.

Blinking in the sunlight, they emerged into the garden and spotted Uncle Ivor heading out to where they'd been digging.

"Uncle Ivor! Wait!" Olive shouted from the path.

He glanced over his shoulder before bending to pick up a spade, then, to her horror, went sprawling sideways onto the ground.

In the seconds it took to dash over to him, he'd unleashed a torrent of Welsh words. One foot was stuck in the larger of the two Hitler traps, and he flailed his arms to try to sit up, like a beetle on its back.

"*Uffern dân!*" he roared, red in the face and hands covered in mud. Olive thought it best not to ask what it meant.

Michael reached out a tentative hand and helped him sit up, then dusted his palms together to remove the worst of the mud. Apart from his pride, Ivor seemed unhurt.

He sent them all a baleful glance, then bellowed, "What do you think you're looking at, then?"

Mumbling apologies, they stood in a line and watched as Uncle Ivor struggled to his feet, still grumbling.

"Pick those ruddy tools up, will you, you little buggers? And fill that hole in so no one else gets hurt." After swooping to grab his cap from the ground, he limped back towards the house.

Relieved that he clearly hadn't broken his ankle, Olive exchanged a guilty look with the other girls.

Peter shrugged and wiped his snotty nose on his sleeve. "At least we know our Hitler trap could have worked," he said.

SIXTEEN

Dodie

Venetia's house in Windsor Avenue was comfortable and modern. Although she didn't own a car, it had a garage attached at the side, where her lodger Maggie Cadwalader kept her bicycle. Unlike its mock-Tudor neighbours, Venetia's stylish Art Deco house had no stained glass. Its corners were rounded and the roof was flat, reminding Dodie of pictures she'd seen of houses in America, or of passenger liners. It even boasted a balcony off the main bedroom upstairs. She suspected that Charlotte, who was always keen to keep up with fashion trends, must be green-eyed with jealousy over its modish look.

Dodie admired the practicality of this new house, compared with Plas Norton's eighty-year-old faded grandeur and extravagant size. Its heating and lighting bills would be a fraction of what it cost to run their old Gothic Revival mansion. No doubt there were some traditionally minded folks who'd disapprove of something so new and up-to-the-minute, with its white-painted pebbledash and its fashionably curved metal-framed window in the front parlour. This was now criss-crossed with strips of tape to protect against flying glass in the event of an air raid, just like the windows in every other house in town these days.

Dodie smiled to herself as she walked up the short driveway with a bundle of books in her hand, knowing she'd be able to relax on the squishy leather sofa in front of the tiled fireplace in the front parlour in a way she couldn't in Plas Norton's more formal drawing room. Her smile widened when Maggie opened the front door and welcomed her inside with a kiss on the cheek. Dodie's former nursemaid – Dolly's elder sister – still held a special place in Dodie's heart even though Maggie's work as a district midwife meant that she was often out when Dodie came to visit.

"I thought I'd call in with Venetia's library books on my way home from work," Dodie explained.

"That's kind of you. She'll be pleased to see you. She's in the study, working as always – but your visit will be a good excuse to drag her away from her letters for once. I've made a shepherd's pie. Do you have time to eat with us? I'm sure we can make it stretch if I peel an extra couple of spuds and carrots."

"I'll need to catch the quarter-past-six bus, otherwise I'll be walking home in the dark. But a cup of tea would be lovely, thank you."

She followed Maggie into the kitchen. It was small, but beautifully appointed with fitted cupboards and a gas stove. As Plas Norton was too remote from town to have a supply of gas, Dodie could only imagine how much Dolly must envy her sister's access to such a modern appliance.

"Miss Summerill isn't back yet, so we've the place to ourselves," Maggie said, laying out cups, saucers and a milk jug on a tray.

"How is she settling in?"

Maggie paused, the lines on her forehead deepening, and Dodie had a feeling she was trying to think of a way to be diplomatic. "She says some funny things sometimes. She wasn't at all happy when war was declared. I mean, none of us were, obviously – but she was quite upset about the prospect of Britain being at war with Germany. Said we've got it all wrong about Hitler, and we should be working with him, not against him. Said the rumours about Jews being persecuted are just propaganda spread by Zionists."

"Heavens. What did Venetia say to that?"

"She said, 'that reminds me, I must send another cheque to help the little Jewish refugees'."

"Good for her." Dodie grinned and followed Maggie into the parlour, where she sank into the comfortable sofa. Maggie set the tea tray down on a side table and disappeared to fetch Venetia, leaving Dodie alone for a few moments. She closed her eyes, enjoying the cosy surroundings and the soft ticking of the mantel clock.

"Dodie! What a pleasure to see you. And you've brought the new Agatha Christie. How marvellous, thank you."

Dodie fancied Venetia's limp was more pronounced than usual as she clumped into the room leaning on her stick. "I hope you haven't been overdoing it," she remarked, concerned, as Venetia eased herself into her armchair with a suppressed gasp of discomfort. The older woman's eyes were smudged with dark shadows, and the lines on her cheeks and around her eyes seemed more noticeable.

Venetia waved aside her concerns.

Maggie pursed her lips. "She always overdoes it. Maybe she'll listen to you better than she does to me," she said, pouring them each a cup of tea.

"Oh, hush your nagging, Maggie. Take no notice, Dodie. She's just cross because she had a trying day."

"Every day's a trying day. Childbearing can make a woman think dark thoughts and do drastic things, especially if life was hard for them before the birth. The mother I delivered today has been depressed for months..."

Venetia cleared her throat and cast a glare Maggie's way. It seemed, inexplicably, like a warning.

Maggie's cheeks turned pink, glancing at Dodie as if to check how her words had been construed. It was odd, but there was no time to mull over what must have been some kind of indiscretion, for Maggie had ploughed on.

"Round here there are too many women with not even two ha'pennies to rub together, having babies they can ill afford or ending up in hospital because... Oh, never mind. Perhaps I shouldn't try to stop you writing so many letters to them in charge, Vee. Lord knows something needs to change."

Dodie sipped at her tea, unsure how to respond, and Maggie bustled out to continue her work in the kitchen.

"How are your young evacuees, Dodie?"

It didn't escape Dodie that Venetia had deflected the focus of the conversation, but there was nothing to be gained from prodding her towards any subject she didn't wish to discuss.

"They're a bit of a trial, I'm afraid. Young Peter is the worst: his language is shocking. He's so different from his sister. Poor Olive is a dear little thing, but she seems so unhappy. Her nightly bed-wetting is creating a huge amount of additional work for Dolly, along with the extra cooking and cleaning of course. We've had to buy a rubber sheet for her bed. She hardly speaks, clings to me like a wounded puppy, and I've noticed if anyone raises their voice or makes a sudden noise, she flinches. Perhaps it's just the upset of being evacuated, but it makes me wonder what she might have experienced before coming to us. I wish I knew how to help her."

Venetia frowned. "If anyone can help her feel safe and cared for, it's you, Dodie. Kindness and fun will be the key to helping her settle, I'm sure. And hopefully her brother will copy your example."

Grateful for Venetia's faith in her, but unsure if kindness would really be enough, Dodie plucked at her skirt. "Olive might feel better if only her parents would send a letter, but she's heard nothing from them in two weeks. I've even tried writing to them myself, to make sure they know our address."

"Have you tried enclosing a stamped envelope and some blank notepaper? Having seen the state of the children's clothes and boots, the obstacle might be something as simple as the cost of stationery and a stamp."

It wasn't a bad idea, but it made Dodie's heart sink to picture a depth of poverty that would prevent a mother from writing to her children.

"I'll give it a try. We've managed to get them some decent boots, at least, so their walk to school and back will be a little easier. Charlotte and her friends in the WVS organised a collection of children's boots and shoes in the church hall, and people rallied round wonderfully." She smiled. "It's been rather satisfying to see how Michael and his sisters have started to put on a little weight. Peter and Olive's legs are already straighter and stronger; they even have a bit of a suntan now. They've been up the mountain helping to collect blackberries and winberries, and Ivor's had them picking apples for making jam."

"Jolly good show. Our jam-making exploits at WI have been tremendous fun," Venetia said, with a twinkle that made her look more like her old self. "It's been quite an operation, organising it all, but most worthwhile when one thinks of the amount of fruit that will be preserved, rather than it going to waste."

Maggie came back in, dusting her hands over her apron. "If I hear another word about jam I'll scream. That's why she looks dead on her feet, you know: from a week of bossing the WI ladies about in the church hall. But then, if there's one thing she loves to do, it's dishing out orders. Should have been a sergeant major, not a local councillor." She perched on the arm of Venetia's armchair and sent a wink Dodie's way.

It amused Dodie the way Maggie spoke so familiarly with Venetia. They were so at ease with one another, but then they'd shared a home in Pontybrenin for years before moving into this house. She supposed living in such close proximity for so long would make formality unnecessary, and Venetia had always been inclined to speak bluntly. As she said her goodbyes and trotted to the bus stop, it seemed to her that they were less like lodger and landlady than an old married couple.

SEVENTEEN

Patrick

Patrick attempted to rearrange his features into something less fearsome than a scowl, conscious that his fists had clenched in his lap. He'd insisted upon this meeting after the end of the school day, as the local teachers had made no secret of their reluctance to discuss alterations to their current arrangements.

There was nothing sweet about Miss Honeycutt, and not a glimmer of radiance shone from the grim visage of Miss Bright. Neither appeared to have learned either patience or tolerance in their years of teaching the local children. Patrick slowed his breathing in an effort to control his temper, frustrated by his failure to make either of them see the need for change. Disdain and resentment seemed to flow from their side of the table on a sour tide of suspicion. So far, they'd blocked every attempt to make them see reason.

"I would ask you to remember that these children have been removed from their homes, their families, and everything comforting and familiar, through no fault or choice of their own.

It isn't right or fair for their education to suffer, or for them to be treated in a way that makes them feel or appear inferior to the local children whose situation is more fortunate."

"What do you imagine we should be doing, Mr Winter, over and above that which has already been done for them? The children are ignorant, rude, and several are even verminous. The behaviour this morning was a disgrace! I've never seen such violence from a child in all my years of teaching. Yet you seem to expect that not only should our community house, feed and clothe the ungrateful wretches, but that it should also squander valuable educational resources on them."

Before he could respond to Miss Honeycutt's withering contempt, Miss Bright fired her own much feebler salvo in support of her colleague. "You see, Mr Winter, it's unfortunate, but there's only so much to go around. Only so much space to be had. And we can't be seen to tolerate the kind of behaviour they displayed this morning. You can hardly expect our pupils to make way for yours, after such a shocking incident."

Patrick opened his mouth to defend the evacuees, but Miss Honeycutt interjected again.

"We can't conjure desks or chairs or pencils or exercise books out of nowhere, any more than we can make the school hall any bigger. Why should the village children be deprived for the sake of incomers who might be gone a few weeks from now? Some have already gone back to London."

"Two," Patrick said, tapping his index finger on the table as he finally managed to get a word in. "Two have gone back. It's hardly an exodus."

Miss Honeycutt stiffened. "I take issue with your tone, Mr Winter."

"And I take issue with your lack of justice and Christian charity."

Ignoring the women's outraged gasp, he pushed his chair

back. If he didn't go now, he might end up saying something he'd regret.

Beside him, Miss Summerill twittered ineffectually, wringing her hands. "Perhaps if our children could use the classroom in the afternoon...?" she said, her voice wheedling in the face of Miss Honeycutt's opposition. "Or perhaps we could get all the children to sit on the floor together, given the shortage of desks and chairs? For singing, perhaps, or reciting multiplication tables or poetry? It's very difficult working outside. The weather will turn soon."

Patrick nodded, his fists clenching at his sides. "When it rained last week, I had to teach arithmetic in the cloakroom, amongst the wet coats, with no paper or pencils, and no blackboard. The situation can't continue."

With an impatient huff Miss Honeycutt rose, giving the others little choice but to do the same.

"I think we've said everything there is to say. The children have been accommodated to the best of our ability. I suggest you take the matter up with the Board of Education, if you're still not satisfied."

He faced her across the table, simmering with anger and more determined than ever to force a change. "Rest assured, ladies – I shall."

He held the door for Miss Summerill as they left, donning his hat before marching to the bus stop. She followed, puffing to keep up with his bad-tempered stride, and mopped her face with a handkerchief before standing beside him in the queue.

Ahead of them was an elderly man holding a newspaper. Patrick nodded to him, but the fellow merely shook the pages and buried his nose further behind them.

Patrick took a deep breath and flexed his fingers. There wouldn't be a bus heading back towards Pontybrenin for another twenty minutes or so; he couldn't help wishing he, too, had a newspaper to dive into, instead of having to endure Miss Summerill's irritating blether.

"I fear you've made an enemy there," Miss Summerill said. She tutted, shaking her head as if at a loss. "I don't know what this world is coming to, lately. Everyone seems determined to fight the wrong people."

It seemed an odd thing to say, but he let it pass, not trusting himself to respond just yet. He needed a few more minutes for his mood to cool.

As his breathing returned to normal, he berated himself for his lack of diplomacy. Miss Summerill was right: the only thing he'd succeeded in doing this evening was making an enemy of the headmistress. He should have found a way to charm her into agreeing to co-operate, instead of charging in like a bull at a gate, fired up with resentment and frustration that his attempts to help the kids weren't being supported.

"I hope you can reach some sort of compromise, Mr Winter, I really do... But in a way, I'm glad this has happened. I've realised this week that this place isn't for me, and this evening's argument has confirmed it." Miss Summerill pressed on, as if he hadn't just gaped at her like a dope. "I miss my family, and my mother needs me. Perhaps back in London I can dedicate myself to the cause of peace. All this nonsense about Hitler wanting to bomb us and gas us – it's been two weeks since we were all sent out here in a panic, and not a single blow has been dealt against Britain. If he was going to attack, he'd have done it by now." She nudged her shelf-like bosom with her forearm, as if hoisting it, and leaned closer with an expression of distaste. "Strictly between ourselves, I've another reason, too. At the risk of being indiscreet, I'll just say that there's something not quite right about the women I've been billeted with."

He rubbed the back of his neck. Where to begin responding to all this? It seemed unlikely that Hitler had such peaceful intentions towards Britain, and he was sure she'd mentioned her landlady had some connection to the Fitznortons. It seemed equally unlikely that they'd be doing anything shady.

Unfortunately, she took his hesitation as an invitation to gossip. "The lodger is more than a lodger if you ask me. She's very over-familiar. I know Miss Vaughan-Lloyd is unwell – something to do with polio when she was a child, I gather – and that's why they say Miss Cadwalader does such a lot for her. But she even goes into her room at night. Sometimes she doesn't come out again until morning. Now, you know I'm not one for gossip or speculation, and I'm not saying anything about what may or may not go on, but with that and the difficulties at the school, it simply confirms what I was already thinking. This place isn't for me."

Patrick frowned, uncomfortable with Miss Summerill's malign attitude towards her hosts. Even if what she'd suggested was true, he didn't see that it was anyone else's business. There was something distasteful about her spreading rumours about people who had treated her with nothing but kindness and generosity.

He couldn't really say he'd miss Miss Summerill, but the children mostly seemed fond of her, and she was at least a familiar face from home. If she went, they'd only have him to look out for their interests, and most of them were frightened of him. The only one of the younger ones who didn't tiptoe around him was Shirley Clarke, who had flung her arms around him once. Olive Hicks, poor kid, still shrank back like a turtle into its shell whenever she saw him issue a glare or reprimand. It was his own fault, of course, for presenting the dour visage of a stern disciplinarian every day, but he didn't dare risk losing his authority by being too soft.

"What about the children?" he asked, hoping to prick his colleague's conscience.

"They'll have you to look out for them, won't they? Anyway,

I expect more and more of them will go back to London. Hopefully all this war nonsense will blow over shortly and the government will make peace with Hitler. It would make much more sense to have him as an ally than as an enemy. He's done wonders for Germany, you know. People really have got the wrong end of the stick about fascism."

Patrick stiffened. Selfishly abandoning her responsibilities and gossiping about her landlady was one thing, but open treason was another. He cast a quick glance towards the fellow with the newspaper; he hadn't turned the page over in a while.

Miss Summerill continued undaunted. "I met Sir Oswald and Lady Mosley at a British Union of Fascists meeting in '36 and I can tell you they're charming. All the fascists want is peace for this country, and an end to corruption. It's terrible the way people set out to make trouble about them. Terrible."

Patrick had been staring intently at a scuff on the toe of his shoe, willing her to shut up, but looked up at the sound of a discreet cough behind them. Miss Bright was there, eyebrows almost up to her hairline, clutching her handbag and looking askance at them. It was a relief to hear the rumble of an approaching bus – regrettably, not the one they were waiting for, but the one heading away from town. It paused for no more than half a minute, its claret and cream paint gleaming, then shifted loudly into gear and continued along the road through the village.

Only one passenger had disembarked. He recognised her at once, with those slender legs and her rich chestnut waves falling to her shoulders. She was wearing a different dress from the last time he'd seen her, but it was equally feminine, and her little hat was at a jaunty angle, a red feather – matching her lipstick – tucked into the band. Their eyes met as she started crossing the road; hers widened before she ducked her chin and veered to the right. Was she avoiding him? It was an uncomfortable thought.

"I wish you well, Miss Summerill," he said. "But if you'll forgive me, I must dash. I've just remembered something I have to do. Have a safe trip tomorrow."

He tipped his hat, then pushed past the man with his newspaper and trotted to catch up with Miss Fitznorton.

EIGHTEEN

Dodie

Dodie thanked the driver and stepped down from the bus at the stop in Bryncarreg. Her feet ached after her day at the library, but she would have to ignore them for the walk back to Plas Norton. Since the announcement of petrol rationing, lifts home after work would have to be a rare luxury. This evening, a walk along the network of footpaths and bridleways crossing farmland on the Plas Norton estate wouldn't be a hardship, but in the weeks and months to come, the dark, wet winter evenings promised to be miserable.

The bus chugged away, diesel fumes puffing darkly from the exhaust, and Dodie looked left and right before crossing the street. She was only halfway across when the sight of a familiar tall figure in a brown fedora hat in the bus queue opposite made her change course, ducking her chin to avoid eye contact. The last thing she wanted was another encounter with the stern-faced teacher whose first impressions of her had been so negative, thanks to Peter.

"Miss Fitznorton!" The deep, distinctive voice hailed her,

making her stomach plummet. She picked up her pace, hoping he'd think she hadn't heard him.

Oh, no. Not only had he seen her, but he was also heading along the pavement as if to cut off her escape.

"Miss Fitznorton! Might I have a moment of your time?"

She paused, knowing she couldn't hope to pretend not to have heard him. He already thought her some kind of monster, thanks to Peter's wild claim that she had made him strip naked. She would like nothing more than to forget that evening. Mr Winter's expression had been as cool and hard as hewn granite, and no wonder. The situation had only grown worse over dinner, with Charlotte's tipsy flirtatiousness, the tense atmosphere, and his surreptitious glances at the peeling wallpaper in the corner of the dining room. Whatever must he think of them? Of her?

"I'm sorry, Mr Winter, but I can't stop. I'm on my way home, and I don't want to be late for dinner. Besides, won't your bus be along in a moment?"

"I'm sorry to hold you up, it's just that seeing you has reminded me I haven't yet collected Reverend Appleton's bicycle. Do you happen to know if Mr Griffiths has been able to fix it?"

"I'm afraid I don't." She swerved past him onto the pavement, but he didn't take the hint, carrying on talking as if this were a friendly chat.

"He did say it might take him a few days, as he had to sort out the bedsteads for the children, and of course since then with the declaration of war everyone's had to put up blackout blinds. I guess your house would have more windows to cover than most. But I feel awful about the bike. As if it wasn't bad enough, me busting it, I guess the Reverend probably needs it more than ever now that petrol coupons have been brought in."

She took in a deep breath. It would be selfish of her to deny the vicar his bicycle, just for the sake of avoiding Mr Winter.

"Now you come to mention it, I believe Ivor might have said something about it being ready. I'm sure he'll be happy to drop it off at the vicarage next time he takes the car into town."

"It seems only fair to save him the trouble. I'm not sure of the quickest way to your house from here, but if that's where you're headed, I could walk with you, then ride back. That's if you don't mind, of course?"

"Oh. Well, I suppose you could. I mean, I am going home. Ivor would be more than willing to deliver it, though..." Her voice tailed off and she risked a peep at him, realising he was frowning. He really was a cold, judgemental fellow. No doubt when he looked at her, he found her lacking, just as Lionel had in the end. And if she didn't agree to let him walk with her, she'd make an even worse impression. It seemed she had little alternative but to give in.

"The quickest way is along the lane on the right," she said, pointing. "We'll get to Plas Norton before sunset if we don't dawdle."

He fell into step alongside her.

She walked faster than usual, knots of tension between her shoulders at this unwelcome intrusion.

"You work in the library in Pontybrenin, don't you?" Mr Winter asked, apparently determined to force her to make polite conversation.

She wished he was content to walk in silence. Now she'd have to pretend she didn't feel unsettled by the proximity of his broad, long-limbed body striding along beside her.

"Yes, that's right," she said. An idea occurred to her that might benefit the evacuees. "Perhaps one day you could bring the children to borrow some books? The older ones should be able to walk there, or they could catch the bus. I've been trying to convince Mr Gibson, the senior librarian, that we should set up a proper children's area. If they were to visit, it might help to show him that it isn't such a silly suggestion, after all."

"I'll have to see how things go," he said.

She stiffened, taking this coolly non-committal response to mean that he, like Mr Gibson, thought her idea a foolish one. If only men weren't so patronising, always thinking they knew best. Inwardly she cursed herself for inadvertently choosing a day to visit Venetia and Maggie when Mr Winter had stayed on late at school. If she'd gone straight home, she could have avoided this.

"Are you usually so late coming home from work?" he asked, as if he'd read her mind.

"No. I visited a family friend, Miss Vaughan-Lloyd, before catching the bus. Your colleague Miss Summerill is billeted with her."

"Hmph. Not for much longer."

"Oh, really? Nothing was mentioned during my visit about her moving elsewhere."

"She's decided to go back to London."

"That will come as a surprise to my friend, I'm sure. Will you go back, too?"

"No, I will not." Perhaps her expression made him regret the forceful way he'd spoken; he continued with a more moderate tone. "The children need someone on their side. Arrangements at the local school are not at all satisfactory, which is why we were there this evening – trying to reach some kind of compromise with the teachers. And failing, unfortunately."

The set of his angular jawline seemed harder than ever. His square chin bore the shadow of brown beard growth, just as it had the first time they met. It must be twelve hours or so since he'd last shaved, of course. Like her, he'd been at work all day. Purple smudges below his eyes suggested he was tired. Teaching must be a demanding job, especially if he had tearaways like Peter to deal with. No doubt that stern, jutting chin and the sharp vertical lines where his eyebrows met his nose struck terror into even the naughtiest children, though. Perhaps his colleagues found him as harsh and abrasive as Dodie did. He certainly didn't seem like someone who would be easy to work with.

Their feet crunched over fallen conkers and the first autumn leaves. Soon they passed through a gate into another lane, too narrow for vehicles, before emerging onto farmland.

"The conflict between the local kids and the Londoners has been regrettable. The incident this morning certainly didn't help," Mr Winter said.

She frowned. "There was an incident?"

"I beg your pardon – I forgot that you haven't been home since the children got back from school, so you won't know. It was one of your evacuees: Michael Clarke. He injured one of the local boys."

"Really, Michael? It must have been an accident, surely?"

He coughed out a sort of laugh, heavy with irony. "I'm not sure it's possible to accidentally knock another kid off his chair and then whack him over the head with it. The fact that he hit the boy twice makes it seem pretty likely that he did it deliberately."

Her heart thumped. This didn't sound right. She couldn't imagine Michael doing such a thing. The boy was always so responsible and kind to his sisters. "Are you sure it wasn't Peter, not Michael?"

"That was my first thought, too. But no. It was definitely Michael. I didn't see it happen; I was taking another group on a nature walk in the woods. But Miss Summerill saw it, and Miss Bright couldn't wait to tell me all about it as soon as I got back. By which time, he'd had a caning from Miss Honeycutt." His voice had a bitter edge.

Abruptly, Dodie stopped walking, her eyes narrowing as she thought of Michael being caned. She could picture his pain and humiliation all too well. What she couldn't imagine was him behaving in the way Mr Winter had just described.

Michael and the other children had only been billeted with them for a few weeks, of course, and she was at work a lot of the time – but still, the boy she knew was gentle and good-natured. He was intelligent and curious about the world and had always shown good manners. When Dodie brought children's books home from the library, he'd shown enthusiasm for the adventures featuring a pilot called Biggles, and had browsed some of the atlases on Plas Norton's shelves to learn more about the exotic locations featured in the stories. Her jaw clenched as she pictured him acting so desperately, and then being punished with more violence.

Mr Winter was waiting; she needed to compose herself. No doubt he would have caned the boy himself if he'd been there. It's what teachers did. The ones at her boarding school had almost seemed to take a spiteful pleasure in being punitive. She could well remember the repeated sting of a cane on her palm or on her behind, like being attacked by a hundred wasps at once.

"What happened before the incident?" She didn't care if he took offence at her accusing tone.

"I didn't get a chance to find out. But I'm guessing the other boy said something pretty bad to make Michael blow up like that." He rubbed his forehead with his hand, looking weary.

"Exactly. He must have been provoked," she said, surprised and relieved that he also saw it that way. "What happened to the other boy? Was he also punished?"

"I'm not sure. Hopefully having a chair smashed over his head will encourage him to mend his ways though."

She set off again at a brisk pace, the upset over Michael making her keen to get home and hear his side of the story.

In the hedgerows, leaves were taking on their autumn hues of orange and gold. The bramble bushes had been picked clean, except for the highest branches, where blackbirds flapped and chattered in alarm at the two humans passing by. Soon they reached open fields and Dodie slowed her steps to appreciate the beauty of the late September evening as she closed the gate behind them. The sun hung low over the wooded hills to the west, daubing the sky with rich crimson.

"Do you ever get used to that?" To her surprise, Mr Winter's expression softened as he gazed across the fields. He wouldn't have struck her as a man who'd get sentimental over a charming view.

"I suppose I have grown accustomed to the scenery around here, but now and then the sunset over the hills still manages to remind me to really look and take notice."

"It's beautiful."

Some of the stiffness in her limbs loosened in their unexpectedly companionable silence.

He had stuffed his hands into his pockets and seemed deep in thought, but roused when she took in a deep breath, filling her lungs with the fresh air as if it were a drug.

"We'd better get a move on," she said. "There's still a mile or so to go."

"How do you think the children are coping?" he asked, after they'd crossed the farmyard and turned north-west on the path towards Plas Norton. "Have they said much about how school is going?"

"Not really. They've adjusted remarkably well in the main and are obviously doing their best to be cheerful. Now and then I've noticed them looking resentful or sad, but it's hard to tell if they're unhappy at school, or simply unhappy at being away from home. Is Michael's behaviour your only concern?"

He shook his head. "I wish it was, but there are so many others I hardly know where to start. I feel strongly that it isn't right for the children's education to suffer when they've already had to adapt to so many changes. We've had to conduct lessons outside, which has been okay on dry days but the novelty will soon wear off when the weather takes a turn. On rainy days they have to sit in the cloakroom among the wet coats. There aren't enough chairs or desks for them all to sit down at once, let alone sufficient exercise books or pencils. No blackboard, no chalk... All my pleas have fallen on deaf ears. I've suggested we set up a new schedule, so that the local kids get the building for half the week, and the evacuees the other half. It's what's happening in some other areas, apparently. But Miss Honeycutt is against it. I just can't see how else we can manage to keep their education going unless we can find another building."

No wonder he looked so down in the mouth. "What about the village hall?" Dodie suggested. They'd rounded a bend now and in the wide green valley ahead the house was in view, its windowpanes gilded by the setting sun.

"It's been taken over by the WVS. There's the chapel – if they'll let us use it. But still, it's not ideal to have the children sitting in pews all day, and where will they eat at lunchtime? What we really need is somewhere we can set up rows of desks and chairs. Some stationery supplies; some story books and atlases... Somewhere spacious. A large room, with facilities to provide school dinners, and ideally, outside space for them to run around..."

His voice tailed off, and Dodie realised he was staring at the house, as intently as a hawk that had suddenly spotted prey. He stroked his chin, then turned towards her, his grey eyes alight with interest.

Surely he couldn't be thinking of bringing the school to Plas Norton? His next words sent her stomach plummeting.

"Miss Fitznorton – I think we may have a perfect solution, right under our noses."

NINETEEN

Dodie

By the time Dodie had shown Patrick to the workshop and located Ivor, whose sprained ankle was still giving him trouble, the children had already eaten and were getting ready for bed. During the past week they'd started a new routine. Dodie would sit on a chair in the boys' room and read a bedtime story to the younger ones while Michael read a book of his own choosing. They'd been working their way through Enid Blyton's *Tales of Ancient Greece*, and had reached the final story of Arachne, whose boasts about her beautiful spinning earned the wrath of a goddess who cursed her to change into a spider. Predictably, Peter found this hilarious, and Dodie had to have a quiet word with him to stop him threatening to leave spiders in the girls' beds.

"There's no need to be unkind," Dodie said. "We should all do our best to be nice to one another and get along."

"Michael wasn't nice today," Peter retorted. "He whacked Brynmor Preece with a chair. Twice. Mind you, that bastard Brynmor had it coming to him."

"Please don't use that kind of language, Peter. Now, I know all about what happened in school today. Michael and I are going to discuss it. But it's time for you to get into bed. And the girls, too." She clapped her hands and sent the girls running to their room ready to clamber into bed.

"One last trip to the bathroom before you go to sleep, remember," she reminded Olive gently.

Poor Olive had been the only one of the children who hadn't yet started to thrive at Plas Norton. She clung to her borrowed doll and followed Dolly and Dodie around like a pale shadow, given the chance. If only her mother would write to her, perhaps it might be different.

As she leaned over Shirley's bed to tuck the blankets around her Dodie sighed, wishing Mrs Hicks would respond to even one of Olive's letters.

"I'm glad you're always kind, Miss Fitznorton," Shirley said, lisping over Dodie's surname through the gap in her front teeth. "It would be horrible having to live with someone mean. Lizzy Marks says her billet isn't as nice as ours. She doesn't get tucked in at night like we do. But Christine Nicholls says she's allowed to call her host Auntie. Can we call you Auntie, instead of Miss Fitznorton?"

"Pleeease?" Barbara added, and Olive, who had just returned from the bathroom, joined in.

"Auntie would be much better than Miss. Miss makes you sound like a teacher."

Dodie straightened. "Well, I suppose if you'd like to. I don't see any reason why you shouldn't. Yes, you may call me Aunt Dodie if that's what you want."

After tucking each girl in and dropping a light kiss onto the top of each of their heads, she left the room accompanied by a chorus of "Night night, Aunt Dodie." She closed the door and leaned on it for a moment. Loulou and Christopher, her niece and nephew, were so close to her in age that they only ever called her Aunt as a joke. The moniker of Aunt Dodie made her sound ancient, but it was sweet that the girls felt sufficiently fond of her to want to give her a more affectionate title. And it did seem silly to insist upon formalities when the children were living in her home. Her lips twitched at the idea that they might also start calling Charlotte "Aunt" or "Auntie". How would that sit with her glamorous sister, who'd been brought up by wealthy Victorians to be ever mindful of her high social status?

Dodie's smile quickly died at the sight of Michael waiting on the landing.

"You wanted to see me, Miss." His tone was flat, as if he had resigned himself to further punishment.

"Yes. Shall we go down to the music room? We can speak privately there."

The music room was Dodie's favourite room in the house. When her mood was low, especially after one of her arguments with Charlotte, or when she brooded over Lionel's cruel words, she liked to retreat there to take sanctuary. Having been told many times how much her mother loved playing the piano, she'd been keen to learn as a child. Music had been the only subject at school in which she had truly excelled, although she'd done her best to hide the fact from her peers to avoid their spiteful remarks. In other subjects her performance had been only average, but her music teacher had described her as possessing a genuine talent, expressing disappointment at her pupil's stubborn refusal to perform in front of anyone else.

Dodie led Michael down the stairs and into the music room, closing the door softly behind them. Gesturing to an armchair in the corner, she waited while he eased himself into it, wincing. The caning had been on his behind, then. She bit her lip at the thought of him being beaten in such a humiliating fashion.

Michael waited, his hands tucked under his thighs, keeping his eyes downcast. One of his knees was jerking in an agitated rhythm, as if he longed to escape.

Dodie perched on the piano stool and folded her hands in her lap. "I hope you'll feel you can be honest about what happened today. The Michael Clarke I've come to know is kind-hearted and intelligent. He doesn't raise his fists to anyone. You're patient with your sisters and even with Peter, who can be – well, difficult, at times. So I'd like to understand what made you hit that boy at school today."

As she finished speaking, the boy's head tipped upwards and his brown eyes seemed to blaze with an inner fire.

"I didn't hit him," he said.

Dodie's mouth twisted.

"I didn't! My mum and dad always tell me not to use my fists, and I didn't."

"From what I've heard from Mr Winter and from Peter, you attacked him with a chair. That's even worse than punching him."

He shifted and gave the tiniest shrug.

"I'm not going to punish you further if that's what you're worrying about. I'd like to try to understand why it happened, because I don't believe you would have done such a thing without a reason."

He looked sullen and angry, not like the child she'd seen at the breakfast table that morning. The knee jerking grew worse, jarring on Dodie's nerves; she was about to remark on it when he finally spoke.

"You wouldn't understand if I told you, Miss. I bet you liked school, didn't you?"

She was taken aback. "Actually, I hated it," she said, leaving him equally surprised. "The other children were spiteful, and most of the teachers were little better."

He nodded. "That can't have been very nice."

"No, it wasn't." If any proof was needed that the kind boy she'd come to know was still inside him, this consideration for her feelings in spite of his own predicament was it.

"None of them would ever have called you a filthy wog, though, miss. Or made monkey noises when you walked past. Or asked you where your bananas had gone. Or told you to get back to the jungle where you belonged."

He'd spoken bitterly, with proud fury in his young face, and no wonder.

Dodie had been insulted many times: called a swot, a goody-two-shoes, a teacher's pet. The words had taken root and festered inside her. They'd made her hate herself almost as much as she despised the bullies who taunted her. As an adult, she still avoided attention and wouldn't make a fuss when someone belittled her at work. She aimed to be quietly helpful and compliant, as she had been as a girl in class. The only person she'd ever really tried to fight back against was her sister, and even with Charlotte she never came right out and explained that she felt let down, instead lodging her protest with indirect remarks that resolved nothing. Yet, as hurtful and damaging as her schoolgirl bullies' jibes had been, Michael was right: not once had she been likened to an animal. The taunts that had been used against him were far worse.

She rose and put her hands on her hips, thinking. What could she say that would help?

"There's a saying, Michael. Sticks and stones may break my bones, but names will never hurt me." But as the words came out, she had to drop her gaze. They sounded so trite; she used the hackneyed phrase only because she didn't know what else to say.

"That ain't right, miss, and I reckon you know it. Words like Brynmor Preece and his mates use don't just hurt you. They smash little pieces of you off inside, like a wrecking ball, until you feel just as small as they're telling you that you are."

She swallowed hard, unable to deny it. "I know. But violence can never be the answer."

"If that's true, why are we going to war to stop Hitler, then?

D'you know what Brynmor and his brothers do, miss? On our way to school in the mornings, they throw stones at us. Not just stones, neither, but bits of dried-up cow pats and sheep's poop. People stare at us in Bryncarreg. Not just the kids, but the grown-ups too. They come to their front windows and point at us when we walk past. The kids run after us and pull faces and call us names. Bad names, ones I ain't going to say out loud in front of you. Sometimes they spit at us. I'm not allowed to use my fists, but I had to show Brynmor because if I hadn't, I know for sure he'd never have stopped. I wouldn't mind so much if it was just me he does it to, but it's my sisters, an' all. So I hope I hurt him, miss. I hope I hurt him really bad, and I hope I scared the others too, so they'll have learned their lesson and Babs and Shirl won't have to hear those words and feel that way again. And if it didn't work and he doesn't stop, well then I'll do it again, and I don't care how many chairs I break or how many times I get caned for it. I won't be treated like dirt."

"I wish you'd told me, Michael."

"Why? What could you do?"

Dodie dropped to her haunches in front of him and took one of his hands between both of hers, squeezing it in a vain attempt to convey how deeply she felt on his behalf.

"I could have spoken to Mr Winter, or Miss Honeycutt. I still shall. They should know what's happening, so they can punish the children who are behaving so abominably towards you."

There was a pause, then Michael withdrew his hand and patted hers, as if he were the adult and she the child. He rose gingerly from the armchair; when she looked up into his face, she was shocked to read pity in the twist of his mouth.

"Can I go now?" he asked, not even bothering to contradict her assertion that the teachers could put a stop to the bullying. It was as if the ten-year-old boy had more understanding of the ways of the world than she, a twenty-four-year-old woman, did.

How bitter must his experiences have been, to make a child so cynical, so young?

"Of course you may. Goodnight, Michael."

The door closed softly behind him. Dodie sank onto the piano stool to lean on the piano and bury her face in her hands. It was painful, knowing she'd failed to protect the children in her care, but she had to face it.

She'd always thought of this valley as a welcoming place. Plas Norton and Bryncarreg village were the places she'd always longed to return to when she was sent away to school, and even when she left to go to secretarial college and then worked in London she'd still dreamed of her birthplace with warmth and nostalgia. It had hit her like a physical blow to hear that the local people who'd always been polite and friendly to her could behave in so hateful a way to young children who had come to the area for refuge. The shame of it – it made her sick to her stomach. She had to do something to ensure that the Clarkes never had to face such intolerance again. But what?

She'd felt flustered when Mr Winter suggested transferring the evacuees' schooling to Plas Norton. Then, her main concern had been to avoid him. There was something about him that disconcerted her. It wasn't that he'd been unfriendly as such, but she couldn't help feeling he disapproved of her. He'd heard Peter say such awful things that first evening, and he had maintained his cool, guarded manner on each of the three occasions they'd met. She couldn't say she'd ever seen a smile soften those stern features. But now that she'd heard Michael's side of today's incident, she was torn. Allowing the children to be educated at Plas Norton with the other Londoners would save the Clarkes from running their daily gauntlet of abuse from the Preece brothers. If they could avoid the village, they'd no longer be an object of curiosity. It could be a solution. But something about it didn't feel right.

On impulse, she lifted the lid to uncover the keyboard and

positioned her fingers on the keys. She'd only play for a few minutes, just a few scales and arpeggios to exercise her hands. The movements came easily from years of practice, bringing her fingers alive even while her mind slowed: while playing, she hardly had to think at all. Soon she delved into her mother's store of sheet music. There was time to play one piece before dinner, she was sure.

Seated at the keyboard, alone with the piano, was where Dodie felt the most like her true self. The self she wished she could be all the time, if real life didn't always have to get in the way with its conflicts and disappointments. She lost herself in the motion and the fullness of the sound, her feet working the pedals while her fingers flew across the keys. The only time that mattered was the tempo of the piece. When a movement at the edge of her vision interrupted her concentration, she faltered, missing the fingering and making a discordant sound.

"Must you play such depressing tunes? It's enough to put one off one's dinner." Charlotte leaned against the door jamb, one hand clutching a sherry glass.

Dodie stiffened and lowered the lid over the keys. "There's a war on. We can hardly use the car for fear of running out of petrol. We've a house full of lonely, angry children whose new school doesn't have room for them and whose new neighbours couldn't be less welcoming. Olive is still bedwetting, and goodness knows how Dolly will keep up with the laundry as the weather gets wetter and colder. And now Mr Winter wants to use Plas Norton as a school. It strikes me there's plenty to feel depressed about. A bit of Beethoven should be the least of your worries."

TWENTY

Dodie

Charlotte frowned at Dodie across the dining table. "What do you mean, Mr Winter wants to use the house as a school? I hope you haven't agreed. It's a preposterous notion."

"I prevaricated by saying I'd have to speak to you about it. Then I spoke to Michael. Did you know, the local children abuse the Clarkes with insults on a daily basis, and even throw stones and dung at them? It's beyond my comprehension. No wonder they seem so glum each morning before school, and brighter on weekends." Dodie's fingers tightened around her knife and fork, any benefits from playing the piano lost.

"I know you like to see the good in everyone, Dodie, but frankly, children can be vile creatures." Charlotte drained her sherry and put down the glass, turning her attention towards the tureens in the centre of the table.

For once, Dodie wished she, too, was a drinker. She didn't really like the taste of alcohol, but this evening she'd take it if it would help to relax the tension in her shoulders.

"After speaking to Michael, my first thought was to agree to Mr Winter's suggestion. After all, we have the space. We could use the ballroom, and it would mean our evacuees wouldn't have to face the local hooligans or trudge across the wet fields each day..."

"For heaven's sake, Dodie! When will you learn that setting yourself on fire won't keep other people warm?"

"Whatever do you mean?"

"We were supposed to have two evacuees but ended up with five. You're reading them bedtime stories and bringing books home for them and arguing with that ghastly Mr Gibson about a children's corner. Now you're seriously considering setting up a schoolroom in our home. Frankly, you'll wear yourself out, not to mention poor Dolly. And there's another factor you haven't considered. The children from London will never be accepted if they don't mix. If we effectively keep them segregated from other children here, it could do even more harm in the long run than if they brave it out in Bryncarreg."

Dodie bit her lip, her fork spearing her pork chop with more force than necessary. The possibility of making the children's situation even worse was an alarming prospect.

"If there's a lack of space in Bryncarreg Elementary School, what about sending them on the bus to the school in Pontybrenin instead?" Charlotte asked.

"Hmm. That might work. But there are evacuees in Pontybrenin, too. What's to say they have any room to spare for more?"

"Don't tell me you've given up without a fight? You, who are usually so prickly."

Bristling at her sister's amused tone, Dodie merely glared at her. She wouldn't dignify or confirm that remark with a response.

"A lesson I learned many years ago from Venetia is that

when you want something to change, start with the people who have influence," Charlotte said.

Dodie tutted impatiently. "If Mr Winter can't terrify Miss Honeycutt into submission, I doubt anyone could."

"Do you think him frightening? Personally, I found him quite appealing. He's terribly handsome – if a trifle reserved. Too young to be interested in me, unfortunately, but I certainly wouldn't be averse—"

Dodie cut in abruptly, colour rising in her face. "Mr Winter's physical charms are hardly relevant," she said. She'd never admit to Charlotte that she, too, found them undeniable.

Charlotte paused before replying, giving Dodie the uncomfortable feeling that her thoughts might have shown in her face.

"If you insist, Dodie. Besides, Mr Winter's physical advantages can't compensate for the fact that he doesn't play bridge with the chairman of the school's governors. I do, however. Mr Johns is a pleasant enough chap. And his wife is a helpful sort, always keen to support the WI. I'm sure he could be persuaded to reconsider the current educational arrangements without too much bother."

Dodie's doubts must have shown in her expression, for Charlotte set down her knife and fork impatiently.

"Really Dodie, I wish you would give me some credit, instead of always assuming me to be useless. Leave the matter with me. And don't go agreeing to any propositions from Mr Winter without consulting me first. Unless of course he makes the sort of proposition that brings that fetching flush to your cheeks. A little more of that sort of excitement in your life would do you no harm whatsoever. It would do us all a favour to see you happy, for a change."

Before Dodie could reply, the dining room door burst open as if a whirlwind had hit it.

"Mummy, darling! And Dodie, too. How lovely. My, that

food smells mouth-wateringly good. I've missed Dolly's cooking."

Charlotte rose so quickly to embrace her daughter, her chair almost tipped over.

"Loulou, darling. What a marvellous surprise. I wasn't expecting you until tomorrow. Haven't you eaten? Come and join us."

Dolly had already appeared with an additional place setting and quickly laid it on the table between Charlotte and Dodie. Her beaming pleasure at Loulou's arrival appeared almost as great as Charlotte's. Within moments she had gathered up the new arrival's woollen coat, leather gauntlets and hat, and bustled from the room.

"I almost thought I wouldn't get here," Loulou said, spooning a generous helping of meat and vegetables onto her plate. "There was a sticky moment just before Gloucester when I thought I might run out of fuel. I'd used my last coupon for this month, but thankfully I managed to charm a dear old chap into topping up my tank with enough red petrol to get me home. It was all terribly cloak-and-dagger. He gave me strict instructions not to tell a soul as we could both get into fearful trouble. Honestly, if I'd realised it was this bad back in Blighty I'd have stayed in Switzerland."

"Don't tell me you rode that ghastly motorcycle all the way from London?"

"Why not? I didn't want to chance the trains with so many of them full of soldiers. You know I'm not one for waiting around, Mummy. Much better just to hop on the bike and get on with it."

Charlotte shook her head and dabbed at her mouth with her napkin, but Dodie noticed she didn't attempt to argue with her wayward daughter. There would be no point, in any case. Loulou would continue to do whatever she liked, unapologetically and unselfconsciously. How liberating it must be to live like that. Dodie gazed at her niece, lost in wistful thoughts as she wondered how it might be to live with so little concern for how one's actions might affect others, or how they might be perceived.

"And how are you, Dodie? Are you enjoying life back in Pontybrenin? I hope you aren't finding it too frightfully dull. I can't imagine being back here permanently now."

Dodie shook her head, knowing Loulou didn't mean to sound disparaging. It was only that her own horizons could never be confined to such a small corner of the country. "I'm keeping busy, thank you Loulou. I'll look forward to hearing about your adventures and plans."

She kept silent, enjoying her niece's retelling of her journey back home from the Continent. With her shiny blonde hair and animated features, her comic talent for mimicry and her dramatic gestures, Loulou made an entertaining companion. Listening to her tales of daring exploits in the Alps and the dangers of crossing the English Channel in wartime, it was easier than usual to feel some sympathy for Charlotte, whose face alternated between frozen horror and a wry, exasperated grimace. Her expression lit up, however, when Loulou mentioned that she had called in at Oxford on her way home to see her brother.

"How is Christopher? Is he well? Studying hard, I hope."

"Oh, I expect he is. We didn't talk about that. I was much too busy telling him about my friend Isobel. I think he'd really like her. I've been rather naughty in singing his praises to her so continuously that I dare say she might be halfway to falling in love with him already. It would be such fun if the two of them were to hit it off. I'm quite desperate to introduce them."

"Now, darling, you know he can't afford distractions."

Loulou carried on, blithely ignoring her mother's frown. "Hopefully it won't be long before Bel and I get leave, and we can visit him in Oxford."

"Leave? Leave from what?"

Oh, dear. This didn't bode well. Dodie's fork hovered halfway to her mouth as she waited for the inevitable fireworks.

Loulou's blue eyes widened guilelessly. "Surely you remember me mentioning it, Mummy? Isobel and I are planning to join the Air Force."

TWENTY-ONE

Dodie

The next morning, Dodie left for work twenty minutes earlier than usual, well before the children set off for school. She made no mention to anyone of her plan, but slipped out of the house without saying her customary goodbye to Dolly or the evacuees. The atmosphere in the house had been tense after Loulou's announcement over dinner. Charlotte had tried to insist that she think it over until after Christmas, but Loulou had been predictably determined. They'd compromised in the end, with Loulou agreeing to wait until after Isobel's twentieth birthday in November. Perhaps Charlotte hoped her enthusiasm would have worn off by then, but Dodie doubted it would. Loulou had always craved adventure.

The air was chilly and damp, the ground boggy in places, and she was glad of her stout walking shoes as she tramped across the fields from Plas Norton towards Home Farm. In a hedgerow, a red-breasted robin eyed her boldly from its perch among the yellowing leaves. Nearby, she glimpsed a pale, spotted mistle thrush plucking dark sloes before it chattered out a warning and flew away to hide in the topmost branches. The path was growing slippery, and as she pushed open the gate to the farmyard, she noticed the cobbles were mossy in the shade of the farmhouse. Skirting around the hens scratching and clucking amongst the stones, she headed for the front door.

As she reached for the heavy knocker a dog barked inside the house, making her jump. The prospect of confrontation had made her jittery, and she'd left the house unable to stomach anything more for breakfast than a cup of coffee. In spite of the unexpected pleasure of seeing Loulou the previous evening, she'd slept badly. Michael's unhappy face filled her thoughts. While she was hopeful that Miss Honeycutt would deal with Brynmor Preece as severely as she'd dealt with Michael, she knew she couldn't just leave it to chance. The bullying had to stop.

The door creaked open, revealing Mrs Preece wearing a grease-spattered apron. Short and dark, with threads of grey in her short hair, which was clipped back from her round face with kirby grips, her eyes rounded in surprise at the sight of Dodie on her doorstep.

"Can I help you, miss?" she asked, her tone polite enough but her expression wary.

"I hope so, Mrs Preece. Sorry to bother you when I'm sure you're busy, but..." Dodie paused. Why was she apologising? If not for the actions of Brynmor and his brothers, there would be no reason to call. She straightened and looked the woman in the eye. "It's come to my attention that there was an incident at school yesterday."

"There was. But it's not you who should be coming round to apologise, is it? It's that boy who's staying with you. Little animal, he is, behaving like that."

Dodie blinked. "I haven't come to apologise, Mrs Preece. I've come to ask you to have a word with your sons. Please tell them to stop bullying the children billeted with us, or else they may face graver consequences than a playground scuffle."

Mrs Preece's shiny cheeks turned florid. "Bullying?" she repeated scornfully. "I don't know what you're talking about."

"I'm talking about throwing mud and stones and dung at other children. I'm talking about using uncouth language. I'm—"

"Save your breath, miss. I've never heard such nonsense. That's not bullying. That's just boys being boys. If it's taking your evacuees a while to settle, that's hardly surprising, is it?"

Dodie gasped. *"Boys being boys?"* she spluttered. "These are hardly harmless pranks."

Mrs Preece cut her off. "If you'll excuse me, I'm in the middle of cooking breakfast. I don't have time to discuss this with you. But if you want to send the boy – Clarke, is it? Send him here and we'll accept his apologies for what he did."

To Dodie's astonishment, the door started swinging closed in her face. With her temper rising, she put out her hand to stop it and glared at the other woman through the gap.

"Mrs Preece, I'm afraid I must insist that you speak to your boys. We have certain expectations of our tenants. And if I hear that Brynmor – or any of your other sons – has subjected our evacuees to insults or violence again, I must warn you that there will be serious consequences. I hope I've made myself clear."

Mrs Preece pursed her lips and folded her arms. "Perfectly," she said, not bothering to hide her resentment.

Well, she could be as churlish as she liked, as long as she sorted her son out. Satisfied that she'd made her point, Dodie marched back to the gate, taking care not to slip on the slimy chicken droppings as she went. The sound of the farmhouse door slamming shut behind her made her wince, and by the time she closed the gate behind her, she felt a little heady as her angry rush of adrenaline ebbed away. Exploiting her position to issue threats sat uncomfortably with her, and she felt out of sorts all the way to the bus stop.

It was only when she reached Bryncarreg that it occurred to her to feel a little proud of herself for sticking up for the children. As a child at school, she'd been cowed by bullies, and part of her had always wished she could have been stronger. Now, she'd struck a small blow on behalf of those who might not easily be able to defend themselves. She'd done what was right. By the time the bus pulled up at the bus stop, her limbs no longer trembled, and she climbed on to purchase her ticket with her head held high and a cheerful smile for the conductor.

Hopefully now the Preece boys would think twice about being cruel to the children in her care.

TWENTY-TWO
OCTOBER

Olive

Olive and the other children had settled into their odd new routine at school over the past few weeks. Now that the school premises were being shared more equally with the local children, each group only had lessons in the classroom for half of the week. The older children, including Olive and Michael, were taught for these indoor sessions by the fearsome Miss Honeycutt, who was quick to stamp down on any slight misdemeanour by rapping offenders over the knuckles with her wooden ruler.

She was especially harsh with Michael since an incident in late September when he'd been driven to violence by one of the local boys. Olive had noticed that the teacher asked him more questions and gave him less time to answer than the other children, as if she was determined to catch him out. Every time she loomed over him and barked out her questions it made Olive squirm with a horrid combination of resentment at the injustice and relief at not being the one singled out.

She much preferred the days when they had outdoor activities if the weather wasn't too wet, or art lessons in the cloakroom during heavy rain. On those days their group was taught by Mr Winter, who had stayed with them even though Miss Summerill had gone back to London.

Mr Winter was strict, with a stern face, but he was at least fair, and Olive had never once seen him strike a pupil. He had only to stand beside a fidgety or whispering child and direct one of his icy glares at them for them to comply. When Olive struggled to keep up in physical education lessons, he didn't bellow critically at her from the sidelines but urged her on. He set up fun lessons with games and organised the teams himself instead of allowing the children to pick their own teammates. It meant Olive never had to suffer the indignity of being the last to be chosen, as had so often happened in the past.

With Mr Winter they'd learned about the local flora and fauna, and Olive now knew how to identify a range of trees, as well as which mushrooms should never be picked. They'd explored the local countryside and knew never to play next to the river, which had strong currents and could be deeper than it looked. He'd organised treasure hunts in the woods near the school, and games of Hare and Hounds, in which Michael, as the boy with the longest and fastest legs, ran ahead scattering tiny paper pieces for the rest to follow.

Mr Winter had even arranged for them to help out on a local farm, spending a whole afternoon gathering potatoes which had been brought to the surface with a machine. Afterwards, Auntie Dolly had been horrified at how muddy they were, but it had been one of Olive's favourite days so far as they'd been allowed to chatter while they worked, and the ride back to school in a horse-drawn cart had made them all giddy with excitement.

Everyone had been rapt with curiosity when a new girl arrived to join their group in school one morning. She was introduced as Eva Fischer, a girl from Czechoslovakia. Eva didn't have to join in the prayers and hymns in their morning assembly, and she wasn't allowed to eat ham or luncheon meat. Olive stole regular peeps at Eva, who mostly kept her chin lowered to her chest and her face shielded by a curtain of dark, bobbed hair. She guessed Eva must be shy, and that her new surroundings must feel even more alien to her, being in a different country with a different language: after all, it was strange enough for Olive being in a faraway town. Still, Olive couldn't match the bigger girls' confidence in taking Eva under their wings and guiding her through the routines of each school day. Olive wished she could be braver. If it weren't for the Clarkes, she would be lonely.

The younger children had their indoor lessons with Miss Bright. At the end of each day, Peter raged about how much he hated her, kicking up stones and spitting out words filled with loathing as they trudged back across the fields to Plas Norton. Barbara and Shirley would merely shrug, acknowledging that Miss Bright wasn't as mild as Miss Summerill had been. They'd quickly learned not to dispute Peter's account of events if they wanted to get home without being pushed or pinched. Olive kept quiet. It had always been the safest course where Peter was concerned. There was too much of their dad in him to risk provoking his temper.

If it hadn't been for the lack of word from her parents, Olive could perhaps be content in her new life. But it had been more than a month now since she'd said goodbye to her mum, and despite writing two letters each week, with help from Aunt Dodie, she'd received not a single reply.

Every night, she held Juliet tightly to her chest, the doll's hard porcelain head tucked under her chin, and said a lengthy prayer beseeching God to help her keep Peter safe, and to make their mother write back. A postcard, even, would do. According to the news on the wireless, London was still safe, even though the Germans had dropped some bombs on Scotland. Their flat couldn't have been destroyed by the kind of raid or gas attack they'd feared when the war began. So what was preventing Mum from writing? If only Olive could go back and see for herself that everything was alright.

Little by little, the wishing for a word from her mother was hollowing Olive out, leaving a gaping void inside. It grew ever harder to smile across the breakfast table at the other children, Aunt Dodie, Auntie Dolly and Uncle Ivor. It was hard to summon the will to get out of her bed in the mornings. What was there to get up for, if her own mother didn't want to write to her? Could it be that some danger unrelated to the war had befallen her? But if it had, why hadn't Dad let her and Peter know? Yet somehow, she kept going. If nothing else, she could keep her brother out of trouble until word reached them that they could go home.

TWENTY-THREE

Patrick

Walking the two miles from Bryncarreg Elementary school to the library in Pontybrenin had seemed like a great idea until the rain started. Not driving rain, fortunately, but still a relentless drizzle that seeped into coats, hats and shoes, and made every footstep a cold, squelchy chore. Although he'd only been in Wales for six weeks or so, and the weather had been clement for a British autumn, by the time they'd walked the first mile he was pretty sure that Welsh rain was even wetter than the rain had been in England. In fairness to the children, not one of them complained, but their forlorn faces said it all. Patrick could only hope that none of them would catch a chill on this miserable mid-October afternoon.

The library itself was, at least, reasonably warm. He wouldn't go so far as to call it welcoming with its institutional green paintwork and stalwart rows of eight-foot-high dark wooden shelving, although there was something cosy about its smell of old paper and leather, supplemented by aromas of wet wool and tobacco from its mostly male patrons. The group of evacuee children trailed along behind him, wet shoes squeaking on the linoleum, between the mock-Doric columns framing the main door with its impressive rainbow-coloured stained glass. They seemed awed by the hushed atmosphere, instinctively whispering to one another instead of speaking up. Most of them gazed about in wonder, a little lost; but he noticed that Olive Hicks' eyes were darting about as if she were searching for something in particular. It was only when they emerged into the central reading area that Olive's sudden smile and purposeful dash to the reception desk revealed she hadn't been searching for some*thing*, but some*one*.

Josephine Fitznorton was standing behind the desk, busy with some task or other. When Olive appeared she glanced up, and her face lit with a delighted grin that made her appear altogether more cheerful than he'd ever previously seen her. Her dark-lashed hazel eyes sparkled as she reached out to cup Olive's chin and bent to speak softly to her across the counter.

An unexpected sensation flared in Patrick's chest. How had he not noticed before how attractive she was? He'd registered her pretty clothes, her wavy hair that looked soft as goose-down, and her long, slender legs that had looked mighty fine marching up the staircase in that horrid crumbling pile she lived in. But that transformational smile was proof that she was a looker, and no mistake. His warm glow was quickly doused when she looked up and saw him, her smile vanishing to be replaced with the anxious frown he knew. Did she really think him so awful? It was a blow to realise his was a face that could make a pretty woman look so glum.

"Good afternoon, Mr Winter," she said, trying to muster a more welcoming expression. "What a pleasure to see the children here in the library. Thank you for bringing them. I'll show them to the children's section."

She hadn't, he noticed, expressed any pleasure at seeing him. Disappointment made his feet feel leaden as he followed her and the children to a corner at the back of the library, where the shelving was lower. Here, some colourful pictures in frames and a couple of jars of flowers brightened the gloom, but there was nowhere for the children to sit and read. Presumably they'd have to join the adults perusing newspapers and periodicals in the Reading Room, or find a space on the floor, if they wanted to spend more than a few minutes engrossed in their books.

Patrick waited while Miss Fitznorton explained to the children how many books they were allowed to borrow. Although they paid close attention to her low, well-spoken voice as she pointed out a display of classic literature, most of the kids seemed more drawn to the recent publications. Patrick leaned against a magazine stand and watched while she bent to chat with each child, commenting on the books they'd picked out.

"I think you'll enjoy *The Hobbit*," she said to Michael Clarke. "It's been popular, and you're a confident reader for your age."

The boy nodded and she squeezed his shoulder before moving on to speak to other children whom she didn't know, taking time to ask them about the kinds of stories they'd enjoyed before and recommending similar books for them to try. Within half an hour or so, each child had found something suitable, and Miss Fitznorton rubbed her hands together, face aglow as if she'd received a precious gift.

"A good day's work," Patrick said to her with an approving nod. He didn't usually mind what people thought of him, but for some reason he found he wanted her to like him. Her unguarded expression earlier had suggested the opposite: he obviously needed to make more of an effort to exercise charm.

"It's such a joy to see them enjoying books," she replied, a faint flush on her cheeks. "I wish Mr Gibson would let me set up a proper children's corner. It would be more inviting for them if the walls were a cheerful colour, and if there were low tables and chairs, or even a few square yards of carpet for them to sit on. I've done my best to make it a little jollier with some flowers and pictures, but..." She lifted her hands palms upwards and gave a heartfelt sigh.

"It sounds to me like Mr Gibson should pay more attention to your ideas."

She threw him a suspicious glance, her expression clearing after a moment as if she recognised that he was being sincere. "Thank you," she murmured.

"Would it help if I said something to him?" he asked.

She snorted. "Who knows? Perhaps he would be more inclined to listen to a man."

He had a feeling he'd put his foot in it, but she was already heading back towards the reception desk, so there wasn't time to add anything that might help to make amends. He dithered a moment and ran a hand through his hair. The children were all behaving remarkably well; it surely wouldn't do any harm to leave them unsupervised just for a moment?

He strode back to the desk, only to find Miss Fitznorton occupied in serving an elderly fellow whose shoulders were hunched forwards as if he'd wrecked his back with years of hard toil. Patrick waited in line, darting frequent glances back towards the children's area and keeping an ear out for any misbehaviour.

"Do you have any books about growing vegetables?" he asked, when the elderly man shuffled away from the desk leaving Patrick at the head of the queue.

"I believe they're all out on loan. It's been a popular subject recently, with the Dig for Victory campaign."

"That's a shame. I was hoping to set up a vegetable patch in a corner of the school yard, to get the children growing some food. But I haven't a clue where to start."

"I could reserve something for you, if you like."

"That would be great, thank you."

She unscrewed the lid of her fountain pen and made a note on a pad.

Patrick bit his lip, wanting to prolong the conversation but unwilling to make a nuisance of himself. "What about books on the subject of outdoor pursuits? Orienteering for instance. Could you show me to the relevant section?"

His heart sank as a thin, officious looking man several inches shorter than Miss Fitznorton practically elbowed her out of the way. This must be Mr Gibson, Patrick guessed from the fellow's dismissive manner and the way Miss Fitznorton stiffened.

"*I'll* help the American gentleman with his query, Miss Fitznorton. There's been a spillage in the men's lavatory which needs cleaning up, if you wouldn't mind," the man said in a reedy voice.

Towering over the man, Patrick followed him to the relevant shelf.

"Thank you," he said, then couldn't resist issuing a challenge in his frostiest teacher voice. "I couldn't help noticing the rather disappointing lack of facilities for my pupils this afternoon. As they're far from their own homes and their own familiar supplies of books, I had planned to bring them on regular visits to the library. But the children's section seems to be in the gloomiest corner of the building. It's such a shame there's nowhere pleasant for them to sit and read, as there would be in the libraries in London."

Mr Gibson puffed out his chest and wobbled his jowls like a scrawny chicken, his cheeks reddening in a way that suggested his blood pressure had risen as quickly as his ire. "Well, might I remind you that you're not in London now, sir. Or America for that matter. And now that I've guided you to the correct shelf, I trust you'll find what you're looking for quickly, so you can go straight back to the children's section. I'm sure you're as concerned as I am about your pupils being left unsupervised in this unfamiliar place... Them being so very far from home."

As Gibson spun on his heel and marched back towards the desk, Patrick sighed. He'd made a blunder there, going in all guns blazing and putting Miss Fitznorton's boss on the offensive. As if offending Miss Honeycutt and Miss Bright hadn't been enough, it seemed he still needed to learn to tread more carefully with people in Pontybrenin.

TWENTY-FOUR

Dodie

It didn't seem to matter how many times Dodie read bedtime stories to the children or sat with them at breakfast and chatted about the day ahead, or helped the younger ones with everyday tasks like tying their shoelaces. Peter was as difficult and disobedient as ever. Ruefully, she rubbed a bruise on her arm that had been inflicted when he had thrown a book at her. She suspected he found reading difficult, and resorted to fits of temper to cover his embarrassment. If only he would be more willing to accept help, perhaps she could get through to him; but he seemed to delight in speaking rudely. It was as if he swore and insulted her all the more because he understood that it offended her; and it was getting harder to maintain any sympathy or patience in the face of such blatant defiance.

She looked at him now as he sat across the kitchen table. Eating the traditional roast dinner with the children on Sundays would be a pleasurable change from eating in the formal dining room with Charlotte and Loulou, if not for Peter's scowling, freckled face with its permanent trail of snot between nostril and upper lip. She wanted so badly to like him. It didn't seem right to dislike a child, especially one whose circumstances deserved compassion. Having suffered more than her fair share of unkindness at boarding school, she'd always taken pride in doing her best to see the good in other people and being kind as a matter of principle. Like Charlotte, Peter was a living reminder that she didn't always succeed.

She frowned as he scratched at his leg under the table. It wasn't the first time since they'd sat down to tea, and she'd noticed the girls scratching too. In the seat beside her, Olive squirmed to reach something on her shin.

"Olive, why do you keep scratching?" she asked. "Is there something wrong?" When Olive didn't respond, she repeated it a little louder. It was easy to forget that Olive was deaf on one side.

"It's just a bite," Olive murmured.

"Let me see."

Sure enough, a trail of red lumps led up Olive's leg.

"Is that what's wrong with you, too?" Dolly asked the other girls.

Strangely, they exchanged a guilty look. Barbara pulled the sleeve of her cardigan down over her wrist, as if to hide something.

"Show me," Dolly insisted, leaning over to inspect Barbara's arm.

Reluctantly, Barbara lifted her sleeve.

"Those are flea bites," Dolly exclaimed. "How have you all been bitten like that?"

Even the thought of fleas made Dodie's scalp crawl.

Barbara's chin lowered to her chest. Next to her, Shirley opened her mouth to speak, but from the corner of her eye Dodie noticed Michael sent a shake of his head and a warning glare in her direction.

There was no doubt that they were hiding something, but

there was no time to ask further questions, as her attention was caught by Peter shoving his plate away so roughly that gravy slopped over the edge onto the tablecloth.

"This is disgusting," he said, his top lip curling. "I'm not eating any more of this crap."

Irritation flared as quickly as if he'd flicked a switch in Dodie's chest. She took a deep breath to calm herself before responding.

Dolly got there first, dropping her knife and fork onto her plate with a clatter. "If you don't like the food I cook for you, you can at least be polite about it."

"I want my pudding, not this shit," he said, folding his arms and cocking his head in Dolly's direction.

Dodie dabbed at her mouth with her napkin. "Peter, please don't be rude to Auntie Dolly," she said, keeping her voice even with an effort.

"Who asked you, anyway? Keep your big nose out of it," Peter responded, sending a contemptuous sneer across the table. "I said I want my pudding. The meat was alright, but this cabbage is horrible. I ain't eating it. So get me my pudding instead."

Uncle Ivor slapped a hand down onto the table, making Olive jump. "You won't get your own way by speaking to your elders and betters like that, boyo. Best you apologise; and if you won't, you can get yourself to bed before you go any further."

For several heartbeats they glared at each other; Dodie only realised she'd been holding her breath when at last Peter shoved his chair back and stormed out of the room.

The other children resumed eating, but the atmosphere around the table had changed. No one spoke for a minute or two.

"*I* think the cabbage is very nice. Thank you, Auntie Dolly," Shirley piped up. She'd almost cleared her plate.

Dolly sent a tight smile her way.

Dodie reached out and patted Shirley's hand. She was a dear little thing, so keen to please, with a sunny and affectionate nature. What a contrast between her and Peter.

Slowly, everyone relaxed and began tucking into their food once more.

"How do you fancy helping me pull up some carrots after school tomorrow?" Ivor asked, and was quickly rewarded with a chorus of offers from all four children.

"Will you show me some more scales on the piano, please, Aunt Dodie?" Barbara asked.

Dodie nodded. She'd been surprised when Barbara had first commented on her piano playing, having hoped it had gone unnoticed. It had been an awkward moment, as Dodie hated anyone hearing her play; but Barbara's enthusiasm had made her let down her guard and she'd agreed to teach her some basic techniques.

"After you've helped to tidy up the tea things," she promised, cheered by the way Barbara grinned and clapped her hands.

The lighter mood was brought to an abrupt end as the door banged open and Peter burst in, wielding a cricket bat.

Dodie jumped, her knife and fork dropping onto her plate with a clatter.

"I *said* I want my pudding!" Peter roared.

Swinging the bat, he brought it down onto the table with a crash. The plate he'd left there smashed into pieces. Gravy sprayed upwards, and everyone started back in fright.

"*Diawl bach!*" Ivor exclaimed, springing up and seizing the bat mid-air just as Peter swung it at the table again. The two of them tussled as Peter used his other arm to aim a punch at Ivor.

Wide-eyed, and with her heart racing, Dodie also leapt from her seat. Catching hold of Peter's arm, she somehow wrestled him away from the table as Ivor sagged onto his chair clutching the bat, his other hand on his chest as he gasped for breath.

"I hate you!" Peter screamed upwards into Dodie's face, his wiry body surprisingly strong as he wrenched out of her grip and ran from the room.

There wasn't time to think. Dodie ran after him. He was fast, but her legs were longer, and she caught up with him on the stairs. Grabbing his wrist, she yanked him around and was horrified when he spat on her.

She couldn't help herself: she shook him so hard he held up his other arm to shield his head.

"How dare you!" she yelled, not caring how his eyes had widened and his mouth trembled. "Don't *ever* behave like that again, do you hear, you beastly little boy! Go to your room and stay there until Auntie Dolly says you may come out again. You don't deserve anything else to eat. As far as I'm concerned you can go hungry until breakfast."

"You can't tell me what to do. You're not my mum!"

"You should be grateful that I'm not. If I were your mother, I'd give you the thrashing you deserve. If I were your mother, I'd be ashamed of you, you hateful little horror." With that, she aimed a slap at his calves that made her fingers sting.

There was a momentary pause in which Peter's chin dimpled as if he was holding back tears. She let go of him to wipe her cheek dry with her handkerchief, taking a couple of steps back down the staircase as her temper cooled. She was horrified at herself. She should never have lost control like that. Not even in the face of extreme provocation.

Peter took advantage of her retreat to race upstairs. To her shame, his calf was scarlet where she'd struck him, white finger marks plain to see against the red. Her pulse seemed to pound in her forehead.

"I'm going to write to my dad and tell him what a bitch you are," he said from the top of the stairs, his voice trembling but still defiant. "And do you know what? He'll come and give you what for. You'll be sorry you ever laid a finger on me."

To her relief, he ran into his room and slammed the door behind him so hard the windowpanes rattled.

Dodie sank down on the stairs, gripping the carved newel post for support. Her heart thumped against her ribs. Only a few minutes ago, they'd all been calmly eating roasted mutton and chatting about Ivor's vegetable patch. Now, she felt sick to the stomach at her own behaviour, as much as Peter's. Hitting a child; lashing out with cruel words... she was hardly different from the boy's vile father. The children deserved to feel safe and to know they were cared for, even when they were naughty. She'd broken her own promise to herself. No matter what happened in future, she must do better.

Trembling, she dragged her hands over her face and drew in a shuddering breath. She needed to go back and check on Ivor and the other children, not to mention help to clear up the damage from Peter's violent outburst, but her legs had turned to jelly. With an effort, she hoisted herself upright, dusted herself down, and took wobbly steps back towards the kitchen.

The children were clearing the dishes away in silence. Dolly was running hot water into the sink in the scullery.

"Is Ivor alright?" Dodie asked.

"He's gone to lie down. This sort of thing isn't good for him."

She couldn't blame Dolly for being curt.

"I know. It's come as a shock to us all. I've sent Peter to his room and told him to stay there. I slapped his legs," she added, hating herself.

"Good. Someone needs to give that boy a ruddy good hiding."

Dodie gaped. She'd never heard Dolly swear before.

Dolly wrenched the tap closed and turned to face Dodie with her hands on her hips. "How much longer will we have to put up with his antics? You've done your best with him, as we all have, but he's proved today that he's out of control. I never saw a child behave so badly in all my days. And my Ivor didn't go through everything he suffered in the trenches to end up getting whacked with a cricket bat by some little lout."

"I'm so sorry—"

"Don't give me your apologies. I know you mean well. But you need to sort it out. I haven't complained about the extra mending when they come home with their clothes ripped or buttons missing from climbing trees. I don't complain about the extra cleaning, or the extra washing and drying and ironing, even with Olive still messing her bed every night. Even the extra cooking doesn't bother me, as long as they eat what's put in front of them and help with the washing up. I'm happy to do my bit. But quite honestly, I'm reaching my limits with that little devil. I've worked at Plas Norton since I was a girl fresh out of school, and it'd break me to leave, but if that boy doesn't change his ways... Well, I'm sorry, but Ivor and I will be left with no choice but to go."

TWENTY-FIVE

Olive

In the girls' room, Olive, Barbara and Shirley stood in a huddle at the foot of Olive's bed.

"What are we going to do?" Olive said, her shoulders slumping as she gazed at the mess.

"You could always say it was you," Barbara suggested, making Olive's cheeks flame.

"I don't poop on my bed. I'd never do that." Olive ignored Barbara's shrug, and the look she exchanged with Shirley that said *well, she pees in it, so it isn't that far-fetched.*

"He didn't mean to do it." Shirley reached out to stroke the furry bundle nestled in Olive's arms. Loud, rhythmic purring vibrated against Olive's fingers as the kitten rubbed its face against her hand contentedly.

In spite of the mess he'd left, Olive couldn't help smiling. "I think he missed us while we were having our tea."

She put him on the floor and he wound a path around her ankles, warm and soft. Kneeling, she delved into her pocket for her napkin and unwrapped the chunks of meat she'd smuggled upstairs from the kitchen.

"There you go, Tyke." While the kitten devoured the meat, Olive stroked his back, entranced by the way his stripy tail stuck straight up into the air every time her fingers traced along his bony spine. His ginger fur felt silky-smooth under her hand and his golden eyes stared appraisingly at her from the moment he finished eating, as if checking in case she had more.

All three girls settled cross-legged on the floor, chuckling as Tyke boldly greeted each one in turn.

"Are you going to keep him?" Shirley asked. "He's lovely. I wish I had a kitten."

"Bet they won't let her keep him," Barbara said, scratching a trio of red lumps on her ankle.

"But why not?"

"He's just pooed the bed, Shirl. Why d'you think?" Barbara rolled her eyes expressively, but put her arm around her sister's shoulders, softening the impact of her words.

Olive's stomach sank. Ever since she'd found Tyke in one of Plas Norton's ramshackle outbuildings, she'd been desperate to keep him. She'd made him a bed in the bottom of the big wardrobe in their room, using a knitted scarf, and she'd managed to snaffle a saucer which she'd filled with water from the glass on her bedside table. But how would she ever persuade Aunt Dodie to allow it? Her mum had always refused any amount of pleading to get a pet.

"Our flat's too small, and in any case they're dirty and smelly," Mum had said, and that had been an end to it.

Tyke wasn't smelly. In fact, his fur smelled lovely when Olive buried her face in it. And he was funny, making the girls clutch their sides as he clawed his way up the floor-length velvet curtains in pursuit of a wayward fly. Olive had had to move a chair across to the window and stand on it to lift him down, unhooking his little paws one by one and holding him safely against her chest in case he was scared.

"Come and see this, Tyke," Barbara urged, tugging one of the ribbons from Shirley's pigtails and trailing it on the ground for him to chase.

The girls were giggling so hard, they didn't notice the bedroom door opening until Aunt Dodie's voice rang out behind them, so suddenly they jumped.

"Whatever have you got there?"

It was unfortunate that Tyke picked that moment to climb the overhanging side of Olive's pink eiderdown and skirt the evidence of his misdeeds, drawing Aunt Dodie's attention to the very thing Olive had hoped to hide.

"My goodness, it's a kitten," Aunt Dodie said, looking dismayed as she answered her own question. "And it seems to have made rather a mess."

"It was an accident," Olive said, scrambling to her feet and scooping him up. "Please don't be cross with him."

Barbara and Shirley dashed to Aunt Dodie's side and took her hands. "Please let us keep him," they chorused.

In the pause that followed, Olive's scalp tightened.

"Oh, girls. I can see that he's very sweet. But look what he's done to that blanket. He's pulled threads all the way up the side, not to mention the mess. And look at you scratching again, Barbara. He must be infested with fleas." She made a face that made Olive's stomach drop.

Resisting all her attempts to hold onto him, Tyke wriggled out of her grasp and pulled himself up onto Olive's shoulder. Not even minding that he was using his claws to hold on, she opened her mouth to defend him.

"Please, Aunt Dodie. He's mine. I've made him a bed in the wardrobe and he's had some meat and some water, and he's been playing like mad. He loves being here with us. We can give him a bath if he really has got fleas, and we can take him outside to go to toilet, or something. Please, please say we can keep him."

Aunt Dodie shook her head slowly, her mouth turning down at the corners.

Olive's breath caught in her throat and tears filled her eyes. It wasn't going to work. That was the trouble with grown-ups: they never listened.

"I'm so sorry, Olive dear. I don't think Mrs Griffiths would be at all happy for him to live in the house. Where did you find him?"

Dumbly, Olive shook her head, her breath hitching in her chest. Words wouldn't come. She reached up to stop Tyke jumping down from her shoulder, her cheeks wet with tears which flowed unchecked.

"Don't take him away, Aunt Dodie." Barbara added her own plea to Olive's, and Shirley burst into loud sobs, screwing her fists into her eye sockets as she bawled.

"Please let him stay! We love him. And I miss Rusty!"

Dodie dragged a hand across her forehead. "I really am sorry, girls. I wish we could offer him a home, but it wouldn't be fair to add to Auntie Dolly's responsibilities." She perched on the edge of Barbara's bed, wrinkling her nose at the mess on Olive's eiderdown. "Where did he come from? I hope you haven't claimed someone else's pet. Imagine if his owner is looking for him – they'll be terribly upset that he's missing."

"He was in one of the barns," Barbara said, hanging her head. "I don't think he belongs to nobody."

"Then I'm afraid that decides it, girls. We can't take in a feral cat. It wouldn't be fair on him to keep him indoors, or on poor Mrs Griffiths, who already has more than enough to do. I hate to see you so distressed, but I'm going to have to insist that you take him back to the barn. Or, better still, take him up to Home Farm and see if they'd like another mouser. While you do that, I'll strip your bed, Olive, and do my best to put things right with Auntie Dolly. We're going to have to vacuum this room thoroughly: we don't want any more flea bites now, do we?"

Olive's feet felt as if they were stuck to the floor. Tyke was balancing on her shoulder like the pirate's parrot in the *Treasure Island* story Aunt Dodie had read to them last week. Now that she had something to love, and something that loved being with her, how could she give him up?

"Off you go to the farm now, Olive. Would you go with her please, Barbara? Shirley, it's a bit late for you to be walking across the fields at this hour. Start getting ready for bed and choose a story ready for when the others get back."

There was nothing more to be said. Olive lifted Tyke down from her shoulder and shuffled from the room with him in her arms. To keep him quiet, she draped one of her plaits over him and let him bat it. Feeling as if her heart had surely split apart, she led Barbara from the house and into the gardens, where the shadows were lengthening.

Up at the bedroom window, Aunt Dodie was watching. She gave a sad smile and a nod of encouragement. Olive turned away. She'd believed Aunt Dodie was different, more kind-hearted and understanding than any other grown-up she'd known. But now she knew better.

Barbara trudged dolefully at Olive's side. "We're taking him to the farm, then?"

"No. I'm not giving him up."

"But... Where will you take him? And how will you look after him?"

"I'll take meat for him every day. And I'll keep him in the summerhouse. It's dry, and we've already put some blankets up there, ain't we? First thing in the morning, I'll take a bowl and some water up, and some sausages from breakfast. I can do it on the way to school, and on the way back I can go and play with him."

"Won't he be lonely while we're in school all day?"

"There's loads of spiders for him to chase, and probably mice too I shouldn't wonder. Tomorrow, we can take some toys for him. Some ribbons, and maybe a little ball. Once he's learned that the summerhouse is his home, and that I'll come back with food every day, I'll start letting him outside to play. It'll work, Barb. I'll make it work."

Ignoring her friend's doubtful expression, Olive concentrated on holding the squirming kitten firmly enough to keep him safe, but not so firmly that he'd be hurt. It wasn't easy. Maybe looking after him wouldn't be easy either, but he was hers now. He'd shown he loved her by clambering into her lap earlier and rubbing his cheeks against her with a look of bliss on his face that told her he thought she was special.

It gave her a strange feeling in her chest, knowing she was being deliberately disobedient. She couldn't remember a time when she'd ever done so before. But she wasn't going to give Tyke up. It was alright for the Clarkes: they had each other. But Olive had no one but Peter, and he didn't even like her. Even her own mum didn't care enough about her to send her a letter. Tyke was different. Tyke needed her. Whatever happened, she wasn't about to let him down just because of some mean old grown-ups.

TWENTY-SIX

Dodie

The hubbub of voices outside the locked doors of the church hall suggested that Reverend Appleton's jumble sale in aid of the Save the Children Fund was sure to be a success. Wooden trestle tables around the edges of the room were piled with donated goods, smelling of dust and mothballs, and several ladies from the church had spent the whole morning arranging items and adding price tickets. The room buzzed with anticipation as final preparations were made.

Dodie and Loulou had been roped in to help on the tea stall, as the Fitznorton-Havard contribution to the fundraising efforts. Already Dodie had stacked cake plates with paper napkins and laid out forty-eight cups and saucers, and a huge electric urn was gently simmering hot water ready to brew tea in the eight-pint aluminium teapot which had been primed with the appropriate amount of tea leaves.

It had been fun having Loulou at home over the past few weeks. Despite her obvious frustration at having to delay joining up to keep her mother happy, Loulou's naturally sunny nature meant she couldn't stay down for long, and Dodie had to give her credit for mucking in cheerfully. There was something incongruous about seeing her young niece wearing an apron over her stylish outfit, her blonde hair held back from her face by a bright silk scarf that emphasised the blue of her eyes. At twenty, Loulou had a petite but shapely figure which looked marvellous whether in slacks or a cocktail gown. Her sunny smile and irrepressible good humour made her a fun companion; it was a shame they hadn't spent more time together when growing up. Dodie had often envied the effervescent personality and prettiness that made Loulou stand out in any crowd, attracting smiling glances from admirers and not a few envious ones from other, plainer girls. These days, Dodie minded less. She was more comfortable remaining unnoticed in the background.

Reverend Appleton checked his watch, then tucked it back into his waistcoat pocket. "Two minutes!" he announced.

Behind him, the doors rattled, making him jump as if a herd of wildebeest was about to trample him in a stampede.

"He'd better make sure he steps back when he throws the bolt. Those women have the bit between their teeth," Loulou remarked. She and Dodie exchanged a grin.

"We'd better start brewing the tea," Dodie said.

"Good idea. Give me a hand with this, would you?" Loulou asked, hefting one of the huge teapots with both hands. "Could you turn the tap on the urn? I never realised making tea for an army of housewives would require the limbs of an octopus."

"If you're joining the forces, you might end up doing rather a lot of mass catering. That's what lots of girls do when they're not marching or polishing their buttons, isn't it?" Dodie joked.

"I certainly don't plan to do any such thing. I shall learn to fly, if I possibly can."

Dodie almost forgot to watch the flow of boiling water pouring into the teapot.

"Do you think they'll let you?"

"If they won't, I'll pester them until they give in." Loulou grunted at the weight of the full pot as she set it down on their trestle table, then gave it a stir and clicked the lid in place.

"Have you told your mother?" It seemed unlikely that Charlotte would be pleased at the prospect of her daughter flying aeroplanes in wartime. Perhaps not even at any time.

"What do you think?" Loulou replied with a mischievous wink.

The doors opened, releasing a swarm of women into the hall, their eyes bright at the prospect of bargains. Dodie was glad that she and the other volunteers had already had an opportunity to peruse the goods on sale. She'd bypassed the White Elephant stall with its assortment of ornaments, kitchen utensils, mismatched crockery, gramophone records and half-used bottles of scent, in favour of the children's clothes stall. In their weeks at Plas Norton, all the evacuees had grown at least an inch. Dodie put this down to a mixture of fresh air and Dolly's cooking, now that they weren't living on bread and dripping or chips from the local chippy.

With the weather turning colder, they needed bigger, warmer clothes, so Dodie had brought a list of their measurements along with her. The items she had selected and tucked away in a parcel under the tea stall earlier would be a boon. She hoped the children would be pleased with them. There was a green woollen sweater which looked unworn, and which she was sure would fit Michael, and a darling pair of red shoes with a strap which were in Olive's size. Smiling at the prospect of Olive's pleasure at seeing them for the first time, she greeted her first customer.

"I'll have a cup of tea and a slice of that Bara Brith," the woman said, handing over a shiny sixpence.

While Dodie counted out her change from their tin and served a slice of the sticky fruit loaf richly spread with butter, Loulou poured the tea.

The next customer in line looked vaguely familiar. With her curly dark hair pulled back into a severe bun, her face bare of make-up and a dowdy, shapeless woollen coat, she had an old-fashioned look about her which belied her relative youth. She couldn't be more than thirty, Dodie guessed, but dressed like a woman much older.

"It's Miss Fitznorton, isn't it? And Miss Havard?" she asked, with a glimmer of a shy smile. "I was wondering if Dolly is here?" Her gaze slid past them to scan the room.

"I'm afraid not. She supplied some of the cakes, but she's back at the house looking after our evacuees," Dodie replied.

The woman's face fell. "That's a shame. I was hoping to speak to her about my own evacuee... Not to worry."

"Wait," Dodie said, noticing the woman's resemblance to Dolly and Maggie. "You're her sister Miriam, aren't you? Mrs Powell?"

"Yes, that's right." She looked surprised that Dodie knew her name. "Well, if Dolly's not here, I'd better be off."

"Wouldn't you like a cup of tea, Mrs Powell? Maggie might be along in a little while. I'm sure her landlady mentioned that they'd be popping in."

But it seemed she wasn't to be persuaded. She slipped away without buying anything, leaving Dodie troubled. The young woman had seemed so different from her older sisters: quiet and shy, flitting in and almost as quickly leaving, as if she felt she shouldn't be there. Dodie recalled Dolly describing her brother-in-law as a stern man, a non-conformist religious minister with strong views about everything under the sun. She hoped he wasn't the reason his wife seemed so anxious to go without buying anything.

Her reverie was interrupted as Loulou nudged her arm.

"Whoever is that?" Loulou's blue eyes twinkled merrily but she seemed to be looking at Reverend Appleton, who was hardly unfamiliar and certainly didn't warrant such excitement. It was then that Dodie realised the vicar was shaking hands with a tall man in a brown fedora. Her stomach lurched in the strangest way as she recognised him.

"That's the teacher who brought the evacuees to Pontybrenin," she said.

"Why didn't you tell me he's such a dreamboat?" Much to Dodie's annoyance, Loulou pretended to fan herself.

"Stop it! He's heading this way." Dodie fussed with the cups and saucers, rearranging them pointlessly.

Beside her, Loulou had lit up as if someone had flipped a charisma switch. Dodie could hardly blame Mr Winter for looking dazzled by the wattage of her niece's smile. She'd long ago accepted the effect Loulou had on the opposite sex, ever since the day she'd taken her sixteen-year-old niece to Contadino's café for an ice cream and poor Johnny Contadino had been rendered tongue-tied, falling over his own feet in the face of her charm.

"Hello there. What can I do for you?" Loulou asked Mr Winter in a breathy voice as he approached their stall.

Dodie resisted the urge to grind a heel into her foot.

Mr Winter sent an inquiring look Dodie's way. "Good morning, Miss Fitznorton. I don't believe we've been introduced, Miss—?"

"Louise Havard," Loulou said, before Dodie had time to respond. She reached out her hand and held onto his for longer than was either polite or necessary.

Dodie cleared her throat. "Loulou, may I introduce the children's teacher, Mr Winter."

"What a pleasure to meet you, Mr Winter. Now, what can I tempt you with? We have some smashing treats on offer."

She really was the most incorrigible flirt. Dodie focused her gaze on the rafters to avoid seeing the way Mr Winter's grey eyes softened and a rather charming dimple appeared on one of his cheeks. He accepted a cup of tea, laying a threepenny coin that was warm from his pocket in Dodie's palm, then pointed to the plate of Welsh cakes, glistening with their dusting of caster sugar.

"I'll give one of those a try," he said.

"An excellent choice," Loulou replied, leaning forward conspiratorially to add: "Our housekeeper Dolly made them."

"Ah. Then I know they'll be good."

Dodie was struck by the gleam in his eyes. She'd never seen him look like that before. But then, it was natural that Loulou's gregariousness and self-confidence would attract a handsome man like him in a way that her own reticence never could. A pang of envy caught her by surprise. She was the way she was. She couldn't pretend to be like Loulou, any more than Loulou could fade into the background. In any case, it wouldn't be sensible to let herself get any silly ideas about Mr Winter having even the slightest interest in her.

"While I'm here, Miss Fitznorton, I wonder if I might have a word with you about the children?" Mr Winter said, his expression turning serious again.

"Oh! Well, yes – of course." Her heart thumped. Had Peter told him that she'd smacked him? Did he think her a terrible person? She still felt awful about her loss of control that day.

Loulou waved her arm carelessly. "Off you pop. I'll hold the fort here," she said with characteristic generosity.

Dodie followed Mr Winter through the throng of bargain hunters to a quiet corner. He had finished eating the Welsh cake by the time they got there, and he dusted crumbs off his tie.

"Your niece was right about that cake. I could eat a whole plateful of those in a heartbeat," he said.

Dodie folded her hands in front of her and waited, painfully aware that Loulou was watching them as if they were the most entertaining thing that she'd seen all week. Dodie's mouth went dry as she wondered what he wanted to speak to her about.

"I was wondering how young Michael has been since our last conversation," he said, lowering his voice.

She nodded, relieved to discuss Michael. "Michael hasn't mentioned any further incidents since the new arrangements at school." She drew a deep breath. The opportunity to discuss the boys' behaviour was too important to let it pass by without also asking about Peter. "It's actually Peter who worries me more. His behaviour has made Dolly threaten to leave. We simply couldn't manage the house and children without her and Ivor. The other day, Peter smashed his plate with a cricket bat."

His eyebrows flew up. "Would you like me to speak to him?"

"Maybe. Until then, could I ask your advice?"

He nodded.

"I'm afraid I haven't handled him well. I was quiet like Olive as a child... I simply can't understand what makes him behave so appallingly. I'd like so much to help him feel happy and at home with us, but at times I find myself losing my temper and – well, I'm ashamed to say I struggle to like him. How should I deal with him? I don't want to resort to smacking him, but sometimes..."

Spreading her hands helplessly, she risked a glance upwards to check his reaction, expecting to be met with cold disapproval. To her surprise, his expression was warm, even compassionate.

"He doesn't realise how lucky he is to have been billeted with you. If you want my thoughts on the matter, I'd say Olive copes by blending into the background to avoid trouble. She's learned that it's the best way to survive, and I have my suspicions about what went on at home to cause that. Peter, on the other hand, is crying out to be noticed. As difficult as it may be with a kid like Peter, try to notice him being good. Even if it's just little things, remark on it when you see him behaving well.

He'll soak up the praise like a sponge and start looking for ways to get more of it. If you think it'll help, I'd be happy to speak to him. Maybe between us, we can work out a way to calm him down and keep Dolly sweet. After sampling her cooking twice now, I can completely understand why you wouldn't want to lose her."

TWENTY-SEVEN
NOVEMBER

Patrick

Of all the hymns which were sung in the school's daily assembly, Patrick's favourite was 'All Things Bright and Beautiful'. The past two months staying in Pontybrenin and teaching in Bryncarreg had awoken in him a new-found love of the countryside which made the words of the song come alive. He could picture the purple-headed mountain, the birds singing, flowers, fruits and the river, vividly as he added his bass voice to Miss Bright's reedy tones while Miss Honeycutt thumped out the tune on the school's upright piano. He was less keen on the verse about the rich man in his castle and the poor man at his gate, but even this had its compensations as his thoughts would inevitably turn to the big house at Plas Norton, and thence to Miss Fitznorton, whose obvious care for the children had made him warm to her. Her sensitivity seemed to be matched by her intelligence and honesty. In their discussions about Michael and Peter she'd been keen to learn the best ways to handle them. Most people would have given up and sent the boys back to the billeting officer, but not her. He'd been impressed the last time they spoke.

As he closed his book and resumed his seat in front of the children, he scanned the rows to ensure they were behaving themselves. He sent Peter a glare which succeeded in quelling his incessant fidgeting for a couple of minutes, then settled back to listen to Miss Honeycutt's chosen story from the scriptures. This morning, she read the story of Judas betraying Christ. It seemed an odd choice, and odder still that as she closed her book she nodded towards the door at the back of the room, which promptly opened to reveal two policemen. He recognised one as Constable Todd, who had questioned him when he first arrived in Pontybrenin.

Excitement rippled across the rows of children as the policemen marched towards the front of the room. Patrick sat up straighter. This was odd. Miss Honeycutt hadn't mentioned a visit from the local constabulary. Perhaps some of the children had been seen getting up to mischief.

As the men reached the front, his attention was caught by a whimper from one of the older children. It was Eva Fischer, the girl who had only recently arrived in Pontybrenin after an arduous train journey from Czechoslovakia. Her eyes were wide, her cheeks ashen. Her fear made his stomach flip. His feet itched to walk over to her so he could reassure her that she had no reason to fear the police in Great Britain, a free country; but before he could move, he realised the policemen had come to a halt on either side of him.

"We'd like you to come with us, if you don't mind, Mr Winter," Todd said. "We have a few questions to ask you down at the station."

Patrick's heart rate quickened. He could hear it thudding so loudly he could almost have believed everyone in the room could hear it, too, above the gasps of the rows of children whose heads were turning as they looked to each other for reassurance.

"Be quiet, Eva," Miss Honeycutt snapped.

The poor girl was crying openly now. If he made a fuss, it would only upset her further. If he protested, it would make him look guilty. Although – guilty of what? They hadn't said he was under arrest, only that they wanted to ask him some questions. Perhaps this time it wouldn't be the way it had been in New York. Sweat prickled down his spine at the thought of going through that again.

He did the only thing he could. He stood, sent Eva a smile that he hoped would appear more confident than he felt, and followed Constable Todd from the room with an appearance of calm. With the younger cop only a foot or two behind him, he tried to pretend his senses weren't screaming at him to run. That there wasn't a knot in his stomach that screwed up even tighter when he ducked his head to slip into the rear seat of the police car. That the policemen's ominous silence as they sat on either side of him didn't make him want to lash out with his fists and fight his way back out into the air instead of obediently allowing himself to be taken away.

TWENTY-EIGHT

Patrick

Patrick had been cooling his heels in a small, bare cell for several hours by the time he was invited to join the police sergeant in another room for questioning. His alien registration card, tie, braces and shoelaces had been confiscated on arrival at Pontybrenin's sombre, grey stone police station. The sensation of his waist band slipping towards his hips and the flapping of his brown leather brogues as he followed the policeman into an interview room added to the feeling that he was beginning to unravel. No one had been unkind, or impolite; he hadn't actually been arrested. But there was no point in fooling himself: he wouldn't have been taken in for questioning and then left alone to contemplate his options for the best part of a day if the local constabulary was convinced of his innocence.

He took a seat on the hard wooden chair indicated by the police officer, who introduced himself as Sergeant Morgan. The officer sat down to face him across the table, on the side nearest the door.

"Now then, Patrick. I have a few questions to ask you. You don't mind me calling you Patrick, do you?"

"I could hardly object to you using my name, sergeant." He wasn't in a position to insist on formalities.

"Excellent. I'm glad we can keep things on a civilised footing." The man took a notebook and pencil out of his breast pocket and made a show of finding a clean page, as if he enjoyed keeping Patrick waiting.

Patrick answered all the standard questions about his identity and his reason for being in Pontybrenin, keeping his responses concise in an effort to remain calm, though he couldn't stop one of his feet tapping out a rapid staccato rhythm under the table. It almost came as a relief when the officer finally came around to a more purposeful line of questioning. This, perhaps, would give a clue as to the reason why he'd been brought in.

"Now, a little bird tells me that even though you sound like an American, you're actually an Irishman, Patrick?"

"Your little bird was only partly correct. My mother is Irish; my father was English. I was born in New York. I've never been to Ireland, myself."

"Nevertheless, I dare say you have strong opinions on the Irish question."

Patrick's mouth went dry. There had been IRA bomb attacks in numerous British cities in recent months. Wartime wasn't a good time to have any doubt cast over his loyalties.

"My only opinion on politics is that it is imperative to uphold democracy," he said.

There was a pause while the policeman stared at him. The expression on his broad face was genial enough. Still, Patrick wasn't under any illusions. The man's attitude might change quickly if he thought something could be pinned on him.

"Are you in touch with this Irish mother of yours?" His pencil was poised above his notebook.

"Sure, I write to her twice a week. She lives with her sister in London."

"And do you also write to your colleague?"

"My colleague?" Patrick frowned.

"The one who's a member of the British Union of Fascists. Which is, as I'm sure I don't have to remind you, a banned organisation. She's quite friendly with the Mosleys, I gather."

His heart sank. "No. I'm not in touch with my *former* colleague."

"But you say you correspond regularly with your contacts in London?"

"With my mother, yes. Not with Miss Summerill." He found himself gabbling to fill the silence that followed, even though he recognised the tactic. "I wasn't aware of my colleague's political leanings until recently. I don't share her views. In fact, I was among the crowd who stopped fascists marching through the East End back in thirty-six."

Sergeant Morgan nodded, but his mouth had a sceptical twist. He leaned back in his chair and gazed at Patrick thoughtfully, as if searching for the truth in his features.

Patrick met his gaze, keeping his expression neutral. In the pause, the sound of his foot tapping against his chair leg threatened to betray his nerves. He set his foot firmly on the floor to stop the involuntary movement.

"You spend a lot of time out in the woods, from what I hear?"

Patrick blinked. Where was this leading?

"You like the countryside, do you, Patrick? Roaming around the forests by yourself. Leaving things hidden amongst the trees. Little messages. Markers, and such. Signs for others to find. You've been quite keen to acquire maps of the local area, too, I gather."

Sweat moistened Patrick's palms. This, then, was the reason they'd brought him in. "Yes, but – that's for the children," he stammered. "I set out treasure hunts, orienteering challenges. For the children," he repeated.

The policeman smirked as he pocketed his notepad and pencil. "I'll just leave you to have a little think, while we wait for the inspector to arrive," he said, then made for the door, his thick-soled shoes squeaking with each heavy tread.

Patrick's mind raced as he was taken back to his holding cell around the corner. Should he ask for a lawyer to be present? Or to contact the American Embassy? Would that make him look guilty? Who might have been trying to incriminate him? He knew from experience that things could get nasty when someone had been squealing to the cops. Despite the chilly air in the room, the hand he dashed across his forehead came away damp.

Perhaps he'd ask to call Reverend Appleton... But the vicar must surely know by now that he'd been taken away in a police car. News like that wouldn't take long to get around a small town. Yet there had been no sign of him. Perhaps he assumed Patrick was guilty. Maybe, in times like these, the principle "innocent until proven guilty" no longer applied. But how could he convince the police that he was harmless?

Patrick slumped down onto the narrow cot and buried his face in his hands. There was no way to let his mother know what was happening. No one else in this country who might believe in him. He'd never felt so friendless and alone.

TWENTY-NINE

Dodie

The sky was darkening by the time Dodie and Mr Gibson left the library. He was in a hurry that evening, not even waiting while she locked the door. It was his wife's birthday, he said, and as Dodie watched his stocky figure rush off down the street in his brown overcoat and hat, she couldn't help speculating as to how he and Mrs Gibson would celebrate. He hardly seemed the sort to make a grand, romantic gesture.

Pocketing the heavy bunch of keys, she turned at the sudden growl of a motorcycle pulling up alongside the kerb. The rider beckoned towards Dodie, then lifted their goggles.

"Loulou! What are you doing here?" Dodie shouted above the rumble of the engine.

To her relief, her niece turned the machine off.

"I've come to collect you."

"You can't expect me to ride on that thing." Dodie had never ridden a motorcycle in her life, and she wasn't about to start now, especially with darkness falling, no street lighting, and precious little illumination from the bike's headlamp due to blackout restrictions.

"Oh, come on. Why catch a smelly old bus and tramp across fields in the dark when you could be home in ten minutes and inject a little excitement into your humdrum librarian's life?" Loulou's eyes twinkled mischievously. "Besides, you're needed back at the ranch. It's all kicked off. Haven't you heard the gossip that's consuming Pontybrenin like a bush fire? The kiddies are beside themselves."

"I haven't heard anything. I've been busy pasting the covers back onto books all afternoon."

Loulou leaned forward, eager to share her news. "It's that teacher chap. The good-looking one you introduced me to at the jumble sale. He was arrested at school this morning, right in front of the children. I heard Mrs Nicholas from the stationer's telling her coven of ghastly chums in Contadino's café earlier that it's because he's been 'spying for the Nasties'. Either that or he's a Fenian intent upon blowing us all up. No one seems entirely sure of anything, except that he's a bad 'un. Apparently, he's been buying maps of the area and laying out messages and codes in the woods for enemy paratroopers. Someone else said he'd been heard talking with a known fascist about the Mosleys, and that he's got dangerous Irish connections. And then, Mrs Thomas said that when her husband was a POW in the Great War, one of the German guards was a Lieutenant Winter. It seems even his name condemns him. People are speculating that he might actually be German, not American."

"It surely can't be true, though... can it?"

"For the good people of Pontybrenin, I'm not sure it even matters if it's true or not. They'll dine out for years to come on having a spy in their midst. Contadino's was doing a roaring trade while they all gossiped over their tea and scones. You must admit, this is the most exciting thing to happen here in – well, probably forever. The children, however, are another matter. I wouldn't be surprised to see Michael and Peter start a riot, they're so outraged."

Dodie hugged herself, and not only because of the chill in the November air. It was frightening to hear that a man who had been in their home, and who had played an important part in their evacuee children's lives, could have been a danger to them all. More than that, she found she was disappointed. There had been something about Mr Winter that gave her a not unpleasant fluttery feeling when they had conversed. Although he'd seemed stern, even intimidating, when they first met, lately he had seemed quite approachable. If asked to vouch for his character, she would have described him as a principled man and a dedicated teacher. But the police must know what they were doing. She'd obviously been mistaken.

"The poor children, finding out that someone they trusted was a traitor. It must have been a dreadful shock."

"I've no doubt it was. So are you going to hop on the back, or do I have to drag you home?" Loulou dangled a spare leather helmet towards Dodie.

It seemed Dodie had little choice but to comply. She needed to get back to the children quickly to offer reassurance. Grimacing, she pulled the helmet over her hair and buckled it under her chin, then ducked her head under the straps of her handbag and gas mask box so they crossed her body securely.

"You'll probably have to hitch your skirt up," Loulou suggested helpfully. It was alright for her: she was wearing jodhpurs and boots.

Dodie muttered under her breath and glanced around, glad of the blackout for once. Hopefully no one would see her riding pillion through the streets with her skirt hem above her knees and her suspenders and stocking-tops dangerously close to being exposed. Against her better judgement, she straddled the saddle behind her niece, who had shuffled forward slightly. The sudden roar as the engine started up made her squeal and throw her arms around Loulou's waist.

"Hold on tight!"

Dodie needed no such prompting. She clung as if her life depended on it, which it undoubtedly did as Loulou drove along at what seemed an irresponsible speed. Undaunted by the twilight's rapid descent, she leaned the bike into each bend and hunkered down to increase their pace on the few straight stretches of road between Pontybrenin and Plas Norton. She was forced to slow down while they passed through the village of Bryncarreg, and on their long, rutted driveway, but by then Dodie's fingers were white and stiff. Her limbs were so rigid with tension that they trembled when at last she was able to stagger off the machine outside the porch.

"Isn't it exhilarating?" Loulou crowed, shaking out her blonde hair with a beaming smile.

"I suppose that's one word for it," Dodie replied with a self-deprecating grin, glad to hand the helmet back and feel the ground beneath her feet. "Thank you for the lift," she added, grateful that at least she hadn't had to trudge over the fields.

As she entered the house, Dodie straightened her clothes and laid her gas mask box and handbag on the table in the hall. She was longing for a cup of tea in her favourite armchair, but she would first have to speak to the children.

She found them in the kitchen, clearing up after their tea while Dolly prepared to serve the adults separately in the dining room.

"Aunt Dodie!" Shirley tossed her tea towel onto the table and dashed over to give Dodie a hug.

Olive stood apart, her chin trembling and her eyes brimming with tears as if Dodie's appearance had sparked a sudden release of tension.

"Good evening, all of you. I gather you've had a rather upsetting day?" With one arm draped around Shirley's shoulders, she beckoned to Olive and gathered her in for a cuddle, choosing to ignore the wet snuffling sounds as Olive buried her face into Dodie's blouse. "There, there, now. It will all be alright, you'll see."

"Mr Winter's been arrested," Barbara said, her dark eyes solemn. "Miss Honeycutt said we must tell her if we've ever seen him do anything suspicious, because he could be a dangerous spy. But we've been talking about it, and none of us think it's true. We've never seen him do nothing wrong, have we?"

Dodie smiled gratefully at Dolly, who had placed a teacup and saucer on the table in front of her.

"Glad to see you made it back in one piece," Dolly remarked wryly. "Can't say I've ever fancied riding pillion, myself."

"Did you ride on a motorbike?" Barbara asked, her mouth gaping.

Even Peter looked impressed, instead of his usual sulky expression.

"I did. It was quite exciting." Now that she was sitting down, safe in the cosy warmth of Plas Norton's kitchen, she felt rather pleased with herself for being brave enough to endure Loulou's riding skills.

"I expect that's why your hair's a bit of a mess," Shirley said, reaching up to smooth it. She could always be relied upon to be honest.

"Tell me more about Mr Winter," Dodie said after she'd taken a sip of her tea. "You say you've never noticed him doing anything wrong… But if he really is spying, he wouldn't do it openly, would he? I'm sure the police know what they're doing."

"You think the police never arrest innocent people?" Michael lifted a disbelieving eyebrow, and not for the first time Dodie wondered what he had seen or heard in his ten years to make him so pessimistic.

The children took their usual seats at the table.

Michael spoke up first. "The thing is about Mr Winter, he's like that boiled egg I ate on my first morning here. He's got a hard shell on the outside, but inside he's a lot softer."

Olive and Peter nodded. Both looked troubled.

"What is it?" Dodie prompted gently.

"I don't know if I should tell you. Mr Winter said it was our secret."

Dodie exchanged a swift glance with Dolly, whose eyebrows had risen. Her pulse picked up, her instinct for trouble aroused by the idea of a grown man asking a child to keep his secrets. It sounded unsavoury.

"What kind of secret?" she asked.

Peter scowled at Michael as if willing him to keep him quiet.

"What kind of secret?" Dodie asked again. "Given the circumstances, I think telling me is the right thing to do. If you know something about Mr Winter's secrets, then it's your duty to say. It isn't telling tales, I promise."

Michael sighed, his shoulders slumping. "Alright," he said. "But I feel bad about it, 'cause he told me not to say nothing to nobody."

"Same," Peter said, before clamming up. He gnawed at his fingernails. Clearly the idea of breaking his teacher's confidence made him uncomfortable.

"Come on. Out with it," Dolly said, briskly no-nonsense as ever. She stood with her hands on her hips, waiting.

Michael huffed out his breath. "Miss Honeycutt sent me to him for a caning. She said I was talking in class, but I weren't, honest. Mr Winter believed me. He didn't cane me, but he said I mustn't let on to Miss Honeycutt or she might just do it herself. He kept me in the cloakroom for ten minutes, chatting. Then he told me to walk funny and act all upset, as if he'd tanned my backside, when I went back into class."

"He was the same with me," Olive piped up, to Dodie's surprise. It was rare for the child to say much at all. "I got stuck doing arithmetic, and Miss Honeycutt said I was lazy. I wasn't being lazy, honest – I couldn't hear what she was telling us, so I got in a muddle. She said I had to go to Mr Winter and tell him I was a lazy dunce, and that he'd deal with me. I was scared. But he gave me a sweet out of his pocket. He said, 'Let's put our heads together and work out what will help you.' And he explained the maths, then sent me back to class. He said I had to keep it a secret, and act upset like he'd shouted at me. He said it wouldn't do for the other kids to know he's a softy, 'cause then they might never behave themselves."

Peter's shoulders sagged as if he'd been deflated. "I got sent to him for fidgeting. That old cow had already whacked me on the hand, and she said Mr Winter would give me a proper caning. But he said if I kept this tiny bit of Plasticine out of sight, I could put my spare energy into fidgeting with that instead of wriggling in my seat. And it does help a bit." He reached into his pocket and pulled out a pea-sized, unpleasantly fluffy ball of red clay.

Dodie searched their earnest faces. Her heart ached for them, being threatened with physical punishment for such minor misdemeanours. Miss Honeycutt sounded horrible.

"I'm glad Mr Winter has been kind to the three of you. What about the things people are saying about him, though? That he leaves messages out in the woods, and that he's been trying to buy maps of the area. You must admit, that does sound fishy."

"That'll be for the orienteering," Michael said.

The others nodded.

"It's fun. Much better than being stuck in the classroom all day," Barbara agreed.

"But what is it?"

"It's like a race to find treasure. We work in teams, and each one gets a map and a compass. We have to find our way quickly through the woods to pick up a different coloured card at each control point. First team to get back with all the cards in the right order wins an extra five minutes' playtime."

"So Mr Winter isn't leaving clues or messages in the woods?"

"Only for us."

"Is that what's got him into trouble? Doing fun things for us? He said it would do us good to get us outdoors, instead of always sitting at our desks. He can't go to prison; it wouldn't be right!" Olive looked as if she was on the verge of tears again. Dodie's throat constricted as Shirley went over and gave her friend a hug.

"It'll be alright, Olive," Shirley said, patting her on the back. "Aunt Dodie will tell the police, and then they'll have to let him go."

THIRTY

Dodie

Dodie went in search of Charlotte. She found her in the drawing room, sipping a glass of sherry and flicking idly through the pages of *Country Life* whilst listening to cacophonous jazz music on the gramophone. Dodie disliked jazz, but now wasn't the time to grumble about her sister's taste in music.

"May I take the Riley out?" Dodie asked, coming straight to the point. She had already donned a coat and hat, ready to venture out again into the chilly evening air.

The needle scraped as Charlotte lifted it, making her wince.

"You'll have to check with Ivor how much petrol is left in it. When do you need it?"

"Now. I'm only going to Pontybrenin and back."

"But it's dark," Charlotte said, gesturing towards the window. The blackout blinds were in place. "How will you see where you're going? Can't it wait until morning?"

"Unfortunately, it can't. I have to fetch something from the library, and then help someone in need. I shouldn't be more than an hour or two, I hope." She turned on her heel, but Charlotte called her back.

"This wouldn't have anything to do with today's events, would it? The suspicions about Patrick Winter, I mean."

Dodie tugged her driving gloves on. "Yes, it does. I've been speaking to the children about it."

Charlotte sighed. "I must say I find all these tales of espionage and treachery rather far-fetched. But I don't see what we can do about it. I imagine the Security Services have already been called."

"Well... based on what the children have told me, I feel I should at least try to convince the police that they've made a grave error."

Charlotte set down her glass and crossed the room to gaze searchingly into Dodie's face. "If you're so sure that's the case, then take the car with my blessing."

A little of the tension in Dodie's shoulders loosened. "I wasn't sure if you'd see it that way. The police might not listen to me, of course."

"In these sorts of tricky situations, I always ask myself: *What would Venetia do?* And you may be sure that she wouldn't sit idly by at home if an innocent man had been accused of treason. Nevertheless, do try not to prang my pride and joy out there in the dark."

Dodie turned to go.

"Should I come with you?"

"No, thanks. It would be better if you could help Dolly settle the children for bed. I usually read them a bedtime story. But don't get their hopes up – I haven't told them what I'm intending to do just in case my efforts come to nothing. It may already be too late."

As she helped Ivor open the garage doors, Dodie had to acknowledge that she wasn't only doing this for the children's sake. Ever since speaking to them her conscience had been pricking her for ever countenancing the idea that Mr Winter could be capable of such a heinous crime as spying. Hadn't he always struck her as a principled man? He'd defied Miss Honeycutt and demanded a fairer system for the children's schooling. Yet she'd simply accepted what the gossips said as true, out of the naïve belief that the police could do no wrong. She berated herself as she edged the car out of the garage and started the mile-long crawl along the driveway through Plas Norton's estate, peering fearfully through the windscreen and cursing the blackout regulations as her eyes struggled to adjust to the darkness.

The car's headlights were almost obscured by masking designed to foil any German bomber crew's attempts to navigate. It was hardly likely that German planes could even reach this part of Wales, let alone that one would happen to be passing overhead and decide to bomb one solitary car – but rules were rules, and must be followed, especially when driving to a police station. She couldn't risk defying the law when she was about to plead for mercy on another person's behalf.

Every pothole and bump made her muscles tense. She was convinced she would land Charlotte's car in a hedge or ditch and be forced to walk for miles alone in the darkness. A badger ran out in front of her, making her catch her breath and slam on the brakes.

It was equally dark in the village, where the windows of each house were all shrouded in blackout fabric or painted over to avoid any chink of light showing, just as they were at Plas Norton. Knowing from the newspaper that there had been a spate of recent road accidents, she prayed that no one would step out in front of the car as it purred towards Pontybrenin.

At last she reached the library and drew the car up level with the kerb, taking a moment to thank her lucky stars for her safe arrival. She unlocked the library door, waiting until it had closed behind her before fumbling for the light switch, to avoid attracting the attention of any passing Air Raid Precautions warden. Within five minutes she had located the items she sought and was back in the car heading to the police station.

Before pushing the door open, she patted her hair into place and smoothed the line of her coat, swallowing her anxiety down. Her hands trembled, and she clenched her fists to make them stop. She'd never been inside a police station before. After surviving the past twenty years by staying in the background, avoiding people's notice, she would have to push herself forward now if she was to have any chance of helping poor Mr Winter. The children's testimonies obliged her to do so. She pushed away the thought that she was glad he had turned out to be a good man after all, unwilling to admit that her own feelings about him might be somewhat complicated.

The police officer at the desk looked up from his paperwork as she approached. She recognised him as the man who had spoken to Venetia in the church hall on the day the children arrived in Pontybrenin.

"Good evening, miss. What can I do for you?"

Dodie fixed a bright smile onto her face, recalling Venetia's maxim that it was easier to catch flies with honey than with vinegar. "I've heard some rather troubling news today about Mr Patrick Winter, a teacher who has been evacuated to Pontybrenin. I understand he's been arrested on the basis of scurrilous gossip, but I'm hoping you'll be able to reassure me that it isn't true, Constable...?"

The policeman laid down his pen and sent her a condescending smile. "Constable Todd. I'm afraid I'm not at liberty to discuss police operations with you, Miss—?"

"I'm Miss Josephine Fitznorton of Plas Norton. You probably know of my sister, Mrs Havard. And I recall that you're familiar with our close friend, Miss Vaughan-Lloyd, the magistrate and former mayor of Pontybrenin. I understand, of course, that you can't give me any details of Mr Winter's case. The last thing I would expect is for you to go against procedure. My only concern is to ensure that the officer in charge is fully apprised of the facts. I'd like to speak to him to present some fresh evidence."

As Todd dropped his gaze, flustered, Dodie stepped forward to shake hands with an older policeman who had appeared from around the corner. His curious expression suggested he had heard every word.

"How can I help you, Miss Fitznorton? I'm Sergeant Morgan. I've been dealing with Mr Winter's case."

"I understand there have been rumours about him. Quite disgraceful rumours, with no foundation in truth."

"Well, miss, I think you'll agree that we should be the best judges of that."

"I most certainly *do* agree. However, it isn't possible to make a sound judgement if one is unaware of all the facts of a situation. That's why I've come to offer you my assistance. Now, I gather some people have tried to imply that the *American* Mr Winter is a Fenian, based on his family connection to Ireland?"

"I can't really comment— "

She cut him off. "I must say I find it quite illogical, myself. In my own conversations with Mr Winter he has been quite open about his Irish mother, but he also has an English father. It isn't illegal to have family connections to other countries, is it? Why, if we did, we'd have to lock up King George and Queen Mary for their German ancestry."

"Ah, well—"

"Of course, the Duke of Wellington was an Irishman, but no one would ever dare dispute *his* loyalty and service to this country. And Winston Churchill, the First Lord of the Admiralty, is half-American. As an American by birth, Mr Winter is a citizen of a neutral nation. It could cause Britain considerable embarrassment were he to be wrongly charged with an offence, based on mere tittle-tattle." She smiled again, as if he couldn't possibly disagree with her line of argument.

He coughed and stammered; Todd's face had turned puce.

She continued regardless.

"Even more incredibly, I've also heard that some people have accused Mr Winter of being a fascist, on the basis that his former colleague has spoken openly about her links to those ghastly Mosleys."

The sergeant nodded and ran his finger around the inside of his collar. "That's one of the angles we're investigating, miss. Do you have any information you can give us about that?"

"Well, only that Mr Winter cannot be held responsible for his colleague's views. Political leanings are not simply absorbed through the obligation to spend time with someone. After all, Mr Winter's *former* colleague Miss Summerill was billeted with our good friend while she was in Pontybrenin, and I assure you Miss Vaughan-Lloyd is as rigidly anti-fascist as she ever was. She would be more than happy to confirm it, should you need to bring her in for questioning on the same basis."

Dodie couldn't help a mischievous smile. Against all expectations, she was almost enjoying herself.

"Colleagues do sometimes have some peculiar notions," she went on, leaning forwards as if sharing a confidence. "One of *my* former colleagues in London believed he saw the face of the Virgin Mary on a piece of toast, yet I remain quite unconvinced."

As she'd hoped, the sergeant chuckled.

"Obviously, if you have evidence to prove that Mr Winter is a fascist himself, then I shall have to change my views. However, I shall be most surprised, given my own dealings with him, and the testimony of the children billeted with me. They describe him as a remarkable teacher: kind, principled and enlightened, far from the kind of brute who would be willing to betray this country. They've also explained exactly what he does when he's out walking in the woods, and I have actual evidence, not mere idle gossip or rumour, to corroborate their story."

She pulled a book out of her bag and laid it on the desk.

"What's this?" The sergeant picked the book up and perused the cover with a frown before flicking quickly through the pages.

"It's a guide to orienteering. That's what he does in the woods. He sets up trails for the children and they race in teams to the various checkpoints using a compass and map to navigate. He borrowed this book from the library a few weeks ago; I checked out the loan myself, so I can testify that what the children have said is true."

"I've never heard of this 'orienteering' business," Constable Todd mumbled, reading over the sergeant's shoulder.

"Neither had I until Mr Winter borrowed the book. But it's popular in Sweden, I believe. And in these troubled times, I can appreciate that teaching children how to read maps and work together to navigate terrain could be valuable skills for later life. We can only hope that the war will end before they're of an age to be called upon to use those skills in military service."

She paused and gestured towards a chair. "Now, I shall wait here while you speak to Mr Winter. I'm sure he will be able to supply further information with regard to the orienteering, should you need it. Unless you have any other concerns – and actual evidence – relating to his character, I shall offer him a lift back to the vicarage. My sister will have telephoned Reverend Appleton to explain the situation by now. Feel free to hold on to the book for as long as you need it, but I'd be grateful if you could return it to the library when you're done."

The two men looked at each other helplessly.

"I'm not sure it's a good idea for you to wait, Miss Fitznorton," Todd said, frowning.

Dodie sat down with her bag on her lap and pulled out a

novel she had picked up at the library. "It's no trouble," she replied airily. "I'm sure an officer of your experience can deal with the administrative aspects of Mr Winter's release quite quickly. In any case, I'm in no hurry. I can read while I'm waiting."

She opened the novel and turned to the first page, although the words seemed to dance across the paper and it was impossible to focus. It was a relief to sit down: her knees were threatening to sag now that she'd done what she'd set out to do. All she could do now was hope that the orienteering manual would cast doubt over the allegations surrounding Mr Winter. While the policemen muttered in the corner and flicked through its pages, she kept her expression neutral and, she hoped, unconcerned, as if there could be no possibility of her being sent away with her quest unfulfilled.

After a couple of minutes, the sergeant once again vanished around the corner, leaving Todd at the desk. Ignoring him, she turned the page of the novel as if she was actually reading it, even though she hadn't managed to absorb a single word.

Now that she'd had a moment to catch her breath, she realised she was feeling quite pleased with herself. Under normal circumstances she would never have dreamed of arguing with the authorities as she had just done, or of exploiting her connections so shamelessly. Still, given the stakes for Mr Winter, a little polite rebellion was surely justified.

At work, she hated confrontation and had found over the years that there was little point in voicing her opinions, as her male colleagues would generally ignore or sneer at them. She was always on the back foot, lower paid and left to languish in a junior role, overtaken for promotion by less competent, younger men, and advised that her progression was less important because she would never be the breadwinner in a household. More than once, a man had taken the credit for one of her timidly expressed ideas, leaving her frustrated but impotent to do anything about it. Mr Gibson wasn't as bad as her colleagues in London had been, but he still had an annoying habit of patronising her and didn't always consider her ideas with the respect she felt they deserved.

This evening, though, she hadn't been cowed. She hadn't held back but had dealt a blow for common sense and justice. She allowed herself to feel a faint glow of pride.

Minutes ticked by, and the warm glow in her breast began fading. What would she do if the police remained unconvinced? She was out of ideas now. She pictured Michael's expression if she had to report that the teacher he saw almost as a hero was still in police custody. Her empty stomach growled, reminding her that she hadn't eaten since her lunchtime sandwich. But this hollow feeling felt like discouragement, more than a lack of food.

A movement in the corner of her vision intruded upon her reverie, making her fumble and almost drop the book from her lap.

"You're free to go with Miss Fitznorton now, Mr Winter, but be sure to let us know if you plan to leave Pontybrenin," the sergeant said, his tone implying he still had reservations about Mr Winter's innocence. "We'd appreciate it if you would call in every week with your registration card."

Dodie jumped up and tucked the novel back into her bag. Mr Winter stood as straight and tall as ever, but his brown hair was dishevelled, as if he'd been dragging his fingers through it, and the purple smudges under his eyes were dark, like the stubble across his jaw. He was staring at her as if he hardly dared believe she was there.

"Would you like a lift to the vicarage, Mr Winter?" The strange, fluttering sensation in her chest was back. She thanked the policemen and led the way to the door, her senses alert to the man following behind.

Outside, she rummaged distractedly for the car key in her

bag, talking nineteen to the dozen to cover her sudden attack of nerves. "Are you alright, Mr Winter? The children will be so pleased to hear you've been released. Do be careful, it's rather dark with so much cloud obscuring the moon."

He murmured thanks and sank into the passenger seat, while she used a torch to find the ignition and start the engine. Its beam illuminated his face only briefly, throwing shadows under his angular cheek bones and chin before she extinguished it and tossed it back into the glove compartment.

He remained silent while she drove, which came as a relief given that navigating the streets between the police station and the vicarage's narrow lane required all her concentration. When at last she drew the car up outside the church and killed the engine, there was an awkward pause.

"I'd like to thank you," he said, at the exact moment she asked again if he was alright.

"Sorry," he said softly. "You first."

"I just... I just wanted to say how sorry I am that you've had so much trouble today. The children were terribly upset on your behalf. I was shocked to hear that suspicion had been cast upon you."

"Miss Summerill did warn me that I'd likely made an enemy of Miss Honeycutt. I was so keen to ignore the rest of the nonsense she spoke that I was probably too quick to disregard that advice."

"Oh, my. Do you think the headmistress reported you?"

He shrugged, looking too weary to care.

"Please don't think we're all so quick to imagine the worst of you. You've made such a positive impression on the children. I hope you won't let today colour your feelings about staying here?"

In the confined space of the car, it would be easy to reach across and touch his hand. She wanted to, but of course such an intimacy was out of the question. Instead, she laced her fingers together in her lap and hoped with all her might that he wouldn't go back to London – for the children's sake, she told herself.

"Miss Fitznorton – would you please allow me to thank you for what you've done for me today? Might I take you out to dinner tomorrow, to show my appreciation?"

Her mouth fell open in surprise. "There's no need," she said, immediately wanting to kick herself. Dinner with him might actually be rather pleasant. "I only mean to say, Pontybrenin isn't exactly teeming with nice restaurants. There's only the Station Hotel, which is rather run down and rumoured to have mice; or Contadino's café, which offers tasty food, but very simple. It won't be up to the standards you'll have been used to in London or New York."

"The cinema, then? There's a movie I'd like to see, and I'd find it much more enjoyable with company."

For the first time, Dodie was thankful for the blackout. It meant he couldn't see the rush of colour in her cheeks.

"Please don't feel obliged," she murmured, for the sake of politeness. Given his previous coolness it was hard to believe he might want to spend an evening with her. She wouldn't want to be asked out of nothing more than a sense of duty.

In the darkness, she heard him take in a ragged breath. His voice came out husky. "That police station was small. I could hear every word you said to those policemen. *No one* has *ever* gone to as much trouble for me as you have done this evening."

"Oh."

"I've been to your house after dark, remember. It must have taken courage for you to drive out here in the blackout and speak up on my behalf. You could easily have done nothing. But you know the thing I'm most grateful for is that you had faith in my integrity when it seems many others didn't."

Dodie blinked rapidly. "Then, thank you. I'd be pleased to

accompany you to the cinema," she said, her voice catching in her throat in response to his suppressed emotion.

"Shall we meet outside the Rialto at six? And if we're hungry after the movie, pie and chips at Contadino's."

It gave her a pop of pleasure to hear a smile in his voice.

"I'll look forward to it. Please don't ever repeat this in front of Dolly Griffiths, but the pies in Contadino's are the best I've ever tasted. It sounds like a perfect evening."

THIRTY-ONE

Dodie

Meeting Mr Winter after work, thereby avoiding the inconvenience of returning to Plas Norton and coming back out in the blackout, unfortunately meant that Dodie would have to wear her work clothes. Still, it wasn't as if she needed to make a favourable impression. He hadn't invited her out because he harboured any romantic feelings towards her. It would be silly to imagine that. It was only that he felt grateful to her for helping him deal with the police.

Nevertheless, she had dressed with extra care that morning, choosing a smart dress of plum-coloured wool that complemented the rich brown of her hair. Tiny pleats down the bodice ended just below her bust, and the padded shoulders and nipped-in, belted waist flattered her figure. A fresh application of powder and lipstick just before she left the library earned her a disapproving glare from Mr Gibson, but she was gratified to see that her appearance had the opposite effect on Mr Winter, who was waiting in the cinema foyer with two tickets when she arrived.

"I got us tickets for *Goodbye, Mr. Chips*," he said. "I hope you won't mind watching a movie about a curmudgeonly teacher."

His grey eyes twinkled, and she smiled to acknowledge the irony before sending a defiant glare towards a couple who had nudged and whispered on seeing them together. Let them gossip as much as they wanted: Mr Winter had nothing to hide, and she wasn't ashamed to be seen on his arm, although of course it wasn't a date as such.

"How are you today?" she asked in a low voice. He looked much better now that he was freshly shaven and rested, but she guessed his hours in the police station must have taken a toll.

"I'm well, thanks to your intervention."

Her senses seemed heightened as she took the seat next to his in the auditorium. She sank into the plush velvet, relishing the spark of excitement when the scalloped satin curtain rose to reveal the opening titles of the film. It was difficult to concentrate all her attention on the screen, however, with Mr Winter so close beside her.

Now and then, she stole glances at him. Could he relate in any respect to the naïve and nervous young teacher on-screen? It was difficult to imagine the granite-hard Mr Winter ever being anything but formidable in front of a class. The stern demeanour she'd perceived in their initial encounters was at odds with the kindness described by Michael and the other children, but she had to acknowledge that their respect and affection for him seemed well-earned. As her negative impressions had faded, her awareness had grown that he was just as handsome as the actor in the film.

She chuckled wryly along with the rest of the audience at the romantic scenes, touched by the change wrought in Mr Chips by his love for his vibrant younger wife. When the woman died in childbirth, Dodie was caught unprepared.

Choked, she fumbled in her bag for her handkerchief, then dabbed discreetly at her eyes. How embarrassing it would be for her companion to witness her sudden outpouring of emotion. But just as she started to think she'd managed to hide her tears, he laid a hand over hers and squeezed it.

She hadn't expected his sympathy. Fresh tears brimmed; she swallowed them down and nodded to let him know she was once again in control. When he removed his hand from hers, she found herself wishing he hadn't. It had warmed her to know he cared. Her fingers flexed, as if they missed the physical contact. It had been months since a man touched her; she couldn't even remember one looking at her with such sensitivity. It would be too easy to misconstrue his kindness for something more... She must be careful to keep a grip on herself.

After the screening ended, they remained seated until most of the rest of the audience had trooped out of the auditorium.

He cleared his throat. "Given the way people have been staring at us, I'll understand if you'd rather not go to Contadino's with me."

She hesitated, unsure how he wanted her to respond. Was this a polite excuse to get out of spending any longer in her company? But his troubled frown suggested his concern was genuine.

She usually had so little fun in her life, it seemed ludicrous to allow baseless rumours to curtail a rare opportunity for it. Surely the best way to dampen down gossip would be to ignore it?

"People will think whatever they want to think, won't they? And besides, my niece says that accompanying a suspected spy on an evening out is the most interesting thing I've ever done. I'd hate to pass up a chance to impress her. Unless... well, unless you'd prefer to call it a night, of course."

"Heck, no. I'm famished," he replied at once.

She was gratified to see his features relax. How had she ever thought him hard and cold?

They walked the short distance to Contadino's café, her hand tucked in the crook of his arm as they carefully followed the edge of the pavement under the dim light of the rising moon.

"I'm sorry the movie upset you. I hope it wasn't a poor choice on my part?"

She shook her head, then realised he might not have seen. Somehow, the darkness gave her the confidence to speak freely. "It's not your fault. I hope I didn't embarrass you by turning on the waterworks. It's only that it reminded me of my mother. If she hadn't given birth to me, she might still be alive today. And I'll never know if… if she felt that bringing me into the world was too great a price to pay for losing her own life. There's always the fear that I might be a disappointment to her. That if she'd had the choice, she might have preferred to live on, instead of giving life to me."

"That sounds like a heavy burden to bear. No wonder the story touched a nerve. If it's any comfort, I'm sure that if she could see you now, she'd be proud of you. You should never feel a moment's doubt about that after everything you've done for your evacuees, and after what you did for me yesterday."

It was impossible to know how Rosamund might have felt, but there was no time to dwell further on her heartache, for they had reached their destination. Mr Winter held the door of the café open for her, and she slipped inside past the heavy curtain that blocked light from spilling onto the street.

"Ah, Miss Fitznorton. *Buonasera*. It's a pleasure to see you this evening. And your friend, of course."

Johnny Contadino smiled as if she was a long-lost friend and directed them to a table. The handsome, raven-haired nephew of the proprietors, who'd arrived in Pontybrenin from Italy several years ago, handled their order smoothly and efficiently. He moved between the gingham-topped tables like an eel through water, remembering each customer's order without needing to write it down, and exerting effortless charm. Dodie suspected it wasn't only the deliciousness of the Contadinos' own-recipe ice cream that drew Loulou to visit the café every week whenever she was at home.

The café was cosy, with a coal-fired stove radiating heat, and mirrors behind the mahogany counter reflecting a warm yellow glow back into the large room. A courting couple sat in a corner, holding hands across the table, their heads close as they murmured confidences. In the back room beyond, a small group of men had gathered to smoke and discuss politics. Italian flags and framed pictures of Roman statues and ruins decorated the walls, but Dodie knew the menu was resolutely British. Few of the Contadinos' customers would be willing to eat anything more exotic than a macaroni pudding.

"This pie is good," Mr Winter said, tucking in with relish.

He wasn't wrong. Light pastry was filled with generous chunks of ham hock in a creamy sauce with leeks. It was easy to see why Contadino's had a reputation for hearty food.

"What did you think of the film?" Dodie asked in between mouthfuls.

"It was a little sentimental, perhaps, but I enjoyed it. I hope to retire before I reach quite such a ripe old age as Mr Chips, of course."

"At the end, when Mr Chips says he hasn't been lonely because his career has given him thousands of children... I found that quite poignant, given that his own child died along with his poor wife. He would so obviously have made a good father."

Mr Winter chewed thoughtfully, then dabbed at his mouth with his napkin before responding. "I guess he would. It's sad that some people who deserve to be parents don't get the chance, when there are others less deserving who make a hash of it."

"It is rather tragic, isn't it? I've no way of knowing how well my parents would have done. My father was an influential man in Pontybrenin, but no one apart from my sister Charlotte seems to speak of him with affection."

"Don't you remember him?"

She shook her head. "He passed away suddenly a few months before I was born. It came as a terrible shock to Charlotte, I gather. She knew him well, being so much older. My mother was her stepmother, but hardly anyone I know remembers her well. Charlotte talks about the past so rarely I suspect it pains her. But that's enough about me. What about your parents? Were you close to your father?"

His mouth twisted as if he'd found a piece of gristle in his pie. "I was not. In fact, if I ever have children of my own, he'd be the last person I'd look to as an example."

She laid down her knife and fork. "Was he really so bad?"

"Oh, yeah. He absolutely was. Let's not talk about him. Some things are best left in the past."

There was no reason why he should confide in her, of course. They barely knew each other. But instinct told her he needn't worry about following his father's example. She repeated his own phrase back to him. "If it's any comfort, I'm sure that you'd be a good father. Based on what your pupils have said about you."

Touchingly, colour daubed his cheekbones. "Thank you. That is some comfort. It means a lot to know I have their respect."

"Peter has started to behave a little better recently. I've taken your advice to heart and keep looking for opportunities to catch him being good. Yesterday, he even helped to tidy up without being asked."

"That's gratifying to hear. Being on the receiving end of

kindness and away from his pa's influence can only be a good thing."

Pleased, Dodie nodded. "Even Charlotte has noticed a difference, and she has very little to do with the children if she can possibly help it."

"If you don't mind me asking, what's your beef with your sister? I get the sense you don't like her very much."

Dodie stiffened and took a sip of her cup of tea before answering. "She sent me away to boarding school when I was only four years old. I hated it there. She kept the twins, but I suppose I was surplus to requirements."

He frowned. "She'd only just been widowed when the twins came along, right? From what I recall her telling me, in the space of – what, a year? – her job running the hospital ended, she gained and lost a husband, and carried and birthed two kids. That's a heck of a lot for anyone to deal with. Must have been a tough time for all of you."

"It was certainly a tough time for me, being uprooted like that. Abandoned, in effect."

He reached a hand across the table and covered hers. His eyes were so expressive. It was as if he understood all of it. Not only the things she had said, but those she didn't have the words to express.

"It's hard to let go of the hurt little kid inside of you, isn't it?"

Somehow, she tore her eyes from his and gave a small nod. It helped, knowing he didn't judge her. But his comments about Charlotte made her feel a little ashamed. She'd been so caught up in her own bitter memories, she'd never actually thought how Charlotte's experience must have been all those years ago. In her heart she had to acknowledge that Patrick was right: they'd both had more than their fair share of pain.

She was sorry when the time came to leave, but she couldn't afford to miss the last bus to Bryncarreg, where Ivor had offered to meet her with the car. Mr Winter held her coat while she shrugged her arms into it, and as she fastened the buttons, she noticed him hand something over to Johnny. A generous tip, judging by the way the young man's face lit up.

Outside, they took a few moments to allow their eyes to readjust to the darkness, standing in a companionable silence gazing up at the stars. He must have sensed her shiver against the chill of the November air, as he moved closer and offered his arm.

"I've had a lovely evening, Mr Winter. Thank you," she said, when they reached the bus stop.

"So have I. But do you think we can dispense with the formality of surnames now that you've rescued me from a prison cell and I've made you suffer a movie that reduced you to tears? Could you bring yourself to call me Patrick? Being addressed as Mr Winter makes me feel like I'm at work."

She wished there was enough light to see his smile.

"Of course. Patrick it is. And I'm Dodie. Or Josephine. I answer to either." She hugged her arms around herself, realising she was babbling.

From the junction on the corner came the distinctive rumble of the approaching bus, its headlights almost blanked out by the regulation blackout shades.

"Your niece is wrong, by the way, Dodie."

"Is she?" Her voice came out as a little more than a whisper. How had his voice made her name sound so much lovelier than usual?

"Sure. And so is anyone who tells you you're not the most interesting woman in town. Any man would be proud to step out with you on his arm. Thank you for a wonderful evening. Thank you for everything."

The bus was already drawing to a halt to disgorge a couple of passengers, and Dodie moved aside to allow them the space to orient themselves on the pavement before she climbed onto the vehicle's step.

"Goodbye," she said. She was on the point of turning away to hand over her ticket when, to her surprise, Patrick pressed a fleeting kiss onto her cheek.

"Evening, miss," the conductor said, distracting her as the bus jolted into motion again.

She stumbled into a seat and pressed her fingertips to her face. It tingled where his lips had touched it.

All the way to Bryncarreg, she gazed at her own dim reflection in the window of the bus and wondered if Patrick's eyes were shining like hers. Did he, too, wish he'd been bold enough to kiss her lips, not only her cheek? Had he meant anything by it, or had he only done it to be polite? Maybe it was the American custom for a man to kiss a woman's cheek at the end of a pleasant evening. If so, he had probably gone on his way without giving it a second thought.

The thrilling jolt she'd felt when his mouth was momentarily close to hers reminded her of how it had been in the heady days with Lionel before it all went wrong. The way her body could melt from the heat of a smouldering glance and a daring caress. The yearning to be touched and kissed; to explore every plane of his body.

You're a nasty little cock-tease. Acting like a slut, leading me on and then leaving me dangling. Everyone will believe we did it, anyway. She could hear Lionel's words as if he were still sneering at her. She'd risked her reputation by agreeing to go to his hotel room but then angered him by getting cold feet. She'd come so close to giving in, driven by longing to have endearments whispered into her ear by a man whose breath was hot against her shoulder and whose lips could blaze a trail down her throat. Fear of a baby had stopped her, when his hands roved past her stockings over the skin at the top of her thigh and pushed under the thin barrier of her panties. She supposed she'd deserved his disgust, but not to be made the subject of office gossip.

She had better resist her desires and ignore the things she'd unexpectedly found she liked about Patrick. He seemed to be a man of integrity, but then Lionel had fooled her at first. If she allowed herself to fall for Patrick, she couldn't bear to upend her life again if he, too, rejected her. Not now, when the children needed her.

THIRTY-TWO

Patrick

Miss Honeycutt's visible disappointment at seeing him back at school was some consolation to Patrick after his brief but frightening sojourn in the Pontybrenin police station. Miss Bright, at least, had the grace to look shamefaced, confirming his suspicions that she had been the one to start the rumour about him being in league with fascists. He remembered that she'd been at the bus stop when Miss Summerill made her indiscreet remarks. No doubt she'd taken the opportunity to gossip with the headmistress afterwards. It seemed he'd dangerously underestimated the consequences of directly challenging their attitude to the evacuees, and of using his acquaintance with Dodie Fitznorton's family to force a change.

Perhaps he'd been naïve in believing they would recognise him as a man of integrity, given British people's customary suspicion of anyone foreign. He should have grown accustomed to it by now, as his inability to lose his New York drawl had frequently caused him problems. Ever since he and his mother returned from America, he'd been particularly conscious of prejudice against the Irish, which had worsened after the recent bombings. It was impossible to be unaware of it, when so many Londoners turned up their noses at his mother's Kilkenny accent. But being accused of having an allegiance to organisations he despised had hurt more than he cared to admit. He understood the desire of many people in Northern Ireland for freedom from British rule, of course he did. But what had that to do with the innocent people in London or Southampton or Coventry who'd been hurt or killed in recent months? Bombings seemed a cowardly way to fight; he hated that anyone could have thought him capable of supporting such despicable tactics.

When his alarm clock sounded that morning, he hadn't been sure if he had the stomach to go into school and face the two women who had so nearly caused him to be handed over to the British Secret Services. Yet, somehow, he'd assumed a professional demeanour along with his suit and tie. He succeeded in ignoring the way his stomach churned, preventing him from eating any breakfast. As the morning progressed, though, his nerves had settled. He couldn't dwell on his own problems when faced with a room full of children who had been wrenched from their families and homes. Although many of them seemed to have adjusted remarkably well, there were a few, including Olive and Peter Hicks and Michael Clarke, who caused him sleepless nights. And as for Eva Fischer, having to leave her entire family behind in Czechoslovakia... Nothing he'd had to deal with could equal that kind of trauma.

Arrangements at school were still far from ideal, but he was determined to make them work. With the weather turning cold and often wet, it wasn't always possible now to send the children out into the woods to run off their energy; and besides, he'd lost some of his enthusiasm for setting up orienteering courses since it had brought him such unwelcome attention.

It had been a week of emotional ups and downs: he was still in a daze of disbelief that Dodie had exerted herself so far on his behalf; he'd previously believed she didn't even like him. When he'd heard her cut-glass British voice ring out in his defence, he'd wanted to seize her by the hand and run away with her. Her unexpected arrival had aroused a relief so fierce he'd pressed his forehead to the bars hard enough to leave marks, rapt to hear every syllable.

She had no idea how marvellous she was. Before that evening he'd seen her gentleness with Olive, and the sweetness of her smile in that unguarded moment in the library. Now that he'd started to get to know her, and to understand some aspects of her past, he was eager to learn more. He'd like to know all there was to know. Her sadness during the film had made him wish he could take her in his arms and kiss her tears away, instead of just holding her hand. Then, when he'd understood the reason for her distress, his heart had ached for her.

And she was a patient listener, easy to talk to. Once or twice he'd had to stop himself telling her more about his past than he was ready for anyone to know. He'd felt remarkably relaxed in her company, as if he could simply be himself. Not Mr Winter the teacher, or Mr Winter the evacuee, the unwelcome, foreign stranger; but Pat Winter the ordinary guy who enjoyed the movies and eating dinner with a pretty girl.

During the midday lunch break, the children raced, yelling, about the school yard, skipped with ropes, or stood in huddled knots against the grey stone walls. Patrick had been meaning to speak to Peter Hicks ever since his conversation with Dodie at the jumble sale; this looked like an ideal opportunity. Beckoning the boy over to a discreet corner of the yard from whence he could watch over the other children, he stuck his hands in his trouser pockets and sent the lad a quick hint of a smile to make himself appear slightly less intimidating.

"How are you enjoying life at Plas Norton, young Peter?"

The boy shrugged, his expression guarded. "It's alright, sir, I s'pose."

"That's good to hear. You've fallen on your feet, having other kids to play with, and being with your sister. And having that great big house and garden to play in must be fun. Not to mention Mrs Griffiths' cooking: I've tasted it, and it's pretty darn good."

Peter pursed his lips, avoiding any eye contact.

"I'll come clean with you. Miss Fitznorton asked me to have a quiet word in your ear. She's worried about you, you know."

That made the boy look up. "She isn't. She hates me. They all hate me. And I hate them, too."

"I'm sure that's not true. If she hated you, she could've asked me to punish you further for the upset you caused with the cricket bat. But she specifically told me you'd been punished and to leave that in the past. That seems more than fair."

"Uncle Ivor definitely hates me. And Auntie Dolly does," the boy said, his freckled cheeks aflame. "I've heard them muttering stuff about me in Welsh, thinking I don't know what they're saying – but I've found out. They call me a little devil. And a little pig. That's what *mochyn* means, in case you don't know. They think I'm stupid, but I ain't." He tapped his forehead to reinforce the point.

Patrick maintained his serious expression with an effort, easily able to imagine how Peter could drive Mr and Mrs Griffiths to utter curses. "You're definitely not stupid," he agreed.

"I'm good at picking up on stuff people say, you know. Anyway, it don't make no difference to me what they think. Auntie Dolly's cooking is horrible. And Uncle Ivor's an old woman, if you ask me."

"An old woman?"

"That's what my dad would say. He puffs and pants like a steam train, Uncle Ivor does. Couldn't fight his way out of a paper bag. It's pathetic."

Patrick drew his index finger across his top lip. "Do you

know why Mr Griffiths struggles to catch his breath sometimes? And why he limps? Have you ever asked him?"

"No, course not. I'm not interested anyway."

"Well, I'll let you into a secret. It's probably more interesting than you might expect. Mr Griffiths was injured in a battle. The kind of battle no one had ever seen before, and we must all hope no one will again. He was ready to give his life for his country. For the sake of your generation and mine. He did that when he wasn't much more than a kid himself. Did you know that?"

Peter shook his head, staring at the scuffed toes of his boots.

"I didn't think so. Ivor Griffiths isn't the kind of guy who goes about bragging how great he is. He just gets on with things. But we know he's a hero, don't we?" Patrick paused to let his remark sink in, then changed tack. "You know, I sometimes ask myself this question, given the times we're living in: is there anything you'd be willing to give your life for? Or even to kill for? What answer would you give to that question, Peter?"

"My dad." There wasn't a moment's hesitation. Peter looked up and seemed reassured by Patrick's nod. His wiry shoulders dropped some of their tension. "What about you then, sir?"

"My mom, I guess. And – maybe – all this."

"What – Britain? But you're a Yank."

Patrick's mouth twitched in wry acknowledgement. "I am, born and bred. So I guess you'd think this place wouldn't matter that much to me. But I like the idea that there's a nation where people can speak in their own language, like Mr Griffiths does when he's cross about something, and live decent lives no matter what shade of pink or brown their skin is, or whether they're Christians like us or Jewish like Eva. That kind of freedom matters, wherever we are in the world. I think so, anyway," he added, seeing the boy's frown.

"I s'pose."

"So tell me about your dad then, Peter. He sounds pretty special to you."

"He's big. Not tall, like you, so much, but strong. People don't mess with him. They look at me and say, 'That's Bill Hicks's boy – better watch your mouth.' And he lets me help him."

Patrick's skin crawled; he folded his arms and leaned back against the wall to keep himself steady. His voice came out as measured as before, thankfully. He wouldn't want it to betray his unease. "How do you help him?"

"I wait outside the pub until he comes out with a message for me to carry. I have to remember it, word for word like, and run like the wind to deliver it. Or sometimes, I'll have to take a package instead of a message. I've never been caught, not once. But if I was, I wouldn't give the message to no one I weren't s'posed to. My dad trusts me, see. He says I'm a chip off the old block."

"Sounds like he can rely on you."

"Yeah. He can. And if anyone gives me cheek, I just tell my dad, and I know he'll fix 'em." The boy stood up straighter, his chest out.

Patrick's gut clenched as he thought of his own dad. Out of long habit, he blocked the thoughts before they could take hold in his mind.

"The kids at that farm can still watch out, even though me dad's not here to sort them," Peter went on. "We'll teach them a lesson one of these days."

"Oh? Why so?"

"They've got it coming to 'em, that's all."

Patrick left one of his pauses, directing a frosty, expectant gaze upon the boy.

"For the way they speak to the Clarkes. They ain't done nothing. Michael's alright, you know? I reckon even my dad would say so."

"I think you should do your best to keep out of trouble from now on, don't you? You wouldn't want your parents to worry about you."

"It ain't my fault if people don't like me. That's their problem."

Patrick supposed it was natural for a boy to use bluster as a self-defence mechanism.

"How would you like things to be?" he asked, keen to find out if the boy's energy could be channelled into more positive pursuits than throwing tantrums and upsetting his hosts.

"What d'you mean?" Peter's eyes narrowed.

"I mean, while you're living at Plas Norton, what would you like to do, if you could do anything?"

The answer surprised him. "Well, I'd like to play football. But there ain't much point with only five of us, especially when three are girls. So instead of that, if I could do anything, I'd like to go fishing."

"Really?"

"Yeah. It looks fun. And I'd like to have a go at shooting rabbits and pigeons. For the pot, I mean. Not to hurt them." He sent Patrick a sidelong, wary glance. It was interesting that he didn't want to be seen as cruel. Perhaps there was still hope for him, while he was away from his father's influence.

"Understood. We could speak to Mr Griffiths and see if he'd be willing to teach you."

The boy's face fell. "'He'll just say no."

"Then I guess it's down to you to convince him that he should give you a chance. You could start by asking him nicely. And what else do you think you could do, to help him trust you to behave yourself on a riverbank or with a shotgun? That's a big responsibility, when you think about it."

Glancing at his wristwatch, Patrick gestured to one of the older boys to fetch the hand bell. Peter was frowning hard, as if he were trying to dredge up ideas out of his boots.

"Well, Peter? Have you come up with any ideas? It's almost time to go back inside."

To Patrick's surprise, Peter's face lit up with a delighted grin, as if he were a scientist who had just found the answer to a particularly sticky problem. He rubbed his palms together gleefully, almost bouncing on the spot in his excitement.

"I've got it, sir! Uncle Ivor's planning to make a bigger veggie patch, but he struggles with the digging. I reckon if I offer to help him with that, he'll be like putty in my hands!"

Patrick patted his shoulder. "Knock yourself out, kid. It has to be worth a try."

THIRTY-THREE

Olive

Olive sat cross-legged on the dusty wooden floor of the summerhouse, tucking her skirt under her bottom to avoid getting splinters in her thighs. Her heart seemed to swell as Tyke climbed onto her lap, purring so loudly she could feel the vibrations as strongly as she could hear them.

"Look what I've got for you," she murmured, pulling her handkerchief out of her pocket and opening it to show him the chunks of pork sausage she had smuggled from the breakfast table. He rubbed his chin against her hand, an ecstatic expression on his face, showing his pleasure before tucking in with enthusiasm. She stroked his back while he ate, smiling at the way this made him stick his bottom up in the air, his tail standing up poker straight.

She was getting good at pretending to eat while hiding most of her meat and eggs under the table during each meal. The seemingly infinite supply of food in Auntie Dolly's kitchen, so different from home, enabled her to fill up on bread and butter. The other children helped her, too, by sacrificing some of their own food for the young cat, whose antics frequently made them roll about the summerhouse floor laughing.

"I'll split my sides!" Shirley would exclaim, making them laugh all the more, as Tyke leapt into the air to chase her hair ribbon.

Over the past fortnight, they'd managed between them to bring some warm blankets, a cushion, and an assortment of toys to the summerhouse, including a stick with a ribbon tied onto it, a rubber ball and a small clockwork car. Every day, whether the other children chose to accompany her or not, Olive climbed the hill, called out Tyke's name, and waited in the summerhouse for him to appear. He invariably did before too long, as if he'd been watching and waiting for her to bring him food. The wooden building's poor state of repair meant that there were plenty of gaps for him to squeeze through, and Olive hoped he made use of the nest of blankets during the cold nights.

Tyke was so funny, the way he loved to play. The slightest movement would make him fix his orange eyes on potential prey, ready to pounce. He would wiggle his scrawny hips and gear himself up to attack, whether it was a spider in the corner of the room, a toy, or Olive's fingers tapping under the blanket. She could play gentle games of rough and tumble with him, and he would stalk a short distance away when he'd had enough, his stripy tail swirling in indignation. She felt she understood his expressions: the movement of his tail and the angle of his ears conveyed his mood as readily as his mewling, purring or little chirruping noises of excitement. When she played with Tyke, Olive could forget that she hadn't received any word from her mum in the two and a half months she had been at Plas Norton.

Every day, she checked the table in the hallway to see if a letter had arrived. It had become a painful ritual. Her expectations had been so crushed by day after day of disappointment that she had to acknowledge there was little point now in getting her hopes up. Every letter the Clarkes received with news of their parents and siblings in London was like vinegar in a cut.

She wouldn't give up on Mum, but hope was gradually being replaced by an insidious fear. Mum had never been one for big shows of affection, but it was hard to imagine what could have led her to ignore her own children for so long. Especially Peter, who had always been the special one to both parents, being the boy. Even if Mum had lost interest in her only surviving daughter, there was no way she would want to lose her son.

Something must surely have happened. The not knowing was worse than being away from home. It was worse, even, than the fear of Miss Honeycutt's hard wooden ruler swooping down on Olive's fingers. It was worse than the horrid children from the farm who threw stones and spat at the Clarkes. The not knowing made Olive lie awake at night, her mind racing with terrifying imaginings as she clung to Juliet for comfort.

Dad had hurt Mum in the past. She'd ended up in hospital once when he broke her arm. She'd told Olive and Peter she had fallen down the concrete steps leading to their flat. But Olive knew the scream she'd heard – covering her good ear hadn't been enough to muffle it – had happened after Dad came home from the pub, when Mum had already been in her nightdress and not likely to be out on the stairs.

Had Dad done something even worse since they left? Or was Mum ill? Either might mean she couldn't write. With no way of finding out, Olive felt she was being subjected to a slow, painful inner death, tortured by thoughts until it was hard to feel any joy at all.

She laughed softly as Tyke kneaded her thigh, pressing his paws firmly and rhythmically, almost like a toy soldier marching. His purring vibrated through her fingers as she stroked his back. After a minute or two, she realised he was suckling on her jumper, enough to leave a damp patch. She hoped he wouldn't make a hole in it.

A picture presented itself in her mind, as vivid as it was unexpected, of Mum in her chair, knitting while Olive and Peter played on the rag rug, well back from the fireplace to avoid accidents. The clicking of Mum's knitting needles, rhythmic like Tyke's kneading paws, creating a garment especially for Olive from yarn she'd unravelled from an old jumper of her own, had made her feel special.

When would life return to normal? Nothing was the way it had been before. She missed the London streets, and the way they were rarely quiet. She missed streetlamps, and the rumble of traffic that could always be heard through their window at night. She missed the neighbours, who all knew each other and looked out for each other, the women who scrubbed the area of landing outside the front doors of their flats at the same time each morning, sharing gossip. She missed the calls of the market traders and the shops she'd grown up with. Wales was pretty, that was undeniable, but it wasn't home. Even though Aunt Dodie was kind and generous, she couldn't answer the questions swirling in Olive's head about Mum, and Plas Norton's large and splendid rooms could never feel like a place where she belonged.

It was only a little comforting that Peter seemed at last to have settled. He had started helping Uncle Ivor in the garden and in his workshop, and now they rubbed along well together with hardly a cross word.

Olive also liked Uncle Ivor, of course, and Auntie Dolly was kind enough, although Olive sensed her irritation at the wet sheets each morning. The humiliation of it felt bitter. Stripping the bed down to the rubber sheet and carrying her bedding and nightdress to the laundry room to soak had become a regular routine. She'd tried going without the comforting cup of cocoa which all the other children drank before bed, but it made no difference. Every night she lay awake in the darkness, praying that morning would find her dry, with a letter on the hall table. Every new morning was another blow to her fragile hopes.

Tyke was the only light in her darkness. He, at least, was easy to understand. He loved food; he loved cuddles – for a short while, at least; and he loved to play. After he had eaten and finished zooming around the summerhouse as if someone had wound him up like a clockwork toy, he curled up beside her on the nest of blankets and went to sleep. She rested a hand lightly on his back, her chin drooping as his rhythmic purring lulled her into her own slumber.

THIRTY-FOUR

Dodie

"I'm worried about Olive," Dodie said to Patrick, over a cup of tea at Contadino's café. His invitation to join him there on Saturday afternoon had made her disproportionately excited. It was only tea and cake: silly to read anything into it. He had made few friends in Pontybrenin, what with the nonsensical rumours which still hadn't entirely been dampened as there were always those who claimed there could be no smoke without fire. No doubt he saw her simply as a friendly face, someone who didn't assume the worst of him. He'd think the same of anyone who showed him a little kindness: she mustn't let herself get carried away.

"I've noticed she's pretty quiet. And she fell asleep in one of my geography lessons. I tried not to take it personally." His mouth lifted a little at one corner in one of the small, self-deprecating half-smiles she found she loved looking at.

"Every morning she arrives at the breakfast table looking as if she hasn't slept a wink. And it's even more rare to hear her venture a contribution to the conversation than it was when she first arrived."

"Do you think she hasn't settled?"

Dodie shook her head, using her pastry fork to cut a bite-sized morsel off her slice of Victoria sponge cake. "I think it's the lack of any word from her parents. I've seen her face when Michael reads out letters from his mother."

Patrick frowned. "I can't understand why they still haven't written to her. But Peter's father sounds like some kind of hoodlum. Maybe they're just terrible parents."

"My niece is planning to go back to London next weekend, to join up for the WAAF. Charlotte isn't best pleased about her going, but Loulou has always done exactly as she likes, so there'll be no stopping her now that the idea is in her mind. I'm thinking of going with her and scouting out Olive and Peter's address. Perhaps I might be able to get news, maybe even speak to their mother and persuade her to write..."

Her voice tailed off as she contemplated a visit to the capital. She hadn't been back there since she'd decided to make the final break from Lionel and her office job.

"You aren't proposing to go to Stepney by yourself?" Patrick's objection came as a surprise.

"Well, it isn't a firm plan as such, but I can't just sit here doing nothing when Olive is so clearly unhappy."

He rubbed a long finger across his eyebrow, looking perplexed. "You'd stick out like a sore thumb with your nice clothes and your educated voice. And you don't know the area. How would you find where the Hicks family live?"

Dodie bristled at his assumption that she couldn't fulfil her plan. "I've got a pocket map of the London Underground, so I can make my way to Stepney easily enough. And I could buy one of those new A to Z maps. I'm not a complete country bumpkin, you know. I lived in London for three years."

"In the East End?"

"No, but—"

He cut her off. "I know the area, after living there for thirteen years. Let me go with you."

Her doubts must have shown in her face, for he pressed on, leaning forward as he tried to convince her. "I couldn't sleep at night if I thought there was a chance you might end up encountering Mr Hicks on your own. That man is dangerous, I'm sure of it. The first time I ever met Olive, she'd just been hurt – you'll remember that bruise she had on her lip when she first arrived? She told me she'd walked into a door, even though it was obvious she'd been hit or kicked. Don't tell me she came up with that excuse all by herself. My guess is she must've heard her mother use it before. If Mr Hicks is the type to get nasty with a woman, as I strongly suspect he is, he'll be less likely to get heavy-handed if I'm with you."

She was torn between resentment at the idea that she needed his protection and excitement at the prospect of having his company for the hours it would take them to travel to Stepney and back. "It seems an imposition," she said.

"It's not. It would ease my mind. And if there's time, I could visit my mother. I'd offer to take you with me, but I couldn't expect you to want to visit an Irish boarding house in Whitechapel." He dropped his gaze, fussing with the butter and jam on his scone as if achieving perfectly even layers right to the edge on each half was of vital importance.

Could he be embarrassed at the idea of her meeting his family? Did he really think her such a snob?

Dodie thought quickly, sipping her tea. She wasn't sure whether the police would allow him to return to the capital, where he could contact his Irish connections. Would such a visit go against him, so soon after suspicions were raised about his loyalties? On the other hand, if he could go, it would be reassuring to have his support if she did encounter Mr Hicks. Just the thought of him being with her made her feel better.

"That's settled it, then," she said. "Provided the police say you may, then I'll get tickets for the three of us to travel to Paddington together. We can split up from Loulou there and go east towards the Hicks' address. It will have to be on the Saturday, as we will both need to be back at work on the Monday morning. Hopefully Mr Gibson will allow me to take the day off: I'm certainly owed one."

His grey eyes twinkled in the way she found so appealing. "I'm sure he will. The woman who managed to persuade him to set up a children's area can surely achieve anything she puts her mind to."

THIRTY-FIVE

Patrick

IS YOUR JOURNEY REALLY NECESSARY?

The words shouted from a poster on the station wall, and Patrick noticed how Dodie folded her arms across her chest as she read it, as if she was determined not to let it make her feel guilty for taking this trip to London. Perhaps the Railway Executive Committee wouldn't see it the same way, but Olive and Peter needed to know if there was anything wrong with their parents as a matter of urgency. If letters weren't achieving the desired result, then there was little alternative but to travel. For Patrick, the main advantages of their trip were a chance to spend more time with Dodie and the chance to see his mother for the first time in nearly three months. He knew from her letters that she missed him, and that in spite of his attempts at reassurance, she worried he wasn't eating enough or making friends in Pontybrenin. Hopefully today he'd get an opportunity to put her mind at ease.

Their journey was straightforward between Pontybrenin

and Cardiff, where they were due to change trains. Loulou talked nineteen to the dozen all the way, clearly excited about the prospect of joining the WAAF. She had grand notions about learning to fly and given her love of speeding about the country lanes on her motorcycle, maybe she'd get the chance. Wartime had a way of opening up opportunities. If not for the war, he wouldn't have been evacuated, and if not for being evacuated, he wouldn't have met Dodie. It was strange to be grateful for having his life uprooted and his work disrupted, but getting to know her was making it worthwhile.

The train from Cardiff to London's Paddington station was crowded with soldiers in uniform, who milled about chatting near the doors and filled the carriage with cigarette smoke. Every seat was full, and Patrick, Dodie and Loulou had to squeeze between them to hunt for a space in the carriage. Only one of the soldiers was gentlemanly enough to offer his seat, laughing off his comrades' jesting as he got up.

"Age before beauty, Aunt," Loulou said to Dodie with an impertinent grin that had her raising an eyebrow. Dodie took the seat, though, and Patrick was glad. They'd had an early start, and he wouldn't have wanted her to have to stand all the way to London.

"You can sit on my lap if you like, my lovely," one of the soldiers said to Loulou. Patrick didn't know whether to be shocked or amused by the way she shook out her blonde curls and perched on his knee with a giggle. Soon she was chatting away with him and the other men as if they were old friends. When the soldier offered her a cigarette, she took it eagerly, allowing him to cup her hand with his as he held the match.

Dodie exchanged a glance with Patrick, pursing her lips with a little shrug as if to say, *what can I do?* He nodded in acknowledgement, but inwardly vowed to keep an eye on the soldier in case of any wandering hands. The fellow looked as if all his Christmases and birthdays had come at once, and no wonder. Loulou was a peach. Too immature for Patrick's taste, though. Her reckless abandon had its charm, but to him it suggested a self-centred streak. She was a girl who'd always be looking for the next thrill, heedless of the risks involved or who might get hurt along the way.

Dodie, on the other hand, struck him as a young woman whose fault, if she had one, lay in the opposite direction. She put others' needs before her own desires. He could see it in the way she fretted about Olive and Peter, and the way she'd driven through the darkness to fetch evidence and present it at the police station to help him.

She was beautiful, but it wasn't the kind of beauty that relied upon a symmetry in the features, an elegant figure, or the smoothness of skin or hair. She had those, but hers was a tender, more fragile sort of beauty, based on a core of kindness. That resolute streak of generosity in her reminded him a little of his ma, whose neighbours were often calling by when in need of something, whether a word of encouragement, a cup of sugar or some sage advice. The Clarke and Hicks kids had fallen on their feet by getting to stay with Dodie Fitznorton, no mistake about it. Kids needed to know someone cared enough to go out of their way for them, whether by listening or by showing them things, or doing things for them, or offering words of affection. And not only kids... but if he had any sense, he'd stop his thoughts heading off in that direction.

As the train trundled on, it seemed to pick up more passengers than it disgorged at every station. The conductor struggled to make his way through the carriage to check tickets. Despite the cold outside, which had fogged up the windows, the smoky air in the carriage had grown humid and even more unpleasant, catching in Patrick's throat and making his eyes sting.

After an hour and a half standing in one place, hanging on to the headrest of the seat beside him to stay upright against the motion of the train, Patrick's feet were sore in his cheap shoes, and his back ached. Even Loulou had quietened somewhat, as if bored now. Perhaps sitting on a strange man's lap had proved less comfortable than expected. Dodie had seemed absorbed in a book, but now she closed it and sent a little beckoning gesture Patrick's way.

"Why don't you take my seat?" she said, raising her voice to be heard over the hubbub of chatter.

He shook his head at once. He'd feel like a heel making her stand.

Loulou was watching. "He's such a gentleman, Dodie. How sweet, letting you sit all the way. I hope you're not suffering too badly up there, Patrick?"

He sent her a polite wave in reply, hoping Dodie would be convinced.

It was obvious from her frown that she wasn't. She tucked her book into her bag and stood up, gesturing for him to take her seat.

"Thanks, but there's no need. Stay there— Hey, what are you doing? Sit back down before someone else takes your seat."

She had come to stand beside him. "It was kind of you to let me sit, but I can't possibly force you to stand all the way. I insist you take it."

It seemed she could be stubborn. Well, she'd soon learn he was as strong-willed as the proverbial mule when there was a point of principle at stake.

Loulou rolled her eyes. "Honestly, you two. The answer is staring you in the face. Patrick, take the seat or she'll never shut up about it. Dodie, sit on his lap. It isn't all that uncomfortable, is it?" she added, addressing the soldier whose lap she'd been perching on.

"It's more than fine by me," the soldier replied, making her giggle again.

Patrick hesitated. His aching body pleaded with him to

agree, but Dodie's cheeks had turned pink in a rather fetching blush. What if she hated the idea of sitting on his knee?

"Oh, for heaven's sake! If you don't hurry up, *I'll* take the seat and then you'll *both* have to stand," Loulou exclaimed.

"Would you mind?" Patrick asked Dodie in a low voice.

A gleam in her eye suggested she could see the funny side of their situation. "Go on, then," she said. "But if you find me too heavy, say, and I'll take my turn standing."

He sank gratefully onto the seat, almost holding his breath when she smoothed down her skirt and perched awkwardly on his knee.

"Are you alright?" he asked, his senses ratcheting up as the train jerked and she shuffled a little closer to steady herself.

"Yes, I'm fine thank you." She was looking down at her hands in her lap as if she was trying to appear prim and proper, but he could just make out the corner of her mouth twitching, all the more so when he spotted Loulou sending her a delighted wink.

He sat awkwardly at first, unsure where to put his hands, hoping his body wouldn't betray the desire that sparked at the scent of her perfume, like flowers, and the softness of her hair whispering past his face when she turned her head. It smelled faintly of rosemary: fresh and clean.

"You don't look very comfortable. Sit back if you like," he said, after a while.

"Well... only if you're sure." Her lashes fluttered down and he sucked in his breath, feeling an overpowering wish that he could kiss the corner of her shy smile as she slid her hips higher up his thighs.

He couldn't stop looking at her, taking in every detail as if he could store them in his memory. The smoothness of her complexion; the gentle curve of her cheekbone and jaw; the sweep of her lashes and the elegant line of her brow. The delicacy of her earlobe, with her tiny earring of freshwater pearl. It was a wonder her throat didn't burn from the scorching gaze he sent travelling across it, all the while longing to use his lips instead of his eyes. Would she arch her neck and close her eyes in surrender if he did? If they were alone, would she feel the same consuming urge that he felt, to nuzzle, to taste, to inhale? His breathing had quickened; inwardly he chided himself.

He shouldn't let his thoughts run in that direction. She was far, far above him. He'd known it all along, of course, given that the first time he saw her she was descending a staircase that wouldn't be out of place in a castle. At the police station, he'd had a further reminder that she was a woman of standing in the local area, with influential connections. She'd told him herself that her old man was powerful. People like the Fitznortons, with their crumbling mansions and sleek, racy cars, thought they were poor when they were down to their last ten thousand in the bank.

But he and his mother had known the unrelenting, crushing fear of not knowing how they'd pay the next month's rent. Of going hungry now and then, or eating the same dull bread and scrape for days in order to meet the next bill. If it hadn't been for kindly old Father O'Leary seeing his potential and helping him complete his schooling, he'd never have become a teacher. It was a respectable job, but still it would be safest to remember that Josephine Fitznorton was out of his league. It didn't matter that she referred to herself as a lowly library assistant, or that she seemed to prefer to stay unnoticed in the background of any situation. Everything about her, from her shoes to the cut of her clothes and the elegance of her voice screamed quality.

"I can stand if I'm making you uncomfortable," she offered, sending a sidelong glance towards him that turned into something more intense as her beautiful hazel eyes seemed to lock onto his. He was faintly aware of her lips parting, as if she'd intended to say more but was as transfixed as he, drinking him in as he was her. For the sweetest moment, everything and everyone else in the carriage was forgotten.

"I'm not uncomfortable," he answered, when at last he could rouse himself to respond with something sensible. His voice came out hoarse, and no wonder: his throat had gone dry with longing. "In fact, I gotta level with you. I could sit like this all day."

His heart was thumping. Had he said too much? If she only saw him as a friend, she'd probably be mortified. She'd avoid him like the plague from now on.

But no. She leaned back, her body feeling dangerously good where it fitted against his. Her hand dropped to her side, coming to rest lightly over his, making his own fingers quiver at the unexpected contact.

"Me, too," she said.

THIRTY-SIX

Dodie

It was strange, being back in London. Dodie had forgotten the hectic busyness of it. Everyone was in a hurry, frowning and absorbed in their own thoughts. No one shoved anyone in Pontybrenin, but here it was hardly possible to negotiate the Tube without being bumped into on its grey, sooty platforms and its plunging staircases. It put her nerves on edge.

They bade farewell to Loulou at Baker Street. She had arranged to stay with a friend in St John's Wood for the weekend and would visit the WAAF recruiting office in Victoria when it reopened. No doubt they'd jump at the chance to take on a girl who spoke several languages and was already capable of handling motorcycles and cars. The only question was how Loulou would take to the discipline of military life.

"Let me know how you get on, won't you?" Dodie urged her, enveloping her in a hug and dropping a kiss on her cheek.

"Of course I shall," came the airy response. As she heaved up her suitcase, beaming with excitement at the prospect of new adventures, Loulou sent Dodie a wink. "Enjoy your time alone with Patrick," she said archly, before stepping off the train and vanishing into the crowd.

Dodie turned back to the man in question, hoping he hadn't heard. A faint quirk to the line of his mouth suggested perhaps he had.

"On to Stepney, then, to find Ansbach Mansions." She hoped she sounded more confident than she felt. She'd purchased a pocket-sized A to Z book which claimed to show every street in London, and they'd managed to locate the Hicks' address. Patrick's mouth had tightened noticeably when she pointed to it, his forehead creasing between his brows. He'd said nothing but given that he knew the area, his lack of enthusiasm had made her nervous.

They left the Tube at Shadwell Station and emerged into the foggy semi-daylight of an autumnal London afternoon. Dodie kept close to Patrick's side. This part of the city wasn't like the parts she knew from her years as an office clerk. There were as many horse-drawn carts as there were vans and lorries. A red-painted bus rumbled past, belching fumes.

On this wide street, market stalls displayed a wide range of produce, the traders in their brown overalls and aprons calling out to attract trade. Delivery boys whizzed past on bicycles, ringing their bells as they dodged dogs and pedestrians. On the corner, a shoeshine man plied his trade from a crate. Union Jacks fluttered from the shop fronts, which were surrounded by sandbags and had taped-up windows like the ones back home. Here, though, the names of the shops were more exotic, a reminder that London was the biggest city in the world, attracting people from every part of the globe to try to scratch a living from its streets.

"I'd forgotten how busy London is," she said, keeping her steps long to match Patrick's stride.

"If we'd come on any other day but Saturday, it would be a whole lot busier."

"Oh? Why should Saturday be quiet?"

"It's Shabbat. All the Jewish market traders will be at home or in the synagogue until they go out for a walk on the Whitechapel Road later this afternoon. If you think it's busy now, you should see it then." He paused at the roadside while a van growled past. "Up that way is Cable Street."

He'd said it expectantly, as if she should know it, but she looked blankly back at him.

"A few years ago, this was where the people of the East End joined together and stopped the Blackshirts marching through our streets. They wanted to send a message that the people who live here don't belong. But we showed them." His jaw set hard, as if he was remembering.

"We?" With his voice more redolent of Irish Brooklyn than the East End, it was easy to forget that he was as much a Londoner as he was an American.

He sent her a look that reminded her of the day she first met him, when she'd thought him fierce and hard. "I'm an immigrant, remember. My father was born in the East End, but that's where my right to claim English heritage ends."

She nodded, wary of the defensive undercurrent she sensed beneath his words. Perhaps he, too, was thinking of the difference between their backgrounds. Maintaining a discreet silence, she tucked her hand into the crook of his elbow as they crossed the street and let him steer her around a heap of horse manure.

"Those people – Mosley and his thugs – wanted to take over these streets. They wanted to send a message that it's not our home, and we don't have anything to give to Britain. But they were wrong. It doesn't matter if it's the black merchant seamen like Mr Clarke, who bring in goods, or the Irish and Indian dockers who unload them, or the Jewish family selling them on a market stall. All those people are creating wealth for Britain and her empire. They're just trying to make an honest living. To create a better life for their kids than they've had.

These people will work sixteen hours a day, six days a week in garment factories to feed their families. When you look at these streets, you see hardship and poverty, and I can't deny that those are here in bucketloads. But I see more than that. I see honest toil and determination, and a steel will to make something out of life. And that's the kind of spirit Hitler will never beat. Just like Mosley's fascists couldn't beat it. The East Enders will fight the Nazis on every street corner if they have to."

"You seem very much at home here," she murmured, after a silence in which the passion in his words sank in.

"The East End was my home for half of my life – until September, of course, when I agreed to go out to the country with the children. In some ways, although of course it's very different, this place reminds me of New York. The energy of it. The mix of people from all over the world. There's a vibrancy in both cities that I like."

How could a small town in Wales compete with the excitement of city life? She'd felt it herself when she'd first returned to Pontybrenin: the dullness of it. How small and quiet everything seemed by comparison with the capital. Since she'd come to know Patrick, life had seemed less stultified. If he left Pontybrenin, she'd miss him.

"Will you be sad to leave, when we travel back to Wales this afternoon?"

She almost held her breath.

"Yes and no." He paused and sent her a sidelong glance, the corner of his mouth lifting slightly. "Pontybrenin has its compensations," he added, leaving her to wonder if he was flirting, or if she had inferred too much.

Things would be far easier if she hadn't started to like him quite so much.

They left the wider thoroughfare where the shops and market stalls stood, the streets becoming narrower and foggier. As they turned a corner, a ship could be seen at the end of the road, its funnel taller than the rows of terraced houses lining the cobbled street. These streets looked as poor as the worst she'd seen in Pontybrenin at the height of the Depression, when a third of the men were out of work and many of the women struggled to feed their families. A rat scurried along the gutter, where litter offered rich pickings. In some of the back yards, laundry hung limply on washing lines, but it was hard to imagine how it could dry out in the damp, smoggy air.

At last they reached Ansbach Mansions. Its name made it sound like an elegant Georgian relic, a corner of continental Europe come to bring a cosmopolitan air to London's foggy heart, but Dodie paused outside, her heart sinking. How had quiet, gentle Olive come from this unwelcoming tenement block built of red brick dulled by smog, with its hard concrete steps and iron railings? A baby was crying somewhere inside, its plaintive wails going unanswered. Ignoring the curious stare of an old woman who rocked to and fro on the bottom step, huddled into a shawl against the cold, they climbed the stairs to the third floor. Above their heads, mould and mildew clouded the ceiling. They checked the numbers on the doorways until they found the flat they sought.

Unlike its neighbours, this front door was grimy. The frosted glass pane was dirty and the step worse. Not a sound came from within. Patrick rattled the letterbox a couple of times, then rapped on the glass with his knuckles. Dodie's muscles were tense as she strained to hear any sound of movement from inside. Nothing.

Patrick bent to peer inside through the letterbox, then called through it. "Mrs Hicks, are you there?"

Dodie jumped as the front door of the next-door neighbour's flat opened. A woman appeared, her bosom covered with a pinafore apron, her hair hidden by a headscarf. It was hard to determine her age: she could have been anywhere between forty and sixty, her heavy-jowled face lined and careworn.

"Looking for Mrs Hicks, are you?" She folded broad arms across her chest and regarded them belligerently. Her own front door gleamed, the step freshly scrubbed, the letterbox polished and the glass shiny.

"We are. I'm Miss Fitznorton. Her children Olive and Peter are staying at my home in Wales." Dodie held out her hand, but the other woman ignored it, raking her and Patrick with a stare like a burn.

"She's not here. She hasn't been here for weeks." The woman turned away, ready to close the door behind her.

"Oh, please – wait just a moment. The children are anxious, you see. They can't understand why their mother hasn't replied to any of their letters. Look, I have a photograph. I brought it to give to Mrs Hicks." Dodie pulled a brown envelope from her bag and opened it to show the woman a picture of the children.

The woman's brown eyes softened a little. "They look like they've grown already. The lad's too much like his father, if you ask me, but Olive's a sweet little thing."

"They're desperate for news. We just want to see their mother, so that we can reassure them that she's well."

"I don't know that she is. Like I said, I ain't seen her."

"What about Mr Hicks?" Patrick asked. "Has he gone, too?"

The woman raised an eyebrow, her lips pursed together. "Oh, he's still living here alright. Moved his fancy piece in for a couple of weeks, 'til she got fed up of him knocking her about and slung her hook."

"Perhaps if we wait, we could speak to him. Do you know what time he's due home?" Dodie asked, desperation making her clutch at straws. Given everything she'd heard about him, she had no desire to meet Mr Hicks. But it seemed he might be the only person who could tell them what they needed to know.

"Look, dear. I can see you mean well. But if I were you, I wouldn't be hanging round here to speak to the likes of him.

Even if he knows where she is, I don't suppose he'd tell you. Leastways, not a truthful answer."

Dodie's face must have shown what she was feeling. Her shoulders slumped. They'd come all this way, and it was for nothing. She'd have to go back to face the children and tell them their mother was missing. The thought of it made her throat hurt with unshed tears. "We'll have no choice but to try to speak to him," she said. "How else will we have any chance of finding out what's happened to her?"

Patrick was shaking his head slowly, his expression rueful. "I'm not sure that's wise."

"You should listen to your young man, dear. He seems to have a sensible head on his shoulders."

"I can't go back to those children and tell them their mother is missing without doing everything I can to find out whether she's safe." Her voice cracked on the words, and she cleared her throat. "Please." She made one last appeal. "If you don't know where she is, and we can't ask Mr Hicks, who else could we ask? Did she have any other family?"

The woman sniffed and looked up and down the landing, as if it paid to be wary. "She weren't one for saying much, but she did once mention a sister who runs a pub up Bethnal Green way. It had a funny name, starts with a W if I remember rightly."

"Thank you! Thank you so much. Maybe her sister will know where she is," Dodie exclaimed, brightening.

"Do you know which part of Bethnal Green?" Patrick asked.

"Somewhere near St Andrew's Church. I know that much, 'cause my eldest is called Andrew, so it stuck with me. Can't for the life of me remember the name of the pub, though. I daresay it'll come to me later, but..." She shrugged and stepped back, ready to swing the front door closed.

"Thank you," Dodie repeated. "If Mrs Hicks does come

back, would you tell her the children would love to hear from her? And please, let me give you something for your trouble..." She reached into her purse, then held out a couple of florins.

The woman's expression darkened. "Put your money away," she said, before slamming the door in their faces.

"I didn't mean..." Dodie's voice tailed off. She looked at Patrick in dismay.

"I know you didn't." He led her back down the stairs and out into the street. "Come on, don't worry about it. It's only that... Well, people around here don't have much, but one thing they do have is pride in helping their neighbours."

THIRTY-SEVEN

Patrick

"You can see now why the women of Stepney won their rent strikes," Patrick said, the tension in his shoulders starting to ease once they were well away from Mr Hicks' front door.

Again, Dodie looked puzzled. There was so much about his world that she didn't even know about, let alone understand. It was a sobering reminder that he shouldn't allow himself to get any ideas in that direction. She might like him a little – her demeanour on the train and on their visits to Contadino's suggested she did – but a girl like her wouldn't be interested in anything more than a little light flirtation with a guy like him.

"Rent strikes?" she asked.

"There was a big one last year, but there've been others," he explained, remembering the charged atmosphere around Stepney at the time. "You've seen this morning the kind of places people have to live in. Damp; crowded; cold. Times have been tough, with a lot of men out of work. Paying rent was hard for a lot of people. Landlords don't maintain the buildings as they should, but still have the gall to raise rents and threaten families with eviction. So the neighbourhood decided they'd had enough. The women held firm and the landlords had to back down."

"If they were anything like her, I can understand why the landlords gave in. I wish she'd let me give her that money. I meant her no insult by it, and I'm sure she would have found it useful." Dodie's tone suggested she was still smarting from the woman's abrupt dismissal.

He shrugged. A grumble from his stomach reminded him he needed something to eat before heading across the East End to continue their search. It gave him the perfect way to change the subject and divert her thoughts back to their quest.

"I'm famished," he said, glancing at his wristwatch. "How about lunch before we head to Bethnal Green?"

"I'm hungry too, but don't you think we should go straight there if we're going to fit in a visit to your mother's as well before our train leaves?"

"If we can't visit my mother, then so be it." He'd be disappointed, but given the uncertainty of their schedule he deliberately hadn't built up his ma's hopes by promising to call in. The sight of him with a pretty girl would have stirred up all kinds of speculations which were safest avoided.

Dodie still looked doubtful, so he pressed his case. "I know a café not far from here which will be open. Have you ever tried jellied eels?"

"Jellied eels?" she repeated, her eyes wide.

He bit his lip to hide his amusement and set the pace, almost dragging her along the pavement. "They're considered something of a delicacy in the East End. You can't really come all the way here and not try them."

"Oh, I'm not sure..."

"Come on, I'd hate for you to miss out. What kind of guide to this part of London would I be if I didn't introduce you to the gen-u-ine Cockney experience?" He strung out the word, playing up his American accent and wondering if she'd catch on to the joke. But no, it seemed her good manners meant she didn't dare challenge him directly. It was tempting to see if she'd eat eels to be polite, but by the time they reached the café she looked so perturbed he didn't have the heart to go through with it.

"Is this it?" she asked, her voice reedy with trepidation as he pushed the door open and stood aside for her to precede him.

"Sure is. Go on in, hopefully they'll have a spare table."

He watched as she picked her way across the sawdust-covered floor towards a table with space for two at the back, staring in barely disguised horror at the bowls of pale, greenish jelly and grey-skinned pieces of fish being devoured by other diners. It was the kind of joint he'd been taken to as an occasional treat since he first arrived in London as a boy, and her expression was a reminder of how he'd felt as a newcomer.

The white-tiled walls and long marble-topped tables with bench seats in this café were as traditional as the food. At the counter, an elderly woman in an apron ladled out bowls of eel chunks. A fishy odour hung in the steamy air.

"Why is there sawdust on the floor?" she whispered as he slid onto the bench opposite her.

"Oh, that's for the bones. Eels are full of them. Haven't you ever heard of the expression 'spit and sawdust'?"

She appeared to have been rendered speechless, but then she wouldn't have frequented this kind of joint when she worked in west London.

"I guess when you lived in the city you went to much classier places?" It was easy to imagine her going out with well-dressed young ladies ripe from finishing school, and handsome men with expensive suits and gold pocket watches who could treat her to the best of everything in gourmet restaurants and fashionable cocktail bars. He could picture her dressed to the nines in a sleek gown, with a fur wrap around her elegant shoulders and a flower or jewel in her hair. She wasn't the kind of girl to be showy or brash, but he had no doubt she'd had her fair share of admirers.

"I didn't go out all that much. I've always preferred a quieter life," she murmured.

Before he could probe further, the waitress appeared beside them, brisk and efficient with her notebook and pencil poised. "What can I get you?" she asked.

"Well?" he asked Dodie. "Are you game to give it a try?"

"I'm not particularly hungry at the moment," she replied, her brows knitting in a frown. "But you go ahead. I'll just have a cup of tea."

"Coffee for me," he said to the waitress. "And pie, mash and liquor twice, please. I'm sure the lady will find she has an appetite once the plate's in front of her."

"Pie and mash?" Dodie whispered, leaning across the table as the waitress whisked away to deal with their order. "And liquor?"

"Don't worry. It's not the kind of liquor you drink. It's a kind of parsley sauce. They serve it instead of gravy. You didn't really think I'd make you eat the eels, did you?"

Her face was a picture. He hid a grin, gratified to see her relax.

While Patrick devoured his minced beef pie and mash with his usual gusto, Dodie took a tiny sample as if still unsure whether this local cuisine could possibly taste good.

"It's actually quite nice," she said with obvious relief, tucking in with the delicacy he'd grown accustomed to from their outings to Contadino's. He was still loath to call them dates, although it would be quite something to be able to think of her as his girl. She'd only gone along that first time to allow him to thank her for helping him, and then the second time she'd wanted to talk to him about the children.

"Did you enjoy working in London?" he asked. There was

so much he didn't know about her yet. He wanted to know everything.

"For a while I did enjoy it, yes. But then, with war on the horizon, it seemed safest to move back to Pontybrenin."

Something in her tone made him suspect she'd deflected him away from talking about her time in the city. It seemed likely that her return must have been driven by something more than rumours of war. After all, she didn't lack courage: she'd been brave enough to defend him to the police when she barely knew him, and to consider tackling Mr Hicks by herself. Something else must have happened. Still, he wouldn't pry if she wasn't ready to tell him. He, of all people, could hardly blame her for having secrets, even though he longed to know more.

"Was your job interesting?" he asked, hoping this would make for a safer topic.

"Not as interesting as working in the library. I prefer being around books. And although Mr Gibson has some peculiar ways, he's starting to recognise that my ideas are worth listening to. I'm winning him over gradually."

"Of course you are." How could anyone fail to be utterly charmed by her? As he cleared his plate and sipped his coffee, which wasn't a patch on that served at Contadino's, Patrick's thoughts turned again to Mrs Hicks. His suspicions about her husband's violent character had left him disturbed by the idea that she had simply disappeared. Would she really have left without a word, and without trying to contact her children? What if Mr Hicks had had a hand in her disappearance? It was a sobering thought, and one he decided to keep to himself. If Dodie hadn't thought of it, he didn't want her fretting about the possibility that it might be too late by now to find Olive and Peter's mother. The girl who took her responsibilities seriously enough to drag herself all the way to London would be heartbroken to have to return with bad news.

Dodie's new *A–Z* book of London showed numerous tiny

crosses in Bethnal Green, but they weren't labelled so it was impossible to tell which might be St Andrew's Church. They agreed that their best option would be to take the Tube once again and disembarked at Whitechapel.

On emerging from the station they found the skies a murky grey. The imposing London Hospital stood on the opposite side of the broad and bustling Whitechapel Road, prompting Patrick to wonder if Mrs Hicks could be sick. It would explain why she'd sent no word to them, but not why the neighbour had been left in ignorance as to her whereabouts. Unless Mr Hicks had injured her, of course. He'd hardly be likely to go telling his neighbour if he'd put his wife in hospital.

Conscious of time, Patrick tried to stop his thoughts running with this kind of speculation. Hopefully they'd find Mrs Hicks' sister soon, and she'd be able to tell them everything they needed to know. They only had a few hours of daylight left, and the gloom of the drizzly November afternoon came as a reminder that they should hurry if they were to get back across the city towards Paddington in time for their train back to Wales. Moreover, they had yet to find the pub, which would have to close at three o'clock. If they couldn't get to it by then, they'd have to wait until it reopened for the evening.

"Didn't Jack the Ripper commit his murders in Whitechapel?" Dodie asked, keeping close to Patrick's side.

"Sure – but that was fifty years ago. You don't have anything to fear now."

"They never caught him though, did they?"

He laughed under his breath. "You're not scared, are you?"

"Only of not being able to find Mrs Hicks. Do you think he's hurt her?"

Patrick stopped abruptly, almost causing the elderly man behind them to stumble. His apology was met with a volley of curses.

Dodie tugged him into a shop doorway.

"Let's not get ahead of ourselves," he said. It bothered him that she'd been thinking along the same lines as him, but then she wasn't stupid. In fact she'd witnessed Peter's violent outbursts more than he had, and she must have guessed months ago what the boy's home life had been like.

She nodded, then nudged his arm. "There's a policeman," she said. "Let's ask him the way to St Andrew's Church."

He let her do the talking, knowing his accent might invite curiosity. His spirits lifted on hearing that the church was only about half a mile away, and the directions they were given sounded straightforward. Walking briskly they could be there in around ten minutes, and provided Mrs Hicks' neighbour was right about the pub, and the news was good, they might even be done in less than an hour.

With their collars turned up against the chill and the damp, they trudged along a lane, little wider than an alleyway, which was strewn with dustbins, then under a railway bridge, the rumble of trains passing overhead rendering conversation impossible. Unfriendly clouds unleashed raindrops to bead on the shoulders of their wool coats, making the feather on Dodie's hat look more limp than jaunty.

Only a couple of doors away from the church stood a small pub, its sign protruding above the entrance and clearly visible from the street proclaiming its name as The Wilberforce Arms. A low, two-storey brick building on the street corner, its facade was decorated with a row of Ionic columns.

"That could be it!" Dodie exclaimed, picking up her pace. It was almost half past two: they'd made it before closing time.

They turned towards the lounge bar, avoiding the tap room from whence a fug of cigarette smoke billowed out as a scrawny man in a patched coat lurched past them. Patrick nodded towards the barman and waited while he finished serving a middle-aged couple who stared openly at the newcomers.

Beside him, Dodie fidgeted with her bag, as if she could hardly keep still.

"Afternoon," the barman greeted them in a gruff voice, his features unsmiling. His neck bulged over his collar, and his red nose veered across his face at an unnatural angle, as if it had been broken more than once.

"Good afternoon," Patrick said. "Are you the landlord?"

"Who's asking?" The man glowered at them, leaning meaty hands on the polished counter. Letters were tattooed onto his fingers in dark blue ink, except for one of his little fingers, which finished in a stump below the first knuckle.

Dodie looked him in the eye, as if refusing to be daunted. "My name is Miss Fitznorton, and this is Mr Winter. We've travelled from Wales this morning to look for the mother of two evacuees who are staying with me. Their names are Olive and Peter Hicks. When we visited their home address, we were advised that their aunt might be the landlady of this establishment."

The man's small dark eyes assessed them coldly. "Were you, now?"

"I have a photograph of the children, to prove I am who I claim to be."

She laid the picture on the bar, but the man barely glanced at it.

"Would you happen to know if Mrs Hicks' sister works here?" she pleaded, trying again.

Anger sliced through Patrick at the man's hostile demeanour. Dodie was trying so hard, her voice strained with nerves as she faced him across the bar. She shouldn't have to deal with this kind of nonsense when she was only trying to help a couple of kids. His fingers curled into a fist in his pocket, and he clenched it hard, pressing his lips together to avoid letting his temper go.

The man sniffed. "She does, as it happens."

"Really? Oh, thank goodness—"

"But she ain't here. You'll have to come back later. She should be in tonight."

Dodie's crestfallen face made Patrick want to put his arms around her.

"Do you know where Mrs Hicks is?" he asked.

The man bridled at his impatient tone. "Like I said, you'll have to come back this evening. Now, if you don't mind, I've got paying customers waiting for their beer." He turned away pointedly and greeted another man holding two empty glasses further along the bar.

It was pointless to stay. The door swung closed behind them with a dull thud.

"What do we do now?" Rain glistened on Dodie's hat and hair. She shivered in the chilly November air.

"We could just leave a message for Mrs Hicks' sister and hope that the barman passes it on to her this evening," he said, not wanting to put Dodie through nearly four hours of waiting on this dreary afternoon.

As he'd half expected, she shook her head. "I don't trust him. You saw how unfriendly he was. Our best chance of finding Mrs Hicks is to speak to her sister." She lifted her chin and he saw a spark of the determination he'd admired so much at the police station.

"Okay. But we need to go somewhere warm and dry, and if we're coming back here this evening, we'll need to consider how we get back to Pontybrenin afterwards. The way I see it, we've got two options: either we find another café and drown our sorrows in endless coffee, or we hail a taxi and head to my mother's."

THIRTY-EIGHT

Dodie

By the time they reached Mrs Winter's boarding house, a tall, thin building of blackened London brick in a narrow back street, Dodie's feet and shoulders ached. The cardboard box containing her gas mask, slung across her shoulder by a piece of string along with her handbag, was in danger of turning soft in the rain, and her toes felt cold and unpleasantly damp in her shoes.

Patrick had been silent in the taxi, his face as shuttered and severe as it had been when she first met him. Now, though, she knew that the face he often presented to the world didn't reflect the real man. He had a soft centre. There was kindness in him, and integrity, and occasional flashes of good humour. He'd surprised her earlier when he took her to the café and made her believe he expected her to eat jellied eels. Who would have thought he had such an impish side to his character? No one looking at him now would believe it. She couldn't help wondering what made him take such care to hide behind a stern facade, and why he stood so stiffly on his mother's pristine tiled doorstep, radiating a nervous energy while they awaited an answer to his sharp raps on the shiny brass knocker.

The door was opened by a diminutive woman in a wrap-over apron, her faded auburn hair neatly set in waves. One look at Patrick had her beaming with delight, and before he had time to say a word of greeting, she flung her arms about him with a squeal.

"Pat! Is it yourself? Oh, my darling, what a marvellous surprise!" she exclaimed against his shoulder in a soft Irish voice. "Why didn't you tell me you were coming? I'd have made a cake. And I'd have kept your old room vacant. Mr Sharma is in there tonight – do you remember the sailor I told you about, from India? Such a lovely feller, quiet as a mouse and no trouble whatsoever. I feel terrible but I can't just kick him out, not with him being one of my regulars. But look at me now, keeping you out on the doorstep. Come on in, darling boy. And tell me now, who's this young lady you've brought with you?"

Mrs Winter seized Dodie's hand and pulled her into the hallway, talking nineteen to the dozen as she gestured for her to take off her coat.

"Let's get you out of those wet things, my dear. My word, it's a long time since Pat brought a young lady home. I'm very pleased to meet you. I wish he'd told me he was bringing a guest. Honestly, Patrick, could you not have mentioned this in your last letter? I don't recall so much as a single word about you coming home."

"How are you, Ma?" he asked, his grey eyes twinkling as she hung both of their coats on the hall stand along with Patrick's hat.

"Sure, I'm grand now I've got my boy home. My, there'll be ructions when your Auntie Clodagh finds out she's missed you. She's gone to stay down Rotherhithe way with a friend who's just come out of hospital. But come on now, you still haven't introduced me to your young lady. I'm Mrs Winter, in case you hadn't guessed," she added for Dodie's benefit.

"Ma, this isn't *my* young lady. This is Miss Fitznorton. You'll remember I told you—"

"Miss Fitznorton! The one who...?" To Dodie's surprise, tears sprang to Mrs Winter's eyes and she threw her arms around Dodie with as much enthusiasm as she had displayed when greeting her son, then planted a kiss on her cheek. "Oh, my dear. He's told me all about you and how you helped him. You can't imagine how I felt when I heard he'd been taken in by the police, and in front of the whole school too... It fairly broke my heart – but then he told me what you did, and I thank the good Lord for sending you to be his guardian angel that day. But Pat, you didn't say what a beauty she is. He did tell me you were pretty, me darlin', but look at you! You're a dote, that you are. That complexion! Those lashes! And those lovely teeth. Hasn't she got lovely teeth, Pat?"

If the effusive compliments hadn't been enough to make Dodie smile, the scarlet hue flooding Patrick's neck, face and ears were more than sufficient.

"Yes, Ma. Miss Fitznorton has perfect teeth. But do you think we could—"

Once again, his mother cut him off, caught up in her admiring observations as she held on to Dodie's forearms, beaming. "And her figure, Pat, in that lovely, smart dress. You've caught yourself a real treasure there, my lad."

"That's awfully kind of you, Mrs Winter, but I'm not actually Patrick's young lady. We're... well, we're friends." Keen to spare him any further blushes, Dodie stumbled over how best to describe their relationship. As much as the idea of being taken for Patrick's girlfriend had given her a fizz of pleasure, it was obvious that he was mortified by his mother's assumption.

"We've come to London together because he's helping me," she went on. "On behalf of the evacuee children who've been billeted in my home."

"Well now, isn't that a shame. You'd make such a fetching couple..." Mrs Winter gave up as her son shook his head decisively. "Regardless, my dear, won't you come in and have a cup of tea with us? It's nice and warm in the back kitchen. I want to hear all about you and why you need my son's help. Which I'm sure he was more than eager to give, after what you did for him."

Mrs Winter led the way along the hallway into a small kitchen where a rich aroma of leek and potato soup came from a gently steaming saucepan. She placed a kettle beside it on the stove. In the middle of the room was a small, square table covered with an oilcloth of gingham check. A brown tea pot covered in a colourful knitted cosy sat in its centre on a metal pot stand, along with a covered earthenware sugar bowl. Beside it stood salt and pepper pots, and a glass bottle of vinegar. It couldn't have been more different from Plas Norton's enormous, old-fashioned kitchen, but it felt homely and clean.

"Will you have a bit of soup?" Mrs Winter asked, reaching up to a shelf for some bowls.

"Oh, no thank you. We had lunch a short while ago." Dodie stopped, disconcerted by Mrs Winter's obvious disappointment.

"Ma hates the thought of anyone leaving this place hungry," Patrick explained, pulling out the chair nearest the fireplace for Dodie.

She sat down gratefully, accepting a cup of tea. Surreptitiously, she slid her feet out of her shoes under her chair, relishing the warmth of the glowing coals on her stockinged toes.

Patrick leaned back in his chair and tilted his head from side to side, as if stretching his neck. He wore a faint hint of a smile, his face softening as he watched his mother bustling with a loaf of bread and a hunk of cheese. As he nursed his tea in his hands, it struck Dodie that he appeared more relaxed than she had ever seen him before.

A plate of biscuits appeared, seemingly from nowhere, rapidly followed by sandwiches and a bowl of pickled onions.

"You'll have to eat something," Patrick murmured, the corner of his mouth lifting as he looked at her, in a way that made Dodie's stomach somersault. "If you don't, she probably won't let you leave." He picked up a sandwich and took a hearty bite.

"Use a plate now, Patrick. Did you leave your manners back in Wales?" Mrs Winter set two plates on the table and he obediently took one, his eyes lighting with amusement.

Dodie looked away, wishing her stomach would behave itself.

Her efforts on their behalf seemingly complete, Mrs Winter sat down across the table and topped up their cups of tea before pouring one for herself. "Now, then – why don't you tell me what brings you here?"

Briefly, Dodie outlined the reason for their trip to London.

Mrs Winter shook her head dolefully. "Those poor little mites. What kind of mother would send her children to strangers and then abandon them without a word?"

"We can only hope there isn't a sinister reason for her disappearance," Patrick said.

"Well, that's true enough. Her old feller sounds like a brute." His mother reached for his hand and squeezed it. A look passed between them that Dodie couldn't interpret; then he patted her hand and pulled his away, as if reluctant to engage in whatever emotions or memories they shared.

"Where will you both stay tonight?" Mrs Winter went on, her brow furrowing with concern. "We've no spare rooms, and even if we did, it isn't what you'd be used to, Miss Fitznorton."

"Please, call me Dodie. I'm sure your rooms are very

comfortable. But your mother has a point, Patrick. Even if Mrs Hicks' sister is at the Wilberforce Arms when we arrive, it will be late by the time we get back to Paddington. We may not be able to get a train this evening."

The cosy but plain simplicity of his mother's home was a reminder that Patrick probably didn't have an abundance of money to splash around on hotel rooms. He had already insisted on paying for his own rail ticket and had treated her to lunch. To expect him to also pay for a room in a respectable hotel would be unreasonable. On the other hand, Dodie didn't fancy the prospect of spending a night in the comparative squalor of the East End, where accommodation would be cheap. From what she had seen so far, rooms as clean as Mrs Winter's might be hard to come by. No wonder she had no vacancies.

"We'll just have to book rooms in a hotel uptown," he said, the line between his brows deepening.

"I disagree. *I* shall take a room near Paddington, but if your mother has even as much as a sofa to spare then you should stay here. It will give you an opportunity to catch up on all your news."

"And let you cross the city by yourself, at night and in the blackout? Not a chance," he drawled.

They scowled at each other, making Mrs Winter chuckle unexpectedly. "Look at you two lovebirds. We'll have no tiffs in my kitchen, if you don't mind."

It was Dodie's turn to flush scarlet, and not only from the gentle scolding and Mrs Winter's misapprehension. There was something thrilling about the determined glint in Patrick's steely eyes and the firm set of his jaw. She lowered her gaze, unwilling to let her unexpected spark of desire, or her pleasure at the way he wanted to take care of her, show on her face.

Mrs Winter pressed her palms onto the table and got to her feet. "I can offer my sofa for this afternoon, at least, even though Pat's quite right that you can't go off wandering the streets at night by yourself. You both look done in. Why don't you rest for a couple of hours until it's time to find the children's aunt? The fire's laid – you can light it, Pat, while I make another pot of tea."

In the small parlour, Dodie was pleased to see a small bookcase filled with what looked like well-thumbed volumes. On the wall above hung a framed print of a ship, no doubt chosen to suit Mrs Winter's guests, whom Dodie gathered were mainly merchant seamen. Behind the sofa was another small table, this one covered by a chenille tablecloth with fringing. Everything was neat and polished, from the dark oak sideboard to the pair of china spaniels on the mantelpiece. Nothing in the room looked new: it had that in common with Plas Norton's thirty-five-foot-long drawing room, but little else.

Dodie sank into one end of the sofa, the horsehair stuffing sagging underneath her so that she guessed she would struggle to get up again. Patrick crouched at the fireplace with a box of matches, giving her ample opportunity to admire the neat firmness of his buttocks where his trousers clung. He had removed his jacket to let it dry on the back of one of the kitchen chairs, but his shoulders looked no less broad with only his pale blue shirt to cover them. Not for the first time, a sensation of longing tugged at her belly.

After a minute or two the fire caught, throwing warm light across the planes of his face, and he stood up.

"Might I join you?" he asked. "The armchair is Ma's."

"Of course. Be my guest." She could hardly object, even though sitting beside him meant that her senses were heightened again, just as they had been when she sat on his lap in that moment of reckless rebellion on the train.

They sat in silence for several minutes, leaning their heads against embroidered antimacassars. Despite its saggy, slightly threadbare cushions, the sofa was comforting, embracing Dodie's weary body like a hug. As the fire got going and the room warmed, the ticking of the clock and the faint sound of Patrick's steady breathing, together with distant sounds of activity in the kitchen, lulled Dodie almost to sleep. Her chin jerked up and her eyes widened as she sucked in a sharp breath, realising she had come close to nodding off.

"Put your feet up and catch forty winks if you like," Patrick said. "I don't mind. I'll keep an eye on the time, make sure we don't stay too long."

Dodie hesitated, then fatigue won out over politeness. She kicked off her shoes and curled her limbs into the corner of the sofa, trying to keep her stockinged feet from resting against Patrick's thigh.

"Thank you. My feet are aching, I must confess."

"Shall I rub them for you? I used to do it now and then for Ma when she'd been working all day. According to her, I did a particularly good foot rub. Not to mention a mighty fine back scratch. Two of life's greatest pleasures, she used to say."

She hesitated, worrying that it wouldn't be proper, and that her feet might smell unpleasant after hours of walking in damp shoes, but those eyes gazing at her like that were impossible to resist.

"Well... if you're sure."

"Stop overthinking it. Just rest them in my lap and lay your head back."

The sudden touch of his hand taking gentle hold of her foot almost made her gasp. She stiffened at first, until the rhythmic pressing of his knuckles under the arch of her foot made her lean her head back. Each toe in turn was kneaded, then gently pulled. This was bliss.

Gradually, she allowed herself to relax and enjoy the sensation of his grip through the thin nylon of her stockings as he worked the underside of each foot from her toes all the way up to the jutting bones of her ankles, then back down her instep. Her calves felt boneless, the tension in the aching muscles in her shoulders and back easing even though he hadn't touched them.

Just five minutes, she told herself, becoming only distantly aware of a murmur of low voices, one deep and the other at a lighter pitch, lilting warmly in the corner of her consciousness along with mysterious, soft clicking noises.

Have you told her what happened in New York?

No, of course not.

After what happened with the police, and seeing how you are together, I thought you might have said something.

What would be the point? Don't go getting any notions, Ma.

Faint heart never did win fair lady, son. And if you don't snap her up, another feller soon will. Did you ever see such a lovely girl?

Whisht, Ma, would ya?

Alright, don't bite my head off. I'm only saying...

"Oh my – I didn't mean to fall asleep," Dodie said, opening her eyes and straightening as she became fully aware of the other people in the room. She hoped she hadn't dribbled or snored in her sleep, or – God forbid – said anything. The girls at school used to laugh at her for talking in her sleep, back in the days when her nights were broken by terrifying dreams.

"It's okay," Patrick said. "We've still time for another cup of tea before we go. And Ma and I had a good chat." He sent his mother what must have been a warning glance; Mrs Winter rolled her eyes and heaved herself out of the armchair, setting some intricate knitting aside.

Sitting up, Dodie set her feet on the floor and reached for her shoes, which had been stuffed with newspaper and placed on the hearthrug in front of the red-hot embers in the fireplace. She was almost sorry to put them back on now that her feet felt so much better, but this pleasant interlude couldn't last. On the table beside Mrs Winter's chair, a single lamp threw out a yellow glow, and the faded chintz curtains had been drawn to keep the dim light contained within the room. The clock on the mantelpiece showed that it was nearly a quarter past five, making Dodie's heart thump in anticipation.

In a little more than an hour, they might have discovered the whereabouts of Mrs Hicks.

THIRTY-NINE

Dodie

The bull-necked man with tattooed fingers was pulling pints at the bar when Dodie and Patrick entered the lounge area. Dodie was glad to be out of the rain despite the chilly welcome as the eyes of every patron turned towards them and the buzz of conversation paused. She was even more grateful for Patrick's commanding presence beside her. He was wearing that stern teacher look again, the one that struck fear into the children at school. She could only hope any would-be troublemakers here would also be put off.

"You're back, then," the barman grunted, after he'd finished serving his customer and finally turned his sour, bloated face towards them.

"We're keen to help the children find their mother. Is Mrs Hicks' sister here now?" Dodie's fingers twisted together as she awaited his answer, pinned by his coal-hard gaze.

"Winnie!" he boomed over his shoulder. "You've got visitors."

Dodie's shoulder muscles knotted. If this Winnie couldn't

tell them anything, Dodie would be out of ideas. She'd have to face returning to Plas Norton bearing the guilt of letting Olive and Peter down.

"You ok?" Patrick murmured beside her. "You're jumpy as a box of crickets."

"Can you blame me?"

After what must have been no more than a couple of minutes – although it felt longer – a woman appeared at the side of the bar. She looked frazzled, as if they'd interrupted her in the middle of something, but she lifted the flap in the counter and stepped out to the public side.

"Pour us some drinks, then Alf," she said to the man, who sent her a mulish look but reached for a pint glass.

"I hear you're looking for me," she said, pointing them towards a table in the corner. Its surface was sticky when Dodie laid her gloved hands on it; she placed them in her lap instead.

"We've been advised you might be Olive and Peter Hicks' aunt. Their mother's sister. Is that correct?"

With obvious reluctance, the woman nodded. "Alf said you've got a picture of the kiddies. Can I see it?"

Dodie fished it out of her bag. "I was hoping to give it directly to their mother."

A muscle twitched in Winnie's face as she gazed at the photograph. Her eyes glistened, then she blinked and looked coolly back at Dodie and Patrick. "She's not here."

"Do you know where she is?"

"Look, dear. I mean no offence, but you could be anyone. For all I know, her husband sent you here with that photo to find out where she is. So even if I knew where she is tonight, I wouldn't tell you."

The barman set their glasses down on the table in front of them: a pint of beer for Patrick, and two smaller glasses of clear liquid for Dodie and Winnie. Picking one up, Dodie detected the distinctive, crisp scent of juniper. Although she disliked gin, she took a sip to show willing. A refusal to partake might offend.

In the corner of her vision, Patrick slipped some coins into the barman's meaty hand. Today must be costing him a small fortune.

"How about we leave the photo with you?" Patrick said, sliding it over the table towards the woman. "If your sister ever happens to come around this way, you can give it to her. The children's address is on the back, in case she decides to write to them. She doesn't even have to tell them her own address. They'd just like to know she's okay."

"Alright. If I see her, I'll pass it on. I'm not promising nothing, though."

"Understood."

They exchanged nods.

Dodie let out her breath in a rush. "What can I tell them, though? If I go back with no information at all, I dread to think how Olive will react. She's been so terribly sad, receiving no letters from home. You can't imagine. Please – I need something to reassure her."

Winnie bit her lip but shook her head. "Sorry, love. I can't help you. Much as I'd like to. I don't like to think of Olive being so down in the dumps."

There was an uncomfortable pause. Patrick rubbed a hand over the back of his neck.

An idea dawned. "What if *you* wrote her a letter? That would be something, at least. You could give them some of your own news and promise to pass on their photograph next time you see their mother."

"I don't know..."

"I'm not asking you to tell them anything that isn't true, or to betray any confidences. But it will be something for them to hold onto, won't it? Something from a loved one back home." On an impulse, she reached out and covered Winnie's hand with hers. Tears welled in her eyes as she sent a silent plea across the table. The prospect of returning with nothing was unbearable.

Winnie drained her glass. "Well... Give me half an hour. I'm not much of a letter-writer, mind. Me spelling ain't up to much."

"They'll just be glad to hold something in their hands that comes from you," Dodie said, blinking her tears away as Winnie got up with a sigh and clumped back towards the bar.

They left the pub with a letter stowed in Dodie's bag.

"Well done," Patrick said. "You gotta hold on to hope now. I have a feeling Mrs Hicks will be getting that picture pretty soon."

She nodded, grateful for his approval. "Thank you for everything," she said. "If it hadn't been for you, I couldn't have got this far. Now – let's see if we can get a train home."

FORTY

Dodie

As a child at boarding school, Dodie was afraid of the dark. The uneasiness returned in the evening murk as they passed under the railway bridge and entered the long, narrow lane heading towards Whitechapel. Her heart rate quickened at the weight of the darkness in the alleyway. Throughout this long day she'd been grateful for Patrick's steadfast presence, but never more so than now, as they picked their way street by street towards home. They'd bought a torch, but its beam was partly shielded by a blackout guard, making it almost useless in this confined area.

The newspapers had been full of reports of accidents caused by the blackout. Vehicles were crashing and pedestrians were being mown down every night, and all because of the fear of German bombing attacks which hadn't even materialised, thank goodness. Perhaps they never would. Dodie crossed her fingers. Other dangers seemed more pressing right now.

She stumbled as her toe hit against an upturned dustbin. Patrick caught her arm and pulled her closer to his side, aiming the narrow torch beam towards the ground. It caught the silhouette of a large rodent scurrying past.

Her nerves were on a knife-edge. The darkness had already made her mind race with fearful imaginings of robbery or murder, or of being crushed by a vehicle careering out of control in the thick smog of a London night. Now there were rats the size of cats to add to her terror.

Somewhere ahead of them, a volley of loud, rough voices made her clutch at Patrick's hand. When the men passed by without incident, she dropped it, cross with herself for being so cowardly. In a couple of hundred yards they'd emerge into a wider road with only another ten minutes or so until they could reach the Underground station and descend out of the needling rain. Besides, hadn't Patrick told her the East End was a close-knit community? They weren't in any danger from the people here.

A few yards further on, a sound behind them made her shoulders stiffen. She half-turned. It was the growl of an engine, increasing in volume as it advanced towards them along the lane. A clanging thud suggested it had hit one of the dustbins, but its pace barely checked.

"Get to the side, quick," Patrick urged, nudging her towards the wall on their left.

She needed no such prompting. With her arms outstretched she made for the edge of the lane, hoping against hope that the driver would see them, or the faint light of their torch, in the restricted vision afforded by the vehicle's half-concealed headlamps.

Pressing her back against the high wall, she was briefly aware of Patrick's body shielding hers, the dampness of his woollen coat and the male scent of him in her nostrils as the engine's noise filled her ears. Then came a thump, and a muffled exclamation. There was nothing in front of her but cold, damp air.

Oh, God – he'd been hit.

"Patrick! Patrick, are you hurt? Where are you?"

The shape of a van was silhouetted in the dim light at the end of the lane as it continued on its way. The driver either didn't realise or didn't care that he'd knocked Patrick down.

The torch was gone. Its bulb must have smashed when Patrick fell.

She stooped and groped for him, relieved to feel the solidity of his body on the ground a few feet away. Kneeling beside him, oblivious to the filthy puddle beneath them, she tore off her gloves and scanned his torso, his broad shoulders, the angular planes of his face, with her hands.

"Are you alright?" she cried, running her fingers through his hair to check for any bleeding. *Oh, Lord – please let him be alright.* Leaning closer, she put her ear close to his mouth to check he was still breathing.

"It was my ass that took a whack, but I won't object if you feel the need to check that over too," he said in her ear, sounding breathless yet amused.

She rocked back on her heels. "Patrick! I thought you were hurt! Are you... good heavens, are you *laughing* at me?"

He sat up beside her with a groan and she grasped his face, tracing the tell-tale upturned shape of his mouth. His breath came out in short puffs as if he were indeed laughing softly.

"You are!" she spluttered, her hands dropping to her lap. The cheek of the man. She'd been thinking he was seriously injured, and he thought her fears were funny.

"No, no. I'm not. Truly. Not in the way you think. Please, don't be offended."

She hoped he was now experiencing a small measure of the worry she'd been feeling a second ago. He deserved it for teasing her at such a moment.

"I'm not offended. I'm merely surprised to find you're

capable of actual laughter. You've never shown much sign of a sense of humour before."

"Ouch! That hurt even more than the whack on the ass. Wait a minute... are you laughing at me now?"

To her surprise, he took her face in his hands, tracing her lips with his thumbs. She couldn't help grinning into the darkness.

"You are!" The timbre of his voice warmed. "Well now, it was worth getting a knock to bring that smile to your face. Although I can't see it, I can picture it perfectly. It being such a beautiful smile, it's lodged in my memory."

Her heart thumped. He hadn't taken his hands away; one thumb brushed against her lower lip in a way that made her stomach turn molten. His other hand swept over her cheek to cradle her head below her ear.

Her breath hitched in her throat. Instinctively she leaned forward just as he did the same. Their lips found each other and clung.

Their surroundings were forgotten as their kiss deepened. The kiss was everything; the warmth and the taste of his mouth on hers, all-absorbing. Her lips parted in response to the gentle probing of his tongue. His arms slipped around her, strong about her back, and she leaned into him, the whole length of her torso pressed against his. She was dissolving into him.

Desire ignited, hotter than she'd known before.

Even with Lionel it had never been like this. She'd wanted him, but this – this was a need. It had an urgency, as if something primal had been awoken in her gut, urging her to draw him in even closer. Her fingers tugged at his hair as the passion of their kiss grew heady. The prickly stubble on his chin scoured roughly against hers, but it didn't matter. All that mattered was this moment with him.

At last he drew back. Their breath came in shaky gasps.

She tipped forward a little, wanting more, but her eyelids fluttered open as her lips met cold air.

He was scrambling to his feet, reaching down to help her up.

Her legs were wobbly from kneeling in the gutter, her senses still dazed in the afterglow of their unexpected embrace.

A sharp intake of breath, quickly stifled, suggested he'd been injured more badly than his joking earlier had implied. But before she could ask if he was alright, he spoke.

"That was a mistake," he said, his voice suddenly hard and cold. The words were a slap.

He brushed himself down, seemingly unaware that she was paralysed with shock, her mouth hanging open. "I apologise. Let's put it down to getting carried away in the heat of the moment, shall we? Rest assured, I won't do it again." He cleared his throat and took a few unsteady steps, widening the distance between them. "We'd better go if we're to have any hope of getting you back to Wales without any further mishaps."

She made a small noise in her throat, gathering up her gas mask and handbag from the wet ground, still reeling from the blow to her shredded pride. With halting steps she trailed behind him, keeping her gaze on the silhouette of his broad back. He was limping, she realised, but found she didn't care. Her emotions were frozen. He'd awoken them, only to douse them in ice.

FORTY-ONE

Patrick

Inwardly, Patrick cursed himself as they crossed the city on the Tube. Dodie hadn't spoken a word to him since that disastrous kiss, and he didn't blame her. He should never have allowed his emotions to run away with him. It was all very well to blame the intensity of the moment, when he'd been shocked by the accident in the darkened lane. He'd been moved by her concern for him, his senses alive to her hands on his body. Flirting had been a stupid way to lighten the tension, leading them both into a course of action she must be regretting even more than he did.

Every minute they'd spent in the East End streets where he'd lived since his teens, she'd been a fish out of water, her bewilderment and nervousness obvious to him even though she'd tried to hide it. When they got to his mother's she'd been as gracious and polite as he could have expected, despite Ma's cringe-inducing chatter. He'd watched her looking around the shabby rooms, no doubt taking in every aspect and understanding, as she may not have done before, the vast gulf between them. He recalled how exhausted she'd looked, and the way she'd curled up on the sofa at his suggestion. If he'd had an ounce of sense, he should never have invited her to put her feet in his lap. It was a level of intimacy that had led his mother to make assumptions about their relationship. Worse, it had encouraged them both to let down their guard.

He'd accompanied her on this trip to help her stay safe, and yet he'd almost got her run over. She'd ended up bedraggled and on her knees in a filthy back street, looking out for him when he should have been protecting her.

No doubt she now thought him a heel for taking advantage of her kindness. It had been wrong of him to lead her on, sweeping her up when she was frightened, when he knew full well there could be no possibility of any relationship between them. He gazed at his feet on the train, conscious of her in the seat opposite. She, too, was avoiding eye contact. Now and then he risked a peep at her, his heart lanced by the wounded, pinched look on her downcast face and the defensive way her shoulders hunched over. She'd tried to cover her knees with her coat, but he'd glimpsed the dirty holes in her stockings. They must have been ruined when she knelt in the gutter to help him.

The sight made his chest ache almost as much as the rest of his body. The blow from the passing van and the jarring fall had bruised him. Now that the initial rush of adrenaline had worn off, his hip, back and shoulders ached. His hat was gone, his gas mask box was crumpled and battered, and one of his shoes was starting to come apart, the sole peeling off at the toe as if it were laughing at him. His coat was stained with God only knew what kind of muck from the cobbles of the lane. Other passengers were giving him a wide berth, and no wonder, given the state of him. He must look like some kind of tramp. Possibly he smelled like one, too.

At Paddington, he let her lead the way and stood beside her while she checked the timetable.

"The next train leaves in less than an hour," she said, in an icy voice.

She turned towards the waiting room, but he called her back.

"Wait. That train will reach Cardiff in the middle of the night. Then we'll be stuck until we can get a train to Pontybrenin, and remember there aren't so many trains on Sundays. You could be waiting around in the cold for hours."

Emotions warred in her features. He could understand her desire to put this trip behind her. She must long to get back to Wales. But common sense told him leaving tonight would be madness.

"Look," he said, pointing to the Sunday timetable. "If we stay in London tonight, with a few changes we can be back in Cardiff mid-afternoon, then find a connecting train to Pontybrenin. It makes more sense."

At last she shrugged, as if she'd given up fighting. Other passengers shoved past, making her flinch.

"Do you have any friends you could stay with?" he asked, wanting to be helpful and blaming himself for making her look so wretched.

A bitter half-smile flitted across her face. It didn't suit her. "No," she said. "When I left my job in London, I had no friends left. My fiancé had made sure of that."

"I'm sorry," he murmured. "I didn't know."

She'd had a fiancé.

She stepped closer, so close they were almost touching. Suppressed emotion made her tremble, energy radiating from her as if she was on the point of exploding with it. With her voice lowered so that no one else could hear, he had to lean forward to catch her words.

"I do my best to help people, and to be a good person. Every time someone I've trusted lets me down, the disappointment cuts a little deeper, because I should have learned by now not to let them do it. I will never allow a man to belittle me, or to criticise my passionate nature, or to use it against me again. I'm not ashamed of kissing you back today. But you should be ashamed for toying with me the way you did."

The words stung. He caught her wrist as she made to turn away.

"I'm so sorry," he repeated, reddening as he realised the intensity of their conversation had attracted attention. "No wonder you're furious with me. I guess you've a right to be. But – let me explain?"

A policeman was drifting past a group of other passengers, heading their way.

Patrick dropped Dodie's wrist.

The policeman looked them up and down. "Everything alright, miss? Is this – gentleman – giving you any trouble?"

Patrick felt nauseous. She could make things very uncomfortable for him if she wanted revenge for his rejection. He kept his mouth shut, trying to appear calm.

"Everything is fine, thank you officer. We were just discussing the best time to travel back to Wales after a rather trying day. I shall book into the Great Western Hotel this evening; this gentleman's plans are not my concern."

The man sent a hard glare in Patrick's direction, then nodded towards the station entrance. "Alright, miss. If you need any further assistance, I'll just be over there."

"Will you hear me out?" Patrick didn't want to have to explain himself, but he owed her that much.

"I suppose an explanation is due," she said, once the policeman had moved out of earshot. "Come along... But you'd better not waste any more of my time."

He had to hand it to her, she was no pushover. She stalked out of the station with her head high, as if channelling the spirit of her aristocratic ancestors. His regrets about the way things had happened earlier deepened. If she'd had a fiancé who'd made her feel bad about herself, he couldn't blame her for standing on her dignity now. She deserved better than she'd got from either of them.

FORTY-TWO

Patrick

They sat in a quiet corner in the hotel's lounge, partly hidden from view by potted palms. A waiter brought them dry martinis, but Dodie left hers untouched on the table between them. Patrick downed his in one, figuring he needed Dutch courage for what he had to say. His hand shook as he set the glass down.

"I want you to know I never meant to make you feel that I was toying with you," he began.

She merely arched an eyebrow and glanced at her wristwatch. This was a whole new side to her, but he could hardly blame her for a lack of patience or sympathy.

He scrubbed his hands over his face and started again, keeping his voice low. "Kissing you was incredible. It was... a moment I'll always remember. But I shouldn't have done it. Because if you really knew me, you wouldn't have kissed me back."

"We've spent almost a dozen hours together today. I've been to your home. I've met your mother. I know where you work, and I live with some of your pupils, who've testified as to your character. We've walked together; been to the cinema together; eaten together more than once. Most people would say we know each other reasonably well. Certainly well enough to be able to trust in one another's integrity."

"But you don't. There are things about my past which... I don't like people knowing."

She sucked in an impatient breath and reached for her drink. "Out with it, then. What could you possibly have done that's so frightful?"

He shook his head. Every nerve and sinew strained against the idea of sharing his past with her. She'd lose any remaining respect for him. But if he chickened out now, he'd lose it anyway. If he was to have even the slightest chance of making her understand, she'd have to be told.

"If you knew, you'd despise me."

"If that's the case, then it's only right that I should know. Perhaps it might help to convince my heart it should never have fallen for you."

Her voice cracked, and his heart along with it. Could she really have fallen for him? Although he was unworthy of her love, he couldn't help rejoicing in the hope of it. What fools they were to allow themselves to get caught up like this when there could be no future for them. He should have stuck with women who only wanted his body and demanded nothing of his soul. Life had been easier then. No one got hurt.

She took a sip of her drink and grimaced. "At least allow me to make my own decision. I'm sick of men telling me what I'm supposed to think or do."

His leg started to jerk uncontrollably, so great was his desire to escape. He leaned forward in the chair, almost far enough to hug his knees, pressing down on his thighs with his elbows and jamming himself against the table.

"Can't you just take my word for it? Why should I lie about not being good enough for you?" he begged one last time.

"If you can't do better than that, I'll go and book my room."

"Alright," he said, almost angrily. "The last person I told threatened to use it against me. But I believe you're different. I'm putting faith in you being a woman of your word. So I'll tell you, but you have to promise me you won't tell anyone else." He hadn't wanted to be pushed into this, had spent years guarding the secret which showed him and his closest family in the worst possible light.

Her fingertips drummed out a rhythm on the arm of her chair while she considered his request. "It depends. If your secret is something that puts someone in danger, then I can't make that promise. If it isn't, then I suppose you have my word."

It would have to be enough. He glanced around to make sure no one else could hear them, then took a deep breath before plunging back into his darkest memory.

"When my mother and I left New York, I was in trouble."

"What kind of trouble?"

He looked at the table, the carpet, his fingers knotted in his lap; anywhere but at her.

"With the law."

He sensed, rather than saw, her tensing her limbs, as if she was about to get up and leave him there.

"I aided my father in committing fraud. I went free because of my age and because we testified against him. You'll remember I told you he wasn't a good man. That was an understatement."

"What happened?" Her tone was guarded.

"He always had one scheme or another to make money, and nine times out of ten they were crooked. When I was about five or six, he decided he could use me to trick people out of their dough. He—"

He swore under his breath and covered his mouth with his hands, hardly able to say the appalling words out loud. "I was a skinny kid. And he determined it would be useful for me stay that way. So he stopped Ma from feeding me properly. Woe betide anyone who broke his rules. She could only give me food every couple of days, and only with him watching, to make sure I didn't get enough to fatten me up." He paused, his stomach knotting with the memory of the hunger that had driven him to desperation.

Dodie murmured something, but he ploughed on with his story, snared in the agony of his memories. Talking about them was like living them again. He could hear his father's voice; smell the booze on his breath; feel the anguish of longing for food and for kindness.

"He dressed me in filthy clothes and told people I was a starving orphan off the streets, to persuade rich folks to give him money. He told them he was helping the church set up a home for kids like me, and I played along. Thanks to me, and the wicked lies I told, Pa must've defrauded kind-hearted people out of thousands of dollars. It went on for years, until someone cottoned on and went to the cops, and Ma went to a priest. He helped Ma and me, and we sailed back to Britain first chance we got. Her sister took us in, and they run the boarding house together. I fear I was a bit of a tearaway for a while, but the church helped us. If it hadn't been for them, I don't honestly know how I'd have ended up. I settled down, got enough of an education to hold down a decent job. Now I help the kids at school as best I can and give what I can to charity to try to make up for some of what I did; but I know I can never undo it. I'll never be able to put it right. It's a filthy stain on my character that can't be washed away in this lifetime."

At last, he dared to look at her face, bracing himself to see the disgust he felt mirrored there. Instead, he saw pity. Pity that was enough to break him.

"Now you know why you absolutely can't throw your heart away on me," he said, his voice harsh with bitter shame and despair.

"But Patrick – surely you see that it wasn't your fault? You were too young to go against your father. You were just a child."

Her hand reached for his, but he flinched away. Better to make a clean break than to drag this out any longer.

Getting to his feet, he shoved his chair back and made for the door, wanting only to be gone. He stepped out of the hotel's grandeur into the hostile rain, glad of it stinging his face and scalp, and welcomed the darkness swallowing him as he crossed the street.

FORTY-THREE

Patrick

Patrick limped up the cobbles to his mother's house, peering at the doors in the absence of any lighting, until at last he found the right one. In the course of his journey across London, his thin woollen coat had given up its struggle against the rain. He shivered on the doorstep, soaked through to his underwear and teeth chattering uncontrollably. One of his big toes had worn through his sock where the sole of his shoe flapped open so badly it had been a constant struggle not to trip over it while negotiating the Tube. He was thankful he hadn't been set upon in the darkened streets, knowing he wouldn't have had the mental or physical strength to fight off anyone determined to steal the remaining couple of shillings in his pocket.

"Who's there?" his mother's voice called from behind the front door.

"It's me, Ma." He was glad she was sensible enough not to open the door to any old stranger at night, but wished she wouldn't take so long to throw the bolts after he'd answered. He was fit to drop.

"Holy Mother of God! What on earth...?"

She flung the door open and he almost fell in through the doorway, staggering as if drunk while he untied his laces and kicked off his wrecked shoes.

She peered out into the darkness of the street, as if looking for Dodie, then closed the door and bolted it again with her mouth set in a firm line.

"Thought I'd use that sofa of yours after all, if that's okay Ma."

"Patrick Jeremiah Winter! The state of you. You're half perished. Get that coat off this minute."

With his limbs still shaking, and the wet wool clinging, she had to help him peel off his clothes in front of the parlour fireplace until at last, he stood in his vest and underpants, his hands crossed over his crotch like an embarrassed little boy.

"Stay there. I'll fetch a towel." With her arms full of his things, Ma marched out of the room.

He was sitting cross-legged on the hearthrug with his face in his hands when she returned with a rough old towel and a dressing gown, reeking of mothballs, that must have been left by one of her paying guests.

"There's a saucepan of milk on the stove. Here's a biscuit to perk you up while I make you some toast. And then, you'd better have a good explanation for why you've come back without that lovely young lady of yours."

His muttered expletive was met with a clip across the ear before she bustled back to the kitchen. Rubbing his stinging ear, he couldn't help a wry laugh at the way she still treated him like a naughty child.

What a day and night it had been. Since boarding the train in Pontybrenin that morning, he'd had more highs and lows than a carousel horse. The thrill of Dodie sitting on his knee, and then, later, resting her feet in his lap while he kneaded them. The kiss, of course: that heavenly, sensual, erotic moment when he'd completely forgotten himself and the realities of life. And then the lows, when he'd had to witness her crushing disappointment at being unable to return with the good news she'd hoped to bring to the children; when he'd rejected her; and then when he'd felt so cornered that he'd had to tell her the very thing he was desperate for her not to know. Genius move, that.

He accepted a mug of cocoa and two doorstep-sized slices of hot toast dripping with butter and jam, eating in front of the fire while Ma busied herself with his ruined clothes. But he couldn't put off the reckoning for ever. She was soon back, perching in her armchair with a determined look he knew of old.

"Now, then. I think it's time you told me what's brought you back to my door with a face on you like you'd dropped a pound and found a penny. You looked on top of the world when you left!"

"It's a simple enough story. We had a fight. As I'm sure you've already guessed."

She tutted. "And where is she now? Safe, I hope?"

"Of course she is. I wouldn't have left her in danger. What do you think I am?"

"I think you're an eejit," she said. "Fancy letting a girl like that go."

He sighed and rubbed his eyes, worn out by the emotions of the day. "I didn't let her go. She was never mine in the first place." He stifled a grunt of pain as he got to his feet and hobbled to the sofa. "She'd never have wanted me," he added, unable to keep the sadness from his voice. He picked up a cushion and hugged it, gazing mournfully towards the fire.

"Know that for sure, do you? You asked her right out?"

"Ma, give over, will you?"

"Don't you tell me to give over. What makes you say she wouldn't want you? Come on, out with it."

"You know why!"

"No, I don't. You're going to have to say it out loud to me."

His scowls had no effect. There'd be no wriggling off the hook now, and he knew it. In fact, she appeared to be enjoying making him squirm.

"Alright. She lives in a goddamn palace, near enough, and drives the kind of car people like us could only dream of. She's educated – properly educated, I mean – and cultured. Her father was a rich and powerful man. A man of influence. Whereas mine was a blaggard, who roped me in to his scheme to defraud honest people, and now I've been fool enough to tell her about it. You'd have to be crazy to imagine she'd consider, even for one second, the idea of stooping so low as to be with me."

The words hung in the air like the stink from the Thames on a hot day; he closed his eyes as they sank and dragged him down.

The sofa sagged as his mother sat beside him. Her arm went around his shoulder and he leaned into her embrace, disregarding the crick in his neck from the disparity in their height. What difference would a bit more pain make? He was already hurting all over, and in need of the comforts of home.

"How long will you let your father rule your life? We didn't leave him behind in New York just to go on as we did before, living under his thumb. He ruined your past, in so many ways; but you can't let him ruin your future."

"You make it sound simple."

"Because it is. When I look at you, I see a fine young man. A handsome man, with a heart as big as a house and the strength to be a good man in a frightful world. A man who tries to make up for his father's sins by working with kiddies and giving most of his money away – oh yes, I know all about where your money goes, so don't waste your energy giving me that look. It's about time you stopped feeling you should pay for what he did."

"It's not just what he did, it's what he made me do. I was

part of it, remember. I was the one parading around with him looking long-faced and ragged, to play on people's heartstrings. It's only right that I should make a few sacrifices by way of recompense."

She huffed impatiently. "He bears the responsibility, Patrick, not you. He was the adult. He came up with the scheme, and you only did what you were made to do."

It was pretty much what Dodie had said. Torn, Patrick rubbed his face. He wanted to believe them, but he couldn't help feeling responsible for his own actions.

"You were a child," his mother went on. "You had no more power than those wee kiddies you work with. Think about them, now. If one of them was beaten and half-starved, and made to do wrong to earn the right to a crust or two, who would you blame? Who would you be angry with?"

He sent her a sidelong glance. The sight of a tear rolling down her cheek made regret prick his own eyes. He pictured the children at school. Would he blame them if their parents forced them into wrongdoing? As much as he struggled to apply the principle to himself, he knew she was right: he'd show compassion if any one of them was ever caught up in such a situation.

"It's time to forgive yourself and leave that skinny, frightened little boy behind." Ma dabbed at her cheeks with a handkerchief, then passed it to him. "You're a man any young woman would be proud to step out with, if she had a grain of sense. A man who couldn't be less like his father, and I should know. So promise me, Pat, that you won't leave things with Miss Fitznorton like this. You weren't raised to be a quitter. Go back to Pontybrenin tomorrow and show that girl what you're made of. Make her see she'd be daft to let you go."

The love in her eyes was as fierce as her embrace, bringing warmth to his body even more than the cocoa and toast by the fire had done. Some of the heaviness in his limbs lightened as her words sank in. He was pretty sure it was already too late to rekindle the spark he'd so effectively doused earlier with Dodie, but he wouldn't know for sure unless he tried one more time.

"Okay, Ma. I promise."

She released him and patted his knee, then nodded as if she were finally satisfied. "Good. I'll light a wee candle for you. Have a bit of faith, Pat. She's a lovely girl, worth putting yourself out a bit for. But for heaven's sake, promise me you'll do one thing."

He nodded.

"While you're on your way back, get yourself a decent pair of shoes and a new shirt. No self-respecting woman will look twice at you if you turn up at her door looking like a vagrant. If you don't believe you're a feller worth having, why on earth should she?"

FORTY-FOUR

Dodie

As soon as Ivor dropped her off outside Plas Norton's grand stone porch, Dodie dashed upstairs to her room. The idea of speaking to anyone else was unthinkable before she'd washed off not only the grime from the journey and her hours in the capital, but also the memories. Memories which included those fateful moments kneeling in a gutter experiencing the most extraordinary kiss of her life.

Flashes of that embrace, and the disastrous time afterwards, couldn't be shaken from her mind however hard she tried blocking them. The way she'd melted against Patrick in the darkness, every one of her other senses magnified in the absence of any light by which to see his handsome face. The giddy relief that he was safe, and the rush of unexpected laughter. Was that when she'd first realised that she loved him? No, that had been creeping up on her for a while.

The tenderness of his fingertips; the pressure of his lips, soft at first and then firmer as if he, too, had awoken an inner passion that defied any hope of restraint.

The movement of his tongue sliding against hers, making everything else disappear.

The stunning blow of his abrupt rejection, leaving her reeling at first and then angry, the molten passion of new love turning to bitterness in the face of pain. He'd made her think he was another cad like Lionel. How could she have known there was so much hidden below the surface?

She unpinned her hat and headed straight to the bathroom, turning on the taps to fill her bathtub. After tipping a generous measure of bath salts into the water she stripped off the clothes she'd been travelling in since the previous morning. Peeling them off felt like a release: a creature shedding a constricting skin or shell. Only after she had washed her hair and scrubbed every inch of her body did she start to feel as if she could breathe again.

Lying in the water, she tried to make sense of her thoughts. In the hours on the train, she'd fretted over where Patrick might be. He'd fled the hotel so abruptly after telling her about his background, there'd been no possibility of catching up with him. She'd barely slept all night, her mind running over and over his story.

She pictured his mother, that generous soul, whom he'd said wouldn't allow anyone to leave her house hungry. What must it have been like for her to watch her own child brought to the brink of starvation through her husband's cruelty? To allow it? Thank goodness the priest had helped her.

She closed her eyes, but she couldn't block the image of Patrick, curled in on himself like a wounded animal as he offered her glimpses into the darkest corners of his soul. What had he said to her once? *It's hard to let go of the hurt little kid inside you.* He'd implied she should let go of her pain and resentment towards Charlotte, and he was probably right. She should try harder with her sister, and let go of the pain of the past. Patrick's case was proof of just how damaging it could be to hold on to past hurts. But Patrick also needed to realise it was time for him to let go of the secret shame he'd carried as a burden for so many years. It was clear that his part in his father's wicked money-making scheme had been no fault of his own. What a fool not to realise it – nor to understand that his plight as a child could only intensify her growing admiration for him. He'd overcome so much.

She was foolish, too, for being so caught up in her own hurt over his rejection; she hadn't considered he might be in agony himself. As her stomach growled with hunger, after having eaten little all day, she contemplated how Patrick's childhood must have been. How could an adult deliberately deprive their child of nourishment, knowing the torment it must cause? She'd often wondered about the stern exterior Patrick had cultivated. Perhaps, she mused now, it was a shield against the possibility of letting anyone else get close enough to hurt him.

He could have grown up to be as cruel as his father, yet the evacuees' testimony was proof that he was kind to children. And apart from that awful moment of damning rejection, he'd shown kindness to her, too. Her feet arched reflexively at the memory of his touch. In those moments on his mother's sofa, he'd revealed his gentle side to her.

All the way home during the long hours on the train, she'd wondered anxiously where he was. Was he safe? Had he gone home to his mother? Or had he taken the late train to Wales after all, and spent a cold night in the station at Cardiff? It would have been too late to find a hotel when he arrived, even if he could afford a room. That morning at Paddington, she'd strained for any glimpse of him, waiting until almost every other passenger had boarded before climbing into the train herself. Since then, it had occurred to her that he might not have come back to Pontybrenin. Perhaps, now his secret was out, he'd stay in London and find another job instead of returning to face her again.

What would she do if she never saw him again? It was a distressing possibility. She sat up and splashed her face with fresh cold water from the tap, then pulled the plug from the tub and rubbed herself dry so vigorously her limbs were red by the time the bathwater had drained away. She couldn't bear the thought of leaving things between them as they were.

Perhaps she could telephone the vicarage and ask to speak to him; but if he had returned, they could hardly discuss his history, or their kiss, over a telephone call. The risk of being overheard was too great. And if he wasn't there... What then? She'd promised to treat his revelations in confidence. If Reverend Appleton answered the telephone, she couldn't explain the real reason for her call.

She tugged a comb through her damp hair. Her first task was to speak to Olive and Peter. If only she could have brought happier news back for them.

Dressed in a simple house dress, she descended the wide, carpeted stairs with anxiety twisting her gut. It was the children's teatime, and she knew they would be gathered around the kitchen table. But as she stepped into the hall, she heard her sister call her name from the drawing room doorway.

Charlotte approached, a speculative expression on her face. "So you *are* back. I thought I heard the car, but then there was no sign of you." Her red-painted lips twitched. "Goodness, you look worn out. Did you have an eventful night?"

Despite Dodie's decision earlier to try harder, her sister's implied meaning made Dodie defensive. "The journey to Stepney and back would tire anyone."

"Hmm. I was intrigued to get your message that you'd be staying overnight. Did Patrick Winter stay, too? Loulou mentioned that the two of you seemed friendly."

"I couldn't tell you." Dodie turned away.

Charlotte caught her arm and held it. She lowered her

voice. "You're an adult, so perhaps it isn't for me to say, but... I hope you were careful."

Wounded, Dodie tugged her arm away. Charlotte's assumption that she'd spent the night with Patrick was a bitter irony, considering he'd made it clear he didn't want her.

"The reason I couldn't tell you isn't to hide anything from you. It's because I have no idea what he did after about half past eight yesterday evening. I suggest you ask him, instead of judging others according to your own standards of behaviour."

Charlotte's eyes narrowed. She lifted her chin, any sign of amusement gone. "It's ironic that you consider *me* judgemental, Dodie, when you're always so quick to think the worst of me. Perhaps you still have some growing up to do." Turning on her heel, she left Dodie standing at the foot of the stairs, wanting to kick herself.

If only she and Charlotte could be more like the evacuees. They might be children, but at least the siblings looked after each other.

Enough was enough. It was time she stopped snapping at her sister and causing an atmosphere that could only cause everyone unhappiness.

The sound of the children's chatter paused when Dodie entered the kitchen.

"Aunt Dodie!" Barbara and Shirley exclaimed. Shirley tossed her half-eaten slice of Madeira cake onto her plate and dashed over to fling her arms around Dodie's waist, as exuberant with her affections as ever.

Olive remained in her seat, eyes watchful. Dodie sent her what she hoped would be a reassuring smile as she took a seat at the table.

"What was it like in London, Aunt Dodie?" Michael asked,

his food apparently forgotten. "Does it seem safe there to you? There ain't been no bombings yet, have there?"

She considered her answer carefully, knowing the boy was chafing against remaining in the countryside. It wouldn't be right to make him believe there was no danger; but neither should she say anything that would make him fear for his parents.

"There haven't been any bombings in London yet, Michael. But you remember bombers did attack Scotland a few weeks ago. And I can't pretend that London feels as safe as we are here. The blackout is horrid. Some of the main roads have had white lines painted along them, but one can hardly see the traffic lights, and cars' headlights are scarcely visible at all. By Christmas, it will be dark by half past four each afternoon, and it won't be safe for you to play outside in the street. You're giving your parents peace of mind by staying here, don't forget that." Reaching out, she patted his hand, but his face remained downcast.

"Never mind the blackout. Did you find Mum and Dad?" Peter asked, with typical directness. The hope faded from his eyes as she shook her head.

"I'm afraid your... your parents weren't at home when Mr Winter and I visited. We spoke to your neighbour..."

"Mrs Solomon?"

"I'm sorry, Peter – she didn't tell me her name." Inwardly, Dodie kicked herself for not thinking to ask. Stumbling over her words, she tried to be both truthful and gentle, but couldn't bring herself to tell the children that their mother was missing. "She told me she hasn't seen your mother recently. She advised us to visit your Aunt Winnie in Bethnal Green, as she might be able to help us contact your mother."

"And did you go to see Auntie Winnie?" Olive spoke up at last, her face pinched with tension.

"We did." Dodie bit her lip. "She's written you a letter. And we left your photograph with her, so when she sees your mother next, she can give it to her. Our address is on the back, so she'll know where to find you. And if you'd like to write back to your aunt, I can post the letter for you on my way to the library tomorrow."

She slid the letter across the table, and Peter snatched it up. He tore it open, frowning as he scanned the words.

"What does this bit say?" he asked Olive, handing it over and pointing.

Olive peered at it, frowning over the words and reading them aloud in her quiet, halting voice. "She hopes we're keeping well and is glad to have our picture. She'll give it to Mum soon to show her how much we've grown. And she says she'll send us sixpence each for Christmas, if we're good and write back."

Olive handed the letter back to her brother. Everyone was silent, acutely conscious of how bitterly disappointed both children must be.

Shirley was the first to speak. Sliding off her chair, she moved around to stand beside Olive and put her arm around her.

"It'll be alright, Olive. You'll see. It's nice to have a letter from your auntie, ain't it? We'll all help you write back, if you want. But d'you want to come upstairs with me and play first? I'm sure Juliet would like to play tea parties with my teddy bear."

"That's a good idea," Dodie said, relieved that Shirley's innocent kindness had offered a way to put this painful conversation behind them. The children seemed to be better at managing their friendships and sibling relationships than she was herself. She'd made a mess of things with Patrick and too often snapped at her sister. Her shoulders sagged wearily.

"Michael, could you find something to do with Peter? You could play with your model plane, perhaps, if you've finished building it?" she suggested.

"It's not painted yet... but yeah, alright. C'mon, Peter."

The children trooped solemnly out of the room.

Dolly had been standing in discreet silence at the stove during the whole exchange; now, she rummaged in the cutlery drawer. Seizing a tea towel, she used it to pick up a plate that had been resting on top of a saucepan, and deposited it in front of Dodie along with a knife and fork.

"You look like you've had a right time of it, flower. I kept a roast dinner back for you. Get that down you, if you don't mind eating in here this evening. I'll make you a nice cup of tea."

Dodie nodded her thanks. At least the task she'd dreaded most was now over. All that remained was to decide how best to deal with Patrick.

FORTY-FIVE

Olive

The school day dragged without Mr Winter to make lessons more interesting. When Audrey bravely put up her hand and asked Miss Honeycutt where he was, they were told he was visiting a relative in London. After pressing for information about when he would be back, the children were told she didn't know, and threatened with a punishment if they didn't apply themselves immediately to their arithmetic.

It didn't make any sense to Olive. Aunt Dodie hadn't said anything about Mr Winter visiting a relative. They'd travelled to London together, so why had they come back separately? But her thoughts were soon occupied with the daily struggle of avoiding a rap on the knuckles from Miss Honeycutt's wooden ruler.

She had written a brief letter to Auntie Winnie, with minimal help from Peter, whose handwriting was less presentable. He had little patience for sitting down to write when he didn't have a teacher forcing him to do it. Olive had some sympathy. After all, it was hard to summon up much enthusiasm to write to an aunt who had seemed nice enough, on the rare occasions they'd met her, but who was by no means close to them. Mum had rarely taken the children to visit her at the pub, and Auntie Winnie had never once visited her sister's flat, as far as Olive could recall. No one visited – not socially, anyway. The rent man knocked the door now and then, causing alarm as they'd have to duck out of sight while he tried to peer through the letterbox. One or two of Dad's friends might pop by to collect him on their way to the boozer, or to leave something at their flat which they said had fallen off the back of a lorry. But no one else ever came. The Hicks family kept themselves to themselves, and Mum said it was better that way, as only trouble could come from letting all and sundry poke their noses into things that didn't concern them.

On their way home from school, it was cold enough to turn the children's breath to mist. They blew out plumes, pretending to smoke cigarettes like the adults they'd seen in movies and around the town. The girls held their index and middle fingers to their lips, noses pointed towards the sky in an attempt at sophistication, while the boys squinted and pretended to cup ciggies in their palms. Peter even tried to blow smoke rings, the way Dad would, coughing out little puffs and clenching his fists when it didn't work, making the others chuckle at his efforts.

Autumn shades gilded the trees, with flashes here and there of fiery orange and red amongst the gold. In places the ground squelched underfoot from recent heavy rain, and they were glad of the sturdy boots and shoes they had been given to replace their worn old shoes and canvas plimsolls.

The evacuees skirted the farm, dreading being seen by the boys there who had recently started taunting them again by throwing stones or clods of earth and shouting rude words. Unfortunately, their efforts were in vain.

"Run!" Michael suddenly yelled, grabbing Shirley by the hand and setting off at a lick.

Without warning, a lump of dried mud sailed past Olive's head. She hadn't heard the farm boys' shout go up when the others did, so was several yards behind them. Her heart pounded as she dashed after them, not daring to stop until she reached the wooded slopes of the hill where the summerhouse stood. Leaning her hands on her knees, she bent double, trying to get her breath back before making her way uphill between the trees.

The other children were already at the summerhouse, calling Tyke. Their breath hung in pale clouds in the November air, and an ominous cloud loomed on the horizon. It would rain soon.

"I hate those bastards," Peter raged, his face red. He kicked one of the wooden walls of the summerhouse, making splinters fly off where the wood was rotten.

"Not as much as I do," Michael said.

Olive slipped inside warily, seeing how both boys were seething with temper.

"I hate it when they shout that word at us," Barbara said, clutching Shirley's hand.

Olive hadn't heard the word, but she could guess which one they meant.

"Ignore it." Anger made Michael fierce. "They want to make us feel as if we shouldn't exist. As if we're not even human. But the worst thing you can do is let them see they've got to you. They think they're better than us, but they're not because handsome is as handsome does, and you ain't never seen us spit on anyone or chuck shit at them, have you? And who are the ones whose dad is out at sea risking his life to bring food into this country? We are! Our dad might not get any medals, and people like them may never see him as a hero, but he's every bit as brave and in just as much danger as men who are fighting for freedom. To people like them, freedom just means being able to tell another human being that they don't count, they're not worth nothing, just 'cause they look different. People like them make me sick." His nostrils flared as he sucked in his breath.

Shirley's lower lip wobbled. Leaning her face against Barbara's shoulder, she sniffled and rubbed her eyes with her fists.

"It's alright," Barbara murmured, patting her.

Olive reached out helplessly, wanting to show she cared but not knowing what to say.

"I'm going to do something," Peter fumed. "They shouldn't be allowed to get away with it. I'll make a catapult and ambush them. I'll wreck their den. I'll – I'll..." He stamped his foot, glowering.

"Don't bother," Michael snapped back. "I can fight my own battles. The last thing we need is for you to go making things worse. I'm just biding my time. They're too cowardly to try fighting me one-to-one, but I'll get my chance, don't you worry. One of these days they'll wish they'd never started this."

Peter subsided, but Olive could tell from the way he continued to scowl and scuff his toes along the floor that he hadn't let go of his anger.

"I'm going back to the house before the rain starts," Michael said. His rush of fury seemed to have dissipated in the wake of his outburst. For a moment he stood silhouetted in the doorway of the summerhouse, leaning his hands on the jamb, as if he had to summon the will to continue walking back to Plas Norton. Then he strode out towards the woods, disappearing among the trees.

His sisters ran to catch up.

Peter stayed, scuffing the toe of his boot along the threshold of the summerhouse where the wood was flaking.

"There's Tyke!" Olive cried, as the cat appeared behind him, his stripy ginger tail standing straight up with a curl like a question mark at the end.

Tyke ran towards her, as if welcoming her back to their own special place. She squatted and her heavy spirits lightened a little as he rubbed himself against her, purring loudly.

Together, the children sat on the floor of the summerhouse and made a fuss of the cat.

"I think he's pleased to see us," Peter said.

She nodded, stroking Tyke's soft stripy fur. "He always comes to me. He loves me."

They'd had shepherd's pie for dinner at school, and she'd managed to spoon some of the minced lamb surreptitiously into her handkerchief while Miss Bright was looking the other way. She unwrapped it now and held it out, smiling at the way Tyke's whiskers twitched. He sniffed it, then took a bite.

"I've been thinking," Peter said.

"What about?"

"Do you think Aunt Dodie and Mr Winter really did try to see Mum and Dad?"

Olive stiffened, unwilling to think about their father. "Well, we know they went to see Auntie Winnie, because she wrote us that letter."

"Yeah, but they could've gone back to our flat after that, couldn't they? They might've been home by then."

Outside, the wind had picked up. It made the door rattle. Tyke shrank back with a start.

"Maybe they didn't have time. I don't think they'd lie to us... Would they?" Olive whispered mournfully.

"I dunno. But I do know one thing. I'm not letting those bastard farm boys get away with chucking stuff at the Clarkes. No one gets to treat my pals like that. It's time to teach them a lesson."

She stared at him, suddenly afraid. "What are you going to do?"

"Promise not to tell no one, or I'll... I'll throw Juliet in the mud."

It sounded like a hollow threat, but Olive made the gesture of a cross over her heart nevertheless.

"Like I said, I know where their den is. It's in the woods. I'm gonna go and knock it down."

"No, Peter – you mustn't. You heard what Michael said. They'll be angry. It'll just make things worse if they guess it was one of us. They'll want to get their own back. They might hurt you."

He wrinkled his nose and scowled at her, then scrambled to his feet. "Stop being such a bloody coward, Ol. I'm not scared of them. I'm not scared of nothing. They'll be sorry they ever picked on the Clarkes, just you wait and see."

FORTY-SIX

Dodie

Dodie scanned the gathering in the chilly church hall, trying to focus on the meeting. There had been no word from Patrick all week, and she had poured her mental energies into her work, so much so that she'd even received rare praise from Mr Gibson for her efforts. However, tedious administrative tasks and tidying bookshelves couldn't help to distract her outside working hours.

Since hearing from the children that Mr Winter hadn't been seen at school since their trip to London, her brain had been engaged in all manner of vain speculations as to his possible whereabouts. Presumably the vicar would have heard if Patrick was missing, making it unlikely that he'd met with any kind of serious misadventure. But he'd been upset, so it wasn't impossible that he'd been distracted enough to fall prey to some kind of violent mugging. Could he be lying in a hospital bed with his memory lost after a head injury? Had he been involved in another road accident, more serious this time? At night, she'd even had to fight away fears that he might have done himself some kind of harm, with vivid thoughts of his body floating face-down in the river. All these imaginings about a man she'd decided she should no longer care for were tying her up in knots.

Reverend Appleton, who sat at the head of the table, might know if Patrick was still in London, and whether he intended to return to Pontybrenin. Perhaps she'd find a way to broach the subject with him after the meeting.

Venetia was seated on the vicar's right, smartly dressed in a tailored coat and with her helmet-like short hair mostly covered by a green WVS hat. On the table before her lay a leather-bound notebook, and she held a fountain pen poised to tick items off a list she had brought to the meeting.

Charlotte sat on the Reverend's left, glamorous as always in red lipstick and fox fur. He seemed content to let the two women do most of the talking, but they faced some competition from Miss Honeycutt and Miss Bright, who made an equally formidable partnership, resisting all suggestions that the committee should provide something special for the evacuees.

"Christmas is only a month away," Venetia said. "It's sure to be a difficult one for the children. Since I've recently taken in a child myself, I've come to realise how poignant it will be for the evacuees in particular. They will be missing their homes and families dreadfully. However, you're quite right to point out, Miss Honeycutt, that it will also be very different from usual for our local children, especially those who have family members in the forces." She removed her spectacles and folded them.

The discussion centred around how to make a wartime Christmas feel festive. There could be no possibility of a midnight mass on Christmas Eve, as the height and number of windows in the church made it impossible to black them out. None of the local shops could light their festive displays, and none of the houses could show coloured fairy lights or candles in their windows. Stocks of some basic groceries like bacon and sugar had been running low in the shops, making Dolly complain that she might even have to limit her Christmas baking this year, and with petrol rationing it seemed unlikely that social butterflies like Charlotte could flit about to their usual number of parties.

Some of the ladies suggested it would be wrong to celebrate Christmas at all this year, what with young men being called up, a spate of bombings by the IRA, and the knowledge that so many people in Eastern Europe now lived under the Nazi jackboot. Others insisted it was more important than ever to have a reason to be jolly, and to pray for peace on earth and good will to all men.

"The evacuees can't go expecting special treatment when everyone is already making sacrifices. They'll just have to accept that there's a war on," Miss Honeycutt argued, rather mean-spiritedly, Dodie thought, considering how completely the children's lives had already been disrupted.

She was struck by how much the war had affected all their lives. No doubt Venetia would prefer to be listening to the wireless at home on a bleak Monday afternoon, not sitting on a hard chair trying to rally this motley bunch of volunteers.

"We need something to bring the community together. Evacuees and locals." As Charlotte spoke up, everyone fell silent – but when had Dodie ever known it to be any different? Her sister had natural charisma and an air of authority. Miss Honeycutt seemed to find this irritating; everyone else hung on her every pronouncement.

"What do you propose, Mrs Havard?" Venetia asked.

"We did it during the last war, and we can do it again. I'm sure some of you are aware that the local children and the evacuees don't always get along quite as well as one might wish. I'm not blaming anyone, Miss Honeycutt; merely stating facts. Christmas offers us a unique opportunity to bring them together and help them understand that they have much in common. I suggest a party on the last day of term. It will give us four weeks to prepare. We could hold it here in the church hall, or at the school, or else I'm willing to offer the ballroom at Plas Norton. Provided we finish mid-afternoon, there should be no difficulty dispatching everyone home safely."

There was a ripple of excitement as options were debated. Dodie noted a secret smile pass between Charlotte and Venetia, as if they'd already planned this. They would have done, of course. Dodie pretended to fumble with her shoelace, so that no one would observe her amusement. She had to give them credit for knowing how to work a crowd.

By the time dusk fell, the meeting was done. The more creative ladies had promised to knit or sew a Christmas stocking and a small gift for every child. A menu had been planned, and the butcher's wife had agreed to support the catering. The grocer's wife had agreed to donate some walnuts and chocolate to ensure each family had something to put into the children's stockings for Christmas morning, and another woman, who was a friend of the stationer, offered to request a donation of colouring books, pencils and wax crayons.

Even Miss Honeycutt had admitted she was looking forward to the planned celebrations. It seemed the prospect of an afternoon in Plas Norton's faded splendour, with sausage rolls and cakes, festoons of paper chains and Father Christmas doling out presents around a decorated tree, was enough to leave the most stuck-in-the-mud sourpuss with a glow of anticipation. Reverend Appleton's suggestion of inviting the evacuees' parents had met with almost universal approval, although Dodie felt a pang knowing there was little chance that many of them could afford to travel all the way to Wales and back.

Charlotte offered Venetia and Reverend Appleton a lift home in the Riley, dropping Venetia off first. While they headed in the direction of the vicarage, Dodie chewed her lip, debating inwardly whether to seize this chance. As desperate as she was to know what had happened to Patrick, she was loath to raise the subject in front of her sister.

In the event, she didn't have to.

"Is Mr Winter alright, Reverend?" Charlotte asked, her tone suggesting she was only mildly curious, although Dodie suspected from the brief glance Charlotte sent towards her in the rear-view mirror that she was enjoying Dodie's discomfiture. "Michael mentioned he hasn't been at school all week. I wondered if he might perhaps still be in London?"

"Not at all. He arrived back on Monday evening," the vicar said.

Dodie released the breath she'd been holding.

"He hasn't been at all well, though," Reverend Appleton continued. "Caught a chill in the rain last weekend. He's been laid up in bed most of the week, poor chap. Barely touched any food. Terrible cough. I've had to keep away from him, I'm afraid. Can't risk catching such a bad cold. Not with my chest." He shook his head dolefully.

Dodie took his place in the front passenger seat when they left him at the vicarage. There was no sign of Patrick. Which room was he in? She wished he would look out of one of the windows. Had he been able to return to his mother's house after leaving the Great Western Hotel, or had he spent the night out in the open, in the cold and rain? Again she felt a stab of guilt for the way they had left things. Perhaps she'd been overly harsh, too concerned with her own feelings to consider his. He was nothing like Lionel really; she'd been foolish to assume that his cold rejection after that moment in the darkened lane had been in any way similar to her former fiancé's cruelties.

"Poor Mr Winter. It sounds as if your trip to London has left you both out of sorts," Charlotte said, as she engaged the gears and set off, speeding through the village.

"I've been perfectly fine, thank you." Dodie kept her voice level, determined not to get drawn into an argument this time.

Charlotte's red-painted lips twitched. "Of course you have, sister dear. If he's been unwell, Mr Winter might appreciate something to lift his spirits. Why don't you pop round to the vicarage after church tomorrow morning with a pot of honey from the larder, and a bottle of whiskey from the cellar? There's nothing so good for a cold as a hot toddy before going to sleep."

"I suppose I could..." It wasn't a bad idea. But she pressed her lips together at Charlotte's next remark.

"Of course you could, Dodie. Although I'm sure Mr Winter doesn't need an excuse to think about you at bedtime."

FORTY-SEVEN

Olive

Aunt Dodie had been behaving quite oddly that morning. On their way to church she carried a basket, its contents concealed by a cloth. The children were surprised when she paused at the vicarage, instead of making straight for the lych-gate at the church as they usually did. It was strange, because they would be seeing the vicar in the service. Why visit him first?

"Wait here," she said. She fussed with her hair and smoothed down her skirt before marching down the flagstone path to the front door.

After exchanging a glance, the children moved as one to follow her, too curious to wait behind.

When the housekeeper answered her knock, looking severe in a black coat and hat as if she were about to head to church herself, Aunt Dodie stammered out a greeting.

"Good morning, Mrs Roberts. We're just on our way to church, so thought we'd... um... pop round with some things for Pat... For Mr Winter. It's not much. Just a little something from the children which they hope will help him feel better quickly.

You will make sure he knows it's from the children?" she insisted.

Olive looked at the others, but they all appeared equally mystified as to what the gift could be. Why should Aunt Dodie say it was from them when they hadn't even seen it?

She started and blushed when she turned and saw them all behind her, striding to the gate so quickly they had to trot to keep up. Olive wondered if they were late for the service, but the clock on the church tower showed as they arrived that they were ten minutes early. It was a mystery to her why Aunt Dodie had seemed so awkward. She'd had an artificially bright, jolly note to her voice as if she was trying too hard to be polite, like Mum used to when the Salvation Army called round and she wanted to get rid of them by saying she was already saved.

The reminder of her mother, never far from her thoughts, added an extra fervency to Olive's prayers in church before the children all trooped out to their Sunday school classes. She prayed for peace, as they all did, and for their families in London, but especially for her mum to be safe and well, and to send them a letter soon.

It had been six days since she and Peter had written to Auntie Winnie, and eight since Aunt Dodie and Mr Winter had visited the Wilberforce Arms and given her the photograph. She'd pushed the letter carefully into the slot of the red postbox on her way to school on Monday morning, putting her hand right in before letting go to make sure it couldn't somehow get trapped. But they'd still had no word back from Mum. It was hard not to conclude that, for some reason Olive couldn't understand, Mum just didn't care enough to write back.

Was there even any point in praying at all? She'd been doing so for weeks, and God still hadn't found a way to get her mum to put pen to paper. Perhaps He was too busy trying to come up with a way to sort out that horrible Mr Hitler.

On the way back to Plas Norton, Aunt Dodie revealed that

plans were afoot to hold a special Christmas party at the end of the school term. Not only were they planning party games and music, but they would also all need to help with the preparations by making paper chains. In a couple of weeks' time, they would be able to help cut boughs of holly, ivy and mistletoe from the grounds around Plas Norton to decorate the house, and if they were good Uncle Ivor might let them help him choose a suitable tree for the hall.

"But that's not all," she said, her face lit with one of her lovely smiles as if she could hardly wait to share the details with them. "You'll all need new party clothes. Auntie Dolly knows someone who will make them if you go up to the attics and find some suitable material. We can look this afternoon."

"What sort of outfit will you wear, Aunt Dodie?" Barbara wanted to know.

"Oh, my. Do you know, I haven't thought about my own yet. What do you think I should wear?"

"A white dress and wings like an angel!" Shirley cried at once, tugging at her hand and skipping in her enthusiasm for the idea.

Aunt Dodie laughed, colour rising in her cheeks as she tipped back her head. "I suppose that would be in keeping with the festive theme, but I'm not sure I'm suitably qualified for the role. I'll have to give it some thought."

They debated ideas for the party all the rest of the way back and while they changed into indoor clothes and snacked on fruit cake and blackcurrant cordial. Later, they followed Aunt Dodie on the steep climb up Plas Norton's attic stairs. Peter barged past the girls towards the front, and none of them bothered putting up more than a token protest, knowing it would make no difference. Even Olive felt a little more energised than usual, although it was clear that the others were much more pleased by the prospect of a party than she.

She was the last to reach the attics, lacking the enthusiasm that had propelled the others to climb more quickly. It was hard to care about a Christmas party which was still a few weeks away. What did it really matter what she wore? The only thing she wanted was her mum.

Her lack of interest irritated the other children, she could tell. They'd been sympathetic up to now, but they must be getting tired of her moods. She couldn't blame them. She was equally tired of feeling this way. Hollow and flat, like a tatty old football that had deflated and been kicked to one side.

While the other kids chattered like a flock of sparrows, delving into trunks and exclaiming over items they'd found, she cast her gaze around the attic and its dusty assortment of items from lives that had no relevance to hers.

"I think I noticed some old clothes in that trunk over there the last time I was up here," Aunt Dodie was saying. She turned, and the sound was lost to Olive's good ear.

Olive had spotted a large bird cage made of wood and wire. It was beautiful, even with so many of its golden bars broken and dented. What might have lived in it? She stepped closer, marvelling at its elaborate domes and towers with their red wooden turrets and curlicues.

She was dimly aware of Aunt Dodie pointing to a box in the corner, and the others nodding and turning to hunt elsewhere, pulling out lengths of camphor-scented fabric from trunks. Laughing, Barbara had balanced an elaborate hat on her tight curls; but Olive was lost in imagining a canary in the cage, or finches perhaps, or even brightly coloured budgerigars with friendly, curious eyes. She'd seen some once in a pet shop and loved the way they bobbed their heads as if they were kissing each other.

While Aunt Dodie left the others to pick out the items that they wanted to use to make their party outfits, Olive knelt in her corner in a dream.

"Aren't you going to look, Ol? There are plenty of things

left," Barbara said, before shrugging and descending the narrow stair with her treasures.

Soon Olive was the only one left upstairs, the others having chosen what they wanted from the trunks which now lay open. Idly, she looked inside, but there was nothing left that caught her eye. Glancing around, she remembered the box Aunt Dodie had pointed out. None of the others had gone to it – perhaps she'd find something nicer in there.

Lifting the lid, she caught her breath at the sight of vividly exotic fabric, covered in flowers of pink, white and yellow. The cloth shimmered under the harsh light of the single electric bulb hanging from the ceiling, and when she touched it, it seemed to slip over its own folds like water. She'd never touched anything so gorgeous before. It was a robe, she realised, finding as she lifted it that it had sleeves and a separate belt made from the same exquisite cloth.

She gathered it up, marvelling at the liquid way it moved, spilling over her hands and feet when she put her arms into the wide sleeves. There was more than enough fabric here to make a beautiful dress. And what's more, it was so long that there'd be plenty to make a matching new dress for her doll Juliet. The idea of it spurred her forwards, excitement igniting in her for the first time in weeks. Quickly, she slipped downstairs to collect a pair of scissors from the kitchen.

"What do you want those for?" Auntie Dolly asked, her hands covered in sticky stuffing mixture for the afternoon's roast dinner.

"I'm planning my outfit for the party," Olive said. She carried the scissors carefully, holding the blades pointing downwards in her fist as she'd been taught. On her way back up to the attics she collected Juliet from the bedroom she shared with Barbara and Shirley, who were nowhere to be seen.

Back in the attic, the exquisite fabric rippled as she laid it on the dusty floorboards and put the doll on top of the bottom hem to help her gauge where to cut. If she cut carefully, she would avoid spoiling the upper part which she could use for her own dress. She'd seen her mum cutting and sewing new items from old clothes so many times, she knew she could save time and effort by keeping the hem intact and reusing it for Juliet's robe. Carefully, she cut out two T-shaped pieces of cloth, making sure they were bigger than the doll to allow for sewing seams up later. A slit up the middle of one of them made the front piece. Now, all she needed was to cut a strip off the original garment to create Juliet's belt.

She poked out her tongue as she snipped, remembering her mum's adage: *measure twice, cut once.* Juliet was going to look so pretty in this new robe. She'd look like a princess.

A noise at the doorway went barely noticed; then a shadow blocked the light from the bulb, falling over the cloth. Olive looked up to see Aunt Dodie standing above her.

"What are you doing?" Aunt Dodie asked. There was a strange expression on her face, one Olive hadn't seen since the day Peter smashed up his plate and tried to hit Uncle Ivor with the cricket bat.

Olive sat back on her heels, lowering the scissors uncertainly.

"I'm making dresses for me and Juliet..."

The silence meeting her reply made her voice tail off. The look on Aunt Dodie's face was so terrible, Olive shrank back instinctively.

"I specifically said... do not touch that box. How *could* you, Olive?"

Olive scrambled to her feet, her heart pounding.

Aunt Dodie lunged past her to catch up the pieces of cut fabric, and now clutched it to her breast, her hazel eyes blazing.

"You've slashed my mother's kimono to pieces! One of the

few, precious things I have that belonged to her. You – *you*, of all people, who miss your own mother so much, should understand how devastating this is. This kimono is sacred!" Her voice snagged, part roar of rage, part wail of anguish.

Tears burst onto Olive's cheeks, dripping onto her jumper. She hadn't realised. She hadn't heard. "I'm sorry," she tried to whisper, but in the face of Aunt Dodie's rage the words stuck in her throat.

"I can't bear to look at you right now, Olive." Aunt Dodie's usually gentle voice came out like a curse as she sank to her knees, buckling in the middle as if the pain Olive had caused was too much for her. "You'd better go, before I say or do something we both regret."

FORTY-EIGHT

Olive

Olive fled. Somehow, her legs carried her down the flights of attic stairs and servants' stairs, along Plas Norton's forbidding corridors with their glaring ancestral portraits, and out to the courtyard. She had to find Peter. They had to go, and at once now that Aunt Dodie had sent her away. Who knew what punishment might befall them if she stayed, having done something so terribly wrong?

She spotted her brother's familiar mop of ginger hair in the kitchen garden, where he was helping Uncle Ivor. He'd started helping as a means to an end, hoping to convince Uncle Ivor to take him fishing, but Olive knew he must secretly like the digging, planting and harvesting, or else he wouldn't have the patience to keep doing it.

"Shouldn't be doing this on the Lord's Day, mind, but it's only a few," Uncle Ivor was saying, as she emerged out of the shadows behind him and waved in Peter's direction. "That's it. Just dig up enough carrots for today's dinner, while I cut a cabbage."

Peter bent over the garden fork Uncle Ivor had used to loosen the soil and pulled up a handful of carrots, wiping the earth off them with his hands.

Olive caught his eye, putting a finger to her lips with a shake of her head to keep him quiet. He looked puzzled but had the sense to say nothing.

"I'll take these in while you cut the cabbage," he called to Uncle Ivor, not waiting for a reply, but heading in Olive's direction with the bunch of carrots in his hands.

"What's up?" he asked, as soon as they were out of earshot.

"We're going home. We have to go *now*." She clutched his arm, shaking and almost dizzy with fright. Somehow, she had to convince him to go with her. They had to stay together, like Mum said. She had to keep him safe.

He stared at her. "You what? I've just pulled up some carrots for dinner."

"We're leaving. Can't stay now. It's Aunt Dodie – Miss Fitznorton – she told me to... to get out. We're going back to London to find Mum."

For once, he took her seriously. He nodded, even though his face was still creased with confusion.

"We'll take the carrots with us," she added, feeling a little braver now that he hadn't refused to go. "We'll need something to eat on the way. You fetch our coats and meet me at Uncle Ivor's workshop in five minutes. Hurry up!"

In less than five minutes, although it seemed longer, he appeared at the entrance to the workshop, wearing his own coat and carrying hers. Her limbs trembled so violently, he had to help her into it.

"What's happened, Ol?"

She shook her head, suppressing a strangled sob. "We need a torch," she said, scanning the work bench.

"Alright. Keep your hair on."

Peter rummaged in the drawers, pulling out a flashlight. He

flicked it on, shining the light into Olive's face and making her squint, before turning it back off and tucking it into his coat pocket. "I nicked us some bread," he said, showing her the contents of his other pocket.

Nodding, she pulled him outside and around the corner of the building. She wasn't proud of herself for stealing from Uncle Ivor's workshop, but they'd need a torch if they couldn't get to a train before dark.

"This ain't the way to London, is it?" he hissed, as they ran across the front of the building, ducking below the windowsills to avoid being seen.

"We're going to get Tyke first. I'm not going without him. And then, once we've got him, we'll go to the station and find a way to get on a train."

FORTY-NINE

Dodie

One by one, Dodie gathered up the pieces that had been cut from her mother's kimono, sobs racking her chest as she cradled them in her lap. It was ruined, this precious memento of Rosamund. Dodie had pictured her wearing it in her private moments, perhaps even when she'd still carried Dodie in her womb and their lives had been connected, two hearts joined by a flow of blood as well as by love. Rosamund might have tied that belt over her swollen belly and caressed it with her hand, transmitting a mother's tenderness through the gorgeous silk and somehow to Dodie's awareness. But now, thanks to Olive, it was in tatters.

It seemed symbolic of so much in Dodie's life. The world was being torn apart by war, families rent asunder. Her own family was broken up, her parents gone and her sister uncaring; her niece and nephew far from home pursuing their individual dreams. Where was the love she so deeply needed?

She was strong enough to recognise that she'd wasted too much emotion on men who didn't want her or care for her as she cared for them, but it didn't stop her craving the affection of someone who deserved her. Lionel had almost destroyed her faith in herself, let alone her faith in men. It hadn't gone so far with Patrick, but it didn't stop her grieving for what they might have had, if he could just have allowed her to love him instead of putting up barriers that existed only in his mind. Yet it wasn't surprising that he didn't want her enough to follow up on that kiss. No one ever did want her, really. Not when it came down to it. Not once they'd got to know her.

And now Olive had let her down, after everything she'd done for her. She'd tried so hard to help all the children. She'd bought them new clothes and shoes; brought books home to them; read to them; taught Barbara how to play simple piano scales and tunes. She'd put up with Peter's wilfulness; tried to support Michael against the bullies; and even spent much of last weekend on a trip to the back streets of London, all on their behalf. Was it too much to expect a little consideration in return? She'd specifically told the children not to take anything from this box, making her instructions perfectly clear.

Unless...

Her scalp tightened, a cold shudder passing over her as it occurred to her that Olive might not have heard her instructions. It was out of character for the girl to be wilfully disobedient, after all; and she did struggle to hear things from time to time.

Perhaps reprimanding her had been a mistake. She could have given her a bit more of a chance to explain, maybe. But she'd been upset and spoken in the heat of the moment. If she had been unfair, she'd find a way to make it up to the child. The fact remained that Olive should have been more careful and asked for permission before cutting into such a beautiful garment.

Dodie straightened and wiped her eyes with her handkerchief. Gradually the uneven, hiccoughing breaths that had overwhelmed her steadied. She picked up Juliet and stroked the doll's hair back in an automatic gesture, then pocketed the scissors and the smaller scraps of fabric. The larger part of the kimono she folded carefully and carried downstairs before laying it on her bed. Now that she felt calmer, she could see a glimmer of a way forward.

The kimono was damaged irreparably, that was true. But it was long, and Olive had taken her pieces from the bottom hem, not the middle, thank goodness. The damaged part could be trimmed off, a new hem sewn, and the kimono would still be wearable. It would be knee-length, instead of falling to her ankles as it once would have done. It would never be the same, but it wasn't irretrievably lost. And maybe it was time to bring it out of storage, to use it herself and enjoy the sensation of its connection to her mother, instead of treating it like a holy relic to be kept out of sight except on rare pilgrimages to the attics. Some good might have come of all this, after all.

A knock at the door roused her from her reverie.

"Auntie Dolly wants to know if you're joining us for dinner in the kitchen, or if you'll eat later with Mrs Havard," Barbara said, sending a curious glance past Dodie towards the bright fabric spread over the bed.

"I'm not really hungry just now," Dodie replied. "Could you tell her I'll eat later, please, Barbara?"

Dodie squashed the feeling that she was a coward for putting off the moment when she'd have to try to put things right; but she still felt she needed time to recover her equilibrium before she could face Olive and apologise for the way she'd spoken.

She took advantage of the children's mealtime to slip downstairs to the music room and shut herself in with only the piano for company. As always, it provided her with a release. First, the muscle memory of the scales and arpeggios, so automatic she barely had to think at all. Then, pieces that reflected her mood, starting with Beethoven. Once that had satisfied her need for the dark and dramatic, she moved on to Mendelssohn's 'Regrets', which seemed apt considering how she felt about that afternoon, not to mention the previous weekend and the situation with Patrick.

At last, she closed the lid of the piano. She'd have to speak to Olive, now that she was feeling better. It wouldn't be right to put it off any longer. And besides, a cup of tea would be welcome: her mouth was dry and sour after her emotional outburst earlier. She was half tempted to take a leaf out of Charlotte's book and indulge herself by pouring a sherry, but she wasn't one for drinking alcohol in the afternoon, however trying the circumstances.

The children would have finished their meal by now and might even have done the washing up. If she went straight to the kitchen, she'd catch them before they dispersed to their rooms.

After smoothing her skirt over her hips and taking a deep breath for courage, she headed for the kitchen, wondering as she passed the telephone in the hallway whether Mrs Roberts had passed on the gifts of honey and whiskey to Patrick yet. Deep down, she'd been hoping he might respond by telephoning her. Several hours had passed. Would Mrs Roberts have remembered to tell him that they were from the children? Dodie hoped so. It wouldn't do to put him under any feeling of obligation to her, or for him to think she'd sent them as a way of courting his attention. If he wanted to draw a line under their fledgling relationship... friendship – whatever it was – then she'd accept it was over.

It was a difficult thought, one that made her mouth feel all the more dry and added to the hollow feeling of dread; but it wasn't as if she'd been looking for romance when Patrick came into her life. She'd proved this week that work could be a useful distraction from such things, and an arena in which she might enjoy a modicum of recognition, if not yet success. She'd go on applying herself to her work and put any silly hopes of love behind her; eventually, one day, she might forget all this pain.

She found Michael and Barbara drying up the last of the dishes in the scullery.

"I'm looking for Olive. Has she gone back up to your room already, Barbara?" Dodie asked.

The two children exchanged a sidelong glance, their brown eyes suddenly guarded.

"Don't think so," Barbara mumbled.

"Do you know where I might find her?"

Barbara shook her head, making her braided pigtails whip to and fro. She bit her lip anxiously.

"I need to speak to her," Dodie said. The children's apparent reluctance to give any information was puzzling. It occurred to her that Olive might have told them about her harsh words. Colour rose to her cheeks. "She's not in any trouble, don't worry," she added, to reassure them.

"I haven't seen her since we were all up in the attics with you," Michael said.

Barbara seemed strangely interested in her toes.

"Have you seen her since then, Barbara? Surely she ate with you?"

Barbara shook her head.

"Do you mean she hasn't eaten? She must be hungry, in that case."

There was another pause. Something seemed off kilter, but Dodie couldn't put her finger on it. On her way out, she paused in the doorway.

"Did you say you'd seen her, Barbara?"

The girl fumbled with the wooden spoon she'd been drying, almost dropping it. She muttered something inaudible.

"You might as well tell her," Michael said, his face a stern mask.

"Tell me what?"

"She's... that is... she and Peter have... gone home."

"Gone home?" Even though she repeated the words, Dodie took several moments to understand them.

"To London."

"To find their mum," Michael added.

She felt as if she were underwater, struggling to hear or to breathe. Her legs trembled; she reached for the door jamb to steady herself.

"To find their mum?" she repeated, not caring how stupid she must sound.

"I saw Peter getting their coats. He told me you chucked them out," Michael said. His voice was flat and cold, not like his usual voice at all. An adult's hard voice, almost, not a boy's.

"But that's not true."

The children turned back to the sink.

Dodie opened her mouth to say more but closed it again. Instinctively, she looked at her wristwatch: it was nearly four o'clock. A glance upwards to the high window in the scullery showed it was already almost twilight, the sky a clear, cold shade of blue grey.

There wasn't time to try to explain. She had to try to find Olive and Peter before dark.

FIFTY

Olive

Olive and Peter dashed across the lawn in front of Plas Norton, hoping no one would happen to look out of any of the front windows while they passed. By the time they'd reached the edge of the tree-lined hill where the summerhouse stood, Olive was panting.

"We don't belong here," she said, as they climbed upwards through the rhododendrons. "Nothing's gone right since we got here. We should be in London with Mum."

"And Dad," Peter said at once.

She merely nodded. She didn't want to go back to their old flat if Mum might not be there. But she couldn't say that to Peter yet. She needed him to come without a fuss. She was responsible for him, as well as for this mess.

It was a relief to emerge at the top of the slope. She'd liked this woodland before, but now it seemed unwelcoming, threatening even, the branches like claws trying to snag at her and prevent her reaching safety. The summerhouse stood in front of them, silent and empty. There was no sign of Tyke.

They called him, over and over, but didn't catch so much as a glimpse of his ginger fur.

"What do we do now?" Peter asked, chafing at this interruption to their plan.

"We'll wait inside until he comes," Olive replied, trying to sound more confident than she felt. "It never takes him long to come when we call him, does it? He'll be busy mousing, but he'll be along in a minute to see if we've got something for him."

"But we haven't. Unless cats can eat bread. Or carrots."

They sat on the bench with the food between them.

Olive watched Peter's feet swinging impatiently. His legs were too short to reach the floor. He, at least, was wearing stout boots. She had her nice shoes on. Aunt Dodie had brought them back from the jumble sale, and Olive had been thrilled as much by the idea that they'd been chosen specially for her as she'd been by the soft red leather. Now, she wished she'd stopped to put on her sensible school shoes instead. They'd be much better if they ended up walking all the way to London. It must be far away because they'd spent hours on the train.

"So what happened, then?" Peter asked. She'd been hoping he wouldn't.

"I did something bad," she whispered, hanging her head.

"What, really? *You* did?" He sounded almost impressed. "Bad enough to get us kicked out?"

Dumbly, she nodded.

He whistled. He'd only learned to do it in the past couple of weeks, and she knew he'd be pleased that she'd given him a reason to do it now. Briefly, his mouth twisted. "I'll miss Uncle Ivor when we go back. He said he'd take me out shooting soon. Still... It'll be nice to be home with Mum and Dad, anyway. Got to look on the bright side, ain't you?" he added, picking up one of the carrots and wiping it clean on his shorts before taking a bite.

She looked away. How could he eat at a time like this? And

where was Tyke? She hoped he'd come quickly, so they could head off towards the village and beyond that to the station at Pontybrenin.

Abruptly, she thumped her thigh with a balled-up fist.

"What?"

"We didn't bring any money. Stupid of me!"

He pursed his lips, then carried on chewing. "We can do like they do on the films, can't we? Catch hold of the back of the train and ride it that way. Or jump off a bridge onto the roof and hang on tight."

She wasn't convinced this would work, but there'd be time to come up with a better plan before they reached Pontybrenin. First, they needed to find Tyke.

Periodically, she went to the doorway to call him. He still hadn't arrived by the time Peter had eaten most of the carrots and all the bread. The sun was hanging low in the sky, its orange orb dipping behind the shadowy outline of the trees.

"We'll have to go without him," Peter grumbled for the third time.

Olive shook her head, but she knew as well as he did that they were running out of time. If they didn't set off for the village soon, it would be dark, and she didn't fancy the thought of walking several miles across muddy, cow-pat–filled fields with only one torch between them.

As she slid off the bench ready to call Tyke again, Peter held her back. It was his turn to put his finger to his lips and look frightened. With eyes wide, he hopped down and tugged at her arm.

"Hide!" he hissed, making her heart race again as it had done earlier.

There was no time to ask what they were hiding from. The only place where they had any chance of concealment was under the bench. They made a grab for the nest of blankets they kept in the summerhouse for Tyke and dived under the bench, covering themselves with the scratchy layers of cloth.

Under the smelly blanket, Peter put his mouth to her good ear and whispered, "It's the boys from the farm. I can hear them outside, talking."

She froze. "Are you sure?"

He nodded, then buried his face in her neck and clung tightly to her, barely smothering a whimper. Every muscle in their bodies tensed.

The door banged open. Olive forgot how to breathe.

"Coast's clear," she heard a voice say.

The door banged again, and the sounds receded.

She waited, feeling as if her belly had turned to mush. It churned so fiercely she was afraid she might wet herself, or worse. The farm boys were wicked, especially to the Clarkes. She prayed Tyke wouldn't choose this moment to appear; the sort of bullies who threw dung at kids just because they looked different might just as easily hurt an animal. And after Peter had destroyed their den, no doubt they'd be out for revenge.

"Have they gone?" she breathed after a couple of interminable minutes had passed. If she had to stay under here much longer, she feared she'd choke.

Peter shook his head. "I can still hear them talking," he whispered. "They're laughing and doing something against the back wall." He paused, then gripped Olive's wrist so hard she had to bite her lip to keep from screaming.

"They want to get their own back for the den. Ol, they've got matches. They're going to burn the summerhouse down."

FIFTY-ONE

Dodie

"You should telephone the police," Charlotte said, as soon as Dodie explained that Olive and Peter were missing.

Feeling dizzy, Dodie put her palm against her chest. She could hardly get enough oxygen into her lungs. If the police were called, they'd want to know what had provoked Olive and Peter to leave, and it had been shameful enough telling her sister about her harsh words. How could she ever explain herself to a policeman?

She drew in a deep breath. "You don't really think it's come to that yet, do you?" she managed to say, surprised that she could still compose and utter a coherent sentence given the state of her nerves. "We haven't looked for them properly. For all we know, they're hiding in the house to punish me, and they'll come out later when they get hungry."

"Perhaps. But it's also possible that they're walking the roads, where they could easily meet with an accident in the blackout. Or they could have fallen into the lake, or the river."

"Don't say that!" Dodie gasped. "They can't have gone far

in a couple of hours. We'll search the house and grounds, and if we can't find them here, then I'll call the police, I promise."

"Alright," Charlotte conceded. "But we'll give it no more than an hour. And in the meantime, I'll telephone Reverend Appleton. I'll get him to take a discreet look around the railway station and ask him to send Mr Winter to help us with the search at this end. He might even see them on his way here if he hurries."

Dodie nodded, desperate enough to agree to almost anything. Only halfway up the stairs did she remember that Patrick was ill, it was cold outside, and he'd made it clear he wanted nothing to do with her. She faltered, then carried on up to the children's rooms. He might not want to see her, but she was certain he would help the children if he could.

"I need you to search the house," she urged the Clarkes, who had huddled together on Michael's bed. "It isn't true that I told Olive to leave. I was cross, but I would never have said that to her. *Never.*" Somehow, she summoned up a stronger voice. "We need her and Peter back safe. We grown-ups will search the grounds. Will you three please check all the hiding places you can think of in the house? And if you find them, tell them I'm sorry and everything is forgiven. There'll be no more cross words. They don't need to worry about anything. We just need everything to go back to the way it was."

The sullen expression cleared from Michael's face as she spoke, as if he understood she was sincere.

"Alright," he said. "We've played hide and seek around the house a few times. I can think of some places to look."

"Thank you," she said. "I'm going outside to search, but there will still be an adult in the house to look after you all," she added for Shirley's benefit, seeing how the little girl clung to her older sister's side.

"We'll start in the attics," Michael's voice drifted towards her, as she ran to her own room, where she changed into outdoor shoes and pulled a warm cardigan over her dress. There was a torch in her bedside drawer, useful in the event of power cuts: she flicked it on to check there was still life in the batteries before running downstairs so rapidly she almost took a tumble.

Charlotte followed as Dodie ran to collect her coat.

"Dolly and Ivor have set off in the car, to see if they're walking along the driveway. Ivor has checked the workshop and garage, and there's no sign of them there, but he did notice that his torch is missing. He thinks they might have taken it."

"Wouldn't they cross the fields if they were heading towards town or the village? The same way they go to school?"

"Perhaps. Patrick Winter is coming that way on the reverend's bicycle, so if they're on the footpaths he'll see them. We don't need to look there."

A rush of relief flooded through Dodie. If Patrick was coming, it was bound to be alright.

Charlotte reached for her own coat, but Dodie put out a hand to stop her. "The other children need an adult in the house in case of an emergency, and to listen for the telephone. You stay here. I'll look around the gardens. And Charlotte..."

"Yes?" Her sister paused, putting a hand to her forehead. Her customary poise had vanished, making her look older.

"Thank you," Dodie murmured, before hurrying outside into the semi-darkness.

Charlotte had every reason to condemn her this evening, and yet she hadn't uttered a single word of criticism. In fact, she'd been a brick, launching at once into sensible practicality. There wasn't time to reflect on her sister's character, however.

Over and over, Dodie called out the children's names, dashing along the gravel paths between the rose beds and through the walled kitchen garden as quickly as she dared. The twilight made deceptive shadows in every corner, and she squinted as she peered around, trying to make sense of her environment. It was remarkable how different everything looked in the dusk.

It took around half an hour to search the gardens nearest the house, along with Ivor's potting shed and the stables, where she ran past every empty stall. Now and then the upstairs windows shone with light in disused rooms where blackout blinds hadn't been installed, reassuring her that Charlotte and the children were combing the building thoroughly. They could only pray that no Air Raid Precautions warden would choose this evening to inspect them, and indeed that the Luftwaffe wouldn't make any unexpected flights over Wales. As far as she knew, Plas Norton was well out of range, but the way her luck was going this week, an air raid could be the final straw.

FIFTY-TWO

Patrick

It wasn't the first time Patrick had navigated his way in the dark from Pontybrenin to Plas Norton on Reverend Appleton's old boneshaker of a bicycle. At least this time he knew a shortcut, having walked the path across the fields from the village before with Dodie on a golden autumn afternoon when his greatest problem had been much less troubling than missing children and his past being known.

He wobbled along as fast as he dared, legs and lungs aching from the exercise after nearly a week laid up with a chill.

If his mother could see him out in the cold night air, he'd never hear the last of it, even though he was well wrapped up with a muffler and a pullover she'd knitted. He could picture her vividly: hands on her hips, as fierce as a miniature tigress.

Don't you come running to me when you're dead with a fever, she'd say.

He'd never quite worked out the logic of that particular saying, but the thought of it was enough to bring a smile to his cheeks in between sporadic fits of coughing that threatened to topple him into a ditch.

On Ma's advice, he'd bought some shiny new brogues and hoped he wouldn't end up ruining them on this expedition by stepping into a cowpat or scuffing them on the bike's chain. There'd been no time to break them in properly, and the hard new leather threatened to chafe his heels raw, but he carried on pedalling. In the circumstances it was unlikely that Dodie would notice his shoes. Her only concern would be to find the Hicks children. She'd be desperate to bring them back. She prided herself on providing the sense of security and safety all kids needed.

What could have possessed Olive and Peter to run away? He guessed the long separation from their mother, without any word to indicate where she might be, had proved too much.

Mrs Havard had given few details on the telephone, her clipped, aristocratic voice taking on an authority he supposed came naturally to someone born to privilege. She and Dodie were different in many ways: where her sister was sophisticated, conscious of her own attractiveness and how to use it, Dodie struck him as more inhibited. She was like a chameleon, with a powerful desire to blend into the background to avoid being noticed. Yet she'd always step forward to help someone else.

She was authentic; honest. Not the kind of woman who'd exploit her charms to manipulate a man's feelings. In fact, she seemed unaware of how lovely she was. When they had kissed, in that brief but shattering moment that he couldn't regret even though it had led to disaster, she'd been acting on instinct. There was nothing calculating about her. She was the kind of person who would despise any behaviour that wasn't genuine or sincere.

His thoughts had returned to her over and over through the week since their trip to the capital. In the throes of feverish dreams, he'd pictured her face. How crushed she'd been by his rejection, and how she'd used her pride as a shield. The guilt of it had hurt far worse than the aches in his limbs or his hacking cough. She'd said in London she was falling for him, but that was before he revealed his background to her. Now, she might well feel differently. This morning Mrs Roberts had reported that Dodie had delivered honey and whiskey to the vicarage and insisted it was a gift from the children. He could only assume she didn't want him to interpret her generous gesture as forgiveness or encouragement. It hadn't stopped him feeling touched that she'd taken the trouble to bring it, though.

The bike's front wheel bogged down as it hit the gravel surface outside Plas Norton, and he hopped off, coughing, before it could topple him.

Rapid, crunching footsteps approached from around the corner and before he could prepare himself, there was Dodie, her coat flapping open as if she hadn't taken the time to fasten it, and her face pale with worry.

She stopped abruptly, her shoulders sagging. "Oh. I thought you might have found them," she said.

"I'm sorry. I kept my eyes peeled, but there was no sign."

"Charlotte wants to telephone the police, but I was hoping you might..."

He batted away the realisation that he'd disappointed her again and listened while she explained where they'd already searched.

"So where's next?" he asked.

"The lake. They might have hidden in the boathouse." She looked doubtful, but he nodded. It had to be worth a try.

She didn't wait while he propped the bicycle against one of the stone columns in the porch, but forged ahead, and he jogged to catch up, painfully conscious of the weakness in his legs after nearly a week in bed. He coughed as he caught up with her, struggling to catch his breath, and was touched by her concerned frown.

"You shouldn't be out in the cold," she said.

"I'll be grand in a minute," Patrick spluttered, falling into step beside her. "The fresh air is probably doing me good."

Neither of them believed it, but he didn't want her thinking him reluctant to help. What mattered right now was the kids. Darkness was thickening around them, lending a sinister air to the bushes, and making the lake look black and forbidding. He shook off the creepy sensation that made him feel as if something was crawling down the back of his neck. If Olive and Peter were somewhere around here, they'd be getting pretty scared.

Patrick trailed Dodie as she followed the lake's edge for a short distance. Twigs and fallen leaves crunched under their feet. Above the silhouetted hills the moon was rising, frost white.

Soon the boathouse loomed in front of them. The small timber structure was in a poor state of repair, planks rotting and frayed at the base, and paint peeling away. Dodie lifted the latch and tugged at the door, pointing the weak beam from her flashlight into the corners.

Even with Patrick's blocked nose, the odour of damp, mouldy wood, earth and vegetation was pretty strong.

"Nothing," she said, flicking the button to extinguish the flashlight.

He blinked, adjusting to the darkness. The sound of her breathing quickened, as if she was nearing despair, maybe even panic.

"Olive! Peter!" she yelled into the silent mist hovering over the lake.

As if by an unspoken agreement, they both strained to listen for any response, not moving a muscle. The only sound was the murmur of a faint breeze disturbing the highest branches of nearby trees.

"Come on," he said after a minute or so, putting out a hand

to shepherd her away from the water's edge. "Let's head back towards the house."

"This is all my fault," she blurted out, taking him by surprise. "If something awful has happened to them, it will be because of me."

"What do you mean?"

"I upset Olive. That's why she's gone. She'd done something – something disobedient, and I was... Still, it's no excuse. I shouldn't have been harsh with her. What kind of person am I, to make a child feel so unwelcome that she'd run away? Only a monster would do such a thing."

Her voice snagged, and he reached out to seize her hands in his. They were half-frozen. He rubbed them, then tugged his mittens off and slipped them over her fingers, giving them a squeeze.

"Dodie, I never met anyone less harsh or monstrous than you. You don't have a cruel bone in your body. Whatever happened, I'm sure you had your reasons."

"I was angry and upset," she whispered. "And I told her to go before I could say something awful. But I didn't mean for her to *leave*, truly I didn't."

"Of course you didn't. Oh, honey – don't beat yourself up for being human. Kids have a way of making the best of us all kinds of angry sometimes."

"If any harm comes to them, I'll never forgive myself."

Unable to help himself, he pulled her close and folded his arms around her.

"They'll turn up, you'll see," he said into her hair, trying to infuse his voice with the confidence he guessed she needed.

For the briefest of moments she leaned on him, her cheek pressed to the lapel of his coat. When she pulled away, he kept his expression steady. Now wasn't the time to reveal how his heart had leapt when he held her in his arms, or to confess how he'd spent most of the past week longing to see her and touch her again. How he'd relived their kiss over and over, imagining he hadn't stopped it when he did, imagining it hadn't been in the dirt of a London gutter, but that it had gone on, gone deeper and ended in an altogether different and more satisfying way.

Pulling her coat about her, she set off without another word towards the house. He sensed she was battling a tumult of emotions.

Whatever had caused Olive to go, he was as certain as he could be that Dodie hadn't behaved as badly as she believed. She could be stern – he'd seen that when she insisted that he tell her the reasons for his own ill-judged behaviour. But having been on the receiving end of deliberate cruelty, everything he'd observed in her told him she wasn't capable of it. She was too sensitive to the feelings of others to deliberately inflict pain on anyone, and especially a child he knew she'd gone to so much trouble to help. He wasn't the kind of man who prayed, not since he was a kid; still, he glanced towards the heavens as he strode towards the big house and sent up a silent plea for Dodie's sake that Olive and Peter would be found.

Light filled the porch as they approached, and Mrs Havard came out, nudging Michael ahead of her.

"Tell my sister what you just told me," she said as they halted in front of Dodie.

The boy's shoulders hunched over defensively.

Patrick pulled his muffler down and tucked it under his chin, then bent his knees to meet Michael at eye level, holding his gaze. "What can you tell us, Michael?"

"They were going to the summerhouse, sir. To fetch Tyke. The cat," he went on to explain after the adults exchanged mystified glances. He pointed an accusing finger towards Dodie. "*She* wouldn't let Olive keep it in the house, so Olive kept it up there instead."

Patrick straightened, glad to relieve the ache in his knees.

Colour had suffused Dodie's face. "It was riddled with

fleas," she protested. "And it messed on the bed. I wasn't being mean; I was just trying to prevent even more work for Dolly." She swung away abruptly and started marching towards the hill, with such speed and determination that Patrick had to break into a trot to close the distance between them.

"I'm coming too!" Michael shouted, pulling away from Mrs Havard's grasp. His footsteps crunched rapidly across the gravel before he fell into step beside the two adults.

"You'll get cold, Michael. You shouldn't be out here without a coat," Dodie said.

But the boy wasn't listening.

"What's that?" he asked, frowning and tugging at Patrick's elbow.

"What's what?"

"That funny colour in the sky."

Patrick followed the direction he was pointing, struggling to work out what he meant. His brain felt slow, as if his cold had blocked his thinking processes as much as it had clogged his nose and lungs.

"Oh, God!" He'd never heard Dodie blaspheme before. To add to his surprise, she started running up the hill towards the trees, elbows and feet pumping like a kid desperate to win a race in a school sports day.

"I think it's a fire," Michael said, eyes wide with alarm, in the split second before he, too, started running.

Patrick took to his heels after them, but his heart quickly started to pound and his lungs gasped for air in a manner that was shockingly unfamiliar to a man accustomed to striding about the countryside. Up the hill they went, Michael soon gaining on Dodie as they followed the narrow track through the dense rhododendrons. Somehow, his lungs almost bursting with the effort, Patrick's long legs carried him past Dodie and into the clearing at the top.

Flames licked the roof of the wooden summerhouse.

As they emerged from the trees, the summerhouse door banged open and Peter ran out, his face stark and eyes bulging with terror.

"Olive's in there!" he screamed, pointing behind him.

Sparks tossed into the air as the flames caught hold, smoke curling upwards into the darkening sky.

Michael had checked his pace at the sight of Peter, but now started towards the building.

Patrick's blood ran cold. He couldn't let the boy risk himself by going inside – but that was exactly what he seemed about to do.

Somehow, Patrick put on a burst of speed. Only a few yards from the building, he made a desperate leap, arms lunging forwards. His fingers snagged on Michael's sweater. He gripped; held tight. Both toppled face-first onto the cold, damp grass.

The tumble had knocked out what little breath had remained in Patrick's chest. His head swam as he tried to scramble to his feet. He had to get to Olive now that Michael was safe. His feet slipped in his new shoes, sending him back to his knees.

He sucked in a rush of air. Wood smoke filled his mouth.

Before he could stagger up again, his heart nearly stopped. Dodie had run past them and through the summerhouse's open doorway.

FIFTY-THREE

Dodie

Dodie's eyes stung, her lungs choking on the acrid smoke. Rubbing her eyes, she instinctively dropped to a crouching position. Squinting, she waved a hand to try to clear the air. Heat scorched the skin on her face, making her raise an arm as a shield.

Where was Olive? She must be on the floor somewhere.

As she reached out, Dodie's hand struck a hard wooden surface. The bench! It was the only possible hiding place. Coughing, she reached into her pocket for her handkerchief and covered her mouth as she bent to peer across the floor.

A red shoe lay just ahead, poking from a pile of blankets. She'd bought red shoes for Olive at the jumble sale. She grasped it and held tight as the foot inside kicked out fearfully.

"It's alright, Olive. It's me!"

The roaring of the flames sent a rush over her skin, a visceral reminder to get out. A timber cracked and fell only feet away, making her flinch.

Through the smoke, Olive's terrified eyes stared at her. The girl was curled into a ball, almost paralysed by fear, and deathly pale despite the hot glow of flames.

Dodie uncovered her mouth so that the child could read her lips. "Come on, Olive. I've got you." She reached for the child's hand, ducking her head as something crashed behind her.

Seizing Olive's hand in a determined grip, she tugged as hard as she could, fighting not to drown in the thick, evil smoke. An almighty heave brought the little girl out from under the bench, and a step closer to the doorway.

Staggering, coughing and with streaming eyes, Dodie dragged Olive the few yards between the bench and the doorway, then scooped an arm under her shoulders. With the fierce heat over their heads, she was scared to stand, but she couldn't lift her from a kneeling position.

Her heart leapt as a tall figure filled the doorway, hands groping towards them through the smoke as he almost tripped over them.

Patrick.

Together, they lifted Olive and stumbled outside with the child's cowering body held between them, before collapsing onto the grass. After the smoke, the cold November air was so sweet it hurt to breathe it in. Dodie took in great gulps of it, cradling Olive in her arms.

"You're alright, darling Olive. I've got you. I've got you," she crooned, holding the girl tightly against her chest.

Patrick's arms encircled them both, and as she leaned into his strength, she allowed herself to cry. Harsh sobs racked her as she rocked the child back and forth. She'd come so close to disaster. To losing Olive for good. To a lifetime of guilt and self-recrimination.

Patrick murmured hushing noises against her hair.

She reached up to touch his cheek and realised it, too, was damp.

"Thank God," he muttered, over and over, as if he could

hardly believe they were safe. She understood: the heat from the burning summerhouse was still fierce behind them, sending its glow into the night sky and throwing golden light and eerie shadows across the grass towards the trees. The timbers hissed and spat, crashing and tossing up billowing sparks as the structure collapsed.

"I'm so sorry," she whispered into what she hoped was Olive's good ear. "Thank goodness you're alright."

Her heart filled as Olive's arms crept around her and clung.

"*Dodie!*" The voice shrieking her name from the edge of the woods was familiar, yet it sounded completely unlike she'd ever heard it before. Hoarse. Wild. Hysterical.

Charlotte ran towards them, dropping to her knees at Dodie's side.

"What were you *thinking?* Peter came running down the hill and said the summerhouse was on fire and Olive was trapped and you'd gone inside and oh – I thought I'd lost you!"

Until her voice cracked on the final few words, Dodie couldn't tell whether her sister was angry with her or relieved to find her safe. Charlotte's blonde hair was dishevelled, and she was out of breath from running up the hill.

Dodie blinked her stinging eyes, stunned by the force of Charlotte's emotion as she covered her face with her hands and let out an anguished sob.

"I didn't think you'd—" She stopped, realising how wrong she'd been. How had she ever believed her sister didn't care?

"Don't ever do anything like this to me again, do you hear?"

Dodie nodded.

"We're all alright," she said, untangling an arm from Patrick and Olive's embrace and reaching out to catch one of Charlotte's hands. It was shaking.

Charlotte never behaved like this. She was always measured, controlled. Even though Dodie frequently had the sense that her sister's nerves teetered on the brink, making her turn too often to the sherry or gin bottle, she'd never once seen her lose her grip on herself. She'd certainly never heard her shriek.

Behind her, Patrick's breathing had slowed, but now he succumbed to a coughing fit that reminded Dodie he'd left his sick room to help her.

Olive's face was still buried against her breast, and Dodie could feel that some of the rigid tension in the little girl's muscles was starting to ease.

All three of them were holding onto Dodie as if she really mattered to them. For a moment, she closed her eyes and absorbed the feeling that she was loved.

Opening them again, she saw Michael dart over to the trees to stoop and pick something up. His face glowed as he carried it towards them.

"Olive!" he called, a broad smile lending a joyful lilt to his voice. "Look who I've found."

"Look, Olive," Dodie murmured. Her own cheeks lifted as she realised what Michael was holding.

Olive rubbed her eyes with her fists. Her mouth fell open in wonder.

"Tyke!" she cried, her voice little more than a croak. "You found him!"

FIFTY-FOUR

Dodie

That night, Dodie retired to her room early, exhausted by the day's events. She'd just climbed under the blankets on her bed and positioned her feet on her hot water bottle when Charlotte tapped softly and poked her head around the door.

"May I come in?" she asked. "I've brought us a little pick-me-up."

Dodie sat up. "Is everything alright with the children?"

Her sister crossed the room and handed Dodie a balloon glass of brandy, then perched on the edge of the bed cradling her own glass, huddled in a silken nightgown and a dressing gown that was characteristically more glamorous than practical for Plas Norton's chilly rooms.

"The children are fine. I helped Dolly put them to bed half an hour ago. I just wanted to speak to you on our own. To clear the air."

Dodie sank back against her pillow, hoping her sister wasn't intending to start an argument. She didn't have the strength to cope with any further upset. "Does it need to be cleared?" she asked.

Charlotte's blue eyes regarded her without flinching. "I think we both know it does. Things haven't been easy between us for a long time. But after what happened today... It's the sort of thing that makes one pause and reflect on what might have happened, as much as what did happen."

"Go on," she said, warily.

"I just wanted to say that I'm so glad I didn't lose you. I've lost so many of those I love. I don't think I would ever recover from losing you as well." Charlotte stopped as her voice cracked with emotion.

Dodie tugged at a ragged cuticle on her thumbnail, unwilling to look her sister in the eye. "I wouldn't have thought you'd miss me all that much. You sent me away as soon as the twins were born. It was never the same after that."

"Oh, Dodie. There's so much you don't know."

"Then explain it to me. I'd like to understand."

Charlotte let out a heavy sigh. She drained her glass in one and set it down on the nightstand, then crossed to the window and pulled open the curtains to gaze out at the night sky in defiance of the blackout.

"After the twins were born, I was in such agony. You can't begin to imagine."

Dodie drew up her knees and hugged them through the blankets. "Do you mean from the birth?"

"Darling, the physical pain was the least of my problems. At least the worst of that was over in a day. No... I mean Kit." She leaned her forehead against the windowpane.

"You must have missed him terribly." Dodie recalled Patrick's words. In less than a year, Charlotte had been a bride, then a widow, then a mother. She found her heart aching on her sister's behalf. It was an unfamiliar sensation – and, she had to acknowledge, overdue.

"I missed him more than I could ever say, and still do. But worse than that, I felt it was my fault he'd died."

"I don't understand. I thought he caught influenza...?"

"His health was delicate. I knew it, but I didn't try hard enough to convince him to take fewer risks. He had such a strong sense of vocation to work with the poor, I didn't want to argue with him about it. He wore himself out, left himself vulnerable, and I didn't stop him. If I had, things could have been so different. Christopher and Loulou would have known their father. You could have stayed here. I wanted to shield you from the pain. From my failings."

Lit by the moonlight through the windowpane, Charlotte's face looked haunted. "I was utterly broken. It's hard to describe... I simply couldn't function. I wanted to die, so the agony would stop. If it hadn't been for Venetia and Maggie, perhaps I would have. Their kindness; their patience; their practical help... They saved me. I thought I was saving you by sending you away to school where you wouldn't have to witness what was happening, but I know that in fact I let you down. I'm so sorry for that. It's one of my greatest regrets."

Dodie set down her glass untouched. Despite feeling bone-weary, she slipped from the bed and padded to the window to wrap Charlotte in her arms. "You mustn't feel guilty. You were doing your best," she murmured, and for the first time in twenty years she realised it was true. Charlotte had had the kindest intentions.

Little things fell into place: not seeing her sister in the days between the twins' birth and departing for school. Maggie's mysterious remarks about the dark state of mind a new mother could find herself in, so quickly stifled by Venetia's warning look. Even Charlotte's drinking, and her short-lived affairs with men in London. Had she been warding off feelings of loneliness and guilt for all these years?

Shivering in the cold draught from the window, Charlotte

leaned her cheek against Dodie. "Do you think you could find it in your heart to forgive me?" she asked, in little more than a whisper.

"If you can forgive me for being such a horrid, resentful little beast."

"No wonder you were. I handled everything so badly."

Dodie smothered a cough, her lungs still sensitive after the smoke earlier. "Come away from the window," she said, once she'd got her breath back. "After the day we've had, the last thing we need is PC Todd paying us a visit to tell us off for showing a light."

Charlotte nodded, but she still looked mournful, her usually elegant face blotchy and streaked with dried tears. With an arm around her shoulders, Dodie steered her back towards the bed.

"Let's get under the covers where it's warmer. You can tell me all about Kit. How you met; what made you fall in love with him. What your wedding was like. I want to know every little detail."

Charlotte's face softened. She wiped her eyes with her thumb and slipped under the sheets, her toes reaching for the hot water bottle at the same moment as Dodie's. They plumped up the pillows under their heads and lay facing each other.

"*Every* detail?" she repeated.

Dodie couldn't help but grin at the irrepressible twinkle in her sister's eyes. "Perhaps not quite everything."

"I'll tell you everything about Kit if you tell me everything about Patrick."

"There isn't much to tell," she said a little ruefully.

"But there is *something*, isn't there?"

"Yes, I think there is. I hope there is."

Charlotte reached across to squeeze her arm. "I *am* glad. I know you don't need my advice, Dodie... But if I may say just one thing, based on my experience... If your instincts are telling you he's the one, then trust them. War may create opportunities in directions neither of you ever expected. But it can steal your chances of happiness, too. It can leave you with a lifetime lamenting the things you didn't do when you had the chance. I wish I hadn't asked Kit to wait for me. We could have had years together, instead of weeks. If you and Patrick love each other, seize the day."

In the past, Dodie might have bristled at being offered advice by her sister. She'd have been angry that the woman who had sent her away felt she had any right to influence the course of her life. But not now. Now, she could see the sorrow in her sister's eyes and hear the regret in her voice. She understood that Charlotte wished her only happiness, and always had done.

"Thank you," she said. "I'll remember."

FIFTY-FIVE
DECEMBER

Dodie

Dodie smiled as she surveyed the Plas Norton ballroom. If everything went to plan, this promised to be a party the children would never forget.

The room hadn't looked so festive since Loulou and Christopher's eighteenth birthday celebrations a couple of years earlier. The plaster mouldings on the high ceiling were draped with yards of colourful paper chains made by the children. Above the tall windows hung garlands of red-berried holly wrapped in trailing ivy.

Wooden chairs had been set up for the children, along with more comfortable ones for the adults. Cloth-covered tables against one wall groaned under the weight of sandwiches, mince pies and cake, thanks to the generosity of the local Women's Institute. Dodie ran through a mental checklist, ensuring that sufficient plates and napkins had been provided for all the children, as well as beakers for the pitchers of orange squash. They'd have to keep Tyke out of here, else he'd scoff the tinned salmon sandwiches Dolly had spent ages making.

In the days preceding the party, Charlotte had been on edge, and although everyone was looking forward to her son Christopher's return for the Christmas holidays, Dodie guessed she still dreaded the prospect of their first Christmas without Loulou, who might not get enough leave to make the trip back.

The two sisters had been getting along much better since the fire. They'd spent a companionable Sunday afternoon decorating the branches of the nine-foot-high Christmas tree which stood in one corner. Ivor had dragged it out of the woods with a tractor borrowed from the farm next door, and now it was pretty enough to put even Scrooge into a festive mood, festooned with silvery strands and bright lengths of electric fairy lights. As they were unlikely to be at risk of bombing, they had hung their usual collection of glass ornaments from its boughs: coloured baubles and drops in glorious colours, little angels and birds with delicate glass tails. These were supplemented by Father Christmases made by the children from crepe paper and pipe cleaners, and thin, crisp gingerbread biscuits with hollow shapes filled with melted boiled sweets, like edible stained-glass windows. Goodness only knew how Dolly had found the time, or enough sugar, to make them. They dotted the tree's branches, enough for each of the evacuees and local schoolchildren to have one.

A generous number of presents waited in a couple of hessian sacks beside the tree, each wrapped in newspaper made cheerful with red and green printed stars. The children had spent hours at the kitchen table cutting halves of potato and using them as stamps with saucers of paint. They had no idea that a special visitor would be joining the party later to give each child a gift.

In another corner stood Rosamund's piano, tuned to perfection by Maggie and Dolly's elder brother Stanley Cadwalader. Stan had been almost blinded in the Great War and now made a living as a piano tuner. Watching him at work, Dodie had tried not to think about how many more young men might need to find new ways to make ends meet after the current war. As she retrieved a stack of festive sheet music from the piano stool for Miss Honeycutt to play later, she could only pray that the conflict in Europe would end victoriously much sooner than the four-year war that had changed Ivor and Stanley's lives and killed the Cadwaladers' eldest brother Leonard. How many more names would be added to the war memorials in Pontybrenin and Bryncarreg?

Venetia's voice carried effortlessly from the doorway, interrupting Dodie's reverie. "Oh, doesn't this room look marvellous? Our evacuees will be thrilled when they see it. I'm glad to see you're preparing the music. I gather Miss Honeycutt and Miss Bright won't be attending after all." She limped across the room and sank down with obvious relief on the piano stool.

Dodie's smile drooped. "But Miss Honeycutt was going to play the carols, and some children's songs for the party games."

"I fear you'll have to step into the breach, dear girl."

"But... but I can't play in front of everyone..." Dodie stammered, clutching the sheaves of music to her chest.

"Nonsense. Your teacher always described you as a talented pianist."

She shook her head. The thought of performing in front of a whole crowd of children and adults made her knees quake.

Venetia sniffed and arched one of her thick eyebrows. "I'm inclined to think a young woman who can dash into a burning building to rescue a child can do anything she puts her mind to."

Dodie's cheeks reddened.

Venetia's round face had taken on a dreamy expression. "Maggie had rescued someone when I first met her – did you know that? It's funny... now that I come to think about it, you're rather like her. Did you know it was being present at your birth that inspired her ambition to become a midwife?"

Dodie nodded, glad that Maggie was now the subject of the conversation and not her fear of performing in public.

"Back then, she had everything against her," Venetia continued. "No education. No money for training or equipment. No connections. But she had remarkable courage and determination. She refused to allow anyone else to determine that she shouldn't use her skills and talents. And upon my word, she worked hard."

Her fondness and pride in her lodger's achievements made Dodie reflect, not for the first time, that they must have become close friends over so many years of living together. Their bond seemed so unshakeable; it was impossible to imagine either of them ever choosing to live alone.

"I can see how much you admire her," she murmured.

"More than you'll ever know. Dodie, I urge you to consider that *you've* worked hard too, to help those children, just as over the course of many years you've worked to develop your talents as a pianist. From what Charlotte tells me, you're perfectly capable of playing music to not only entertain the children but also to lift people's spirits. In these troubled times we need all the festive cheer we can get, and for each one of us to play our part in keeping morale up." She sighed, making Dodie hope she'd drop the subject, and then shrugged. "It's up to you, of course; but it does seem rather a shame to let all that talent and practice go to waste for the sake of jealous and petty remarks made by less gifted girls more than a decade ago."

The words were spoken without malice, but Dodie felt them chafe like grit in a shoe.

"Don't let her boss you about," came a dry Welsh voice behind her. Maggie and Charlotte had come in while they were talking.

Venetia rolled her eyes. "I'm merely pointing out that if Josephine here won't play, and Miss Honeycutt can't, then who else could do it even half as well? The children need music for their party, don't they? How else will they play musical chairs or sing carols?"

Maggie tutted. "I'm sure there's a gramophone somewhere. Now, come and see what my clever sister has done with the cake."

Ever tactful, Maggie took Venetia's arm and steered her towards the table of food.

Dodie remained where she was, leafing through the pages of sheet music.

No doubt Venetia was right. She had allowed those horrid girls at boarding school to influence her feelings about performing. She'd never again risked exposing to criticism anything so intensely personal as her love of music. Her stomach curdled as she laid a hand on the smooth varnished lid of the piano and flexed her fingers. Could she bring herself to do it, if there was no one else to play? Could she?

An excited hubbub of bright young voices came from the corridor outside. Dodie's ears strained as she turned to face the door. Yes, there it was: the deeper voice she'd hoped to hear, the one that made something in her chest fizz and pop with pleasure, and all her anxieties melt away.

As the children filed in behind Charlotte, dressed up in their party clothes and with exclamations of delight at the gaily decorated ballroom, Dodie's eyes sought out and then lingered on Patrick's handsome face. Although he was firing off instructions to the children, his attention was on her. And when she stepped forward and greeted the evacuees and local schoolchildren, her senses were locked on him as if magnetised.

The children's respect for him was obvious in the way they lined up quietly and obediently.

"Good afternoon, Mrs Havard. Good afternoon, Miss Fitznorton," they chorused as they must have been taught. The nod of approval from their teacher made them all stand a little taller.

Charlotte stepped forward, smart in a scarlet dress that clung in all the right places. Her blonde hair was expertly styled and her make-up perfect. Dodie felt unsophisticated by comparison. Yet a glance at Patrick showed he had paid her sister no more than cursory attention. His grey eyes slid again and again to meet Dodie's gaze, giving her a warm feeling inside.

"Thank you, children," Charlotte said. "Good afternoon to you all, and welcome to Plas Norton. You all look awfully smart in your party outfits, I must say. We hope you'll enjoy spending the final afternoon of the school term with us. We've planned lots of fun party games for you, and later we've arranged for a very special guest to join us. I wonder if any of you will be able to guess who it is?"

Speculative whispers of *Father Christmas* swept along the rows of children, but Charlotte merely responded with an enigmatic smile.

"Naturally, it wouldn't be a Christmas party without plenty of delicious treats for you to eat and drink. How many of you like jelly and blancmange?"

Their answering cheer made all the adults laugh.

Patrick thanked Charlotte, Dodie and Dolly on behalf of the school. "Before we eat, we've prepared a little performance to thank you for hosting our Christmas party," he added.

At his nod, two children stepped forward and recited the first lines of 'A Visit from St Nicholas' with such solemnity that Dodie's heart squeezed. The group took it in turns to perform, each child getting their chance to shine, before taking their seats with the exception of Michael, who pulled a nightcap from his pocket and put it on. He performed the role of Ebenezer Scrooge with zest, and Dodie couldn't conceal her pride as others joined him to act out an abridged version of *A Christmas Carol,* Peter in the uncharacteristically angelic role of Tiny Tim.

As they took their bows, to everyone's surprise the loudest

applause came from the doorway, where Miss Bright had appeared.

"This is an unexpected pleasure," Dodie said to her while the children scattered towards the tables of food. "I heard you were unwell."

Miss Bright winced and looked down at her feet. "Oh, I'm much better now, thank you. And I really didn't want to miss the party, when the children were all looking forward to it so much."

Patrick had moved to stand beside Dodie, his proximity sending her senses into a tailspin. "I'm so glad you were able to join us, Miss Bright," he said, reaching out to shake her hand and making her stammer and blush.

While his colleague went to supervise the children at the tables, he bent to murmur in Dodie's ear. "Interesting to see Miss Bright has wriggled out from under Miss Honeycutt's iron fist."

"Do you think they weren't really ill?"

"They were no sicker than you or I. The old battle-axe just hated the thought of the kids having fun together. But look at them all now, mixing like old friends and enjoying the craic. You'd never know which ones were local and which were evacuees."

Dodie followed his gaze. He was right: the children seemed on good terms. She heaved in a sigh, relieved that the conflict which had reached its climax with the torching of the summerhouse had finally fizzled out. Perhaps Sergeant Morgan's subsequent visit to the school and the farm boys' punishment had been enough to make them understand the disastrous consequences of their rivalry. Perhaps they had found unity in the shared pleasure of anticipating Christmas and performing together. She was glad.

"You look beautiful, by the way. But then, you always do. I

can hardly tear my eyes from you. Do you think we could snatch a moment to talk before the end of the party?"

"I'd like that," she said. Her heart skipped as his gaze dropped to her lips. She couldn't think of anything she'd like more than time alone with him.

"Who'd like to play a game?" Charlotte called out, clapping her hands to get the children's attention. "We'll start with musical statues. Find a space in the middle of the room, ready to dance to the music. The last one to freeze when the music stops is out."

As one, Charlotte, Venetia and Maggie turned to stare at Dodie.

Her mouth went dry. The children were already moving into position around the room, and there was no gramophone to play songs for them.

"Does Miss Bright play piano?" she whispered urgently to Patrick.

He chuckled. "Sure, but her playing is even worse than mine, and mine is atrocious," he replied. He sent her a curious look, no doubt wondering why she had suddenly turned pale.

Across the room, Barbara was watching her with wide, trusting eyes. What would she think if Dodie spoiled the party by refusing to play? The children had shown courage in facing up to bullies; could Dodie fail to do the same now, when hers had passed out of her life long ago?

"Oh, to hell with it," she muttered, and crossed to the piano stool before she could think too hard about it. If she gave herself time to panic, she'd never do it.

"Turn the pages for me?" She sent Patrick a wild-eyed look over her shoulder, and he sprang to help.

Having him standing beside her made her feel a little better. She flexed her fingers, rolled her shoulders and launched into 'What Will Santa Claus Say?' His look of surprise was so gratifying, she started adding some jazzy embellishments, and before she knew it, she'd started to enjoy herself.

The children jigged and hopped, waving their arms and laughing, and soon Dodie was laughing too, stopping at unpredictable moments and giggling as the children froze in silly poses. She played 'Winter Wonderland' and 'Deck the Halls' until Charlotte changed the game to Pass the Parcel, then continued with 'Good King Wenceslas' and 'Jingle Bells'. At last Barbara tore off the final layer of crepe paper with a triumphant grin and held up her prize of a magic painting book.

"You're a marvel," Patrick said when the games were over. "How did I not know you could play like that?"

"I don't play in front of people," she said, blushing.

"You do now," Charlotte remarked, sending her a wink before addressing the children again.

"It's time to welcome our special visitor, children."

As this announcement sent them into a frenzy of cheering, Patrick intervened. With his sternest voice he got them to sit up with arms folded and legs crossed. All were agog, their excitement tangible.

Ivor opened the door to reveal the Reverend Appleton, come to read the children a story. He beamed at them in his kindly way, and Dodie hoped he wouldn't notice when one of the evacuees grumbled rather loudly: "Bloody funny looking Father Christmas, that."

"Shhh!" Patrick said at once, plastering a frown onto his face. She watched him, loving the way his silver-grey eyes gleamed when he was trying not to betray his amusement. He caught her looking and his lips twitched in a way that made her stomach perform all kinds of gymnastics.

What an afternoon it had been – and it wasn't over yet. As the vicar's story ended, the door opened again, and this time the children were not disappointed.

"Ho! Ho! Ho!" boomed a jolly Welsh voice. "*Nadolig Llawen* – Merry Christmas!"

In walked an old man in red, sporting a fine white beard and Wellington boots, and carrying what looked suspiciously like a potato sack. The vicar vacated his seat and the children each had their chance to tell Father Christmas what they wished for, and to receive a small gift donated by the local villagers. Softly, Dodie played Christmas carols until the gift-giving was complete, then slipped away to offer her own thanks to whoever had played the role so capably.

She caught him by the front door, where he was shaking hands with Ivor.

"Thank you so much," she said, holding out her right hand.

He grasped it in both of his and, to her surprise, didn't let go. The way he gazed at her was oddly intense, as if he wanted to capture the details of her face to be stored up for the future.

"It was my pleasure – to tell the truth I should be thanking you for the invitation. My, you've grown into a beauty. And your playing... well, that was a treat to hear. Just like your mam. She used to love her piano."

Dodie's heart leapt. "You remember my mother?" There was something familiar about him, but she couldn't recall his name.

"Aye, I remember her well." His green eyes misted. "From what I've been told, you're just like her. You have the same intelligence. The same care for other people. And I suspect the same strength. She'd have been so proud if she could see you now." He appeared lost in memories. "It damn well broke my heart the day I had to take you off to that school. It was no place for a little one like you. When I think what you must have gone through..."

Dodie beamed with pleasure. "You're Mr Cadwalader. Dolly and Maggie's father. And my mother's driver. Ours, too, of course, when I was small. I still have the toy car you made for me. How lovely to see you. It must be fifteen years or more since I saw you last."

On an impulse, she kissed his whiskery cheek. He must be a sentimental old thing, to judge by the way tears filled his eyes in response, but as she waved goodbye it was comforting to know he remembered her and Rosamund with such affection.

She drifted back along the corridor towards the ballroom, reflecting on how her long-held views of the past had started to change. Not only understanding the reason she'd been sent away, but also coming to realise that her departure had been felt as a loss by those closest to her. She'd been missed. It was a poignant realisation, but it felt good. Finally, twenty years on, she was starting to heal.

Patrick was waiting outside the study. "I couldn't leave without trying to catch you alone," he said, pulling her inside the room.

It was late afternoon, the remaining daylight filtering through the window watery and grey. Soon the party would end. Tomorrow morning, Patrick would catch the train back home to London. How she would miss him. His wry sense of humour; his strength and dependability; the way he looked at her, as if she was the glamorous heroine of a story, not a mere library assistant in a small, insignificant corner of Wales.

She moved unhesitatingly into his embrace. His lips brushed her temple, into her hair, then their faces tilted to join lips in a kiss that was as tender as it was passionate. A soft moan caught in Dodie's throat as his hands splayed across her back, pulling her close against him. Reaching up, she snagged her fingers in the softness of his hair, relishing the masculine scent and taste of him, the roughness of his suit and the hardness of his body against hers.

"We've had so little time," he murmured, his voice hoarse with regret.

"I know. But we'll have more when you come back. And you'll be glad to spend Christmas with your mother."

"I will. But..."

She waited, almost holding her breath. This close, he was beautiful. The lines of his face which had once seemed stern and forbidding now struck her as intensely sensitive.

"London doesn't feel like home anymore. Nowhere can be home to me now, unless you're there. As much as I love my mother and owe her more than I can ever repay, my heart will be at Plas Norton with you."

It was such an unguarded thing to say. How could she feel anything but love for a man prepared to expose his vulnerabilities with such honesty? His words lodged in her heart, making it swell with joy. She responded the only way she could: by kissing him, the kiss quickly deepening and becoming breathless, their bodies pressing as tightly to each other as they could, leaving no possibility of doubt as to the level of their passion.

She'd forgotten how thrilling it was to feel desire, and to be desired in return. All over her body, from the tips of her toes to the scalp, her skin tingled, aware only of him. She wanted more – so much more. Nothing she'd experienced with Lionel had ever come close to this.

Patrick straightened with obvious reluctance, cradling her face in his hands as he regained control of his ragged breathing.

"I've gotta level with you. And this room seems the right place to do it, knowing your love of books."

He glanced around at the yards of bookshelves. The smile curving the edge of his mouth was so delicious she had to reach up to kiss it again.

"Go on," she said, her hunger to taste him only momentarily assuaged.

"I know I'm not worthy of you, but nothing would make me prouder than to be yours, Josephine Fitznorton. Being with you... it's like being a character in an adventure story. I'm spellbound, enthralled by the way you keep on surprising me, making me want nothing more than to keep turning the pages and find out what happens next. The world could end, and if you were in my arms I wouldn't even notice."

"Darling Patrick... There's no one I'd rather have as the hero in my love story."

She laughed as he picked her up and swung her around for one more kiss before they'd have to return to the ballroom and real life. Her heart was full.

If this was a story, she wanted it never to end.

FIFTY-SIX

Olive

Olive sat quietly, turning the pages of her new book carefully so as not to bend them. It was called *Adventures of the Wishing-Chair*. She'd borrowed it from the library a few weeks ago and had been sad when the time came to return it. The idea of being able to jump in a chair and transport herself safely home through the power of wishing had captivated her. Now, she had her very own copy, one she could keep and re-read as many times as she wanted.

When Father Christmas asked her what she'd like most of all for Christmas, she'd had no hesitation in telling him what she wished for.

"I want to see my mum," she murmured in his ear. If anyone had the power to make it happen, he did.

"She's in London, is she?"

"I think so. If I can't see her... if that's too much to ask for... Well, then I'd like a letter from her, so I know she's alright. Please," she added, belatedly remembering what Auntie Dolly always called the magic word.

"I'll do my best," he said. "In the meantime, this present here has your name on it." That was when he handed her the book, wrapped in newspaper with potato prints, just like the wrapping paper she and her fellow evacuees had made a couple of weeks ago.

It struck her later as strange that Father Christmas had a Welsh voice. In the toy shops back home he'd always sounded like a Londoner. Perhaps he had to change the way he spoke to suit the places he went. As he left, waving goodbye, he instructed them all to be good, and to go to bed early on Christmas Eve. Even Peter had promised solemnly to obey, though Olive guessed he'd struggle to stick to it.

Still, he hadn't been so horrid to her since that terrifying night at the summerhouse. For nearly a week he'd insisted on sleeping in the same bed with her, like they used to at home. He hadn't even mentioned the wet sheets in the mornings, just helped her tug them off the rubber-covered mattress and carry them downstairs for the laundry.

Where he'd been clingy, she had retreated into herself. She was glad Aunt Dodie still wanted her, and thankful to have been saved. But thinking about that led her to thoughts of the sister she hadn't been quick enough to save from a fire. The memories had rushed back to torment her ever since she first smelled the smoke and saw flames licking up the summerhouse wall beside her. Perhaps if she'd been braver, instead of curling up and freezing like a frightened hedgehog under the bench that night, Aunt Dodie wouldn't have had to risk her life. If she'd been braver, more like Aunt Dodie, and rushed to the rescue on that chilly evening four years ago, Irene might have lived.

Without her mum, there was no one she could speak to about it. Without her mum, it didn't really feel like Christmas, even with a new book and all the games they'd played today, and the songs and the wonderful food. Without Mum, nothing was right. Olive put on a smile and joined in the games, but her heart wasn't in it.

Four o'clock came, signalling time for the local children to go. There'd been no hostility from the farm kids since the fire. After word spread around the village that two children could have died, and the police had dealt with the Preece boys, there'd been no more trouble on the walk to and from school. Michael, Barbara and Shirley looked almost relaxed now as they walked past the farm, although Olive was sure none of them would ever be able to forget the humiliation of being spat upon and pelted with lumps of dung.

As the Bryncarreg children trooped out, Olive was able to bid them farewell and wish them "Happy Christmas" quite sincerely. Soon, only the evacuees were left in the ballroom.

Reverend Appleton appeared at the door, and Olive heard Barbara tut beside her.

"I hope he isn't going to read us another one of his boring stories," she whispered in Olive's good ear.

Olive shrugged.

"Gather around, children," he called in his brisk way. "Hurry, now. We have one final surprise for you." He beckoned towards the doorway, where Aunt Dodie stood with Mr Winter and Mrs Havard. They were whispering together, but with their hands covering their mouths Olive couldn't tell what they were saying.

She exchanged a glance with Barbara. Whatever it was, there was little chance that it could top a visit from Father Christmas, especially now that the Bryncarreg kids had gone home.

Mr Winter opened the door, and after a moment's pause a line of grown-ups filed into the room, some singly and some in pairs. They were wearing coats and hats, as if they'd only just arrived.

A squeal from Barbara made Olive jump.

"Mum!" Barbara screeched, flinging herself at a red-haired woman who had come in leading a small child by the hand. She laughed as Michael and Shirley piled equally exuberantly into a group embrace that made some of the other adults stare. Perhaps they were startled that Mrs Clarke looked so different from her children, whose deep brown skin and black hair were nothing like hers.

There was no doubting the love between them, or their joy at being reunited, however different they looked. Watching them together gave Olive a jolt like electricity.

Her breath came in gulps. Around her, children were starting to move, some hesitantly and others barrelling towards the assembled parents. Snotty-nosed Sidney was beaming with joy, shaking hands with his father and having his hair ruffled by his mum. Jimmy had his face buried in his gran's coat, his skinny little arms not quite reaching all the way round her.

Only Eva Fischer looked as downcast as Olive felt. There'd be no chance of her parents turning up from Prague. Olive had overheard Auntie Dolly talking about her once, saying the girl's family might be dead, for all anyone knew. She took a step towards her and held out a hand.

With a nod, Eva took it. They looked at each other, standing in silence and shared understanding.

"My host comes for me," Eva said. She patted Olive's arm and walked to join a kindly-looking woman in an expensive coat and smart hat near the door.

Olive realised that the local host families had sent someone to collect their evacuees and their parents. They must have invited them to stay, or perhaps they were taking the children and their parents back to the station to catch the train back to London. How many of them would return after Christmas, if they had the chance to go home now? Given that there'd been no bombings in the capital, many felt, like Michael, that there'd been no point in sending so many children away to strangers, where they might be in more danger than they faced at home. Perhaps only Peter and Olive would be left to start the new school term at Bryncarreg Elementary School in January.

She turned away with a sigh, her feet dragging, looking for the chair with her book on it. Her own wishing-chair, where she'd wished so hard for her mother. If only real life could be more like a story with a happy ending. But when she reached for the book, a bump against her arm knocked it from her hand.

"Watch out," she growled at Peter, who had appeared beside her.

His freckled face was lit by a wild grin. "Ol! Ol – what are you doing? *Look*, will you?"

She followed the line of his finger, and her heart nearly stopped.

At the back of the line of parents and hosts stood two women dressed in shabby coats, looking lost. Aunt Dodie was walking towards them, her steps speeding up as if she recognised them. Her lovely smile lit her face as she scanned the room and made eye contact.

"Mum!" Peter yelled, shock giving way to excitement as he flung himself towards them.

She looked different, her nose misshapen, more crooked than it had been before. Peter was right, though. It really was Mum. She patted him on the head and said something, then put her arm around his shoulders. She was smiling. It made her look younger, somehow. She'd rarely smiled before.

Beside them, Auntie Winnie laughed and dabbed at her eyes with a hanky.

With her pulse pounding in her ears, Olive followed Peter across the room. This was surely a dream – a dream too wonderful, too perfect, to be true. She stopped in front of her mother, almost swaying, delirious at the unexpectedness of it all.

Mum's face crumpled in a mixture of sadness and joy. "Hello, my Ol. My, you've grown. I ain't half missed you."

"Where's Dad?" Peter asked, looking towards the door.

Mum bent awkwardly and put her hands on both of his shoulders to gaze into his face. "I'm sorry, Peter. He ain't coming. He's got himself a new family now." She pulled him close, not seeming to care that his snotty face would be buried in her coat. Above his head, the look she exchanged with Auntie Winnie seemed full of secrets.

Olive's eyes flooded with tears, so many it was like looking at her mum through thick glass. She didn't care if Dad had a different family, or even if she never saw him again. But seeing her mum after so long made her throat feel like it was closing up.

"You didn't write," she murmured, her voice emerging strangled and strange. "We didn't know where you were." Somehow, she managed not to voice the other fear: *we thought you were dead*. The torment in Mum's face was already painful enough to see.

"I was ill. I was in hospital, and then Auntie Winnie got me back on my feet again. But I'm here now. Mrs Havard and Miss Fitznorton have said we can stay for a few days, as long as you want us to."

"Yes, stay!" Peter's eyes, swollen and red, looked up hopefully.

Olive nodded. "I kept Peter safe, like you said." She watched her mother's face, needing to know she'd done well.

"I know. I knew I could rely on you, Ol. I am so pleased to see you."

Mum had never been one for hugs. She wasn't like Mrs Clarke, who'd cuddled her kids the moment she arrived and sent letters twice a week telling them she loved and missed them. But now, still with one arm around Peter, she held out the other.

Olive wiped her eyes with her sleeve. "I'm pleased to see you, too," she said, and stepped forward into her mother's embrace.

EPILOGUE

It was always warm in the kitchen. A kettle simmered on the range and the smell of toast and coffee made Olive's mouth water as she trooped in for breakfast behind Barbara and Shirley. On their way downstairs, they'd been giggling about Tyke, who had a habit of lying in wait for them at the foot of the stairs and pouncing on their feet as they passed.

Michael was already seated at the table, his cheeks bulging as he chewed. In the seat beside him, Peter was making Uncle Ivor chuckle by mimicking Miss Bright leading a gas mask drill. He still hated her lessons.

The girls took their usual seats at the table. Olive reached for her cereal bowl and poured in some cornflakes. The first time Auntie Dolly had offered them, she'd tried to eat them with a knife and fork. But even though it was only four months ago, September now seemed such a long time ago. So much had changed since then.

"Is there any bacon?" Uncle Ivor asked Auntie Dolly, who was busy slicing more bread.

"Not today," she said. "If I use it today, there'll be none left for the rest of the week. And before you ask, you're not having any butter or sugar either. I'm keeping it for Barbara's birthday cake."

"Well, well," he said. "No bacon. No butter for my toast. No sugar in my tea. By the time this war's over, I'll be half the man I was." He patted his tummy mournfully, earning himself a severe look from his wife.

"You'll have to make do with margarine or dripping. And be grateful you can still have tea. Lord help us if they ever ration that."

A draught swept over Olive's calves as Aunt Dodie came in, looking fresh and pretty in a cherry-coloured knitted sweater teamed with a checked skirt.

"The postman has been," she said cheerfully, causing a ripple of excitement around the table. "There's one for you, Ivor, one for me that looks like Loulou's handwriting if I'm not mistaken, and one for Master Michael Clarke." She handed the letters out and pulled out the chair beside Olive, reaching for a cup and saucer.

Olive couldn't hide her disappointment.

Aunt Dodie grinned. "Oh, wait a minute – look what I've just found. There's one for Miss and Master Hicks, too." She passed it to Olive, hazel eyes sparkling, and Olive beamed back, her mood immediately lifting.

Michael had already torn his letter open and he began reading it aloud. Barbara and Shirley were rapt, enjoying hearing news of their parents and siblings in London. They'd gone home for a week at Christmas, and on their return the girls had whispered to Olive after lights-out how funny it was to be back in a big house with proper bathrooms indoors and carpets everywhere, even on the stairs.

Olive and Peter had felt a little guilty about just how much they'd enjoyed being at Plas Norton for Christmas. After Mum and Auntie Winnie went back to London, they'd stayed on and all the adults had made a fuss of them. They'd eaten like kings and the stockings they'd put out on Christmas Eve had been bulging the next morning. The atmosphere in the house had been warm and loving, and they'd met Mrs Havard's son Christopher for the first time. When it snowed, he'd showed them all the best places for sledging.

Now, Olive held her envelope in both hands, enjoying the anticipation of reading her first ever letter from home. She traced her fingers across the dark blue inked words, picturing her mum sitting down to write.

"Go on, Ol. Open it. Tell me what Mum says," Peter urged.

Ivor smiled and ruffled his hair indulgently. "Give her a chance, boyo. She's getting to it."

Aunt Dodie used a knife to cut a neat slit in her own envelope, then slid it across the tablecloth to Olive. Picking it up, Olive carefully slipped the point under the edge of the flap and tugged it along the fold, then almost held her breath as she pulled the letter out and opened it.

"*Dear Olive and Peter,*" she read aloud. A glance around the table revealed that everyone was smiling. It gave her a warm feeling to know they were all happy on her behalf. She sat up and cleared her throat importantly, then continued reading in a more confident voice. "*I hope you are well. I am staying at the Wilberforce Arms with Winnie for a bit longer, until I can find another flat. Every day we talk about how lovely it was being able to stay with you both at Plas Norton for those few days before Christmas. Please pass on my regards to Mrs Havard and Miss Fitznorton and thank Mr and Mrs Griffiths for looking after us. I'll always be thankful to them for taking such good care of you both and inviting us to stay.*"

The adults nodded, looking pleased.

"Go on," Peter said.

"*Now that I'm so much better, I've decided to volunteer to be an Air Raid Warden. It will give me something to do while you are away and I would like to feel useful and do something for the war, instead of just cleaning at the pub."*

Olive paused, unsure how she felt about this idea.

Aunt Dodie patted Olive's hand as if she understood. "It's good to hear that she's feeling well enough to work again. You must be proud of her for wanting to do her bit, Olive," she said in her soft voice.

"We've had lots of snow in London, which was a surprise, but things are getting back to normal now. Did you have much snow? I hope you have been having fun. Be good for your teachers and work hard at school. Write back soon. I like getting your letters. With love from Mum. She's put two kisses at the end." Olive swallowed down the lump in her throat and passed the letter to Peter.

"We'll have to tell her about sledging in our next letter," he said. "And our snowman. Although I looked out of our bedroom window when I woke up, and it looks like he's nearly melted. I'll go out and fetch your cap and scarf back in after breakfast, Uncle Ivor."

"Good lad. Your mam will enjoy reading about it. Probably best not to mention the time you fell off the sledge head-first, though," Ivor replied, sending him a wink.

Auntie Dolly flapped a tea towel at Tyke, who had jumped onto the table. "Oi! Get down, you," she exclaimed.

He jumped down, stripy ginger tail held high in the air as he stalked off to wrap himself around Olive's ankles. She reached down and scratched his back before carrying on munching her cornflakes. It didn't escape her notice that Aunt Dodie tickled his chin too.

"What did your letter say, Aunt Dodie?" Shirley asked.

"Oh, mostly that Loulou is having tremendous fun despite the rules being terribly strict. She's hoping to get some leave soon so that she can visit." She laid down her napkin and pushed back her chair to get up. "I'd better go and get ready," she announced, tucking her chair back under the table. "Charlotte and I are going shopping in Pontybrenin this morning, and then I have a lunch date at Contadino's."

"Oh, yes? You wouldn't be meeting a handsome American, by any chance?" Auntie Dolly teased.

Interestingly, her cheeks turned a fetching shade of pink, but her only reply was a grin before she wished them all a good day and left the room.

Barbara gave Olive a nudge. "I hope Aunt Dodie and Mr Winter get married," she whispered in Olive's good ear. "Maybe they'll ask us to be their bridesmaids."

It was an exciting prospect. Olive swallowed the last mouthful of her cornflakes and set her spoon down in her empty bowl. Who knew what the rest of the year would bring? Besides the possibility of a wedding, there was lots more to look forward to. The end of the war, maybe, and then returning to London to live with Mum in her new flat. In the meantime, regular letters, and the fun of seeing the countryside in springtime. Aunt Dodie had already told them about the flowers they'd see everywhere: snowdrops should be appearing any day now, then camellias and daffodils and primroses. Soon there would be lambs in the fields, too, and ducklings on the lake. She almost hoped the war wouldn't end before she'd had a chance to see it all.

Even if it ended tomorrow and they had to go back to London straight away, she and Peter had made friends for life with the Clarkes. And as she leaned back in her chair, gazing about the kitchen and at the familiar faces of the other people seated around the table, she knew for sure that her time at Plas Norton would forever hold a special place in her heart.

A LETTER FROM THE AUTHOR

Dear reader,

Huge thanks for reading *What We Left Behind*. I hope you were hooked on the story of Dodie and the five evacuee children. If you want to join other readers in hearing all about my new releases and bonus content, you can sign up here:

www.stormpublishing.co/luisa-a-jones

If you enjoyed this book and could spare a few moments to leave a review that would be hugely appreciated. Even a short review can make all the difference in encouraging a reader to discover my books for the first time. Thank you so much!

Thanks again for being part of this amazing journey with me and I hope you'll stay in touch – I have many more stories and ideas to entertain you with!

Luisa

www.luisaajones.com

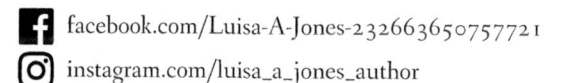

facebook.com/Luisa-A-Jones-232663650757721
instagram.com/luisa_a_jones_author

AUTHOR'S NOTE

Early in 1939, with the prospect of war with Germany seeming increasingly likely, the British Government made plans to protect the populace. Germany had used gas as a weapon in the First World War, and it was feared that this would be used again, with bombing raids causing mass casualties that could result in the emergency services being overwhelmed. The devastating bombing of Guernica in Spain in 1937 was an example of what the Luftwaffe could do to cities within its range. It was therefore decided to evacuate large numbers of people from areas most at risk.

In the countryside, the Women's Institute carried out an accommodation survey which determined the number of evacuees Rural Councils could be expected to accommodate. Billeting officers were appointed to allocate evacuees to potential host households. The evacuees included school-age children and their teachers, pregnant women, mothers with young children, disabled people, elderly people, and workers in a range of government departments. Many schools, businesses, government departments, and even hospitals relocated. At the same time, military camps were set up, buildings were requisitioned, and tracts of land were earmarked for military use. In some rural areas, the evacuation programme which swung into action days before the outbreak of war on 3 September 1939 almost doubled the local population, causing intense pressure on services such as education, health and sanitation.

Many host families resented having to house strangers whose way of life, habits and attitudes were very different. Householders could be fined up to £50 or given a three-month custodial sentence for refusing to house evacuees. In South Wales, where this novel is set, many people had experienced dire poverty during the Depression of the 1920s and 30s. High levels of unemployment had caused hundreds of thousands to move away from the area in search of work, and in August 1939 more than fifteen per cent of insured Welsh men were out of work. Life was hard, with few modern conveniences, and many families were struggling to survive. Although they received an allowance for hosting evacuees, there were concerns that it wouldn't be enough to cover the costs of feeding and clothing them, laundering soiled bedding, repairing their clothes, and replacing their shoes as they grew.

Some families made their own private arrangements if they knew someone willing to take them or their children in. Others relied on the official evacuation programme. This offered no guarantee that siblings would be kept together, and many were separated. While there are many happy stories of evacuees loving their time in the countryside and being treated well, not all had a positive experience, and some estimates suggest that around ten per cent of evacuated children were physically or sexually abused by their hosts.

As a mother, I couldn't contemplate ever sending my children away to live with strangers. However, many families felt they had little choice if they were to give their children a chance of avoiding worse trauma or even death if they stayed in the city. Government communications sought to persuade parents that their children would not only be safer but happier in the countryside, and that keeping them at home would play into the enemy's hands. It must have been an agonising decision to relinquish a parent's control and influence, and to depend on the kindness of strangers, especially when there was no way of knowing where the children would end up, how well they would be cared for, or how long they might be away.

It would be easy to assume that all of the evacuees in 1939 were white, English-speaking, and from Christian backgrounds. Yet Britain had a more diverse population in the 1930s than is often recognised. I read about several interesting cases in the course of my research. Some children with Chinese heritage, from London's Chinatown, were evacuated to Oxfordshire. Many Jewish children were evacuated, some to non-Jewish families who had little understanding of their needs. Some evacuees included refugees from Eastern Europe who had suffered the trauma of Nazi oppression. In North Wales, some communities spoke very little English, and evacuees had to pick up the Welsh language quickly in order to communicate with their hosts.

The cosmopolitan East End of London was home to families from a wide range of backgrounds, including Jewish, Irish, Indian, Chinese, Japanese, and many black and mixed-race families. A recent film, *Blitz*, by director Steve McQueen, was apparently inspired by a photograph of a black child evacuee. Coincidentally, before I knew about the film, I found the same photograph on the Imperial War Museum's website. I had already become fascinated by a snippet of testimony about a family of evacuees from a mixed-race family in London who arrived in a small Welsh industrial town. Sources suggested they faced racism at first, yet despite this they settled in the area and were eventually accepted into the community. Through social media, I was able to find and speak to the daughter of one of these evacuees. It was a privilege to hear her family's remarkable and moving story, although painful to hear about the prejudice they faced when they first arrived in Wales, which contradicted the accepted idea of "a welcome in the hillsides". This family's experiences inspired the characters of Michael, Barbara and Shirley Clarke, and I hope to write more about the Clarke family in a future book.

ACKNOWLEDGMENTS

It isn't possible to write a book without the support of others. For this book, a number of people deserve a mention. I owe them all a debt of gratitude.

Firstly, I must thank my husband Martin for his unfailing encouragement and faith in me, as well as for bringing me countless cups of tea. He supports me in so many ways, both practical and emotional. My best friend, beta reader, motivator, and adviser on all things relating to vehicles, he is indispensable.

My kids Sam, Ben and Anna helped me choose Patrick's surname. It had to be one which could be either British or German to suit the purposes of the plot. When I struggled to decide between a couple of possible options, they sold me on Pat Winter. Now I couldn't imagine him being anything else.

Through his daughter Lowri, John Harris shared recollections of his time as an evacuee. He was patient with my questions and generous with his time, showing me photographs and written materials to help me understand what he and his brothers experienced.

Helen Blackmore shared her family's remarkable story with me, which influenced my depiction of the Clarke children. I was so touched by her account of her mixed-race family's evacuation to the Welsh Valleys, and grateful for her permission to draw upon it as inspiration for this and potentially a future book.

Roger Wrapson from the Riley Register provided information about the Riley Kestrel and confirmed it would be a suitable car for a woman in Charlotte's position. (If any readers are interested to know more about Charlotte's car, there is an example of a 1930s Riley Kestrel at the Cotswold Motoring Museum and Toy Collection in Bourton-on-the-Water, Gloucestershire. I can definitely recommend a visit.)

Rebecca Coote confirmed that my family's story of a grass snake biting her hand and hanging on under the cold tap was indeed true. The internet says they don't bite, but Becca knows from experience that they do.

Ruth Jones and Lowri Graham helped me invent fictional Welsh place names. Ruth Lloyd helped me with suitable Welsh phrases for Ivor's more stressful moments. Diolch yn fawr iawn i chi. Any mistakes are my own.

My beta readers Jan Baynham, Jessie Cahalin, Natalie Normann, Jenny O'Brien and David Hobday gave me invaluable feedback on an early draft. Thank you all for your friendship, encouragement, and constructive suggestions.

Three friends provided me with extracts from family histories. Thank you to Jayne Hall for extracts from her mother's memoirs, and Isobel Brown for extracts from her grandmother's. Alistair Pitt shared part of his uncle's story with me. All provided wonderful snippets to illuminate my research into life on the Home Front during the Second World War.

Dr Emma Sherrington helped me research rickets and sent resources about civilian morale during the war.

Once again, I'm grateful for the exceptionally talented, insightful and supportive members of the Cariad chapter of the Romantic Novelists' Association, without whose collective wisdom and cheerleading I would not be writing acknowledgements for my fifth novel today.

The team at Storm Publishing have ensured that this book is brought into the world in the best possible shape. I'm especially grateful to Emily Gowers and Kathryn Taussig for their brilliant editorial guidance and feedback.

Lastly, and most importantly, thank you for taking the time to read this book. Without readers, there would be no point in writing. It's been a joy to return to Plas Norton and Pontybrenin in a fresh series, and I can't wait to continue writing about the impact of the Second World War on South Wales in my next book.

Printed in Great Britain
by Amazon